THE HAPPY SAPPERSTEINS

Carol K Howell

Palm Beach Press

PBP
GEP

Golem Bookworks
Engender Bookworks
Palette Bookworks
divisions of
Palm Beach Press Inc

ISBN-13: 9798832782515 softcover

ISBN-13: 9798832784687 hardcover

Library of Congress Control Number: 2022948782

Cover design by: Sheila Hollihan-Elliot

Printed in the United States of America

Imprint: Golem Bookworks for

Palm Beach Press, Inc.
PO Box 531
Palm Beach, Fl, USA
33480

DEDICATION

For my children

CONTENTS

FOREWORD

This is a collection of mostly autobiographical stories that I have put together for one reason: I wish to be known. I loved both my parents—eventually—and I'm pretty sure they loved me, but I can't say we knew each other. We never talked about belief, opinion, point of view. I did hear family tales and bits of recollection, but I never had access to their interior lives, nor they to mine. In part it might have been fear of opening Pandora's box, of the damage that secrets and interior voices can inflict. For example, I was over sixty when I learned that my mother had had a mentally retarded brother, the only boy after five girls, who was put in an institution as a child and whom they never saw nor spoke of again. I was the same age when I learned my father's father had had a first wife and family whom he left behind in Russia. But really I think the problem was that my parents didn't know how to ask or answer the kind of questions that would make true intimacy possible. I believe that you cannot really love without knowledge of the beloved: to love, to be loved, is to *know,* and you show it by telling. What lay between my parents and me was necessarily shallow, but I don't want to repeat the same pattern with my own children or grandchildren. Hence this collection of stories.

It may be hard for the reader to tell what's fictional and what's autobiographical without some help. The fictional details, while made up, are nevertheless true in spirit. Sometimes you just have to change or add things to make the story better. However, I've added a headnote to each story to clarify some of the distinctions. This is an imperfect system. Though I tried for consistency, some stories have character names or facts that contradict other stories. For example, Lev is Asher in one story, and sometimes he has no children and sometimes he has a son. But the essential truth of him—why he is present in the collection at all—remains the same. In some stories Owen's occupation differs. I found I could not make such things consistent without damaging the fabric of the stories.

You may also notice that many of the stories take place during a family function of some kind—a seder, an anniversary party, an unveiling, a bris. That's because we had so many functions when I was growing up and also because a special event gives the story a natural framework.

I must also point out that this collection is by no means exhaustive. I didn't write about the spooky reconciliation between my mother and me when I was forty. I didn't write about her sudden death (in the hospital elevator on her way to surgery) or my father's terrible decline and death: by the end, neither of us recognized the other. I could say these subjects were too weighty to take on, but the whole truth is: they were too weighty to take on, and I was too lazy to try.

There. You're starting to know me already.

THE HEBREW SCHOOL GIRLS' ROOM

This story is almost reportage. The events and persons it describes really happened, and if this is not the precise moment when I became a writer, it's damn close.

T hey were singing the song in the Girls' Room before Hebrew School—*Where oh where can my baby be? The Lord took her away from me*—a tragic tale about a young man who lost his true love in a car crash. It could have come straight out of Child's Ballads, which is what I'd spent my birthday money on because it was the thickest book of poems in the store. *I held her close, I kissed her our last kiss. I found the love I knew I would miss.* Caryn and Beth were singing it. They both had nice voices, unlike me. And nice figures, unlike me. We were the only Jewish girls in seventh grade, but we never talked except at Hebrew School. Caryn's parents had given her a nose job as a bat mitzvah gift. Beth was petite and pretty, a JV cheerleader. They'd both found ways to set their Jewishness aside that were a mystery to me.

The cryin' tires, the bustin' glass, the painful scream that I heard last. The lyrics echoed nicely in the Girls' Room.

"Where did you hear that?" I blurted when they paused.

Beth was putting on lip gloss from a pink pot shaped like a strawberry. Caryn was wetting her bangs. I wanted to tell them about Child's *Ballads* even though I knew better.

"The crow," Caryn said. She probably thought I couldn't see her roll her eyes, but she was standing in front of the mirror. "It's been number one all week."

Beth was kinder. "WCRO," she added. "The CRO. You know, 1450?" When I still looked blank she exchanged a glance with Caryn, who went into the single stall, letting the door bang. "The radio station, all the latest music. Don't you ever listen?"

I shook my head, blinking back tears of stupidity. "I will now, though."

Beth gave me a smile that was mostly wince and turned back to the mirror. She had a mother who was cute and wore miniskirts. Caryn had two older sisters. I didn't have anyone to clue me in. We had a radio in the kitchen that my father turned on for the morning news while he made breakfast for my brother and me. Why hadn't someone told me to find the cool stations and start memorizing songs? Or to buy lip gloss in a pink pot and come to seventh grade wearing pantyhose, not cotton socks? My mother lived in her own world, whispering to her psychiatrist twice a week. She was no help. Yet being cool was more than just learning what to do. Once in Sunday School when we were reading aloud, Caryn came to the word "Nazi" and pronounced it to rhyme with "phase-eye." The boys hooted, but Beth and I just looked sympathetic, and soon it was forgotten, and no one teased her about it, ever. Why? Because *she* wasn't weird. She was cool. It was more than what you did. It was what you were. How did you change what you were?

The stall door opened halfway and I backed up, but Caryn just stuck her head out. "Beth," she called. "Can you hand me my purse?"

As Beth did, I caught a glimpse of the toilet behind Caryn and saw that it was full of blood.

Red blood, like in the song they'd sung. *Somethin' warm a-runnin' in my eyes.* If you saw it on the road, you'd think *death.* If you read it in Child's ballads, you'd think *death.* But here in the pristine white toilet it meant the opposite—it meant Caryn had a woman's body, capable of bearing life, something my body had shown no sign of. Not even a hair.

The buzzer in the hall went off. Time to squeeze ourselves into old-fashioned desks and study an ancient language no one but me cared about. But today I wouldn't be listening. I wouldn't be taking notes or raising my hand. Today I would be copying down as much of that song as I could remember. And if those lines weren't bitter enough to suit me, then perhaps I would just start writing my own.

REDEMPTION

or Pidyon ha-Ben Rides Again

The events in this story are invented, though the characters are based on real people. But the spirit of the story—the attitudes and relationships and history—sticks pretty close to truth. My insights into certain characters—Mel, for instance—remain just that: my own insights. The part about being Kohanim, however, is absolutely true.

My father is in demand most weekends, driving to Akron, Cleveland, even Pittsburgh, where people have heard what a beautiful ceremony he makes and how well he translates a barbaric ritual into terms even the most secular Jew feels comfortable with. After all, through modern eyes, the Pidyon ha-Ben can seem a little hinky: a transaction in which a newborn son is redeemed—purchased, actually, with five silver dollars, unless you've got shekels handy—from a member of the Tribe of Levi, preferably a Kohane, a high priest like my father. Actually, my mother is Kohanim as well, so since I'm first-born, if this were 1445 B.C.E., I would be hot stuff—definitely Top of the Tribe material. If I were a boy, that is.

My father's so good because he's funny, he's reassuring, he gives the new mother tips for presentation of the child (you think "on a silver platter" is a joke?), he gets everyone involved, he makes new friends, new contacts, even ferrets out distant cousins—if not his own, then somebody else's. And he loves it, the same way he loved being president of Temple Sinai, all five terms. It's because what he loves best in the world is *mishpocheh*—family—everyone connected, everyone getting along, *genipt und gebinden*—knotted and pasted—no one left out. Families Getting Along is his most sacred concept: nothing distresses him more than feuds and cold shoulders —he works tirelessly to reconcile the parties, who sometimes give in out of sheer exhaustion. I speak from experience.

I started going with my father to the ceremonies after my mother, chronically depressed, made it clear that I was not the daughter she'd had in mind. She'd imagined someone daintier, prettier, more artistic, more like her. More dateable, less clumsy. Probably another boy would have been preferable, one like Jonathan, my handsome younger brother, who'd had girlfriends since sixth grade and conquered every club and team high school had to offer. My mother and I tried to be civil to each other for my father's sake when he was home. But when he was gone we rarely occupied the same room.

At first my father would go alone. But we had a joke: whenever I saw him pack his kit, tuck a *yarmulke* into his pocket, and jingle his car keys like spurs, I'd say: "Yee haw! *Pidyon ha-Ben* rides again!" and he'd say: "*Oy vey!* Ride 'em, Rabbi!" Then one day he just held the door open and said: "Want to come along?" From then on I rode with him.

So it's a surprise when my cousin Josh asks not my father but Uncle Mel to perform the *Pidyon* for his newborn son. Mel has the same pedigree as my father, of course, but no one's ever seen him conduct the ritual. And this one's particularly important. First of all, it's going to be combined with the *bris,* the ritual circumcision, which breaks all kinds of rules and puts the conservative faction in the family at odds with the progressive. On the one hand, the *bris must* be performed on the eighth day of the baby's life, while the *Pidyon ha-Ben* is supposed to be done on the thirty-first. On the other hand, these rules were formulated at a time when child mortality was fifty per cent; furthermore, Josh and Suzanne, who live in an $800,000 house, need to consolidate the events because Suzanne only took a two-week maternity leave and has to go to Seoul on business for her bank.

*Further*more, this is the first grandchild for my mother's sister Lois and her husband Lev, the only member of his family to walk out of the smoke of Auschwitz. Josh is Lev's only child, so this grandson is important in all sorts of ways: the blood goes on, the Jews go on, we dance on Hitler's grave. The baby will be named for Lev's father, lost to the ovens.

All of this adds up to one potent Jewish party: prayers, blood, Hebrew documents, camcorders, hankies, bear hugs, masses of food, and, once the schnapps come out, some roaring Yiddish songs as well. Lois and Lev have chartered a bus to take friends from their synagogue; caravans of relatives have hit the road from all directions; and Josh and Suzanne have invited their bosses and co-workers, friends from their gym, and their entire wine-and-cheese club. It's a mix that would challenge even as seasoned a diplomat as my father, which makes it all the more puzzling that Josh has chosen Mel.

Josh's house is the family Versailles. We've heard stories, we've seen pictures, but no one is really prepared for five bathrooms, upper *and* lower decks, digital showers, and closets, Lev says, his whole *shtetl* could live in. He gives us the grand tour. Downstairs, guests congeal in four uneasy corners, chattering in some foreign tongue for all I can tell. It reminds me of a school play I was in where the townsfolk had to mill around discussing the hero's innocence or guilt. Actually what we said was: "Rutabaga, rutabaga, rutabaga, rutabaga." The drama teacher said that from a distance, it sounds just like conversation.

In the center of the room, occupying all of the furniture, is *mishpocheh*: aunts, uncles, cousins, the chartered-bus crowd, the blissful new grandmothers, and now one extremely wired new grandfather. Lois holds the sleeping baby while Lev runs around making light and sound checks for the video.

Near the door, people from Josh's office partially mingle with people from Suzanne's bank, like one amoeba digesting another. Each cell has a nucleus that, judging from the expensive suits, must be the respective bosses. The others stop and pay thoughtful attention when the nucleus speaks, but never shut up when it's only each other—like rabbis and their courts of Talmudic scholars.

The cheerful wine-and-cheese crowd is easy to spot, though they seem a little lost with no glasses to hold onto. Rabbi Flah is the young guy in the denim shirt and the tie with smiley faces. He's working the room, shaking hands, touching arms and elbows, a roving ambassador of *Yiddishkeit*. When he reaches the conversation pit, where my relatives and their friends occupy every sittable surface, he is swallowed up and roams no more.

"So where is this *moil*?" Lev pops up beside us. "This *kreplach*. Where is he?"

"*Kreplak*," says my father gently. "No *ch*, or he'll take offense."

Of course he'll take offense: a *kreplach* is a meat-filled dumpling, delicious in chicken soup.

Lev ignores my father. "Half an hour late already. Maybe he stopped for a bite to eat?"

Anyone who's been to a *bris* would recognize the scornful implication: there are always mountains of Jewish delicacies, the kind that come only from the kitchens of Jewish matrons; it would be insane to dull the appetite with so much as a cracker.

Mel winks at me. "Maybe he had a professional emergency."

Lev is incredulous. "An emergency circumcision?"

"Sure—on the way over, he passes a car wreck, which turns

out to be new parents taking their son to a *moil,* only now they're going to the hospital instead, and they beg him: ʻ*Reb Kreplach,*' they say, 'you know what emergency rooms are like —a boy could grow a beard waiting for the doctor—please, *Kreplach*, won't you perform a *bris* on our son? Otherwise, we're going to miss the eighth day!'" Mel shrugs. "What can he do? He can't refuse to make the child a Jew."

He loops a long arm around Lev's shoulders, but Lev, much shorter, stands stiffly apart, looking like a man wearing an arm. He wants to worry, not be distracted.

Mel is the tall one, the family jokester, the uncle with the drooping hound-dog face who always pulled nickels out of our ears. "Ask me why I'm sad," he'd urge, then say: "I'm not sad— I'm smiling upside down!" He did impressions of Donald Duck telling Yiddish jokes. When he sang *Bei Mir Bist du Schoen* with my father in flawless harmony—just the two of them, his hand on my dad's arm to steady them both, knees dipping to the beat—I could see them as boys, running wild on the streets of Pittsburgh when the Hill was still a Jewish neighborhood, sneaking into movie theaters because they didn't have the nickels my uncle now pulled so freely from our ears, and playing some elaborate game he'd invented that involved footballs, long passes, and streetcars. Their father died when they were small; their mother spoke no English; they had to protect their younger sister, Frieda.

The day after graduation Mel ran off and got married, leaving my father, who had just turned sixteen, to support my grandmother and aunt. It was 1941: as soon as my father graduated, he was sent to France. Mel, drafted late because he was married, spent the war safe at the naval base in Virginia.

When my father returned from Europe, he thought about using the G.I. Bill to put himself through college: medicine, maybe, or even—he laughs when he says this—rabbinical school. But Frieda had been diagnosed with diabetes, and their apartment building was being torn down, and my grandmother had grown deaf. He stayed. Mel got him a job at the carpet warehouse where he worked. On Sunday afternoons, Mel and Shirley came over and sat in the dim living room of the little house my father had bought for his mother with a G.I. loan. As yet there were no children, but that was not, Mel explained, for lack of trying.

Then my father met my mother at a cousin's wedding. She lived two streetcars and a bus away, so their courtship consisted of Saturday night movies and Sunday afternoons in the dark living room. By then Aunt Frieda had met Uncle Hersh in the diabetes doctor's office, and that living room was getting pretty crowded. My mother wanted to go to art school, but her father—who had five daughters and no sons—didn't believe in paying to educate girls, so she was trying to teach herself with books from the library. She wanted to spend her Sundays wandering around with her sketchpad, but she also wanted to be with my father. He wanted to be with her, but he also wanted—well, it's the same thing he wants today: *mishpocheh*, everybody together, preferably in the same room. The war and his father's early death had taught him there was nothing more precious than family. They were all in their twenties and, except for Mel and Shirley, still living with their parents. When Frieda and Hersh announced, sadly, that they wanted to get married but couldn't afford it, Mel proposed The Plan. The Plan involved the buying and selling and rebuying and reselling of carpets from the warehouse—it was nearly as elaborate as those football plays he used to call—but when the dust settled, he and my father would be launched in the carpet business themselves.

And, amazingly, that's just what happened, except that my uncle ended up with most of the money. He explained it was a special commission—and the explanation, apparently, was so complicated that no one has ever wanted to explain it to me. The upshot was, Hersh and Frieda got the house and my grandmother; Mel got the business; and my parents got married in City Hall and moved to Ohio the next afternoon, where my father found a job in a carpet store and my mother sold lipstick at the local Rexall, where she was said to have a very good eye for color.

But Mel's life was not carefree. He had a lot of *tsuris* from the IRS, and Shirley couldn't conceive. Eventually they adopted a boy and a girl: Ross and Rochelle. The children, as the saying goes in my family, gave them nothing but heartache. Rochelle ran off for good when she was still in high school and has very little contact with Mel: he has a grandchild he's only seen twice. Ross left home when Shirley died of breast cancer. He's a ski bum, a surf bum, a rock-climbing bum—half the time Mel doesn't even know what part of the country he's being a bum in.

Things seemed to be looking up again when Mel met Norma, a glamorous blond widow in Palm Beach. For a few years they were happy, spending winters in Florida and summers in Pittsburgh, taking cruises, playing golf, e-mailing their brokers. Then Norma was diagnosed with Alzheimer's. When he could no longer keep her from wandering into traffic, Mel put her in a home. Now he divides his time between his two condos: he always seems to be just leaving or newly arrived. You don't ever ask him: "How's Norma?" or "What's Rochelle doing?" or "Where's Ross these days?" You ask: "How was your flight?"

"Hey," Mel is still going strong, and I can see he's wired too, even for Mel. "Did you hear about the *moil* who said `The pay's lousy but you get to keep the tips?'"

"I heard," Lev says.

"Well, I bet you didn't hear what he did with them. He started a business—" Mel glances at me. "Esther, *maideleh*, come over here." Dutifully I present myself and he claps both hands over my ears. "He turned them into wallets, and they sold like hotcakes. You know why? Because when you rub them, they turn into suitcases!" He lets out a big Mel laugh; my father smiles, embarrassed, and suddenly I know why Mel is doing the *Pidyon*: my father must have asked him to, because he needs it—he needs *something.* He goes to the nursing home and sits all day with Norma and she doesn't know who he is. He needs to feel connected.

Now it makes sense. But I wonder what Lev thinks about it. Lev is extremely big—huge—on family tradition: understandable, since he has no graves to visit or dates for lighting *yahrzeit* candles. His superstitions, cherished and polished like fragile souvenirs, are one way of keeping his lost family close by. He wouldn't let Josh and Suzanne bring a crib into the house before the baby was born—why tempt the Evil Eye? They compromised by buying the crib but storing it, unassembled, in the garage. The night the baby came, Lev and Josh went back to the house and stayed up till dawn, getting loaded on schnapps, fooling around with the cordless screwdriver, and somehow putting the thing together. My father told me Lev insisted on tying a bit of red yarn to the underside—where Suzanne wouldn't see—to keep demons away. He said that when Frieda was born, his own father drew a chalk circle on the floor around her cradle. Newborns who were ill or otherwise at risk were called *Alter* or *Zayde* —Old Person, Grandfather—to confuse the Evil One. And you didn't name a baby after a living relative because the Angel of Death might make a mistake and take the child instead of the grandparent.

"Wait, wait, that's not all," Mel is saying. "If there's a pretty stewardess when you check your bags—" but Lev, staring at the door, says *"Shah!"* and then we all hear it: a muffled but determined *thud, thud, thud.* Either Death has come for the Archbishop, or Kreplak the *moil* has arrived.

Kreplak turns out to be a slight elderly man with the fearsome disposition of a waiter in a kosher restaurant. Grimly determined to get the show on the road and just as grimly convinced that no one else can do it, in very short order he arranges the blobby cells of guests into a concentric and complex organism. The two custom-tailored bosses may feel some chagrin at not being seated ringside—or at all—but Kreplak has his own idea of hierarchy: colleagues, oenophiles, personal trainers and such form the outer circle along the walls; cousins, aunts, uncles, and synagogue friends come next; then grandparents and parents; then in the center, Kreplak, the rabbi, and the baby himself. All I can see of the latter is a busily working pacifier and the tiny skullcap Lois crocheted. No doubt there's a strand of red yarn skillfully worked within. Lev distributes—he is not *offering*—skull caps to all the males, who meekly put them on, regardless of tax bracket.

And then we are ready. Kreplak and the rabbi ceremoniously wash their hands, Kreplak *dovening* and muttering a prayer that, apparently, need not concern the rest of us. Then he lifts the baby and hands him to Suzanne's mother, who hands him to Lois, who hands him to Lev, who kisses him and hands him to Suzanne, who hands him to Josh, who hands him back to Kreplak. The rabbi begins the usual prayers of gratitude, flattery, supplication. I'm watching Suzanne. I've seen a lot of new mothers at these things. Some are right there, front and center, chiming in with the *Omains*, but most retreat, averting their eyes. Some get sick. Some flee. Suzanne is tough, disciplined—aggressively slim again only a week after childbirth—but her animation has evaporated and she is an interesting shade of wan.

The rabbi, doing his ecumenical best, explains to the guests that during the long years of bondage in Egypt, Jews would have become completely assimilated if they hadn't held onto two things: their Hebrew names and the rite of circumcision. He explains that the Hebrew word for foreskin—*orlah*—is also a metaphor for obstructions of the heart that prevent us from hearing God. "The Midrash tells the story that Adam was born without the *orlah*, signifying the absence of any barrier between him and God. Of course that was before he developed a taste for apples," he adds, smiling around the room.

Rabbis talk; *moils* work. Swiftly Kreplak lays out his tools—scalpel and socket wrench, cotton balls and disinfectant, gauze and ointment. I try not to look at the socket wrench. He dips his finger in the kosher wine that tastes like cough syrup and gives it to the baby to suck, then beckons Lev. It's easy to see from the way Kreplak drapes the prayer shawl around Lev's shoulders how comfortable they are together. Each recognizes a *landsman*, more Old World than New, despite the Nikes each happens to be wearing. Watching them, I remember something my father told me about watching his own father in *shul*. During the holiday service, all male *Kohanim* would rise, cover their faces with their prayer shawls, and bless the congregation with the triple benediction of the ancient priests of Israel. My father said it gave him shivers and he could hardly wait until he was *bar mitzvah* so he could rise and do it too. He showed me the special hand sign *Kohanim* make when they give the priestly blessing—four fingers raised, separated into two's—which looks amazingly like the Vulcan greeting on "Star Trek" when Mr. Spock says: "Live long and prosper." My father never got to stand beside his father and give the blessing, though—by the time he came of age, his father had been dead three years.

There is a distinct surge forward as Kreplak goes to work —the synagogue crowd presses close, anxious to observe a master, a *moil's moil*—but I let myself be sifted to the back. The baby's sharp, surprised wail tells me he has just become a card-wearing member of the tribe. Aunts, uncles, and synagogue friends all shout *"Mazel tov!"* The other guests are more subdued; the men look a bit green.

I find Suzanne leaning against the back wall, as far away as you can get without actually leaving the room. She looks at me without trying to smile, which impresses me no end, and I offer her one of my dad's huge handkerchiefs. Kleenex is useless.

"Thanks," she says.

The rabbi raises his voice, chanting in our direction: "May his father rejoice in the issue of his loins, and his mother exult in the fruit of her womb."

I'm careful not to look at Suzanne, who is feeling anything but exultant at the moment, but Mel's face catches my eye, maybe because he's taller than anyone else in the room. He is wearing an expression I've never seen before. His loins had no issue and Shirley's no fruit, and the children they acquired anyway have somehow been lost. My father is right: he needs something.

"May this child, *Yaakov ben Yeshua*, grow into manhood," the rabbi concludes. "As he has entered the covenant, so may he enter the study of Torah, the wedding canopy, and the accomplishment of good deeds."

With mingled cries of "*Mazel tov!*" and "*Omain!*" the crowd breaks up. The *moil* shows Suzanne how to change the baby's dressing, then she whisks him off to nurse. There is an exodus of women to the kitchen to see about the feast, while the older men huddle in the middle of the room, Mel at the center. "Hey, ever heard what they do with the tips?" I hear him say, and the huddle grows tighter. I amble out to the kitchen to see what looks good.

Everything. Platters of corned beef and pastrami, whitefish and lox; homemade bagels, bialys, and pumpernickel; high twisted crowns of challah; noodle kugel and potato kugel; stuffed kishkes and kasha varnishkes; blintzes and honey cake and sticky buns and strudel...a Taj Mahal of Jewish food that gives even an $800,000 house a run for its money.

I ask if I can help. Help? Of course I can help! My job will be explaining to the *goyim* that the dining room is going to be *fleischedig*, with its own plastic dishes and utensils, and the kitchen is going to be *milchedig*, with *its* own plastic dishes and utensils, and that non-kosher-keeping guests can have whichever they want, but *under no circumstances are they to mix things together*. It is my job to repeat all of this to the well-groomed people waiting patiently in the living room for their refreshments. I hope they weren't expecting cookies and punch.

Josh and Suzanne's Jewish friends smile when I tell them, as if one of the children has done something cute. Their gentile friends look worried, and Lois and Lev's synagogue friends nod grimly. *If you didn't have a rabbi here, even a half-baked rabbi like this one*, their expressions seem to say, *we'd never let you get away with this.*

But before we can eat, we have to have the *Pidyon*. I'm keeping an eye on Mel, who's doing Donald Duck doing Barbra Streisand, performing finger tricks, and telling jokes about rabbis, priests, and golf. I hope and pray he will not tell the one about Clarence Thomas's wife's gynecologist. Not even Mel could be so reckless.

In the meantime Rabbi Flah, in the hushed yet resonant tones of a PBS narrator, continues instructing the guests. It boils down to this: when the Jews were slaves in Egypt, God sent plagues to force the Egyptians to release His people, the worst of which was the death of all Egyptian first-born sons. After the Red Sea closed over the heads of the pursuing army, God told Moses that from now on, in memory of this rescue and its terrible price, all first-born Jewish sons would be dedicated to the Temple as priests. Trouble was, while Moses was up on Mount Sinai taking dictation, the scurvy Israelites were down below, losing faith, melting their jewelry, and casting an idol to worship. All except for the Tribe of Levi, who refused.

Well! When Moses came down from the mountain, was he ticked off! He smashed the brand-new tablets of the Ten Commandments into a million pieces, and...(here the rabbi notices that the younger portion of his audience is drifting)... oh well, we've all seen the movie! Anyway, God punished the eleven faithless tribes by condemning them to wander in the desert for forty more years, long enough for a new generation to grow up. And he rewarded the faithful Levites by declaring *them* a tribe of priests who could take all the other tribes' first-born sons to serve in the Temple. Unless, of course, the child were redeemed from a *Kohane*.

"That's my cue!" cries Mel, grabbing his duffel bag and rushing off.

I catch my father's eye—he's smiling: *this is doing Mel good; see how happy he looks?* A little too happy, if you ask me, which no one does because I'm good at keeping my thoughts to myself. The murmuring resumes: work, time-share, day-care, free weights—rutabaga, rutabaga—until Mel makes a spectacular re-entrance. He has dressed himself in a voluminous purple caftan with gold sashes and straps holding a breastplate adorned with fake gems and engraved with the names of the twelve tribes of Israel. Everyone stares as he struts and turns like a model on a runway. Lev looks as if he might combust. The *goyim* exchange glances: the afternoon is turning out to be even more exotic than anticipated.

The rabbi is the first to recover. "An *ephod*!" he exclaims. "I've seen pictures, but..."

"Priestly robes," Mel translates proudly, adding: "I had it custom made."

"Well," someone says, "it's stunning!"

"Make sure to have it dry-cleaned," says someone else.

"You can always wear it again for Halloween," a third person says, and the young people laugh.

Mel looks at my father. "I wanted to be authentic."

"You are," my father says. "You're the real thing. Wear it in the best of health."

At this point Mel is upstaged by the baby, who arrives like a swaddled sultan, reclining upon velvet cushions on a great silver tray, surrounded by purple grapes, pomegranates, and chunks of marble halvah. The tray is borne carefully by his father, whose eyes bug out when he sees Mel's costume. Then he stands before him and offers the tray.

"This is my son, my first-born, who opened the womb of his mother," he recites tensely. "As it is written: consecrate unto Me all the first-born; whatever is the first to open the womb among the people of Israel."

There is a faint titter at "open the womb," but Josh keeps going. I'm sure Lev's been drilling him, probably springing pop quizzes in the middle of the night: "Blessed with the sacred trust of new life do we thus dedicate ourselves to the redeeming of life."

Now the rabbi chants, but I'm watching Mel. His face has gone pale and sweaty. Is it stage fright? An allergy to purple dye? An obstruction of the heart?

"May we create a home where love, compassion, and righteousness abide," Josh continues. "Where the hearts of the parents and the hearts of the children shall always be turned to one another."

The rabbi chants. Mel looks ill. From his height he can see the young people at the outer edges, the ones with their great days still to come: children not yet born, triumphs still in the making—all the joy and glamour of life before them. How does that look to him from there?

Again Josh lifts the tray, arms trembling from the strain, and declares: "This is my first-born son, whom I wish to redeem according to the ancient law of Torah!"

Mel reaches for the tray but his grip is weak; Josh lets go at the wrong moment, and the tray drops for one heart-stopping instant, before they catch hold of it again. Everyone gasps; the grandmothers shriek. The baby isn't hurt, but he's been jolted and he wails. Mel lifts him to his shoulder, shushing him, smoothing his little back, swaying gently like any parent, every parent. "*Shah, shah,*" he murmurs. The baby scrubs his face against Mel's neck. Mel cups the velvety head, closing his own eyes, and they sway together for a long blissful moment. But the moment stretches on until it becomes uncomfortable. There is shuffling, murmuring, a cough. The five silver dollars clink in Josh's hand as he holds them out, but Mel doesn't open his eyes. Finally, my father steps forward and lays his hand on his brother's arm. Mel jerks, startled, and the baby cries again.

"*Shah*," Mel murmurs, patting him and backing up and backing up. He keeps backing up while Josh looks helplessly at Lev, and Lev looks indignantly at my father, and everyone else is frozen, staring, until Mel turns around and in two strides of his long legs disappears into the powder room with the baby. We hear the lock turn.

We all stare at each other.

"What just happened?"

"Is this part of the ceremony?"

"He refused the money!"

"He can't do that. Can he do that?"

"He refused to give the baby back!"

Suzanne, Josh, Lev, the rabbi, my father, and Kreplak go into a huddle. The rest of us keep staring at the bathroom door. At one point we hear Lev say: "Get the key!" and Josh reply: "*What key?*"

"Try a butter knife," someone says.

"A credit card,"

"Call 911."

"Please," says my father, holding up his hands. "Everyone relax. Let's not make more of this than it is."

"But what is it?" someone asks, and the arguing starts again.

"What if he tries to go out the window?"

"A guy that big? He'd never get his shoulders through."

"Yeah, but the baby—he could drop the baby out."

At this both grandmothers shriek till Josh remembers there *is* no window, and my father presses his ear to the bathroom door.

"But wait!" A lawyer has a question. "What I don't understand is whether he's allowed to *keep* the baby? I mean, is that an option?"

Everyone looks at the rabbi, who shrugs helplessly. "The question never came up at Hebrew Union. I'm not sure about

Midrash, but I can tell you this: I've never seen anything in Scripture that says he *can't*."

Suzanne grabs Josh. "He's got our baby! Break down the door!"

"It's solid oak!" says Josh.

"What if a splinter flies across the room and hits the baby?" Lois demands. "He could go blind!"

"Tear gas is out," someone says thoughtfully.

Now Suzanne's mother hurls herself against the door. "Come out of there, you maniac! That's my grandchild! What do you want with him?"

Kreplak, oddly quiet, is stroking his chin, which, a hundred or so years ago, would have sported a full rabbinical beard. I get the feeling from his noncommittal gaze that he thinks Mel just might have a claim.

My father leads Suzanne's mother away from the door. "Please," he says. "Everybody sit down. He's my brother—I'll talk to him."

"Your brother!" Lois weeps. "You couldn't have done the *Pidyon* yourself? You had to turn it over to a rookie?"

This from Lois is strong talk. My father throws me a beseeching glance, and I am suddenly inspired. "Hey, anybody want a drink?"

We haven't had so much as a *kiddush*, let alone a *shehechiyanu*, but I break out the bar, pulling unblessed bottles from Josh and Suzanne's liquor cabinet, popping open cans of tonic, emptying ice cube trays, pulling corks, slicing limes. There's an enthusiastic bustle as the guests converge. Spritzers and martinis for the bank-and-office crowd; schnapps for the synagogue delegation; wine for the oenophiles, which I sample freely myself though the crowd keeps me busy. I could like being a bartender—here but not here, essential but invisible.

Drinks in hand, the guests retreat into their separate groups. Suzanne migrates among them, half hostess, half object of compassion, smoothing things over with the work crowd and offering herself for hugs of consolation from the family. When the rabbi sits her down for professional counsel, she clasps her hands and drops her head. I get the feeling she doesn't know just what to be at this moment—probably a new sensation for her. I want to take her a stiff drink until I remember that she's nursing. I take it anyway, and she looks up, startled.

But business is brisk; people are already bringing me glasses for refills. I wish I could set out a bowl of peanuts and turn on a baseball game. I wish someone would ask me for a fancy cocktail, something with a silly name and a garnish. The atmosphere is tense but *festive*.

Meanwhile, Josh and Lev are locked in furious consultation, Kreplak's tucking away schnapps, and my father is glued to the bathroom door, lips moving, as he pleads with his brother the joker. My father feels responsible. He has always felt responsible, leaving Mel free to feel any way he wants.

I think I can guess what's going on with Mel. There are times when something comes over you, powerful emotions that seem to have a will of their own. It happened to me once when I left home to be a camp counselor. It was a *relief* to leave— I'd been counting the minutes—but when I said goodbye to my parents, I burst into tears that wouldn't quit. I cried for three hours, and it made no more sense than hiccups. Oh, I suppose a drugstore psychologist might say it had to do with feeling like the odd duck who notices too much, or leaving the comfort of my father's tenderness, or guilt that the friction between my mother and me hurt him. Just like you could say Mel snapped because he'd broken a trust, abandoned his mother and sister, cheated my father, lost his children, failed to save Shirley from cancer or Norma from dementia; because the only bends left in his road are the ones he'd rather not see coming.

But I keep this speculation to myself. Nobody wants to hear what the bartender thinks. Besides, the guests are getting boisterous, making jokes: so far three people have told me they hope this doesn't mean we all have to wander in Josh's backyard for forty years.

"By the time they get that kid outta there they could've had another one!" someone calls.

"Maybe he'll be *bar mitzvahed* from the bathroom!" calls another.

Lev and Josh are louder too. Lev's ready for a Swat Team. Suzanne is holding hands with her mother and Lois. I don't know how she and Josh can ever go back to work after this: they'll have to go into the Jewish Witness Protection Program —dress like *Hasidim*, move to Brooklyn.

"All right, enough—I'm breaking the door down," Josh says finally, stripping off his jacket. Immediately, his gym buddies line up behind him. I look around for a battering ram; the guys get into rushing formation; the rabbi drifts to the back of the room; even Kreplak drops back; the whole room collectively takes a breath; then Suzanne releases her mother's hand and says sharply: "Wait."

It's as if a director yelled "Cut!" Everyone drops what they're doing and turns around—her voice is that commanding. You can see why her bank is sending her to Seoul.

"Uncle Mel." The room is so quiet and her voice so sure that he must be able to hear. She stands by the door. "Uncle Mel," she says, as if she's been saying it all her life. Nobody moves or even clinks ice. "Uncle Mel, it's time to change the baby's dressing."

Not a sound. Her voice softens a little.

"Uncle Mel, his diaper must be wet. The cut will start to sting. He'll be hurting."

Another moment.

"Uncle Mel, he'll want to nurse. You know that's the best possible thing for him." Then she adds with what sounds like a note of surprise: "And I'm the only one who can give it to him."

A moment. Then the lock turns and the door opens. Mel gives the swaddled baby to Suzanne. "I was saying a special prayer for him," he says. "It's an ancient *Kohane* custom." He looks at all of us. "You're supposed to do it in the Holy of Holies, but"—he holds out his arm, introducing us to the powder room —"this was as close as I could get."

The crowd, deciding he is not a dangerous maniac after all

—the Holy of Holies, where God speaks to priests, *would* have been about the size of the powder room—bursts out laughing; the baby is whisked away to be changed, and everybody has another drink. I take one to Mel, who is standing so close to my father their shoulders touch.

"Hey Uncle Mel," I reach up to whisper in his ear. "How come you're smiling upside down?"

"It's a long story," he whispers back. "And so am I."

The baby returns: just baby—no tray, jewelry, or fruit. My father lays his hand on Mel's arm. "Come on, let's get him redeemed before Lev has an aneurysm."

"You do it," says Mel.

My father smiles. "I'm underdressed."

The guests gather around as Josh, firmly tucking the baby like a football under one arm, holds out the five silver dollars with the other and says again: "This is my son whom I wish to redeem according to the ancient law of Torah."

This time Mel accepts the coins, jingles them over the baby's head, and declares: "This instead of that, this in commutation for that, this in remission of that." He looks at Josh and Suzanne and makes the ritual proclamation: "Your son is redeemed. Your son is redeemed. Your son is redeemed." Then, laying the tips of his fingers gently upon the baby's head, he gives the blessing: "May the Lord bless you and keep you. May the Lord make His countenance shine upon you and be generous unto you. May the Lord lift up His countenance upon you and give you peace."

Just as I am wondering why it's equally desirable to have the Lord shine his countenance upon you *and* take it away, the rabbi adds softly: "What God wants, humans cannot fully understand."

I'd like to shout "Amen, brother!" but we don't have that kind of religion. However, when the rabbi blesses the crowd, and Mel and my father hold up their hands with their fingers spread in the Vulcan greeting, I do it too, discreetly, murmuring: "Live long and prosper." I may be a girl, but I am also the real thing: I am *Kohanim*, I am first-born, and I know something about blessings.

Then Lev shouts: "Let's eat!" We race through the *kiddush* and the *hamotzi,* and everyone sits back down, jabbering and laughing, holding out their cups for wine, taking fragrant chunks of challah from the silver tray as it comes around, and dipping them in honey for a sweet life.

THE UNVEILING

The unveiling actually took place, though the stone was for my Bubbe, my father's mother, and I only thought about running away. The girl asking for money really existed too, though many years later in another city. Again, I only thought about slipping her the twenty. (Not just lazy but cowardly—you really are getting to know me.) And this is the only story in which Esther has a sister rather than a brother. But everything else—rage, confusion, disgust, doubt, longing, compassion—is completely autobiographical. Almost.

O n the first anniversary of my uncle's death, we went to the cemetery to unveil his stone. Fresh snow had fallen overnight. We had to wait while the caretaker shoveled a path to the grave. My mother and sister and aunts all stood shivering in their skirts and heels, but I'd brought only jeans home from college. My mother and I had one of our major battles about it, but this time I won, mainly because I was too big to wear anything of hers. Physical fact represented a truth even she couldn't contradict.

Jeans were all I ever wore now, jeans and sweatshirts and big ugly boots. I gave away the pleated skirts and plaid jumpers my mother sent me off to school with when I was seventeen and still hoping that college would be full of people like me, dressed in matching accessories by their mothers but seeking the *rapport*, the intellectual fire that would burn all false layers away. At Thanksgiving that first year I was afraid to go home, lest the radiation of family love undermine my progress, so I made excuses and stayed in the empty dorm. At Christmas I managed to sublet an apartment and find a job, my first, at a restaurant in town, where I mastered the skill of carrying four loaded plates lined up on my arm.

When Asher entered the hospital for the last time, I took the bus home to see him, but I refused to come back for the funeral. My mother called me "heartless" and hung up without saying goodbye. At the end of the term I persuaded my father to pay for summer school and resumed my job at the restaurant. Now I was finally home and nothing had changed. My sister was still as nervous as if *she* were the black sheep, and my father was caught in the middle as usual, trying to negotiate a truce.

When the path was clear, we picked our way among the tombstones to the top of the hill. More relatives arrived, the slamming of their doors muffled by snow, the aunts huddling together, clutching their fur collars. We were waiting for the rabbi. The new tombstone was covered by a cloth staked to the ground. Now and then a gust of wind made the cloth billow and strain at the ropes as if eager to be gone. More relatives teetered up the hill.

"Everyone's coming back to the house afterwards," my mother announced. Her invitations had a way of sounding like commands. "Nothing fancy, just coffee and cake."

Nothing fancy, just what she'd been up all night preparing. By the time I woke up she'd made chopped liver with egg, potato knishes, two coffee cakes, rugelach, and a pan of strudel. And cleaned the house, of course. My mother cleaned each bathroom every day, whether it had been used or not. And every day she patrolled the house with a garbage bag, emptying wastebaskets which hadn't had time to accumulate more than a tissue. I think a visit from my sister or me threw her into a genuine crisis: on the one hand, we were her children; on the other, we might use one of her toilets.

Of course she didn't need to worry about Miriam, who was truly her mother's child, erasing every trace of herself as she went. She even kept her toothbrush in her suitcase. Last night

I watched her spend ten minutes lacerating her gums with a piece of dental floss, then an hour in front of her magnifying mirror with her tweezers. This morning she painted her fingernails mauve. Her hands looked like they belonged to someone who didn't get enough oxygen.

Now, watching my sister shiver in her sleek wool coat, I remembered something I saw in one of my textbooks. I was reading ahead, trying to see how it all came out, when a quote caught my eye. The author, a scientist named Marie Bichat who lived two hundred years ago, wrote: *What is life? The totality of those functions which resist death.* It was almost funny. As if life's some kind of slapstick joke: you're moving along, picking up speed, finally starting to get somewhere, then—wham—banana peel underfoot and everything's over. I watched the aunts chatter among the tombstones, chiffon scarves protecting their hair. What kept them from howling through the streets, clawing at their eyes?

The rabbi arrived at last, apologizing from the moment he popped out of his car: the bar mitzvah ran late, there was a phone call, a traffic jam. He was a plump little man with red lips and rosy quivering cheeks. Breathless, he climbed the hill and shook hands all around. Then he drew a book from his pocket, peeked at his watch, and looked up, his face suddenly and expertly severe. We huddled closer, surrounding the grave.

He began by reciting a psalm in a hushed monotone. Was this the voice that got God's attention? The tombstone's cloth snapped in the wind like the sail of a grounded ship. Beneath the snow and frozen earth lay Asher, wrapped in a prayer shawl in a plain box with holes drilled in the bottom. Though we were modern Jews, and Asher himself an unbeliever, he had been given a traditional burial. Miriam told me the aunts wore old blouses so they could tear real clothing instead of the token strip. After the cemetery they rinsed their hands with a garden hose before going inside to eat the funeral meal of eggs and potatoes: eggs for life, potatoes for death. For seven days after the funeral the men met to recite Kaddish, the famous prayer which affirms the great justice of God and the great meaningfulness of life and contains no reference to the dead. When I asked Miriam why they did all this for Asher, who no longer believed in God—let alone a just and compassionate God—she replied: "Because that's what he wanted." This made as much sense to me as Marie Bichat.

The rabbi enunciated with exquisite precision, shaping each syllable lovingly, prolonging the vowels as if reluctant to let them go. "At Thy command, O God, we have laid to rest one dearly beloved," he intoned, getting a lot of mileage out of "beloved" for someone who never even met Asher. "We murmur not at Thine inscrutable decree."

I wanted to hiss: *Speak for yourself!* But I held it in. Wasn't that what Asher wanted? Hadn't he spent his entire life holding it in?

He wasn't really my uncle. He was my father's cousin, part of the family that stayed behind when the rest emigrated to America. Asher was sixteen when the Nazis came. He survived Auschwitz by strangling an officer's pet dog, digging a hole to hide the corpse, and sawing off morsels with a sharpened spoon. He made the dog last a long time. He did not share. After the war he traveled between DP camps, looking for family, finding no one. My father, who came to Europe with the occupying forces, tracked him down and persuaded him to come to America. Asher started a small grocery store with money raised by his American cousins, who were eager to make amends for not having been turned to smoke. The little store flourished, despite the threat posed by supermarkets, from sheer loving care. Asher weighed seventy pounds when he was liberated: he could imagine nothing more precious than groceries.

He married late. Aunt Tilly was past the point of having children. When she died, Asher the unbeliever tore his clothing, covered the mirrors, sat on the floor, and, as he did each year on the anniversary of his liberation, recited Kaddish to the empty air.

"Why do you do it?" I asked when he lay in the hospital, wasted to a skeleton again. "Why go through the motions?"

He gave a shrug so weak it barely disturbed the tubes. "My family went to the ovens because they were Jews," he said in a hoarse whisper. "If I don't act like a Jew, what did they die for?"

I looked at his arm where dark blue numbers rippled over the loosened skin. "Asher, how can you?" I said, harshly, so I wouldn't cry.

It took him a moment to gather his strength. Then he said: "What else can I do? I have no graves to visit."

The nurse made me leave. I got on a bus and went straight back to school without stopping to see my parents. Asher died three days later. I couldn't bear to attend the funeral, but he alone of the European family whose name I shared had a grave that could be visited, and that was the reason I'd come home this weekend.

Wind swept snow into my eyes, making them sting. The rabbi talked on, smacking his lips over every syllable. "Those of us who have not yet tasted the bitter cup cannot know how soon we may be called upon to drink of it," he said serenely. "We are travelers on the same road leading to the same end."

He nodded to the caretaker, who crouched and tugged at the pegs anchoring the ropes to the earth. The cloth leapt away and everyone shuffled forward to get a good look. Those standing behind the stone craned their necks to gawk at it upside down, like tourists at a historical monument, ready to pull out a camera and take snapshots. The stone was a plain smooth block of granite, rounded on top, standing upright like a closed book. Seeing my name on a fresh tombstone made me queasy.

"As day follows night, and hope follows grief, so does death sweeten life," said the rabbi, closing his book and gazing moistly at his small congregation.

I gave him a bitter stare. This was the wisdom of Torah? This was what Asher's family died for? It made no more sense than the principle of the vacuum, than Asher surviving Auschwitz so he could die of cancer. What happened to him was a hellish acceleration of what happens, eventually, to everyone: if you're lucky enough to live long enough, you lose everyone you've ever cared about. Then you're obliterated. And the real question is, knowing that, how does anyone bear it? What keeps all of us standing in our shoes?

The rabbi concluded with a speedy Kaddish, anxious to get out of the cold and taste my mother's strudel. I itched to throw a rock at that face just to spoil its serene expression. Then, as if reading my mind, everyone began groping under the snow for stones. But instead of pelting them at the rabbi, they filed past the grave one by one to lay them on top, and I remembered that we'd done the same for Tilly. The stones were a calling card, my mother had said, to let other mourners know you remembered the dead. But Asher had another explanation. In a voice rough from weeping, he told me that in the old days mourners had to pile rocks on a new grave to keep wolves from digging up the body. I was fifteen then, and his words made a strong impression: truth is bitter and always concealed. I should have asked him more questions—he had energy left only for the truth—but I was too young.

Abruptly, I dropped my stone and broke into a run, skidding down the hill, ignoring my mother's call. I wanted to lose myself in the traffic outside the gates. I did not want to sit in an overheated living room, eating pastry and answering questions about how I liked school.

"Esther, wait!" my mother cried again, the aunts joining in like a tragic chorus.

It takes a certain amount of nerve to run away when your mother is calling, but once you start, the easiest thing is to keep on going. Before I knew it I was through the gates and across the street, dodging a taxi which barely slowed down. *What the hell's wrong with you?* the driver yelled from his window. I wished I had an answer for him. I kept running. When a bus pulled up to the curb, I jumped on without a thought. I had no idea where it was going.

I rode the bus a long time, trying to think. I'd never run away before, never given in to the urge. I'd thought college would be running away, but apparently it wasn't far enough. I wondered if perhaps I was cracking up.

Then I caught sight of my face in the driver's mirror, a long morose face with stringy bangs, and I let out a laugh that made the old woman across the aisle edge away. That was cheery old me in the mirror, all right: *Esther Fester* my father called me when I brooded.

At the next stop some girls got on, laughing all the way to their seats—normal laughter, the kind that doesn't make old ladies flinch. Listening to them reminded me of something that happened when I was eight. On the playground one day, a group of snickering classmates surrounded me, daring me to sing "Yankee Doodle" with all F's. I began cautiously: "Fankee Foodle fent foo fown, fiding fon fa fony—" then paused. For a moment I teetered, sensing disaster, then proceeded doggedly over the edge. I didn't know what that word meant, that F word that made the others shriek with laughter, but the perverse sense of inviting disaster seemed utterly familiar, even then.

When the bus reached Sherwood Square, the girls got off. On impulse again, I followed. But when they entered a boutique whose windows displayed bald mannequins draped with garbage bags and chunky silver jewelry, I kept walking. The dull afternoon was fading. Soon the shoppers would be gone and the night people would take over. I walked around and around the Square. The obvious answer was to go back to school, but philosophy and physics class hadn't taught me what I needed to know. Nor had listening to the rabbi or watching my mother scour her bathrooms or my sister police her body for imperfections. But neither had lining up plates on my arm, which is all I'd be equipped for if I left school now.

I forced my steps in the direction of the bus station. My nose began to run, scraped raw by the icy mitten I used as a handkerchief. Snow pelted my face: another squall building up. I hunched my shoulders and kept walking.

The girl spoke twice before I realized she was speaking to me.

She was small, about my age, wearing a pilly purple beret. She laid an ungloved hand on my sleeve.

"Excuse me," she said, squinting against the snow. "Could you spare some change for me and my kids? We need food—"

Automatically, I shook her off and kept moving—it could have been a set-up for a mugging. Yet as I put distance between us, I kept seeing that face and hearing that earnest voice. Did she really have children? Could they really be so desperate that she had to go out in a storm and beg for food? She didn't look any older than me, and she'd spoken politely, like someone who'd been brought up well. Didn't she have family?

I looked behind me. All I saw was snow. I walked a little more, remembering how Asher had taken groceries from the shelf every Sunday morning, filling bags for poor families. He left them just inside the back door, where they were quietly picked up. Nothing was ever disturbed, nothing else ever taken.

I'd almost reached the bus station, but I turned around and headed back. It took a long time to find her. I asked a few women if they'd seen a girl in a purple beret, watching as they drew back, taking tighter hold of their purses. At last I spotted her in a bus shelter gnawing on a frozen bagel. I opened my wallet and counted my money: a twenty, two ones, and forty-nine cents—just enough for a ticket back to school. I palmed the twenty, folding it into a tight square. Then I sat on the other end of the bench. She barely looked up. I waited as long as I could stand it. Then I glanced at my watch, let out a theatrical sigh, and got to my feet.

"Darn bus is late," I said. "Guess I better find a cab." To my ears I sounded just like the rabbi, but the girl paid no attention. Then I said: "Oh, look! You dropped this." I stooped as if plucking something from the ground. The girl drew back. Then she saw the folded twenty in my fingers and slowly put out her hand to take it, not looking at my face. She was not a stupid girl at all. I left my mittens beside her.

At first I felt so light, walking back toward the Square,

you'd think the twenty had weighed twenty pounds. But then I remembered my parents, who'd seen me nearly get run over by a taxi, and I stopped in the middle of the sidewalk. My nose was running. My boots leaked. My fingers ached. When I saw a bright coffee shop with a sign in the window advertising a bottomless cup for forty cents, I knew that was what I needed: a bottomless cup.

The coffee was strong and steaming. I loaded it with sugar and gulped the first cup straight down just to thaw out. This amused the counterman and he poured me another. When my fingers worked again, I borrowed a pen, took a paper napkin, and wrote: *Life is the totality of those functions which resist death.* I studied it for a long time while I drank my coffee. There it was, the essential fact of life, a natural law like gravity or inertia. What goes up must come down. A body in motion tends to stay in motion. An empty belly must be fed, cold hands warmed, a sore heart soothed. If life was the problem —short, arbitrary, unfair—then life was also the solution: life was what distracted you from the awful and essential fact of life.

"So what's it gonna be?" said the counterman, topping my cup. He was a gruff wiry little man with silver stubble dotting his jaw like permafrost. "You gonna eat something or just drink up all my coffee?"

"I'm not sure," I said. There were exactly two dollars and forty-nine cents in my wallet. Forty for the coffee, fifty for the tip, sixty for subway fare. That left only ninety-nine.

The counterman gave me a knowing grin. "How 'bout the Breakfast Special? Two eggs and home fries. Ninety-nine cents. Tax included."

I stared at him. Eggs and potatoes, the mourner's meal. Coincidence? Telepathy? Another cosmic joke?

"Yes please," I said faintly. "That would be great."

"How do you want 'em?" Then he added impatiently when I continued to stare: "The eggs."

"Oh," I said. "Scrambled, I guess." Under the circumstances, it seemed the appropriate choice. "And can I use your phone?"

He shook his head but pointed to the wall and busied himself at the grill. I dialed, hoping Miriam would answer, and she did. In the background I could hear the familiar buzz, gossip about health and finances, punctuated now and then by a peal of laughter from the aunts. "Just come home," Miriam said. "Let Mom yell and Daddy make peace, then eat some strudel and everything will be okay."

Afterward, I went to the window to peer out at the night. There were more people on the street now, some striding briskly as if they knew where they were going, others just wandering. I didn't see the girl in the purple beret, but twenty dollars wouldn't last long, and tomorrow or the next night she'd be back. Nothing had changed, really. Even if the smallest human connection or the most trivial coincidence did make the universe seem less random and cruel for the moment. My breath fogged the glass. "Rest in peace, Asher," I whispered, though I knew there was no "rest," or "peace," or even "Asher" anymore.

The counterman set my food down, saying gruffly: "I threw in some toast. Eat while it's hot." He filled my cup and went back to his newspaper. My belly growled. Steam rose from the plate. I took one last glance outside. The veil of snow had lifted, but it could drop again at any moment. Still, I might have just enough time to eat my eggs and potatoes and get myself home before the next storm.

THE SEVEN-LEAGUE BOOTS

This is the story of my first marriage. Everyone, including me, had trouble understanding why we eloped so abruptly and kept it a secret, even from our parents, for six months. The marriage itself lasted four years, and though I struggled to fool myself, I'd known it was a mistake from the start. This story is my attempt to explain things to myself. Professor Moon is based on one of my favorite teachers of all time, Harry J. Mooney. And I did work in a preschool for a while. Chip's promised job was an invention, and Esther's chance to study art history at the Sorbonne is on par with attending the University of Iowa's Writers' Workshop, which I eventually did and which is where I met my second husband.

*I*f *you don't give them Bristol Cream Sherry, how will they know you care?* Esther slides beneath the covers, reaching for the fraying end of a dream. But the voices pursue and penetrate. *You better not pout, you better not cry.* Chip must have left the radio on again. Stations fade in and out, overlapping. *Only four more shopping days!* Esther opens her eyes. Four shopping days till Christmas means eleven days till the end of the year, the end of the decade. The papers have been full of talk about what the eighties will bring: war, economic boom, New Realism Among Youth. Everyone wants to cast the horoscope of the new age. No one suggests that everything might remain the same.

The clock says 8:10, but that's not right. Chip is constantly turning it ahead so he won't be late for work, then forgetting he's turned it and turning it again. When the buzzer goes off, he catapults out of bed, stumbling into walls, furniture. Once he broke his toe, but most days he just gets bruised.

Now Perry Como is singing "What Child Is This?" Esther lets her eyes drift shut, but Myron hops onto the bed and begins biting her earring. She doesn't have to be at work till ten, but Myron wants breakfast now. Esther gives up, pushing the blankets aside. Myron makes himself a nest, purring.

In the bathroom she picks up towels and underwear, straightens the rug, puts the soap back, uses the Pooper Scoop in the litter box, and wipes little hairs out of the sink. She stares out the window as she brushes her teeth. More rain. More thin dark indecisive rain that never quite makes it to snow. She ought to go anyway, put on her slicker and go for a run. Her jeans are getting cranky about zipping. By the time she's had a few kids she'll have to wear caftans, like Chip's mother. Of course, having majored in art history, Esther knows that cultural standards of beauty are arbitrary and ephemeral. But that doesn't make her any happier about her classical waistline and baroque thighs.

On the way to the kitchen Myron makes practice attacks on her ankles, leaping and dashing away. He thinks he's still a kitten—yet another case of arrested development, as Tamar would say. Esther drags the sack of cat chow out from under the sink. When the Mormon Tabernacle Choir bursts into "Winter Wonderland," she reaches over and snaps off the radio. Then she yanks the plug out of the wall.

"Which hand holds the prize?"

Pressed against Esther's legs, Jessica regards the two fists Esther is holding out. Tears still wet her round cheeks and she remembers to hiccup, but she is more interested in the prize than in the boys who decapitated her Barbie and played

Keepaway with its head. She hovers over one fist, then the other.

"Come on, Jess, you have to choose," Esther says.

"All right!" Jessica sounds like a cartoon mouse. "I choose this one—no, this one!" She seizes the left fist. It opens, empty. "No, this one!" She seizes the other, pries Esther's fingers open to uncover the candy cane.

Esther lets her take it. "I said to choose. You made the wrong choice."

"No, I didn't," Jessica says firmly. "I choosed both." Sucking loudly, fragrant with mint, she climbs onto Esther's lap. The playroom is full of four-year-olds kicking balls, slamming blocks, ramming trucks into walls. Every one of them except Jessica is roaring.

All at once the lights go out. Mrs. Moss, the director, is standing at the door, hand on the switch. A ragged hush falls over the room, and Mrs. Moss turns the lights back on. With her pinafore apron and 1950's bob, she looks like the mother in the Quaker's Oats ad.

"Boys and girls," she says sternly. "When the lights go out?"

The response comes in unison: "The mouth goes shut."

"A little faster next time, please." Turning to Esther, she adds: "You have a phone call, Mrs. Hutchins. I'll cover for you here."

Jessica climbs onto Mrs. Moss's lap, settles herself, then bursts into tears. "The boys chopped off Barbie's head," she wails as Esther leaves the room.

Chip is calling from work. In the background Esther hears the racket of knitting machines and wonders how someone used to spending hours enclosed in a soundproof room with his flute and Rampal recordings can bear it. For the past year Chip has worked in a hat factory. Before that he was a doughnut maker, a carpet cleaner, and a parking lot attendant. Twice he went briefly back to school. Now, before his veterans' benefits expire, he is trying again.

"I filed the forms," he tells her. "But there's a new fifty-dollar fee. Can you stop on your way home and pay it?"

"It'll have to wait till I get to the bank," she says. What makes him think she has fifty dollars in her wallet? They don't even have a checking account because they can't manage the $500 minimum.

"IBM was on campus interviewing seniors," he goes on. "You should have seen those kids lined up in three-piece suits. Every one of them holding a briefcase. What could they have in a briefcase besides their lunch?"

Esther takes a breath. "Listen. You don't have to go through with this. You can change your mind."

"I'm running out of time," he replies, so softly she can barely hear. For a moment they both listen to the clatter of machinery. Then Chip says: "I better get back or they'll dock me. See you tonight."

There is music coming from the playroom--Mrs. Moss whacking out "Frosty the Snowman" on the wheezy piano as the children sing. She has even distributed the tambourines and sand blocks—a reproach for Esther, who never organizes anything besides art projects. Mrs. Moss finishes "Frosty" and slides into a strident "Jingle Bells." Esther calculates that she has time for coffee.

The coffee pot is kept in an empty supply closet big enough for two chairs and a tiny table. Tamar is there already, regarding her large feet propped far away on the second chair. Tamar is six feet tall, with ruddy cheeks and a long black braid the children love to yank. She used to be a revolutionary and was actually expelled from college for teaching other undergrads how to make firebombs. These days she lives quietly with her boyfriend and never discusses politics except to groan when Reagan's name is mentioned. The children call her The Giant and love to hurl themselves at her knees and tumble her to the floor, where she stretches out in comfort. In fact, she is so often horizontal that Esther is rarely conscious of their difference in height.

"How's Joel?" Esther says, filling a cup with Mrs. Moss's bitter coffee.

"Contemplating law school and the good life," Tamar drawls, moving her legs so Esther can sit.

Esther's never sure when Tamar is joking, but she grins and says: "Chip's going back to school too."

"Why? I thought he finally decided to let your father teach him the carpet business."

"My dad thinks a college degree will give him more confidence." Esther feels herself flush. "Anyway, one of Dad's clients is building a mall, and Dad convinced him to include a day-care center for shoppers. They're going to put me in charge. Of course it means moving back to Akron. But everyone feels that way about their hometown, right? Unless they come from Paris, maybe." She waits, but Tamar is still regarding her feet. "Also my father's got his eye on a little house he says would be perfect for our first. We could move in as soon as Chip graduates."

"Well, great," says Tamar. "Made in the shade."

"We could start a family."

Tamar arcs her paper cup into the trash. "So what's the problem?"

"No problem. Everything's falling into place." She sips the nasty coffee.

"Well, great," says Tamar again. She takes out a cigarette and lights it, defying the Surgeon General, the fire marshal, and Mrs. Moss all in one economical gesture.

Esther watches the smoke curl into the air. "Can I have a hit of that?"

Tamar raises an eyebrow but hands her the cigarette. "I didn't know you smoked."

"I don't. This is only..." The sharp bite of menthol brings back the taste of summer three years ago, that strange summer when her life took an unexpected turn and strayed off the map. She remembers lying on Chip's bed at sunset, sharing his cigarette and beer, watching the sky turn the color of raspberry jam. That she can picture clearly. But the girl on the bed—just graduated, fresh from the triumph of a prize-winning thesis, headed for Europe to study art and perfect her French—she's a little out of focus. Esther holds in the smoke, but her head seems to float away from her shoulders and she has to let go. "Woo," she says. "Dizzy."

"You know you need a degree in Child Ed. to run a licensed daycare center."

"I know," Esther slides down in her chair. "I'll have to hire someone else to be in charge till I get the damn degree."

Tamar grins. "I'm sure it'll give you more confidence."

Esther flushes again. "It's just—I never expected to spend my life in nursery school."

"Oh well, expectations." Tamar shrugs. "At some point you just have to call it: this is your life, this is how you turned out."

"But at which point?" says Esther, reaching for the cigarette again. "How do you know when?"

Just as she takes another hit, the door opens and little Mrs. Finkel pokes her head in. Instantly, Esther drops the hand holding the cigarette out of sight.

"There you are, Mrs. Hutchins," says Mrs. Finkel in her fluttery voice. She is frail and elderly and wears a monstrous ginger wig. "And Miss Malinsky, too. Did you girls know that Mrs. Moss is looking for you?"

"Of course," Tamar says coolly. "Why do you think we're hiding in here?"

Mrs. Finkel gives a fluttery uncertain laugh. "But isn't it time for Art Table?"

"Tell her I'm on my way," Esther manages to say around the smoke in her lungs.

Mrs. Finkel withdraws. Esther lets out a sputtering cloud,

and she and Tamar giggle like a pair of four-year-olds.

A collective groan goes up from Art Table when Esther takes Christmas tree cutouts from the filing cabinet.

"We did Christmas trees *YES*terday," Jessica squeaks.

"Yesterday we did wreaths," says Esther. "We haven't done Christmas trees for almost a week."

"I don't want to color," declares Matthew. "I want to go outside!"

"Me too! Me too!" comes the chorus.

"It's raining outside." Esther rummages through the cabinet. "I know what—" She pulls the fat book of fairy tales from its hiding place. "You color your trees and I'll read you a story."

"What kind of story?" says Matthew suspiciously.

"One you've never heard before." The book, Esther's own, is so old that corners of brownish pages break off in her fingers. Mrs. Moss would definitely disapprove. Esther found it in a used bookstore when she was sixteen and fell in love with the glossy medieval-style illustrations, glinting with silver and gold. She can't imagine actually giving such a thing to children, however, for it contains terrifyingly faithful translations of the original tales. There is one about a boy whose tongue is plucked out by ravens because he invents extravagant lies and another about a girl who neglects her duties for love of dancing and is condemned—-by an angel, yet—-to dance without ceasing in red-hot slippers until she falls down dead. But there are a few...Esther carefully turns pages until she comes to a story that won't give the children nightmares.

They listen, crayons moving slower and slower, as she reads them the tale of a clever courageous youth who goes into the world to seek his fortune. After many gory but educational adventures, he rescues a princess from an ogre by stealing the ogre's magic boots, which cover seven leagues with each step. Though the boots cruelly fatigue the wearer, and the ogre places many obstacles in his path, the young man perseveres. Holding the princess in his arms, he goes striding from hilltop to hilltop, stepping over rivers as if they were streams and oceans as if they were puddles, until he arrives at the kingdom of Heart's Desire, where the grateful king lavishly rewards him with treasure and the hand of the princess in marriage.

Enchanted, the children leap up to strut about the lunchroom in magic boots. Esther lures them back to the table by announcing that she is about to draw a portrait of the glamorous new couple. Taking a big sheet of manila paper, she draws a blond blue-eyed princess with dainty feet and a tiny waist. The princess wears a crown, a ruby necklace, long gloves, lacy skirts, and carries an armful of flowers. Esther makes the prince tall and broad-shouldered with dark hair and a sensitive cleft chin. He wears his crown, sword, cape, and, of course, the wonderful boots. She has drawn Barbie and Ken. Art is something she *studies*.

"Where's the ogre?" asks Matthew.

"He must have killed it," says Esther, knowing she lacks the skill to attempt an ogre.

Matthew is crestfallen. "Why did he have to kill it?"

The girls answer promptly: "So he could marry the princess!"

"And get all the treasure!"

"And keep the magic boots!"

"And live happily ever after," says Esther, laying down her crayon, exhausted.

Clutching keys, purse, gloves, and two damp bags of groceries, Esther trudges up the stairs. As usual, Myron bolts for the bedroom when she unlocks the door. He is not a heroic cat —burglars may take whatever they like. The apartment is crowded, with floors that slant like the deck of a grounded ship. Bare wood shows through bald spots in the carpet, and none of the doors close properly. Still, it's cheap and has a small spare room, which Esther thought could serve as a study, a kind of sanctuary. But sanctuaries cannot be shared, and since the room belongs to both of them, neither uses it. It is occupied instead by Chip's hoard.

Chip is a natural forager whose talent for finding things made him a valued supply clerk during the war and kept him safely in the rear, where there was so much unofficial trade that a more ambitious young man might have made a small fortune. These days he scavenges in trash piles and dumpsters. The kitchen radio, slightly defective, was one of his finds. He has also brought home leaking bags of birdseed, a wig stand, a garden hose, enough end tables and lamps to furnish a small hotel, and his greatest prize: an old-fashioned beehive hair dryer on wheels. This last he was willing to donate to the day-care center.

"What do you expect the children to do with a hairdryer?" Esther asked.

"Turn it into a spaceship." He gave it a pat. "That's what *I'd* do."

Perhaps in reaction, Esther has come to take great pleasure in throwing things away, even an empty tub of margarine which she'll have to replace. It gives her the illusion that she's making some kind of progress. But then Chip will come struggling through the door with another ottoman or box of squashed papayas, looking so pleased that she will do no more than remark: "Other people take the trash *out*."

Tonight, however, he comes in empty-handed while she is making the meatloaf. "Hey," he says, shrugging out of his coat. This is their evening ritual. Her response is "Hey." They used to exchange pecks, self-consciously, as though waiting for the applause of a studio audience.

Chip drops his keys on the table, his wallet on the bookshelf, his coat in the vicinity of the sofa. He twists off his wristwatch, puts it vaguely aside. Esther notes its location. Tomorrow he'll wake her to ask: "Have you seen my wallet? I can't find my watch." Then he'll rush off, leaving behind the lunch she packed the night before. Maybe not altogether by accident, either. He's tired of bologna and egg salad but can't think of what he'd like instead, and if she tells him to make his own lunch, he won't bother. He'll get a candy bar from the machine. And he's so skinny already. Marriage seems to have starved him and surfeited her.

Myron emerges from the bedroom to sit discreetly before his dish. Chip slings him over one shoulder and wanders into the living room to pick out a Rampal record. Esther only hears a few notes before he plugs in the headphones and sinks into the beanbag chair, legs asprawl. His long hands, sticking out of the flannel shirt, are scarred with burns from the pressing equipment.

After putting potatoes on to boil, Esther sits down to make a list. Tomorrow is her day off, but the laundry hamper is full, the bathroom needs scrubbing, she ought to get some exercise, and there's Chip's errand at school. *Laundry*, she writes, *bathroom, litter-box, bank, school, run*, then puts down her pencil and looks at Chip, trying to remember what she'd expected, what she'd thought married life would be like. But everything happened too fast. He proposed on a Sunday night, she said "Maybe someday," and by Thursday they were married. Esther was so stunned that she spent the next six months impersonating a happy bride. And when that delusion finally burned out, she was left with a persistent feeling of displacement, as though she'd wandered by mistake into someone else's life.

Chip suddenly opens his eyes and gives her one of his rare sweet smiles. Startled, Esther smiles back. After all, he is not the enemy. He's the same boy who smiled at her four years ago, the boy who sat in a tree and played his flute and lured her away from her dream of foreign cities and great museums. Theirs is a compelling love story: romantic, impetuous, improbable—-the kind women read about in magazines. When Esther remembers it this way, she feels a flutter. But Chip closes his eyes again and sinks back into the music. It was the flute that made him smile—-he must have forgotten that she cannot hear it. Esther picks up her pencil and stares at her list. When the kitchen timer goes off, she jumps up as if there is not a moment to lose.

The university is deserted. Classes have been suspended for the holiday, and tomorrow the offices will close. After paying Chip's fee, Esther takes a detour through the Fine Arts building. Last term's student paintings and sculptures are on display, looking all too familiar. She wanders past empty studios and practice rooms until she comes to the big picture window overlooking the courtyard. There in the middle of the yard, naked and smaller than she remembers, is the tree. If it hadn't been for this tree...but then, if it hadn't been a prematurely hot spring, and if she hadn't been lying among the new dandelions, listening to the flute instead of studying her French. If she hadn't looked up and caught him looking down. If they hadn't smiled.

But how could she not have smiled to see him straddling his branch, shy and sleepy-eyed in his camouflage fatigues, his hair curling to his shoulders, his chin tipped with an absurd sandy tuft? He was so clearly not to be taken seriously—-a late-blooming flower child, an uncomplicated summer fling—-that the waters closed over her head before she knew she was in trouble. Instead of going home to work in her father's office and save every penny for the pilgrimage to Europe, she stayed and let summer slip by in a haze. Spring seemed to linger that year. Even in a city full of fumes and exhaust, a persistent fragrance hung in the air, and the gaudy poisons sent up by the mills made for spectacular sunsets. Chip was the first boy she had ever had so much power over. Soon enough she would be in Europe. What was a month more or less?

She cannot remember—-standing here in Fine Arts, her hand laid flat against the glass which shuts out wind, rain, and history—-exactly how the subject of marriage came up, but she remembers saying: "Wait till I come back." And Chip saying: "It will be too late." Day and night he badgered her: they would go to Europe together, they would *live* in Europe, it didn't matter if she wasn't sure: he was sure enough for both of them. And so one fresh morning more like May than August, Esther found herself on a bus going to the magistrate's office, clutching a handful of pink carnations and staring at the other passengers, hoping some psychic would take her arm and tell her what to do. She knew she wasn't in love, not like he was, but perhaps that kind of mutual rapture was simply a cultural fantasy, or else so rare that, like the goodness of saints, it passed instantly into myth. Surely no educated person labored under such illusions. Even so, in the middle of the ceremony she began to cry so hard that the magistrate buzzed his secretary for Kleenex. "Would you like to sit down and think it over?" he asked Esther, looking pointedly at Chip's hair. Esther looked too. He wasn't what she'd expected, what she'd been waiting for, but how often did someone who loved you come along? She was afraid it might only be once.

The rain is falling harder now, staining the tree fresh black. Esther turns her back on the window and walks down the hall of eerily empty classrooms. Everything looks the same as it did three years ago, even the notices on the bulletin boards. She stops at Professor Moon's seminar room and smiles, remembering how he always greeted his students at the door as if he were hosting a banquet and they were his dear guests, how he seated them at the long table, and offered coffee from his own thermos before plunging into a lecture which mostly consisted of thinking aloud. Now and then he would invite a comment, saying: "Just wade in here anywhere, Miss Sapperstein, anywhere at all." He would listen to what she said with unflinching attention, make one of two standard replies

—-either "You have gone straight to the heart of the matter" or "A point or two about that and then I shall have done"—-then resume his monologue exactly where he'd left off. Often he got up to pace, and the students would follow him with their eyes as he wandered around the table, hands clasped behind his back. Once he became so engrossed in what he was saying that he strayed out of the room into the hall, still talking. The students smothered their laughter and strained their ears to hear him. Eventually he wandered back in.

Impulsively, Esther turns and hurries up the stairs to his office. She has never failed to find him there. Legend has it that he sleeps on the couch and never goes home, although she has also heard that he shares an apartment with his aged mother and takes her to early Mass every day.

His is the only office door without a poster taped to the glass for privacy. Esther can see him inside, holding a slide up to the light. As always, he is wearing a baggy gray suit, white shirt, and black bow tie, as though he himself were a study in chiaroscuro. When Esther taps on the glass he jumps, and his thatchy gray eyebrows shoot up. In two strides he is flinging the door open, grasping her hand, and declaring with great conviction: "But it isn't Miss Sapperstein!"

"Actually, it isn't," says Esther. "It's Mrs. Hutchins now. How are you, Professor?"

"Mrs. Hutchins?" he repeats, mystified. "Well, of course you must be right about that. But how long has it been? Two years? Three?"

"Four, I'm afraid."

"Four years!" He shakes his great head, adding dubiously: "Well, you must be right about that too." Seating her on the visitor's throne, he offers a peppermint from the ancient Near East burial urn on his desk, then leans forward to fix her with his intent gaze. "Now then, Miss Sapperstein, you must tell me where you have been and what you have seen."

Embarrassed, Esther tells him about the day-care center, but under the nourishing light of his attention, her experiences there acquire new life and humor. She even manages to laugh when she describes the "art" projects: macaroni glued to paper plates, necklaces of cut-up straws and string. Then she tells him about Chip's series of jobs and his decision to go back to school, adding: "I'm thinking of going back myself."

At this Professor Moon hitches his chair forward again, exclaiming: "But do you believe in kismet, Miss Sapperstein?"

"Kismet?" The old Broadway musical?

"The Greeks called it *moira*—fate, happenstance, serendipity." He gives a happy laugh, and before she can explain about Child Ed. and the licensing laws, rushes on: "I confess I believe along with Pope that `all Nature is but Art unknown.' Or Dryden, perhaps. Or no, no, Pope." He is sorting rapidly through the mass of papers on his desk. "You see, just yesterday I had a letter that made me instantly think of you...and today here you are!...but where is the letter? Ah!" Triumphantly, he extracts the right page and drops it back on the heap. "The Mandelbaum Foundation! Six new post-graduate fellowships, very private—-one has to be invited to apply. Well, that's it, you see? They've asked me to recommend a candidate."

Esther is stunned. "Mandelbaum. The collector?"

"The *great* collector," he corrects her. "Now, I believe the terms are generous..." Again he gropes for the letter and Esther discreetly nudges it forward. "Yes, tuition, stipend, travel, and so on, `for indigent students of exceptional promise." He peers anxiously at her. "But *are* you indigent, Miss Sapperstein?"

"Oh yes," says Esther faintly.

"I am very glad to hear it! Now, the selection will be based upon the sponsor's recommendation and—" the eyebrows shoot up and stay up—"an original critical essay."

"But Professor, I haven't done anything in three years. I haven't been to a museum. I've scarcely looked at a picture."

He waves her protest aside. "Your thesis on Myron of Eleutherai's sculpture was the best piece of work to cross my desk in twenty years, particularly your insights about the crucial moment of rest between completing one motion and beginning another. All you need do is bring it up to date."

That thesis. When Esther was little, she'd wanted to write stories—fairy tales like the ones in the gold book with the crumbling pages. But in junior high she'd gone to her first art museum and simply fallen into the paintings. Later, in college, she'd shown talent for writing about them—and about sculpture, especially Greek and Roman figures, which seemed to just be waiting for her to breathe them out of their stilled enchantment.

Professor Moon coughs discreetly. Startled, Esther swallows her peppermint, which leaves a tingling trail down her gullet. "But Professor, even if you're right, even if I got my master's, what then? There are no jobs in fine arts. My father's always sending me articles from *The Wall Street Journal* about it. And in the eighties it's supposed to get worse."

"My dear Miss Sapperstein," says Professor Moon. His chair will go no further, so he leans forward to pin her with his gaze. "There may be few jobs, there may be fewer jobs than ever before, but *there are never no jobs at all.* Even *The Wall Street Journal* will tell you *that.* There will always be a place for someone who is good enough."

"But that's just it—" She stops, shaking her head. She looks around at the statues of Isis and Enki and Marduk on his shelves. How can she tell him that he is well known for judging students in light of his beatific personal regard? "You're telling me just to do it. To go ahead as if I knew it would all work out."

"As if!" The words electrify him. "As if! Miss Sapperstein, you have gone straight to the heart of the matter. To act in hope. To profess faith in the beneficence of the unknown. Because what is the alternative, Miss Sapperstein?" Instead of answering the question, he asks it again, thoughtfully. "What is the alternative?"

Before he can slip further into reverie, Esther gets up, murmuring something about catching her bus, which is absurd since buses run every twenty minutes. But Professor

Moon hands her the application form, beaming.

"I shall expect great things of you in Paris," he declares.

Esther's arm freezes mid-sleeve. "Paris?"

"Of course. Where else would they put the Sorbonne?"

"The Sorbonne?" She stares at him. "I thought—-I assumed I'd study here."

"Oh, they can do much more for you at the Sorbonne. And think of the museums just a train ride away—why, the finest Discobolus is in the National Roman! And I know you have a particular weakness for Etruscan vase paintings—think of all you could see first-hand—the real things!" His smile fades when she doesn't respond. "Does Paris present difficulties?"

Esther looks up into his kind puzzled face. "No," she says after a moment. "No difficulties." It's true: she's always loved vase paintings, with their circular stories. Always hoped to save up enough to buy one herself someday. To own a piece of history, mythology, art—it's almost too much to ask for. Like stealing fire.

She gives him her hand at the door, jams on her damp woolen hat, and trots briskly out into the rain. Not until she is wedged into a bus packed with Christmas shoppers does she permit herself to think: *Paris.*

They eat hot dogs for dinner and watch "A Christmas Carol" on TV. When Ebenezer Scrooge stands shivering beside his own grave, Chip turns it off and begins laying out a game of solitaire. Before he can put on the headphones too, Esther offers to play a little Back Alley Bridge. Warily, Chip re-shuffles the deck. He knows she doesn't like card games.

She learned Back Alley Bridge the day she met his parents: it replaced the need for conversation. The family named the game for the house they lived in before Chip's father had the heart attack which forced his demotion from bus driver to dispatcher. Now they live in a trailer so crowded and dim that

Esther has to take a deep breath before she can step onto the concrete block and enter.

Chester Hutchins Senior, a shorter and denser version of his son—a man whose veins you can almost see clotting with anger—spent eighteen years as a drill instructor in the army. At home he was given to rages which ended with smashed lamps and dry sobbing. To escape, Chip took his flute and disappeared into the woods. His sisters sought refuge with neighbors, and his mother—a pale blond mound of a woman—learned to sit before the television as though she were floating, tranquil and oblivious.

But when, in a fury at being passed over for promotion, Chester quit the army before his pension came due, humiliation knocked some of the fight out of him. His heart attack a year later did the rest. Now he contents himself with black coffee and bitter disparagement of federal government, company management, and union leadership. He resents all forms of authority. When Chip enlisted in the army so that he could go to college, his father refused to speak to him for a year.

Esther's parents, on the other hand, are middle-class Jews of the Depression generation that grew up anxious and ambitious. Her father, trim and well-tailored in suits her mother picks out, owns a carpet business in Akron. Esther's mother, who wears long earrings and custom-made eyelashes, takes classes and lessons and therapy. Currently, she is studying color analysis. She makes collages for Esther from magazine pictures of fashions and accessories she thinks would look becoming. At first Esther's parents were bewildered by the elopement, but they consider themselves progressive thinkers and know of far worse fates that have befallen their friends' children. Besides, the person who would have taken the news the hardest—Esther's Yiddish-speaking grandmother—had, sadly but conveniently, passed away the year before.

"Your bid," says Chip.

Esther is gazing at her cards. "I'm thinking."

"Want to quit?" He shuffles his cards and flips them in the air for the entertainment of the cat, who swipes at them wildly. Chip laughs. He is losing and wants to catch up, but he's willing to quit if she's tired. He doesn't have his father's temper. And he doesn't drink or gamble or sleep around. He can even be romantic on occasion. A lot of women would gladly trade places with her.

"Not yet," she says. "Let's go on a little longer."

It is not until they are lying in bed with the lights off that she tells him about the Mandelbaum Foundation. He shows polite interest in the news.

"I'd have to live in Paris," she adds to make sure he understands.

"Well," he says. "It's a little far to commute."

The room is so quiet she can hear the electric whine of the clock. Myron hops onto the bed and settles on her pillow. A loud, comfortable, familiar purr rumbles into her ear. Esther's throat tightens. She is sure cats cannot go to France.

"I have to let him know right after New Year's," she tells Chip.

He yawns. "It's a great opportunity. Chance of a lifetime, probably."

"Well, I haven't decided to apply yet," she says irritably.

Chip says nothing more but keeps scrupulously to his side of the bed. Esther lays her cheek against Myron's warm fur, closes her eyes, and pretends she is telling the children a story: *Once upon a time there was a clever and courageous youth who went into the world to seek his fortune...*

She wakes confused, thinking someone has urgently called her name, thinking she has overslept and will be late for work. Then she hears the familiar thin moan. Chip is having one of his nightmares.

"Wake up!" she whispers, grasping his shoulder. The eerie moan continues. "Stop it! Wake up!"

He gives a sudden gasp and jerks up, shuddering. "I was blocked. I couldn't get back in till you touched me."

Ever since childhood Chip has believed that while he sleeps, his spirit leaves his body and travels through the astral plane, moving through natural and supernatural dimensions, released from the constraints of mortality. Mostly, it's a great adventure. But if anything should prevent his spirit from re-entering his body, or if his body should be discovered and occupied by another wandering spirit, he would be exiled, marooned: a premature ghost.

"First I floated toward the window," he goes on. "But something kept me from leaving. So I turned and saw a figure standing by the mirror. Its back was toward me and I couldn't see a reflection. So I went a little closer...and I felt this tremendous wave of..." He swallows. "I don't know...something ice-cold. I froze. I couldn't move." His voice sinks to a whisper. "Then the figure began to turn around...very slowly...and do you know what I saw?"

"No!" Esther shouts, startling them both. "And I don't want to know!"

They stare at each other. Then Chip says bitterly: "Right. After all, it's not *your* nightmare."

"I'm sorry," says Esther. "Those dreams give me the creeps."

"Forget it." He turns over, pulling up the covers. "Have a nice night."

Esther snaps on the lamp. "Why don't you just say it? You think I'm a selfish bitch—and not just because of the nightmare. Because I want to go to France."

"Well, how would *you* feel?" He turns over to face her. "Besides, I thought you hadn't decided yet."

"I haven't. Not about us."

"What about us?"

She hesitates. "Well, what would happen? Would you come with me?"

"And live on what? Am I supposed to press hats in France?"

"So we'd split up? That's what you're saying?"

He sits up, tossing the covers aside. "Don't put words in my mouth."

"Well then, tell me what you think!"

Again they stare at each other. Then Chip heaves a sigh and drags himself out of bed. "I don't know what I think."

Esther follows him into the kitchen, where he pours himself a glass of milk.

"How can you not know? You were always so sure. I kept asking and asking, remember? I said if you had any doubts, we wouldn't go through with it. And you said—"

"I said I was sure enough for both of us. What else could I say? You laid the whole responsibility on me." He chugs down the milk, adding bitterly: "It was all right for you to moan and worry, but I was supposed to be some kind of *rock*."

"But you were the one who insisted on marriage. If we'd just lived together—"

"If we'd just lived together, you would have been off to Europe like a shot as soon as you had the money. You wouldn't have given me a second thought." He wanders into the living room and drops onto the beanbag chair.

Esther follows. "Just answer a simple question. Why did you want to marry me?"

Chip rubs his eyes. The milk has left a slight mustache. "But it's not simple," he says after a moment. "I'd just gotten out of the army. I was in college, a place I used to think was only for rich kids, and had no idea what to do. One thing I did know: I wasn't going to end up like my father. But I didn't want to be swallowed by some coat-and-tie job either and spend my life doing something I hated. My life was finally my *own*—not the army's and not my father's—and I didn't have a clue what to do with it." He slides further down, staring at the ceiling. "Then I met you, and it was like...you know that old movie about the runaway princess and the commoner who fall in love? I mean, maybe she's dressed in rags, but he can still tell. She just seems to know, instinctively, how life should be lived."

"What are you talking about?" says Esther. "I was just a middle-class Jewish girl. I still am."

"You brought home flowers the way other people bring groceries. You taught me how to eat an artichoke, remember? And I had champagne for the first time." He smiles faintly. "I had a lot of firsts with you. Remember those white dresses you used to wear?"

"One," says Esther. "I had one white dress."

"But the best thing was the way you taught me to use my eyes. There's a whole other world camouflaged by this one, you said. You showed me the patterns of leaves and shadows in the woods. And the buds that looked like green scrunched-up faces of little old men. And the paintings at the museum, the specks and dabs that came together and made the illusion of a whole —like atoms, you said, like the universe." He shakes his head. "I'd never looked at things that way. I'd never met anyone like you. You seemed to have some special knowledge or talent or *something*. Something to protect you from ordinary life..." He runs out of words and they sit looking in silence at the slanted floor and buckling carpet.

Then Esther says without meaning to: "Poor Chip."

He stirs irritably. "But you could have backed out. Why didn't you? Why did you marry *me*?"

"Because you were so much in love." She shrugs. "Or so I thought. I thought it was the most romantic thing that would ever happen to me." She is quiet for a moment, watching the cat. "I think we created our own mythology."

Chip laughs softly. "Maybe we could sell it to the movies."

"But we don't know how it turns out yet."

He turns to look at her, his face with the milk mustache haggard in the graying light. "What does that mean? You want to stay together?"

"I want to be sure we don't make another mistake. Aren't you the one always telling me not to throw things away? I mean, let's not rush out of anything."

He doesn't smile. After a moment he says: "All right. Let me know what you decide."

"But what do *you* want?"

"I'd wait for you. I'd wear a tie and learn your father's business and give the regular life my best shot. Or if you'd rather, we'll call it quits and no hard feelings. But this time it has to be your decision. No pressure from me. *You* have to be sure."

"But...what are you saying? You still love me?"

"Love," says Chip, as the alarm goes off in the bedroom. "I have no idea what to call it." He turns to look out at the granite sky. "Christ. I've got to go to work."

On numb feet Esther goes to start the coffee. She turns on the radio. Nothing happens.

"Chip," she says, staring into the empty pot. "What if I'm never sure?"

He doesn't answer. Then he says: "It was you in front of the mirror, Esther. That's what I saw."

The radio suddenly comes to life with a burst of static and a voice shrieking that there are *only two days left.*

Today is the children's party: four hours of shrieks and tears punctuated by sugar breaks to fend off total mayhem. Tomorrow the vacation begins. There is still no snow, though the radio plays "White Christmas" constantly as if invoking the weather gods, and the children keep running to the window to check. They disdain Mrs. Finkel's attempts to organize a game of Pin The Star On The Tree, preferring to become ogres, lurching about the room, curving sticky fingers into claws, and falling on one another with hungry snarls. When they fall on gigantic Tamar, she allows them to bear her to the floor and drag her to their lair, the playhouse in the corner, where the task of stuffing in her long limbs is so hilarious that Mrs. Moss has to flick the light switch five times before they come to order.

"It seems that some people have not made the connection between knowing and doing," Mrs. Moss announces with a severe glance at Tamar, who is trapped in the little house, limbs sticking out the windows like Alice after she drinks the White Rabbit's potion.

After the last child has been collected by his mother, Mrs. Moss invites Tamar into the coffee room for a chat. Esther wonders if Tamar will avoid a scolding by announcing her wedding plans. She has announced them to Esther already.

"Heard the one about the retired anarchist tying the knot with the former draft-dodger?" she'd murmured while they were passing out cards for Animal Bingo.

It took Esther a moment to decode the irony. Then she said in astonishment: "Joel proposed?"

"Well, he didn't get down on his knees in the moonlight," Tamar replied. "Let's just say that the topic came up for discussion and a resolution was drafted."

"Congratulations!" Esther said. "I hope you'll be happy."

Tamar grinned. "About as happy as most married people, I expect," she said, and Esther realized that Tamar used cynicism the way some people use alcohol: to insulate herself, to flatten things out and reduce them to manageable size.

Esther volunteers to clean up the lunchroom so the other ladies can go home. Alone, she wanders, sponge in hand, till she finds herself up against the window, forehead to the glass. When she was little, she used to press her nose against the TV screen, trying to get close enough to fathom the magic, to see the dancing dots in a pointillist painting. But all she makes out is a fuzzy string of lights inching up the ramp to the expressway. The sky is black already. Yesterday was the shortest day of the year.

Her breath has fogged the glass. She rubs it clear again,

trying to imagine Chip ten years from now: confident, fleshed out, playing his flute on a Sunday afternoon, perhaps, while she weeds the garden. The grass is chrome green, the sky Chinese blue, the flowers bright dabs of red and yellow. She looks up, he looks down, sunlight flashes on the silver flute...but it's the past she's seeing, not the future.

"Tired, Esther?" says Mrs. Moss.

Startled, she turns. "No, just thinking. About the holiday and all." In the hall Tamar passes by, bundled up for outside. She pauses long enough to grin and give Esther the power salute, one fist raised straight in the air.

"Oh, the holiday." Mrs. Moss sinks wearily onto one of the tiny chairs. "Every year my children try to send me on a cruise, but I tell them: what's the point of going somewhere just to turn around and come back? Nothing changes." She begins to rub her hands, finger by finger. "My big mistake was letting them talk me into selling the house. It's too much work, they said, but work is my secret vice." Then, with unexpected humor, she adds: "But maybe you know that."

Esther smiles, sitting beside her. "There are worse vices."

"Last year I gave in and while I was gone, my daughter had my apartment redecorated. Pink and white, as if I were sixteen." Mrs. Moss sighs. "Sometimes at night I go home and sit on my pink couch and stare at my polka-dot curtains and think: now what?"

Esther picks up the sponge and gives the table a half-hearted swipe. "So you're...on your own now?" This has been a topic of much speculation among the staff. Everyone knows that something happened to Mrs. Moss's husband, but no one knows the details.

"Well, I have my children. Of course, you can't really call them yours after they've grown up. When they're little, they stay close and you know what they need. But then they grow up, they get complicated, they have secrets—they turn into somebody else. Sometimes I catch a glimpse of the children they used to be, looking out of their eyes, and I want to warn them. But then I think: be quiet, old woman, no one can warn anyone else."

Esther scrapes a blob of jelly. "You must have been married a long time."

Mrs. Moss takes the sponge and applies it herself. "Let me tell you a little story," she says, switching to her usual cheery voice. "Once upon a time, I married Henry Moss, a nice boy from a good family. He was smart, handsome, full of promise, every girl's prince. Henry started a business with his brother, and we had our first child. The business made money. We bought a house and had the twins. The business made more money, so we bought a bigger house and had another baby. We planned to put in a tennis court and swimming pool, to learn to ski and sail, to take the children on a fabulous safari.... But by the time the twins started junior high, none of us was seeing much of Henry. He would be gone overnight, then weekends; he was funny about bank accounts and phone calls and—oh, it's an old familiar story. The judge awarded half of everything to me. Henry never protested. I told him to leave town and he did. I went back to teaching and discovered that a person with a crater in her chest can still function with perfect efficiency."

She lifts a hand to smooth her hair, and suddenly Esther understands why Mrs. Moss, with her pinafore apron and Mamie Eisenhower bangs, looks like a relic from the fifties: it's her way of commemorating the time in her life when she was happy, when the children were small and her husband came home every night.

"But you know," she goes on. "I missed him badly. He was my oldest friend, after all. When he began calling late at night, I started to think maybe he wanted me to ask him back. But then I remembered all the pain he'd caused, and I thought: no, let him stew a little longer." Her voice trails off, and for a moment there is no sound except a click from the clock on the wall. "One night he went out jogging. It was freezing, but he'd quit smoking and he was determined to get back in shape. `You're trying to recapture your youth,' I told him, but he just laughed.

He went out to jog and fell dead on the sidewalk. Just like that. No more Henry Moss." She gives Esther a bitter bewildered smile.

"I'm sorry," says Esther. It's all she can think of to say.

"Oh, sorry, we're all sorry—I'm sorry for burdening you with this sad tale." She reaches over and rests her hand on Esther's. The bent fingers resemble the children's make-believe claws. "Young people don't like to hear that life plays dirty tricks. They don't really believe it." She pats Esther's hand with her dry one. "But I've heard some talk. I thought maybe you needed to hear this story. Now go on home to your husband. I'll finish cleaning up."

Esther doesn't want to leave her alone. "I don't mind staying."

But Mrs. Moss is firm. "No, no, run along. He'll be wanting his dinner."

Esther gets her coat. On her way out she pauses at the lunchroom, but Mrs. Moss is scrubbing tables and doesn't look up.

On Christmas morning, Esther wakes early to find that the invocations have paid off: clean white snow paints the muddy streets and soggy lawns. It will be a pretty Christmas after all. She slides out of bed quietly and gets dressed. Chip is still asleep, sprawled across the bed. Last night he had another nightmare. Who will wake him if she is no longer here? What if his soul remains trapped outside his body?

Myron accompanies her briskly down the hall but flees back to the warm bed as soon as she opens the front door. Outside, the air tastes like Professor Moon's peppermints. There is little traffic. She walks one block, then breaks into a sluggish trot, skidding a little, forcing her knees up and letting her feet thud back to earth. She passes window after window of bath-robed families gathered under their Christmas trees. By day, the electric lights strung along rooftops look dusty and dull. Yards and porches are ringed with paper bags filled with sand and splotched with melted wax. Last night these were fairy lanterns.

Her muscles resist as she starts up a hill, and she imagines them as giant teeth, grinding up the distance. This makes her think of a proverb she once found in a fortune cookie: "To finish a journey of a thousand miles, take a step." But the proverb doesn't tell you what to do when the road forks and there are good reasons for choosing either path. Not only reasons, but risks—if she leaves, she could lose everything. On the other hand, staying has its own costs. Which hand holds the prize?

Running comes easier now, and she is no longer cold. When the street slopes downhill, she takes it with great loping strides, sliding in the snow, pretending that her battered Nikes are magical boots, that each step carries her hundreds of miles. She sails across the world, whole continents passing beneath her feet, each sidewalk square a country, each crack a river, each iced-over puddle a frozen sea. She laughs into the minty air. Running is effortless now. Fearless, she opens her arms and skims down the hill into the intersection.

Out of nowhere a station wagon appears, swerves, skids, and goes into a spin. Esther freezes. The car finally jerks to a stop, half up on the curb, only inches from a big oak, and the driver raises shaky hands to his face. The back seat is full of children, all gaping at Esther. After unbearable moments, the car bumps down off the curb and pulls slowly away.

Esther's heart is still slamming. The air sears her throat. She tries to jog, hobbled now by a cramp. She keeps picturing the shaky driver, the shocked faces of the children. They could have died, all of them, just like that. *Just like that. No more Henry Moss.* Life is precarious. There's no time for a wrong turn, a bad decision. But how can you be sure of making the right one?

The light turns red as she reaches the next intersection.

This time she waits for it, jogging in place. You can't, she tells herself. You can only keep moving, keep going, as if you believe it will all end well. Because what is the alternative? The ache is sharp beneath her ribs as the light turns green, but still she remains there, lifting her feet and letting them drop, running in place on the corner.

DYED TO MATCH

When my little brother was three, we used to stand him on the front seat of the car and say: "Which way, Jonathan?" And he would always point in the right direction as if, even then, he knew just where he was going. When I was seventeen and getting ready to go away to college, he sat in my room helping me write my name on my cherished record collection. At some point I looked over and saw that he was signing his own name, not mine. Thinking he'd done it on purpose, I stormed out to my mother to complain. Now I understand that he'd never have done anything so malicious: he was simply revealing, the way a boy plucks an apple from a tree, his instinct to assume possession, to grasp the desirable things in life.

Unlike me, Jonathan was receptive to my mother's lessons in etiquette and ritual. He was the child of my parents' late affluence, and they took him everywhere. At seven he knew how to seat ladies at the table. At twelve he could order wine. At sixteen he borrowed my father's Lincoln to take girls to dinner at elegant restaurants, which he paid for with his own credit card. The bills, of course, went to my father.

Jonathan's taste for the good life sharpened when he attended a private college in Boston: he just seemed to gravitate naturally toward scions and heiresses. He was without self-consciousness or doubt, good-looking, sweet-natured, and glad to talk to anybody, including small children and elderly women. He was not conceited, but he expected to be liked, to be valued as a fine commodity himself.

At twenty-one my brother stood six feet three inches tall, and everything he wore, from jeans to tuxedo, was exactly right. His summer tan, acquired on friends' sailboats, lasted till December, when he refreshed it skiing at Mittersill and Stowe. His only physical flaw, in fact, was the strawberry birthmark on his cheek, which he'd camouflaged with a splendid glossy black beard that made him look ten years older—an important factor in the commodities business, where investments are made as much in the broker as in the commodity itself.

When he graduated that June, he had a wonderful job waiting for him at a small brokerage so exclusive it didn't even advertise. He'd worked there as an intern, doing so well that they wanted him back. But by June he had met Delilah Sugarman, and Delilah refused to spend another winter anyplace where the temperature dipped below seventy degrees.

Delilah was from Palm Beach. She was also from Toronto, Beverly Hills, and the Bahamas, where her father kept his legal residence for tax purposes, though he had houses everywhere and a yacht besides. Abe Sugarman's portfolio was said to be as thick as a phone book—another reason, perhaps, why Jonathan's brokerage was sorry to see him go. For by June it was public knowledge that Jonathan was about to become Abe's son-in-law.

Delilah, nearly six feet tall herself with a headful of frosted blond curls and a permanent tan, was my brother's match in physique and sartorial splendor. In fact, she had studied fashion merchandising at an expensive school for those who wish not to be burdened with the liberal arts. After the wedding, the newlyweds would move to Palm Beach, where her family wintered every year and where Abe had bought them a Ralph Lauren store as a wedding gift. Jonathan, dazzled by the prospect of true wealth instead of mere affluence, agreed to move to Florida to live in a permanent state of air-conditioning and sell expensive blue jeans to expensive women.

The wedding invitations, all creamy parchment and raised gold, named the date according to the Hebrew calendar: "The ninth of Av, 5740 years after the Creation of the World," as though the two events were of equal significance. The wedding would be held in Toronto, where Abe and Regina Sugarman had grown up in traditional Jewish homes and where they had family still. By all accounts, it was going to be a spectacular affair. Everyone who could claim passing acquaintance with the Sugarmans had been invited, and everyone, it seemed, had accepted. Abe had reserved three floors in the same immense hotel where the reception would be held, discreetly inviting those in need to stay as his guests. My parents, whose list was somewhat smaller, immediately reserved half a floor for our own impoverished relations, which included me and the man I was married to at the time.

"Of course, we're not in the same league as the Sugarmans," my mother conceded with dignity. "But we try to do things nice."

Doing things nice became the byword of that memorable weekend. It was nice to have twelve bridesmaids, with twelve ushers in white tie and tails to escort them; it was nice to have wedding programs, a silk *huppah* imported from Israel, and a formal dinner afterward with white glove service and rolling bar carts so that none of the guests would have to suffer the indignity of standing in line for drinks.

The color scheme was going to be the nicest thing of all: Delilah, who had minored in window dressing, was designing everything herself. The bride would be in white, of course, with a huge bouquet of white orchids and trailing green ivy. Green was Delilah's favorite color because it matched her eyes, which was why she had a whopping emerald for an engagement ring. (I did wonder how my brother could afford that ring, as I didn't think my father's American Express card stretched quite that far. But it was not nice to ask such questions.) All the bridesmaids would be dressed head-to-toe in their own shades of green. Delilah was having the gowns made with sashes, gloves, headpieces, handkerchiefs, and shoes dyed to match. The outfits would be ready weeks before the wedding so there would be plenty of time to have them altered, if necessary. All we had to do was send her a complete set of our measurements.

I balked at that. I didn't want to *know* my measurements, let alone send them off to a perfect stranger, even if she did plan to marry my brother. In fact, I didn't want to be in the wedding at all. I hated being on display. My mother found this attitude appalling and made a speech about getting my priorities straight: what was a little humiliation, compared to my brother's happiness? So I sent the measurements, along with paper cutouts of my hands and feet for glove and shoe sizing. I was not sanguine about the shoes, however, as I take a double width when I can find it, and even then have never put on a pair of pumps that didn't blister my toes and rub my heels raw.

"Why don't I get my own shoes?" I asked Delilah on the phone. "I'm hard to fit."

"Oh no," she said warmly. "The only way to make sure we get a uniform look is for me to control the whole thing myself. Don't worry—you'll have lots of time to break them in."

When I hung up, my mother said in the quiet voice she reserves for her most dramatic statements: "This wedding means a great deal to your father and me. We would like to see *one* of our children, at least, stand beneath the *huppah*."

This was a strategic blow. She was alluding to the fact that Chip, who is not Jewish, and I had simply wandered into a city magistrate's office one day and legitimized our union, then gone out for corned-beef sandwiches afterward. We didn't tell our families for six months. Although both sets of parents took the news calmly, relieved that we were no longer living in sin, there was no denying the fact that I had cheated my mother of the chance to stage-manage one of the great events of her life. I owed her one, a big one, and my cooperation at Jonathan's wedding, I was beginning to realize, was just a small down payment on the debt.

For their part, my parents were pledged to give the rehearsal dinner, which they were determined to make relentlessly nice. Throughout July, my mother spoke daily by phone to the hotel catering department, negotiating food, drinks, flowers, service, decor. She marshaled the home-forces as well, instructing each relative who would be present at the dinner to prepare an anecdote about Jonathan, then calling a conclave at the house to rehearse the rehearsal.

By August everything was arranged and proceeding smoothly, except for one small hitch: the bridesmaids' ensembles had not yet arrived. A week before the wedding, I dug out an old pair of white flats, extra wide and fairly run-down, had them tinted pale green, and began wearing them around the apartment. By the time we packed our bags and caught our flight to Toronto, I could almost walk without limping.

Abe's son-in-law Artie picked us up at the airport, sitting self-consciously behind the wheel of Abe's Rolls sedan. Artie was married to Camilla, the oldest Sugarman daughter, and seemed to spend most of his time running errands for Abe or helping Camilla through one of her crises. All the Sugarman girls suffered from nerves. Ten years earlier, the girls had been kidnapped for ransom and held in the trunk of a car. They were freed and the kidnappers caught, but the experience had warped all three of them. Delilah, the tallest and most robust, had a pathological fear of being confined in small places. She could not go to movies unless the rows behind and in front of her were unoccupied, nor could she even contemplate boarding an airplane without heavy tranquilizers. Camilla had been left permanently scatterbrained by the ordeal. She'd attended a number of finishing schools without finishing any of them and couldn't think of anything she wanted to do besides shop and lie in the sun and have lunch with her mother. Although no one had ever kidnapped Artie, he was much the same, which was probably why Camilla had married him. They seemed to spend their lives trailing after the elder Sugarmans.

Belinda, the baby of the family, was the most disturbed. She had yet to complete a full year of high school; her parents tried one specialist after another, but no form of therapy seemed to take. She was terrified of men, threw screaming fits, and frequently locked herself in the bathroom. Oddly enough, though she despised Artie and even her father at times, she adored Jonathan.

On the drive into town from the airport, Artie never once mentioned the wedding. Instead, in reply to a polite inquiry from my mother, he discussed in detail his and Camilla's efforts to conceive a child: what tests they'd had, what therapies they'd tried, what the specialists had said. He seemed to feel no qualms about sharing Camilla's menstrual history with us. My mother had a nice way of explaining it afterward — "He considers us family already"—but of course this was early in the weekend, when she was still committed to seeing everything in the best possible light.

At the hotel, my parents went straight into conference with the catering department. Chip, who was making one of his periodic attempts to finish college, said he was going to study, but when I left to report to the bridal suite he was lying on the bed studying the TV guide.

The Sugarman daughters, plus Artie, were staying in one suite, while their parents had another across the hall. The living room in the girls' suite was strewn with clothing, magazines, cans of Tab, and bags of M&M's. Delilah was sitting on Jonathan's lap in the one chair large enough to hold them both, Belinda was in her room with the door shut, and Camilla, Matron of Honor, had propped her feet on Artie's knees while he colored her toenails with green Magic Marker.

All through that long afternoon, while my mother mobilized

the catering forces—personally rearranging the tables, the seating plan, the platters of salmon beignets and miniature quiches, even re-folding the napkins—I waited in the suite as the other bridesmaids trickled in. They all seemed to be named Staci or Traci, although perhaps I was introduced to some of them twice. We were waiting for the dressmaker, who had promised to bring the gowns over the moment they were finished and fit them to us on the spot. Soon the groomsmen arrived and carried Jonathan off for his last hours of freedom. Delilah made them wait while she gave him a lengthy kiss goodbye. When he turned to go, she smacked his bottom, and the bridesmaids erupted into giggles.

"It's *so* nice to finally have a man who's big enough," she exclaimed after the boys left.

"Now, now!" said one of the Staci's or Traci's, wagging her finger. "You're not supposed to know anything about that until the wedding night."

"Well, you know what they say," Delilah retorted. "A hard man is good to find."

The girls shrieked with laughter. I went to the window, looked out at the city glinting in the sharp August sun, and thought of all those snowy Ohio winters when I used to pull Jonathan behind me on a sled—his black curls peeping out of his hooded snowsuit, his chubby delighted face bright red from the cold, so red that the strawberry birthmark disappeared. I wondered if Delilah knew about that mark. I hoped Jonathan would never shave off his beard.

When the girls calmed down, they phoned room service for more Tab and M&M's. Belinda opened her door, looked at us, and slammed it again. Delilah rolled her eyes. I was on the point of making the unsisterly suggestion that I wait for the gowns in my own room when there was a brisk knock, and in marched the triumphant dressmaker followed by two assistants and a string of bellhops carrying so many boxes it looked like the Queen of Sheba checking in. The bellhops deposited their burdens and left, untipped, as the girls shrieked afresh, each feverishly hunting the box with her name and shade of green written on front. Despite cries of caution from the dressmaker, the floor was soon covered with tissue paper, sashes, gloves, floral wreaths, and streaming satin ribbons.

Delilah was in an alarming state of excitement as she raced from one girl to the next, holding up the gowns and naming the colors: "Water Lily, Celery Seed, Olive Haze, Dried Moss, Mint Froth, Lagoon Mist, Chaste Fern,"—more giggles at this — "Winter Pear, Lime Fizz, Beach Grass, Budding Bough for Belinda, and—" She stopped short in front of me. "Esther, where's yours?" Silently, the dressmaker handed her the only intact box. "Lettuce Heart!" she finished happily, presenting it to me. "Well, what are you waiting for? Try them on!"

The girls promptly shucked their clothing, adding to the layers of debris, as the dressmaker and her assistants pulled out their pincushions and went to work. Delilah tucked Budding Bough under her arm and knocked firmly on Belinda's door. No answer. She rattled the knob. She pounded. From within came a muffled scream. Some of the bridesmaids looked up, startled, but Delilah only continued to pound.

"Belinda, you have to be fitted! Belinda, get out here!" She stepped back and gave the door a kick. "I can't believe you're doing this to me! Do you want to ruin my wedding?"

Camilla joined Delilah at the door. "Belinda," she coaxed. "It's just us girls out here and everybody wants to see how nice you look in your gown."

Silence.

"Do you think she's all right?" someone said.

Delilah gave the door another savage kick. "Of course she's all right! She just can't stand not being the center of attention!"

While Camilla continued to scratch at the door, Delilah stomped across the hall to her parents' suite. "Mother!" we heard her yell. "Come make Belinda try on her gown!"

I hastened into the bathroom to try my own gown on, lest Delilah next turn her attention to *me*. The extravagance of her rage had me shaking. It reminded me of my mother's rampages when Jonathan and I were young, before she started taking the medication that evened out her moods. I remembered how we sat in the basement Saturday mornings, watching cartoons on the old black-and-white TV. I was too old for cartoons, really, but Jonathan liked them, so we sat together in the big easy chair with the rip down the middle and kept the sound turned down low so we could hear when she began to scream. If we didn't answer at once, it was worse. She always used our full names: "Esther Jean Sapperstein!"—if it was me, which it usually was— "*Get* up here!" With a look of sympathy from my brother to warm my freezing blood, I would dash up three flights to find my mother in my bedroom, yanking drawers out of the bureau, dumping them on the floor, or pulling armfuls of clothing out of the closet. The transgressions usually had to do with untidiness. Though the medication helped, and my mother did develop quite a good rapport with Jonathan after I left home, I have never gotten over my fear of female fury, and I had to wonder whether Jonathan had either. Could he have forgotten that moment of terror as we huddled together on the chair? Had he ever seen Delilah this angry? Should I warn him?

But he would not appreciate such a warning on the day before his wedding. Anyway, I thought as I struggled with layers of taffeta, I was in no position to be handing out marital advice, as everyone would know soon enough.

When I came out of the bathroom, Regina Sugarman was standing at the bedroom door negotiating with Belinda. Regina was a tall, sleepy-eyed, *zaftig* blond with the same thick sensual features as her daughters. She was known chiefly for looking gorgeous and being late. Abe made a practice of telling her to be ready two hours before they were actually due for an engagement and had suggested that we do the same. Nothing, least of all Abe's displeasure, seemed to ruffle Regina, who moved and spoke so languorously that I suspected she was on Valium--yet another aftereffect of the kidnapping. Her slow even voice coaxed Belinda into opening the door enough for

Regina to slip inside with Budding Bough. After a few minutes she poked her head out to call the dressmaker, who approached the bedroom with some trepidation.

Mollified, Delilah at last turned her attention to us. "Oh, it's fantastic!" she cried. "What an effect!"

The gowns were voluminous, with pouf sleeves and sashes tied into extravagant bows. Mine fit well enough, though the sash was so tight I wouldn't be able to eat. But the shoes were another matter.

"But they're your size," Delilah exclaimed when I told her. "Eight-and-a-half wide, isn't that what you said?"

"I told you my feet are wide," I said. "But I take EE and these are just C's." I did not add that dying makes shoes even tighter or that the four-inch heels made my feet stand pointing downhill. My toes actually overlapped.

"You can stand it for one night, can't you?" Delilah said. "Put some Band-Aids on."

At that moment Regina threw open the door, crying "Here's Belinda!" and out came a shorter, younger, wobblier edition of the Sugarman Blond, with bad skin and reddened eyes. As the bridesmaids obligingly crowded around, Delilah put an arm around her younger sister and squeezed, saying loudly: "*That's my girl!*" Then finally the rest of us were dismissed.

Chip wasn't in the room when I got back, and the stack of books on the table seemed undisturbed. I laid my hand on the television: warm. My marriage was turning me into a detective. A few weeks earlier I'd seen an unfinished letter lying on our kitchen table. It was from Chip to his army buddy and said, among other things: "I spend most afternoons in the library trying to study, but it's hard to concentrate. You wouldn't believe how many beautiful girls go to this school." I knew it was wrong to read the letter, but why did he leave it out? Why did I find it on my side of the table? The answer was obvious, but somewhere along the way Chip and I had tacitly agreed not to bring it up until after the important weekend. A wedding, after all, was no place for family discord.

◆ ◆ ◆

Because of the delay with the gowns, there would be no time for rehearsing before the rehearsal dinner. Instead, we would rehearse two hours before the wedding itself. Chip and I were assigned to greet guests on behalf of my parents, who were still supervising operations in the kitchen. The bridesmaids reappeared in civilian clothes; the groomsmen, somewhat flushed and noisy, delivered my brother; and various relatives began arriving. Chip and I kissed so many people it seemed like we were the ones getting married. Though both of us were shy and hated making conversation, we dutifully circulated, freshening drinks and urging guests to try the pistachio triangles and smoked trout rillettes. Of course this too was mainly for form's sake, since my relatives seldom need encouragement to eat. There was plenty of food, and the bar stayed busy. The plan was to have cocktails and canapés for an hour, then sit down to dinner. Between courses, guests would offer up their homage to the groom.

Chip and I kept our own drinks fresh and hoped that beatific smiles would compensate for impaired social skills. As we worked through the crowd, we heard much whispered speculation about the cost of the wedding, which seemed to escalate as the hour wore on. Finally, to my great relief (and, no doubt, the chef's), my mother emerged on my father's arm like a bride herself, and the entire Sapperstein clan surged forward with praise and congratulations.

Released from duty, Chip and I went to sit in the corner with Uncle Lev, my favorite uncle and the only member of the family Chip felt comfortable with. He raised his glass joyously as we sat down and said: "*L'chaim,* children," and we drank to life. Then he said: "To the *chossen* and the *kallah,* may they live to dance at their great-grandchildren's wedding," and we drank again. "To the whole *mishpocheh,*" he went on, still gathering momentum, but this time I barely tasted my drink.

I was not used to alcohol; already I felt hot and a little heedless.

"It's been a long time since we had a wedding in the family," said Uncle Lev, smacking his lips over the vodka. I felt my face get warmer, but he didn't mean Chip and me—there was nothing subtle or malicious about Lev. "There will be a *huppah*?"

I assured him there would be a *huppah*, a rabbi, and a glass to break. "A real Jewish wedding," I said.

Lev shook his head wistfully. "A *huppah*, a rabbi—it's nice, but it's not real tradition. Not like in Krakow when I was a boy. There the whole family would come to witness the *ketubah*, the marriage contract. To seal the act they broke a dish; then there would be a party. There were many parties." He laughed softly, refilling our glasses from the bottle he'd stowed beneath his chair. "They lasted from a whole year before the wedding to a whole year after. On the wedding day, there was singing and dancing when the first guest arrived, when the *chossen* signed the contract, when the bride received her friends, when the groom came to lower her veil just before the ceremony. Ah," he said, looking into his glass. "That was a moment. The groom looks into her eyes, the family and friends crowd up close, holding candles, singing...."

He trailed off, and I knew he was remembering his own bride, long vanished into smoke. They had been married only a year when the Nazis came. Lev alone survived the camp and eventually came to America, where he married my mother's younger sister. My aunt was a plain, quiet woman who soothed and comforted Lev, but that early marriage in that far-off place, the glad young face turned to his as he lowered the veil, the candles and singing and beloved faces of so many ghosts— these would always haunt him.

"Why is it the groom who veils the bride?" I said too sharply. The vodka had made my voice unreliable.

Some of the mistiness left his eyes. "So he can make sure he's getting the right girl. Nobody wants a Leah when he's expecting a Rachel." His face brightened and he held up one finger as if reciting from the *Pirke Avot:* "What you see ain't always what you get." Then he roared with laughter as he always did when he demonstrated his command of American idiom. He filled our glasses again and clapped Chip on the shoulder. "Tomorrow I dance with your wife—okay, *boychik*?"

Chip smiled shyly. He had once interviewed Lev for a journalism class. The resulting article earned him his only college A. "Sure," he said. "I don't dance anyway."

I thought of those torturous shoes. "I'm not much of a dancer myself."

"So what am I, Fred Astaire? It's a *mitzvah*: you dance at a Jewish wedding, you dance on Hitler's grave. Who knows when we get another chance?"

Across the room I could see Delilah feeding Jonathan canapés, cramming them into his mouth faster than he could chew, smearing them into his beard, until, laughing, he pushed her hands away.

By eight-fifteen the food was gone, everyone was loaded, and Regina Sugarman had still not appeared. Between bouts of gracious conversation, my mother sent scorching glances at the clock. Finally, she disappeared into the kitchen while my father had a word with the bartender. Then both of them conferred with Jonathan, who took the problem to Delilah, who listened with a smile on her frosted-pink lips, then glided across the room to where Abe stood nursing a drink and chatting with the young men. Jonathan said Abe had always wanted a son, and apparently Artie didn't count. It was my private opinion that this was the reason Abe had bought Delilah and Jonathan the Ralph Lauren store: it would keep them in Palm Beach, where the Sugarmans spent a lot of time and where, no doubt, Jonathan would need to call frequently on Abe for fiscal and fatherly advice.

Delilah deftly hooked her arm through her father's and drew him aside. As Abe left the room, I could see by my parents' worried faces that they were wondering whether to close down the bar. The noise level had increased considerably in the last half hour, and the younger guests especially were flushed and hilarious.

Regina made her entrance in time to prevent this embarrassment. She looked stunning in her white lace dress—worn to steal a little thunder from the bride, perhaps—but not worth waiting two and a half hours for. My mother barely gave her time to kiss a few cheeks before herding us all over to the table. Immediately, waiters were setting plates of shrimp and smashed cucumber in front of us and filling the first of a trio of wine glasses. Beside each bridesmaid's plate lay identical long narrow packages wrapped in shiny green paper with matching bows.

"Now what could this be?" I said to Chip, rattling my box.

"Pen and pencil set?" he guessed.

"Not romantic enough. Got to be jewelry. The question is, how many karats?" We studied the Sugarman females, who all sported pearls, emeralds, or diamonds. "About the only thing Camilla could possibly need is a fertilized egg," I said, then laughed so hard I choked. My mother looked over with what she imagined was a subtle glance of disapproval.

"Oh Chip," I said, wiping my eyes. "What makes me so mean?"

He answered with the little smile and shake of the head that meant he agreed I was mean but had no idea why. Chip intoxicated was no more forthcoming than Chip sober.

With Delilah's permission we unwrapped our packages, plucking carefully at the paper and smoothing it out in order to maintain the illusion that weddings are about loftier matters than who gives what and how much everything costs. Inside was a shining heart-shaped locket set with emeralds and engraved with Jonathan's and Delilah's initials. I thought it would have been nicer to have a locket with my own initials but joined the others in squeals of gratitude.

We finished the shrimp and Riesling and went on to Unborn Veal with Pear Sauce and Sauvignon Blanc. My stomach turned. Artie pronounced the wine superb. By the time we got to the Fig Mousse and champagne, I could no longer remember what had been funny at the start of dinner. In fact, everything seemed unbearably sad, especially the anecdotes about Jonathan that Sapperstein guests were getting up, one by one, to tell.

When my turn came, I had trouble pushing my chair back, then almost walked into a waiter. I didn't look at the faces turned expectantly up at me, especially my mother's. I was trying to remember the polished little nugget I had rehearsed. It began: "When I first met Jonathan, I was impressed by the certainty with which he knew his own mind even then." But past that point I could remember nothing.

"When I first met Jonathan," I began and stopped. There was a ripple of laughter. I'd intended to be funny, but now I couldn't remember the joke. In fact, I felt an awful ache in my throat that couldn't be due completely to stage fright.

"When they brought him home from the hospital, I used to sit in his room and read him stories," I blundered on. "Just on the off-chance that he might be a genius." There was a bigger laugh this time, but I had no idea where I was going. "When my parents let him cry at night, I used to lie awake in the dark, petrified, imagining a vampire bending over his crib sucking all the blood out of him. I kept thinking: how do they *know* there isn't one? Why don't they get up and *see*? I was too scared to get up myself, so I would lie there and cry in the dark, afraid that the vampire would get my baby brother..." I stopped, struck with the horrifying realization that the vampire *had* got him after all, and my voice gave way altogether. The guests got to their feet and applauded what they took for a loving sister's tears of devotion. Even my parents clapped and beamed: I was a success. There was nothing to do but sit down and hide my face in Chip's shoulder, while he patted me awkwardly, acting his own assigned role.

After the speeches, he steered me through a thicket of smiles and praise and solicitous glances into the elevator and up to the room, where I tumbled into bed with a groan.

"Can you get undressed?" he asked.

"Of course I can get undressed," I said rudely. "I've been doing it for twenty-seven years."

Chip didn't fight back. He didn't even correct my math: if I'd been undressing myself for twenty-seven years, I must have been an infant prodigy. Why did he let me get away with so much? I didn't want a husband I could bully the way my mother had bullied me. Chip disappeared into the bathroom and I fell asleep without undressing.

I awoke to the sound of sharp rapping. At first I thought it was coming from inside my ravaged head, but then I heard my brother's voice. He was knocking on the door of my parents' bedroom.

It was a little past two. I got up and cracked the door open just in time to see Jonathan hurry my bath-robed parents through the living room and out to the hall. I thought perhaps Abe had had a heart attack or Belinda had jumped off the roof or one of the ushers had been arrested. Whatever it was, there was nothing I could do, and my head hurt too much to try. So I gulped down six aspirin and a carafe of water and groped my way back to bed, hoping the wedding would be called off so I could sleep straight through till Monday.

The wedding was not called off, but afterward my mother insisted it had come close. Jonathan had fetched her to negotiate an armistice in the Sugarman war that erupted around midnight in the daughters' bathroom. My mother said later, in a dramatic reenactment of the event, that it looked as if a bomb had gone off in the suite. Abe was dangerously red-faced, while Regina, still in her elegant white dress, lay crumpled on the loveseat, weeping. Belinda, who'd had hysterics and tried to beat up her parents, was being restrained by Camilla and Artie, but as soon as she saw Jonathan she broke away and ran to fling her arms around him in a fresh storm of tears. This sent Delilah over the edge. Her yelling was so loud that nobody could hear the phone ring. It was the night manager, calling to ask them to quiet down. He came upstairs and knocked on the door, but nobody heard that either, so he went away.

By now Abe was stomping about, shouting to make himself heard above the weeping. The tumult had begun when Abe and Regina looked in to say goodnight. There was a preliminary skirmish over the mess in the living room, which the girls countered by attacking Regina's tardiness at dinner, but the real battle began when Abe visited the bathroom. "He has his own goddamn bathroom across the hall!" Delilah shrieked, but that, apparently, was not the point. This even-tempered, dry, slightly ironic little man, so generous with credit cards and jewelry, came raging right back out, shouting about hair in the bathtub.

My mother personally inspected the site and said he was quite right. All three girls had washed their hair, and no one had wiped the long tawny strands from the tub. Towels, underwear, cosmetics, and toiletries were scattered everywhere. Still, the maids cleaned every morning—how bad a mess could it be? "That's not the point," my mother told me. "Nobody should leave a room in that condition. They should respect each other too much."

One thing, at least, was clear about the Sugarmans: they were in no danger of respecting each other too much. Delilah was the fiercest. At one point she up-ended the loveseat, dumping her mother on the floor. That was when my mother hustled my brother out to the hall, took hold of his lapels, and said: "Jonathan, you do not have to go through with this wedding."

"But Mom," he said unhappily. "I love her."

"You're going to have to live with that temper," she warned. "It's not going away."

"I love her," he said again. "I do."

My mother stood there, looking up at her child. At one time he'd been small enough to fit in the crook of her arm. He'd had a head full of ringlets and the strawberry mark, a flaw which made him vulnerable to the cruelty of the coarse, the crass, the unworthy. Now he was tall and dapper, sleekly bearded, perfectly behaved, a son to be proud of, and a mystery. She sighed, released his lapels, and marched back inside to negotiate terms.

She was able to dispatch Abe and Regina by promising to take over the management of the wedding, thus relieving Regina of any responsibility other than beautifying herself. She sent a yawning Artie and Camilla off to bed, and then, with Jonathan's help, persuaded Belinda to take two of her mother's Valium and lie down. Only Delilah raged on about her father's intolerance, her mother's unreliability, her sisters' disloyalty, and her own special pressures and burdens, until my mother, who has observed many a nervous bride, made a shrewd deduction.

"Delilah," she said delicately, "what time of month is it?"

Delilah stared at her until, comprehending, she collapsed on my mother's shoulder in tears. "It's supposed to come *next* week!" she wailed. "I've never been early before, never!"

At five-thirty, my father and brother were sent out into the Toronto dawn to forage for tampons. My mother packed Delilah's clothes for the honeymoon, put her to bed, and cleaned the bathroom just in case Abe dropped by again. Then she phoned the kitchen for coffee, found some hotel stationary, and began, with lists and diagrams and misgivings, to plan her son's wedding.

By mid-afternoon, the hungover members of the wedding party had straggled into the synagogue and embarked upon the arduous ordeal of getting dressed. The bridesmaids were using the Sisterhood Room, which looked surreal with mounds of floaty green fabric and white ruffled petticoats obscuring the podium and folding chairs and portraits of Jewish dowagers. Delilah was still at the hotel, but I, being my mother's daughter, had arrived early and was already dressed. I felt like a walking birthday cake in all those tiers of ruffles and sugar-icing rosettes. My mother made me stop and stand like a child with my arms raised while she re-tied my sash. She re-tied everyone's sash. The girls all rolled their eyes and made faces when she wasn't looking.

Chip, who was not an usher, had been commissioned with the distribution of Lifesavers to the wedding party, but, feeling nervous and wanting people to like him, he compulsively gave them away to the florists, the musicians, the film crew, the photographer's team, and anyone else he met wandering the halls. By the time my mother found out, it was too late to get more, and she told the bridesmaids firmly that to prevent dry-mouth they would have to rely on the time-honored device of dabbing a little Vaseline on their back molars. This suggestion re-activated several hangovers, however, and pushed the girls over the line into mutiny.

By three o'clock my mother realized there would be no time at all for rehearsal and hurried around to each member of the wedding party—except for Delilah, who had not yet arrived—to explain strategy and logistics. The bridesmaids paid scant attention to her diagrams and laughed at her when she hurried away. This put me in an awkward position. It's one thing to have your own scores to settle with your mother, but another thing entirely to see her insulted by strangers. Then again, she was self-important and officious and deserved to be laughed at. I solved the dilemma by concluding that I hated everybody and everything and went out to wander the halls myself.

In the sanctuary, the string quartet was tuning up while the video crew made light-checks. This would not be any rinky-dink home movie, Regina had assured us, but a real film, edited and titled, with background music and professional narration.

It would be called *The Delilah and Jonathan Story*. And the stills photographer had an "international reputation," she'd added—meaning, I suppose, that he worked both sides of the border. His specialties were multiple exposures and soft focus, so flattering to older faces. The photo album, too, would be a work of art.

The sanctuary, dark and cavernous with huge stained-glass windows and a Jewish Star the size of a spaceship suspended from the ceiling, had been transformed by the white and gold *huppah*, the orchids and ivy, the feathery palms and white silk ribbons. I saw Chip watching the musicians and went up and touched his arm. We exchanged a look of bleak recognition, one POW to another.

"Well, Chip, this is it," I said. "This is what we deprived ourselves of."

He made no reply, but I thought I detected a shudder. "What are these supposed to be?" he said, tracing one finger along the *huppah's* gold embroidery.

"Doves and pomegranates. Peace and plenty."

Chip thought this over, then said: "Well, they'll have plenty of plenty, at any rate."

I laughed, and as if on cue the string quartet burst into "Stranger in Paradise," and then we both laughed. It had been a while since we'd laughed together, and we prolonged it, shaking our heads.

"How are the feet?" Chip asked when we ran out of chuckles.

"Holding out, so far."

He stepped back to see. "I don't think she'll notice."

"She'll notice," I said grimly. "She probably did post-graduate work in accessories."

Then one of the ushers poked his head in to say that the wedding party was mustering in the Sisterhood Room for final inspection. I was not anxious to be scrutinized, but I went glumly along and found the bridesmaids in revolt against my mother. They did not wish to wear their long gloves or carry their dyed-to-match handkerchiefs or be bossed around. When they decided to take their grievances to Delilah, who had finally arrived and was being dressed in the library, my mother huffily gathered up her hairpins and emery boards and combs and tissues and smelling salts. "They can do as they please," she said. "I've got my *own* eyelashes to put on. Come on, boys, it's late."

She herded the sheepish young men into the Ladies' Room to instruct them while she did her face. I tagged along. "An usher never escorts more than one lady at a time," she said, pressing a spidery black fringe to her eyelid. "And men sometimes faint during the ceremony because they stand so rigid, so keep your knees flexed and wiggle your fingers behind your back, like this." She showed them. "Now you try."

We heard running footsteps in the hall; then the door crashed open and a teary-faced Belinda came to a dead halt at the sight of so many tuxedoed young men in the Ladies' Room, bending their knees and wiggling their fingers. Frantically, she checked the door to make sure she had the right place. "What is *wrong* with everybody?" she shrieked, then wheeled and raced back down the hall.

My mother sighed, pressing her other eyelash into place. "Make sure your coats are buttoned," she continued. "And keep in step when you come out with Jonathan." She eyed the stunned young men in the mirror. "Well?" she said, blotting her lipstick. "Practice!"

After that, things began happening very fast. The music played; the cameras rolled; the synagogue filled up with guests; the ushers meekly escorted ladies, one at a time, to their seats; and the rebellious bridesmaids were corralled again in the Sisterhood Room. Each wore her gloves and carried her handkerchief. Delilah had accused them of trying to ruin her wedding day and issued a blistering tirade. The florist handed out the bouquets, and my mother demonstrated how to carry them, how to hold our heads, how to walk—step, pause, smile; step, pause, smile—starting with the right foot.

As instructed, an usher tapped on the door to let us know the guests were seated. We could hear the string quartet delivering a weepy rendition of "Sunrise, Sunset."

"All right, this is it," said my mother tensely. "Anyone need smelling salts?"

There was a faint titter, which she pretended not to hear. She marched us down the hall and lined us up outside the sanctuary door, then gave the sign to one of the dressmaker's assistants. A few moments later, the library door opened and the bride stepped into the hall. She waited for the assistant to gather up the end of her train; then, like a queen with lady-in-waiting, moved gravely and serenely down the hall to meet us.

The gown alone could have housed a tribe of nomads. There were yards and yards of satin silk encrusted with crystal and pearls, a high illusion neckline which looked bare but wasn't, and a veil cascading to the floor. The high heels and crystal tiara gave her the stature of an Amazon.

As the bridesmaids broke ranks to surround her, breathing admiration, one girl skidded on the smooth carpet. Instantly, my mother pulled an emery board out of her tiny white bag and made the girl take off her shoe, which she vigorously went to work on, roughening the slick surface.

"This will give you some traction," she whispered, handing the shoe back. "Quick, anybody else?"

To my horror, both my mother and Delilah looked directly at our feet. I held my breath, preparing for the showdown. But I was wrong. Delilah glanced at our shoes, then asked the dressmaker to adjust her veil. Chip had been right: she wasn't aware of anything but herself. I had sweated over nothing. It was almost a disappointment.

The quartet started "Sunrise, Sunset" over again. It was time for my mother to be seated. As the usher led her away, she hissed over her shoulder: "Start with the right!" Somehow the rest of us got down the aisle on our own, though Delilah had to give Belinda a shove. I was next to last, and as a matter of principle, started with my left. I risked one glance at the front row, where my parents sat. My mother seized the opportunity to point discreetly to the corners of her mouth. She was telling me to smile.

I took my place on the steps and watched Camilla come down the aisle. The ushers across from us looked upright and elegant in their white tailcoats and green ties and cummerbunds. I checked to see whether Artie, my date for the evening, was indeed wearing Lettuce Heart, but it was impossible to tell. I wondered if all the ushers were busy flexing their knees and wiggling their fingers, and I hoped the video crew would get it on tape. Jonathan, all in white and wearing a silk top hat instead of a *yarmulke*, was pure eager confidence as he waited for his bride.

There was a pause. Then the quartet broke into Mendelssohn's Wedding March—written, I longed to point out, by a Jew who had himself baptized a Lutheran—and Delilah glided down the aisle on Abe's arm, dwarfing him. Behind me, I heard whispered exclamations about how stunning she looked and how clever she'd been to design the whole ensemble. At the *huppah,* Abe reached up to kiss her veiled cheek, which she graciously inclined, and formally passed her hand to Jonathan —with, I imagined, a sense of relief. Then he took his seat beside Regina, who looked enraptured, though my mother, who has theories about everyone, thought that she really resented her daughters for getting married because she wasn't ready to be a grandmother.

Jonathan took Delilah's hand and they stepped under the *huppah,* which had been built higher than usual to accommodate them. In his top hat and her tiara, they looked like two young giants. The cantor chanted, invoking God, and the rabbi began to speak in that deliberate, ringing, over-enunciated style favored by rabbis of rich congregations. The six-pointed star loomed over our heads like a flying saucer.

When Delilah turned back her veil to sip the wine, I saw that her face was serene, even a bit sleepy. Jonathan, on the other hand, was wildly excited. I could tell by his ramrod legs and the tension in his shoulders—as if he were about to break loose and go out for a pass. I wondered if grooms ever fainted at their own weddings. When Jonathan turned to get the ring from his best man, he was grinning hard, unable to restrain his glee.

The ring was the traditional plain gold band with no holes. It had to be one solid piece, Lev had explained, to represent the *shlaymut*—wholeness—of the newly united couple, and it had to belong to the groom and no one else. But this plain ring was just a stage prop. The real ring, which Delilah would put on after the ceremony, was platinum set with emeralds and matched her engagement ring. And everyone knew that Delilah's father had "helped " Jonathan buy it so that Delilah could have what she wanted.

Even so, when Jonathan slid the ring onto her finger and said clearly, first in Hebrew, then in English: "Behold, thou art consecrated unto me with this ring according to the law of Moses and of Israel," I was glad my mother had made us carry our handkerchiefs. I remembered my own hasty wedding, where the justice of the peace kept offering me Kleenex while I tried to convince us all that I was crying for sentiment's sake. Long afterward I kept up the pretense because no one in her right mind would run off and do what I'd done if she weren't in love. And when that no longer worked, I decided that true love was a product of the imagination anyway—that people fall in love with what they think the other person thinks. I had thought Chip would devote himself to me the way my father devoted himself to my mother so that I could be a matron, someone's cherished wife, adult at last. But that delusion wore off almost as fast as the sexual intoxication, which was why I didn't trust the joy on my brother's face.

When the cantor finished his sweet moaning, the rabbi stepped back, linked his hands across his round belly, and looked at the congregation with the patient foreboding air of a man about to preach. But instead of a sermon, he talked about the Jewish saint of laughter, the Baal Shem Tov, who spoke of the light within human beings.

"From every person there rises a light that reaches straight to heaven," the rabbi said. "And when two souls who are destined for each other find one another, their streams of light flow together"—here he lifted the two candles and merged their flames, which leaped— "and a single brighter light goes forth from their united being."

I wanted to laugh out loud at this— "destined for each other" indeed—but instead I felt a painful thickening of the throat. It made me remember what I sometimes caught a glimpse of in other couples—the intimate glance, the touch in passing which hinted that they lived in a *context* of love, something I could only dimly imagine. And this thought made me resort again to my dyed green handkerchief, which prompted cooing sounds from the ladies behind me.

The rabbi raised the empty goblet, intoned: "As this glass shatters, so may this marriage remain whole," wrapped it in a cloth, and placed it carefully on the floor by Jonathan's foot. "Hand-cut lead crystal," I heard one of the ladies murmur with a cluck of satisfaction at the waste. Then Jonathan raised his right foot and stomped. As the glass smashed, the guests shouted "*Mazel Tov!,*" Uncle Lev loudest of all.

The string quartet burst into "Ode to Joy," and suddenly everyone was on their feet and the wedding party was in motion again. Artie, my escort, gave me a loony conspiratorial grin as he offered his arm. "Now comes the good part," he whispered, meaning the food and drink, which is what Artie seemed to live for. It reminded me of a Talmudic proverb Uncle Lev liked to quote: "Take what you want ...and pay for it." I wondered how long it would take Artie to work off his debt.

Back at the hotel, corks popped like gunfire as the orchestra kicked off with "Daddy's Little Girl" and the bride and her father box-stepped around the floor, dreamy smiles on their faces as if they were the happy couple. Lev stowed a bottle under his chair and showed me how to polka, whirling and stomping, sweat flying off his face, shouting in defiance as if Hitler himself sat at one of the little tables, sipping champagne and nibbling an artichoke fritter. I stumbled about trying to follow, then danced dutifully with my father and cousins and Artie, who discussed famous hotels where he had stayed. By this time my feet were so mangled it hardly mattered which shoes I had on.

Belinda refused to dance with anyone but Jonathan, who was working his way through the bridesmaids, taking only a hurried turn around the floor with each one, because of course the wedding had run late, and he and Delilah had to catch their flight to Maui. "I think it's very inconsiderate of Abe not to have bought you an airplane," I told him during our brief spin. He laughed, and I felt a little guilty because I knew what lay ahead. So I squeezed his hand and said: "Be happy."

I also danced, for the first time ever, with Chip. I was afraid to move too much, lest he think I was trying to lead; he was afraid to move too much, lest I not be able to follow. So we merely swayed back and forth. After four years of marriage, we'd found a new way to embarrass each other. I was the one who suggested the dance, not because I enjoyed being conspicuous, but because I knew it would please my parents. As far as they were concerned, anything I'd done—eloping, marrying a gentile, keeping it a secret, giving up a chance for the Sorbonne—was justifiable if done for love. The truth, or a palatable version thereof, would come out soon enough: let them enjoy while they could the illusion of happy couples, loving families, and healthy well-adjusted children. I think Chip knew what was on my mind, but neither of us wanted to say it. So we just shuffled back and forth over the same tiny space, gratifying my parents and setting an example for the young people.

The dancing stopped when the wedding cake, ablaze with sparklers, was wheeled in on a silver cart. While the cameras rolled, the happy couple went through the ritual of cutting cake and stuffing it into each other's mouth. Jonathan had so much white frosting on his beard it looked as though marriage had aged him already. He and Delilah went off to change clothes while the waiters, gloved in white like Mickey Mouse, served the cake and brought extra slices wrapped in napkins to the mothers of marriageable daughters. Once my mother, too, used to bring home such talismans to put under my pillow at night so that I would dream of the man I would someday wed. I never did have the dream, perhaps because the cake never lasted till morning. A little sweet consolation in the middle of the night is a hard thing to resist.

The orchestra went on playing, but without the bride and groom the party seemed pointless: we were just a crowd of people who didn't know each other very well. Even Lev grew morose and went on with his drinking in silence. It was as if everyone had suddenly remembered the blankness of ordinary life waiting for us when the magic weekend was over.

There was a brief revival of excitement when the newlyweds, dazzling in matching suits of tropical white, looked in to say goodbye. Delilah held up the bouquet of orchids, and there was the usual fuss as the bridesmaids jockeyed for position. Delilah, already doped up for the plane trip, raised the bouquet high above her head, pretended to cover her eyes with one hand, then hurled it at Belinda, who shrieked and let it drop as though it were a bundle of snakes.

Then, clutching our little bags of rice, we trooped through the lobby and followed them outside, arriving just in time for a cloudburst. The sudden wind whipped back the bridesmaids' frothy skirts and demolished our hair. The ushers pulled their jackets over their heads. Jonathan and Delilah gave a last hasty wave and piled into a white limousine festooned with green tissue flowers. Dutifully, we pelted the car with rice, though they couldn't have heard in the rain, and watched as it pulled away from the curb, the flowers bleeding already, leaving long ugly smears of green against the flawless surface.

The aftermath was predictable enough. My mother was offered a job with the catering department—a flattering and quite safe proposition, since they knew we lived in Ohio. My parents did not die of shock or shame when I told them, soon after the wedding, that Chip and I had split. All members of the wedding party received a copy of the videotape, for endless viewing pleasure, and engraved thank-you notes with a photograph of Jonathan and Delilah striding down a corridor of trees on the golden afternoon of their wedding, as confident as two young giants. I keep the photo on my desk as a reminder.

The marriage lasted almost two years. When it ended, Abe's lawyer arranged for the Ralph Lauren store to be sold and the company, of which Jonathan was president, to be dissolved. Earlier, when they first opened the store, Abe had taken Jonathan to the bank and arranged for a million-dollar line of credit for the business and, as befitting an Executive Officer, a personal line of fifty thousand. At that point, of course, Jonathan was still cast in the role of Crown Prince, the spiritual son who would someday pick up where Abe left off. Jonathan signed the agreement, making him responsible for any debts incurred, then promptly forgot all about it. He also forgot to dissolve it when he filed for divorce.

But Delilah did not forget. Wasn't everybody always saying what a clever girl she was? She waited until two weeks before the divorce was final, borrowed $49,500 against his personal line of credit, and spent it. Nine months later, the bank caught up to Jonathan, who now deals in futures on the West Coast. He is being sued and would like to counter-sue Delilah, but she, mysteriously, cannot be found. None of her friends has any inkling of her whereabouts. She could be in any of half a dozen countries, they say, or floating in international waters on her father's yacht. Abe's lawyer, too, is hard to reach these days: he doesn't return my brother's calls. Meanwhile, the interest on the debt keeps climbing, along with Jonathan's blood pressure. He is twenty-five years old and already on Inderal and ulcer medication. Of course, he's doing well in his new job, but the tastes and habits acquired during life with the Sugarmans are not easily discarded, and he spends what he makes. The girls he dates tend to be voluptuous, well-heeled, and strong-willed. Jonathan is still warm and loyal, though not, perhaps, quite as sweet as he used to be.

My mother has a theory about it all. Delilah's problem is a compulsive fear of being controlled, she tells Jonathan over the phone. "After the kidnapping, she made a subconscious decision that no one would take her or anything belonging to her ever again. That's why she tried to control every little detail about her life *and* yours, no matter how much damage she did. None of it was your fault, darling. You married a sick girl."

That's also why Delilah suffers so terribly from constipation, she tells me, having pried this detail from Jonathan during one of their post-mortems. "That girl willingly gives up nothing, not even body waste, and certainly not something as precious as your brother." She shakes her head wisely, then adds with a sigh: "I wish I knew what makes him keep falling for that type."

But I, even wiser than my mother, know enough to look down at my shoes and keep my own counsel.

SAVING SOVIET JEWELRY

"**S**top!" shouts my mother. "Nobody sit! We have to take a picture of the table!"

Hastily, we all back out of the dining room. My mother calls instructions to my father, who climbs onto a chair, adjusting his lens. The table is an artful clutter of china, crystal, silver, and flowers, with the big Seder plate in the middle. All the chairs from upstairs, including the little stool from my old vanity, are jammed in with the others. My mother's golden raisin wine gleams in the decanter as she lights the candles, murmuring a blessing. The only time my mother murmurs is when she prays.

Owen and I have just arrived. I take his elbow, introducing him to my father's sister Frieda, here as usual without Uncle Hersh, my cousin Marla, her husband Seth, their children, my mother's sister Goldie, her husband Moe, and Mr. Malik Tunador, professional guest, who pulls an extra *yarmulke* from his breast pocket and proffers it with a flourish. He is humming.

"Thank you, sir," says Owen, patting it into place. Mr. Tunador makes him a little bow.

"What was the name again?" Aunt Goldie asks. "Cohen?"

"Owen," I say firmly. "Owen Muldoon."

Goldie is shocked. "Muldoon!"

"It means *descendant of Saint Duin*," I add unnecessarily, and Goldie looks extra shocked. Passover is no time to be mentioning saints.

"Say *cheeze!*" my father tells the table, making the children giggle. When the flash goes off, Marla's baby begins to wail. The aunts shout out helpful advice.

"Sit! Sit!" my mother shouts above the tumult, and we all squeeze in at the table. Somehow I end up on the vanity stool with a table leg wedged between my knees— divine retribution, no doubt, for bringing a boy named Muldoon home for Seder.

My father pours the first cup of wine as my mother beams a smile around the table. "Isn't this nice," she says. "The whole family together."

I would like to point out that we are scarcely the whole family: my brother Jonathan, now an L.A. broker, is celebrating Passover with the West Coast branch of the family, with whom—though no one admits it—we are deadly competitive; Uncle Hersh, always unsociable, has scarcely left home since Sears retired him; my father's brother Mel is off on his third honeymoon; none of my mother's other sisters would come because they're all giving splashy Seders of their own; both sets of grandparents are gone, the entire European branch of the family vanished into greasy smoke; and what about Cousin Richie? But my mother twists the truth into silly putty, and we're all supposed to beam and nod like Aunt Goldie. That's why Goldie is her favorite sister.

I catch Owen's eye and he takes my hand under the table. I get the message. I'm trying. That skullcap perches atop his hair like a small hummock.

As my father recites the blessing, Mr. Tunador hums along. He is a small dapper person with a bald head shaped like the Kremlin. Since he has no family of his own, he belongs to the Jewish community and is passed from house to house for holiday meals. Being a *Kohain*—tracing his ancestry back to the tribe of high priests—he never turns down an invitation, feeling that his presence confers an extra sanctity upon the occasion and thereby does his hosts a service.

We drink my mother's raisin wine, which fizzes slightly on the tongue, and eat parsley dipped in salt water to remind us of the tears shed by our ancestors while they were slaves in Egypt. Owen examines the parsley, lifting an eyebrow: the parsley is inferior. He takes a professional interest.

Then Michael, Marla's oldest, begins his struggle with the Four Questions, coached in whispers by his parents. "Why is this night different from all other nights?" he stammers, and the question makes me gulp my wine before you're supposed to. Michael labors on. He is only five, but Marla and Seth are ambitious parents. After Richie, Marla took over the role of family achiever. She was a straight-A student, president of everything, dated future dentists and accountants from respectable Jewish families, married a podiatrist right after college, and—in a family where there is often gloomy talk about the Jewish people dying out—promptly produced three babies, two of them boys. My parents keep so many snapshots of the children in the house you'd think *they* were the grandparents.

When Michael stumbles to a finish, everyone applauds. Then Marla's middle child, perhaps jealous, announces that he has soiled his pants. Marla hustles him off to the bathroom. Seth apologizes. Aunt Frieda alternately defends her second grandson and praises the first.

"I've lived to hear my grandchild ask the Four Questions," she says, eyes filling. Aunt Frieda is a weeper. "Believe me, I could die tomorrow."

My mother noisily gets up to check the brisket and motions me into the kitchen. "That woman has death on the brain," she whispers, forking a bite of meat into my mouth before I can duck. "As sick as she's been, she runs all over the city attending funerals. Friends, friends of friends, total strangers—it doesn't matter: as long as they're Jews. She goes and wails like an old woman, like her mother used to do." My mother bangs lids, stirring and tasting. "You remember last fall? In the hospital? She had a different kind of pneumonia in each lung. She kept lapsing into Yiddish, breaking the needles off in her arm. The woman is completely *tsetummelt*! Who needs such *meshugas*?"

"Why does she do it?" I whisper.

My mother gives me a level look over her half glasses, which means she is about to say something she considers extremely perceptive. "Because she has a deep-seated death wish, that's why. When she was so little and her father died, she wanted to die for him, felt guilty that she couldn't. And you were too young to remember how she carried on at her mother's funeral. Screaming: 'Take me, not her!' Trying to climb into the grave." Absently, she aims a spoonful of soup at me. I flinch and it spills.

"What's the matter, Esther?" she says. "What are you so *shpilkes*?"

"I'm not nervous," I mutter, dabbing my collar. Yiddish sits awkwardly on my tongue. "We're going to be stuffing ourselves all night. Why start now?"

She shoots me an offended glance.

Back at the table, where Mr. Tunador is chanting the story of Pesach in his high thin voice, I look at Frieda's gaunt face. My mother must be right. She is always right about such matters, having long established herself as the family sage, a combination of shaman and historian. She even claims the gift of prescience. Recently, for instance, she announced the death of my father's last uncle an hour before the phone rang with the news. She'd been listening to the radio, she said, and suddenly the music turned into a funeral march.

My father begins to sing "*Dayenu*." He has a pure tenor, the only true voice in the family, but he cannot resist clowning, bobbing his head to make the children laugh, and the song becomes comical. My father is a man of two passions: business and family. He has no other vices, hobbies, sports, clubs, vocations, tastes, or interests. His devotion to my mother goes beyond love: it's more like patriotism. He was very upset by the news about his uncle.

Now Mr. Tunador is making a speech about the fourth matzoh. Normally there are only three on the Seder plate, one for each division of Jewry, but Mr. Tunador insists on a fourth to symbolize the oppressed Jews in Russia. Holding it aloft, he beseeches God to free them. Everyone says "Amen," except Uncle Moe, who says "God forbid." Mr. Tunador turns as pale as my mother's wine.

"What's this?" he croaks. "*Antisemitisch?*"

"Now Moe," says Aunt Goldie in the tone of the long-married.

"It's simple," says Moe. "Jews will survive as Jews only as long as they're being persecuted somewhere. Why do you think we've lasted this long?" He ticks off the reasons on his fat fingers. "The Egyptians, the Syrians, the Philistines, the Persians, the Romans, the Crusaders, the Cossacks, the Nazis, and now the Soviets." He shrugs. "When oppression disappears, so do the barriers to assimilation."

I glance at Owen to see if this talk of assimilation embarrasses him, but he is listening intently. To him argument is a spectator sport, and he has been a fan ever since his undergraduate days at Harvard.

Mr. Tunador glares at Uncle Moe. "And what about the Covenant? What about our bargain with God?"

"*Bubemeinses*," says Uncle Moe. "Superstitions."

"Atheist!" hisses Mr. Tunador.

Moe shrugs. "I prefer to think of myself as a humanist. Instead of celebrating supernatural events, I celebrate human dignity, human courage, human ingenuity."

"Since when does he like humans so much?" Goldie asks my mother.

Mr. Tunador rattles off something in Yiddish. Owen looks at me, so I risk a free translation. "The Talmud says that on holidays we should honor strangers and fools," I whisper. "Are you sorry we came?"

"Not at all." Owen laughs. "At least I'm the stranger."

We drink the second cup of wine and eat Hillel sandwiches, made with matzoh, horseradish, and honeyed *charoset*, and named for a woodcutter who knew a good deal about mixing the sweet with the bitter. We are now halfway through the Seder, and though we've been eating ever since we sat down, it's time for the actual meal. My mother rises purposefully to her feet.

"No one leave the table," she commands. "I'm coming right out with the eggs. Esther, you can carry."

Now the procession of food begins in earnest: chopped egg in salt water, matzoh ball soup, *gefilte* fish, brisket and potatoes, duck in cherry sauce, sweet-and-sour cabbage, stuffed *derma*, *tzimmes*, asparagus and baby peas, three kinds of salad. Owen is bug-eyed. When we visited his mother, she fed us cottage cheese and sliced tomatoes. My mother graciously assists him, explaining what everything is made of, how it is prepared, how many people have tried to pry the recipe out of her. They discuss seasonings, and my mother looks pleased. She is thinking that he is one of my more palatable suitors. Ever since my divorce, there have been so many different young men that my parents have stopped bothering to learn their names.

Mr. Tunador eats diligently. Seth jiggles the baby and describes a case of Morton's Neuroma he treated this week — such pain between the toes that the poor man had to wear his wife's bunny slippers to work. Aunt Frieda shakes her head, communing with the sufferer. Marla cuts up food for the boys and tells us about a new Richard Simmons exercise tape that features the parents of famous movie stars, all over sixty. Marla says she and the children exercise to Richard Simmons every morning. She uses the baby as a free weight.

My mother rolls her eyes and motions me into the kitchen again. As we reload serving platters she tells me that Frieda is worried because Marla and Seth and the children always have colds. They all seem scrawny, but Marla won't let Frieda bring over any food except raw fruits and vegetables. What's more, Marla has joined an over-achievers' therapy group which consists of ferociously well-groomed people discussing their compulsion to get out of bed in the middle of the night and sand the garage door. My mother shakes her head, looking at Marla's narrow face, so much a younger version of Frieda's. For the first time in my life it occurs to me that it's possible to feel sorry for Marla.

We circle the table again with the platters, but no one can oblige save Mr. Tunador. Uncle Moe, who has been rolling a cigar between his fingers waiting to light it, lets out a sigh. While Seth discusses the Saachi merger with my father, Marla starts the children on their hunt for the *afikomen*, the piece of matzoh my father has secretly wrapped and hidden away sometime during the meal. Until it is found and redeemed for a prize, the Seder cannot be finished. I am considering ducking out and joining them to speed up the process when Goldie leans over and catches my hand.

"So tell me, Esther, how's the travel business? Any good bargains coming up?"

"The only place I travel these days is in my head."

"Oh?" A look at my mother.

"I work with Owen now." I feel myself redden, which has always bothered me. Jews don't blush.

"Is that right?" she says, flashing my mother another look, then addressing Owen with exquisite courtesy. "And what line are you in, young man?"

"I'm in herbs," says Owen, then smiles. "I've got a greenhouse on the Lower East Side."

"That wilderness?" Moe exclaims. "Nothing down there but junkies and rubble."

"I got a special city loan for building in an underdeveloped area."

Mr. Tunador bristles over his brisket. "Wilderness? I was *raised* on the Lower East Side!"

"You been down there lately?" says Moe.

"Is there much demand for a business like that?" my father asks.

"Chefs all over the city depend on him," I answer. "Sometimes we have to use couriers to rush them some basil or cilantro."

"Good tax breaks, I'd imagine."

Owen grins. "I'm classified as a farmer."

My father nods, eyebrows raised. He's impressed.

"You know, my friend Valerie runs a cookie business right out of her kitchen," Marla remarks from the doorway. Her children are ransacking the living room. "She's making a fortune, isn't she, Seth? And another girl just started a housecleaning service. She uses college kids, runs it on a shoestring, and the money's just pouring in." Marla breaks off, looking thoughtful. Seth gulps some water. Now *he* looks *shpilkes*.

"In my day, you didn't rush into business," says Mr. Tunador, helping himself to another potato. "You worked for someone else, you listened, you learned."

"Well, I think it's wonderful," Goldie declares. "If young people have talent, why shouldn't they use it? My Richie had such talent." She leans forward, fixing her bright eyes on Owen. "He could have run ten businesses, that boy. A genius. He thought up inventions long before their time. Self-cooling beer cans, flip-up toothpaste caps, flushable kitty litter—he just pulled ideas out of thin air, didn't he, Moe?"

"Pulled them out and threw them back in," Uncle Moe says, sour. "Like fish too small to keep. If he'd bothered to apply for even one little patent, the way I told him, he would've been a millionaire."

"*Alav ha-shalom*, may he rest in peace," Aunt Frieda murmurs. My mother blows softly over two fingers to prevent the dead from being disturbed.

All I remember of Cousin Richie is the haze of glamour which surrounded him. While I was lumbering painfully through adolescence, he was winning awards, driving a

Mustang, going off to college. He was especially attractive for a Jewish boy: tall, fair-haired, cheerful. A little like Owen. Then of course he got killed, and that was the most glamorous thing of all.

"Richie died in Vietnam," I tell Owen in a low voice.

He nods, puzzled. "He was drafted?"

"No," says Uncle Moe. "He enrolled."

"Enlisted," Aunt Goldie corrects him sadly.

"Enrolled," repeats Uncle Moe. "For him, it was an education. Oh, he marched in the demonstrations with the other kids. But he had doubts, and this was not a boy who could leave doubt alone. He had to see for himself. So he went." Uncle Moe shrugs. "His third week there he stepped on a landmine."

"A beautiful boy," Aunt Goldie mourns. "A brilliant boy."

"A boy, period." Uncle Moe's voice is flat. His bitterness imposes a brief silence.

Suddenly Marla's kids burst in, shrieking that they have found the *afikomen* wrapped in a napkin and taped inside the clothes hamper. I think of the times my father hid it there when I was young. The boys bargain with him, first demanding a trip to Disney World. My father counters with a trip to Chuck E. Cheese after Passover. The boys confer, then up the ante: Chuck E. Cheese *and* a Light Saber for each of them. My father agrees, adding a silver dollar—the traditional gift from his own father—to seal the deal, and the aunts shout "*Mazel Tov!*" as though it were a wedding. Then my mother announces firmly that it is time for coffee and dessert.

After cake and three kinds of cookies, made without leavening from powdered matzoh, plus a fruit pyramid glazed with pink sugar, we manage to wedge in a bite of the *afikomen* and say the Grace After Meals. We have no trouble giving thanks that the food has finally stopped coming. However, we still have to drink. Marla's baby begins to fuss and she takes her upstairs to nurse while we bless and drink the third cup of wine. Then it is time to open the door for Elijah.

My father recites the legend of Elijah the Tishbite, fierce

prophet and miracle-worker, whose reappearance on earth will herald a second Paradise, when all Jews will return to the Homeland. That is why we end every Seder with the words: *Next year in Jerusalem!* We open the door for Elijah, my father says, to invite him inside, to show that we are ready at any moment to give up our worldly concerns and follow him into Paradise. There is a special cup of wine for Elijah on the Seder plate. When I was a child, the adults always made a big fuss about the level of wine going down in the cup. "He's here! He's taking a sip!" they would shout, and I would rush over from the door to see, always a little too late.

This year, when Michael opens the door, the evening air is so unexpectedly balmy that no one tells him to close it. We just sit there feeling it flow across our faces, until Aunt Goldie stirs herself and sighs: "Sometimes it's a *mitzvah* just to breathe."

"You want to breathe air?" says Mr. Tunador, as if she might want to breathe something else. "You should breathe the air in Israel. Milk and honey, I'm telling you!"

"I don't know," remarks Uncle Moe, rolling his cigar between his fingers. "There are some who think Israel don't smell so sweet at the moment."

Mr. Tunador stiffens. This is worse than insulting the Lower East Side. My mother turns hastily to Owen and begins one of her lectures-for-our-Christian-friends on the customs of Passover. But Moe interrupts: "Tell him that in the Middle Ages, when they opened the door for Elijah, it was to make sure none of the *goyim* had dumped a body on the stoop."

My face turns as red as the horseradish, but Owen only says: "Oh yes, a Christian child's body, so the Jews could be accused of using the blood in their Passover rites. It was an excuse to start a pogrom." He glances at my mother's raisin wine. "That's how the custom of using white wine originated. So no one could be mistaken about what it was."

Everyone stares. We are a family of starers, shruggers, and interrupters. If they had bothered to draw him out, they might have discovered that he's a scholar, working on his astronomy Ph.D. while running his business—his specialty is the origin of the cosmos. As soon as we met, he began reading the *Encyclopedia Judaica* and asking me questions I couldn't answer. He even chose to meet my parents on Passover, rather than some ordinary night when we might have had dinner at Spaghetti Warehouse and discussed things rationally, because he wanted to see a traditional family Seder.

My mother is the first to recover. "Technically," she goes on, resuming her lecture, "it's forbidden even to own anything that's not *Pesadich*. My father, for instance, was a macaroni salesman, and every year he had to lock his entire product line in a closet and sell it for a dollar to the Italian barber at the corner. After the holiday he bought it back."

Mr. Tunador leans back and sighs. "*Oy*, what my mother had to go through every April. Weeks and weeks of scrubbing and polishing everything from top to bottom to make sure there were no crumbs. Not a speck of anything with flour. Special dishes just for *Pesach*, special pots and pans, special silverware. Everything else had to be packed away. She even had a special *Pesadich* set of false teeth."

"You think that's something?" says Uncle Moe. "My mother was such a fanatic she took a blowtorch to her oven."

"My father always brought the poorest Jews he could find home to Seder," says my father. "They were old and not always well, and sometimes they never left. My mother had to give away her shroud three times."

"I remember once she took a splinter out of my finger and swallowed it so no one else would pick it up," Aunt Frieda says, adding softly: "When our papa died, she wept so hard she went blind in one eye."

"My father was a cantor, a great *chazzan*," says Mr. Tunador. "His voice was so beautiful, when he sang at a wedding even the groom would cry."

"My father had an insurance business," says my father. "During the Depression, I used to go with him when he collected payments. If the people couldn't pay a little something each week—a quarter, fifty cents—their policy would be canceled and their children would have no protection. I can't tell you how many times I watched him take a quarter from one pocket and transfer it to another. Then he'd record a payment: 'Twenty-five cents.'" He pantomimes writing in a notebook, then shakes his head. "He was a *tzaddik*, my father."

I look at Owen to translate, but he already knows. "A righteous man," he murmurs.

"Well, my father spoke fourteen languages," says Uncle Moe. "He just worked in the rail yards, but they were always calling him down to the courthouse to interpret. In Europe he was trained as a rabbi—we go back six generations as rabbis—but here, of course, he had to earn a living."

"I don't see what Moe's getting so excited about," Aunt Goldie says with a wink. "When Richie's school had an Ethnic Fair and they asked all the parents to send in some symbol of their heritage, Moe sent a bunch of bananas. He said we were descended from the apes."

Amid a burst of laughter Uncle Moe loudly asserts himself, but this time I interrupt. "Well, Owen's Great-Aunt Prudence went to the electric chair," I say. "For setting her husband on fire."

There is a startled silence.

"She was a singer too," I tell Mr. Tunador. "On her way to the chair she sang 'Danny Boy' so beautifully that the guards wept. They refused to execute her. The warden had to threaten to discharge them."

"She was only an aunt by marriage," Owen assures my family. "And the guy deserved it."

"And his mother's taking a course in hieroglyphics," I go on. Passover might not be the most judicious time to bring up the Egyptians, but I don't care. "She's trying to write a poem, but it's terribly difficult—there are sixty characters just for `bird.' She has to make a rhyme by matching up beaks." I glance around the table to see if anyone can be unmoved. "Tell them about Grandpa Jack and the family fortune," I say, nudging Owen.

He takes a sip of water. I know him. He's giving them a chance to interrupt, to stop him. But no one says a word. "Well," he begins, "My great-grandpa Jack was a traveling salesman back in the days when drummers traveled the West by train and carried pistols." Young Michael, lolling in boredom on the couch, drifts back in to lean against his father's chair, drawn by the promise of a cowboy story. "He sold telephone systems when phones were brand new. There was a lot of competition, but the salesmen all played cards and drank together on the trains. One night they got to town and set up their usual game, but Grandpa Jack bowed out, saying he had a toothache. He slipped out of the hotel, paid a railroad man five dollars to use the handcar, and pumped himself down the line to the county seat. He ferreted out the Town Fathers' regular poker game, got himself dealt in, and sold them a system for the entire county. Next day when the train pulled in, his competitors were getting off and Grandpa Jack was getting on. He gave them a 'Howdy, boys!' and a big grin, because he knew his drumming days were over."

Everyone is still staring. Why are they so surprised? Did they think Jews had cornered the market on colorful family history?

"Grandpa Jack started a small phone company in Troy," Owen goes on. "When AT&T came along during the Depression buying up all the little companies, they offered him fifty thousand dollars: twenty-five in cash, twenty-five in virgin stock. But my great-grandfather insisted on the entire thing in cash."

My father lets out a groan, and Owen smiles. "Grandpa Jack put the money into a traffic light business, which is why to this day there's a traffic light on every corner of the city of Troy. I don't know if that had anything to do with his being run out of town one night—no one knows the truth about that. But he landed in Boston and went into the electrical parts business. He lived very well. At one point he even bought his own golf course. Finally he announced his retirement and his son, my grandfather, took over the business. Two weeks later, he declared bankruptcy. He never told us what happened and he never said a word against Grandpa Jack. He just went out and got a job—with the phone company, as a matter of fact. Grandpa Jack continued to live well till the end of his days. Women loved him. They thought he looked just like JFK. He died at the age of 102, outliving all his children."

My father shakes his head, still thinking about that virgin stock. Aunt Frieda wipes her eyes. I sit waiting for some acknowledgement of Owen, some sign of recognition that he is a product of a past as rich as ours. But Mr. Tunador is the next to speak, and he speaks about himself.

"That story reminds me of my own *zayde*," he says. "He went to Palestine to die, but when he got there he decided that Israeli Jews weren't Jewish enough, and it made him so mad he came back home and lived fifteen more years."

Uncle Moe stirs in his seat. "Israel is making itself a modern Western nation. It can't afford to be too Jewish," he declares, and suddenly we're back to the argument my mother tried to avert. It is the nature of Jews, apparently, to relate everything to Jewishness: we are a wholly self-centered tribe.

"One day the Law will be restored," Mr. Tunador insists. "A movement is underway."

Uncle Moe laughs. "Yeshiva boys throwing stones at cars on the Sabbath."

"There has been violence!"

"You really think they'd turn the country over to a bunch of fanatics? That would make a big hit in Washington."

"Those 'fanatics' have kept us alive for five thousand years!" Mr. Tunador thunders.

"That's right, and brought us to America where we prosper so well we're disappearing. Face it, my friend: history is ringing down the curtain on Jewish life."

"Very nice," says Mr. Tunador bitterly, glaring around the

table. "And what about the rest of us? Are we all turning into *meshumadim*?"

"Apostates," I whisper to Owen before he can tell me. It would have been scary if he'd known *that* one.

"A world without Jews is not inconceivable," Uncle Moe goes on. "I predict that within the next hundred years the American Jewish population will shrink to a tenth of its size. So you'd better pray the Soviets *don't* let up. They're what's keeping Jewish awareness alive."

"*I* should pray for such a thing?" repeats Mr. Tunador in amazement. "*I* should pray for oppression and persecution? What are you, a pharaoh? *Narishkeit! Mishegoss!*"

"What's foolish and crazy?" says Marla unexpectedly. She is standing in the doorway, dabbing at her blouse with a damp cloth. "What's going on? Why is the front door still open? Haven't you finished the Seder?"

There is a sheepish silence as everyone looks over at the door.

"We wandered a little," Aunt Goldie admits. "Maybe it's the wine."

My father makes a joke about wandering Jews, then clears his throat to signal that it's time to get back to business. We bless the fourth cup of wine and read from the Book of Psalms. Mr. Tunador chants in Hebrew for what seems a vindictively long time but looks calmer when he's done. Then my father recites the final prayer, we give the traditional response: "Next year in Jerusalem!" and close our books. The service is over. For a moment everyone looks a little lost, except Mr. Tunador, who says: "Aren't we going to sing?"

"Owen and I have to go soon," I say, hoping to get out of the singing. "Tomorrow's a work day."

My mother, remembering her obligations, casts a gracious eye upon Owen. "We're so glad you could join us," she says. "It was so interesting to hear all about your father."

"His great-grandfather," I say through my teeth. If Owen were Jewish, she wouldn't be so polite: she'd be grilling him about his grandmother's maiden name.

Then Owen surprises me. He says: "Actually, I was just thinking about my father."

"There, you see?" says my mother. "I read his mind."

"I was wishing he were still alive so I could introduce him to Esther," Owen goes on. "He would have liked her so much."

My face turns as beety as the horseradish. I give Owen a look that means *Maybe this isn't such a good idea.* He just smiles.

"In fact, there's something we'd like you all to know," he continues, speaking gently. "And that is that Esther has done me the honor of consenting to be my wife."

Jews don't talk this way. Everyone stares. He's got their full attention now.

"We've had such a good time tonight that we wanted to share our news with all of you."

I grab his hand under the table. This will be my second marriage, but right now I am sixteen again, afraid to look my parents in the eye.

"Well, isn't anyone going to say anything?" booms Uncle Moe, looking around the table in disgust. He shakes his head, turning to us. "*Mazel tov*, children—long life and good health. In honor of your engagement, I'll re-light my cigar."

My father clears his throat. "Well," he says. "Your mother and I—" He hesitates, trying to catch her eye.

"Owen is a very nice young man," my mother says quietly. I am surprised that she remembers his name. This has been a night of surprises. "But you should stop and think, both of you, before it's too late—" She breaks off, looking at me. "It's not too late, Esther?"

"Mom!" I say—two syllables, just the way I said it at sixteen. "No, I'm not pregnant."

My father and Aunt Frieda also turn horseradish red. Well, that's where I get it from.

"I had to ask," my mother says.

"Well, don't ask any more."

"I have to ask how you plan to raise the children."

I wince. "We'll raise the children, if there are any, as civilized human beings. I hope."

"You know what I mean. You'll tell the stories? You'll make the holidays? *Brisses? Bar mitzvahs*? If you don't— She pauses, a long and terrible pause. Where are the interrupters now?

"Listen," I say desperately. "*I* haven't even kept Passover since I was fifteen."

"How can you say that? We always—"

"No, *me*, Mom. Not you. I was on a date and the guy suggested pizza. I remember hesitating, thinking: 'Does it really make a difference?' And the answer came back clear as a bell: 'No. It really does not.'"

My mother pounces. "You see? None of this would have happened if you'd only stuck to Jewish boys."

I stare at her. Where is her prescience now? "He was Jewish," I say. "It was David Margolin."

"Margolin!" Mr. Tunador breathes, shocked. Of course he knows the family.

"We were both sick of it. All those years of Hebrew lessons, pretend 'tests' and 'report cards' no one took seriously. As if you could fail Sunday School! Listen—" My hand flies out, knocking over an empty glass. "Remember the banner that used to hang across the front of the Temple? The one that said *Save Soviet Jewry*? I always thought it said *Save Soviet Jewelry*. That's how out of it I was. All those years I took a quarter to Sunday School to put in the *pushke*, I kept thinking: what's so damn special about Soviet jewelry?"

"And Auschwitz?" says Mr. Tunador softly, bringing me up short. "And Dachau? And Treblinka? They don't matter either?"

That argument is unfair, but even so, I have to speak around a lump like one of my mother's matzoh balls stuck in my throat. "Yes," I manage to say. "They matter. Of course they matter."

"That's good to hear," says Mr. Tunador. "If we forget the Jews in Auschwitz, they died for nothing. If we forget the Jews in

Russia, they suffer for nothing. That is what makes a Jew a Jew. He remembers. For five thousand years, he remembers."

"I'm not forgetting anyone," I say. "But they died for something I don't believe in. I don't believe we're the chosen people. I don't believe in God or Moses or any of that stuff—"

There is an outcry, but my mother's voice soars above the rest: "Not everyone believes everything, but we share the same traditions—"

"Do we? Are you the same Jews your parents were?" I look around the table. No one answers, and now I feel ashamed. Low shot.

"What can I do?" I say. "I have to be what I am."

Then Goldie says soothingly: "What's everybody getting so excited about? Any child of a Jewish mother is Jewish. That's the Law. And it's not as if there's no one left to teach the children. *We're* still here."

"That's right," says Owen unexpectedly. "And besides, who knows? Maybe I'll convert."

Everyone turns to stare. The Cup of Elijah being drained before their eyes couldn't have made them stare any harder. I stare too. Despite all the wet matzoh in my belly pinning me to the stool, I just might tip over.

Mr. Tunador is the first to find his tongue. "Oh no," he says persuasively. "You don't want to do that."

"Why do anything hasty?" Aunt Goldie chimes in. "What's your rush?"

Uncle Moe leans forward. "Don't take it personal," he tells Owen. "Jews don't encourage converts. We figure they got to be half out of their minds."

"We do think you're a nice young man," my mother says anxiously, afraid they've been rude. "Your manners are lovely."

"Thank you," says Owen.

"Every family has its own little ways," Aunt Goldie adds. "I'm sure you understand."

"Sure," says Owen. "I remember a story Grandpa Jack used to tell about a woman who always cut one end off the ham before putting it in the oven to bake." There is a little squirming at the mention of ham, but Owen doesn't seem to notice. "No one could figure out why she did it, and when they asked her, she said: 'Well, because that's the way my mother always did it.' So they went to the grandmother and asked her, and she said: 'Well, because that's the way my mother always did it.' So they went to the great-grandmother and asked her, and she said—" He pauses, smiling around the table. "'Well, I had to do it that way because my pan was too small.'"

To my surprise, everybody laughs. My mother looks at Owen and me, her eyes moving from one face to the other. Suddenly she claps her hands and says: "The fourth cup of wine!"

The laughter is renewed. "We already had it!" they tell her.

"Maybe you've had enough!"

She is undaunted. "Then we'll have a toast. Why shouldn't we have a toast on *Pesach*?" She looks at my father, who rises at once to fill the cups. "We'll drink to family, absent and present. How's that? Is that something everyone can drink to?"

Out of habit, we bless the wine. Then we drink to what we have and what we have lost, and set the cups down empty. I think we might actually get to leave now, but five cups of wine have made Marla chatty. "So," she says. "How did the two of you meet?"

Owen and I exchange glances. *You tell the story. No, you.*

"In the university library," I say at last, losing the toss. "We were working at different tables across the room, but when I left, apparently the draft of my Phizzies for Dizzies paper slipped out of my notebook. Owen picked it up."

"Phizzies for Dizzies? Is that a drink?" says Aunt Goldie.

Marla laughs. "They still call it that? No, it's the basic physics course for non-majors to fulfill the science requirement. You know, like Rocks for Jocks. They don't expect too much. No offense, Esther."

"Anyway, I found the paper and returned it the next night," Owen breaks in smoothly.

"Yes, but not before he covered it with red ink, correcting all my mistakes, rewriting sentences, and suggesting an entirely new approach." I can't help it: I still have to glare. I don't consider it supportive that the entire table laughs.

"What grade did you end up getting?" my father asks.

I lose my glare. "An A. And Owen became my tutor. To pay him back, I started helping out in the greenhouse."

"We did so well together that eventually she left the travel agency and came to work for me," Owen adds. The way he says "for me" implies something so tender and possessive that all the blushers in the family instantly glow.

Worried that if any more blood rushes to the head of my elderly relatives, one of them will stroke out, I say firmly: "Enough talk! This is Passover! On Passover we sing!"

So we open our books and sing the familiar Passover songs, which include "America The Beautiful." I hate singing in groups—everyone plods along, inventing the melody as they go—but when we come to "The Four Sons," which is sung to the tune of "My Darling Clementine," I can't resist a little harmony on the chorus. Mr. Tunador sings with the fervor of a Hasid, while Uncle Moe raps the table with his heavy knuckles, singing around the cigar clenched in his teeth. My father's clear tenor rises above the rest, and it occurs to me that I have never heard his voice raised except in song. Goldie claps her hands to the beat, or so she thinks, and Frieda sings with tears glittering in her eyes. Marla and Seth sing, exhausted, from behind the children sprawled on their laps. My mother sings triumphantly, although what she's got to be triumphant about I have yet to discover, and Owen studies the musical notation, humming along, holding my hand.

For the benediction, my father defers to Mr. Tunador, perhaps assuming that blessings delivered by a senior *Kohane* have more staying power. I have my doubts, but, unlike Cousin Richie, I can leave doubt alone.

Then, finally, it is time to leave. We say goodbye. We thank my mother and she hands us one of her Care Packages—leftovers, plus a box of matzoh though I just told her I haven't kept Passover since I was fifteen. We say goodbye. Marla and I promise to keep in touch. Everybody shakes Owen's hand. They gather on the porch to see us off. We say goodbye. My father walks us to the car, watching to make sure we lock our doors and fasten our seatbelts. We make plans to meet after Passover at Spaghetti Warehouse. We thank my mother again. We say goodbye.

"Goodbye, children!" they cry. "Happy Passover! Have a good week! Drive safely!" And, rising above the others, Mr. Tunador's high, thin, hopeful voice pursues us out of the driveway and into the street: "Next year!" he is calling. "Next year in Jerusalem!

THE CUTTING

This story is extremely autobiographical—in fact, I sat down and wrote it the very night my relatives departed. It was written out of intense complex emotion and proved to be excellent therapy. There is no satisfaction quite like pinning your tangled thoughts and feelings with the right words. This is not a funny story, nor is the one that follows, but they each voiced truths I'd spent my childhood suppressing and enlarged my perspective enough to let me combine both humor and pain in my ultimate family story, "Fool at the Feast," which comes later in this collection.

The door shuts behind Esther's relatives at last and she is alone in a room cluttered with boxes and gift wrap and chairs brought downstairs for the guests. The door harp is still jangling. Esther's mother once expressed great admiration for this harp, so Esther spent a year searching out crafts fairs till she found another like it, made of pear wood and sculpted to a delicate point. She and Owen gave the harp to her parents as a thank-you—a token, really, since nothing they could afford would equal what her parents have given them: the baby's furniture, his stroller and car seat, most of his clothes. They even paid for the circumcision.

When Esther's mother unwrapped the harp she said: "Oh! A zither!" in a bright tone that meant: *Why on earth would you give me a zither?* Esther didn't try to correct her. You didn't correct Esther's mother.

She stacks little boxes in big ones, smooths out blue-is-for-boys gift wrap, untangles ribbons. Owen, usually so genial, took Jesse upstairs without a word as soon as they got back from the doctor's. He wouldn't come down to lunch even though Esther's family was toasting the baby with champagne. When she looked in, they were both asleep under the fluffy white quilt, Owen's face still grim, his hand cupping Jesse's head. Jesse, whose face is never still even in sleep, was pursing his lips, raising his barely visible eyebrows, and making his usual snuffles and grunts. Except for a shaky little sigh, there was no hint of what he had just been through. Esther wanted nothing more than to crawl under the quilt and sleep, the three of them together, but her family—her other family—was waiting downstairs to congratulate her. Her son was now a certified member of the Chosen People.

Although she isn't supposed to exert herself or lift anything heavy, Esther yanks the extra leaf out of the dining room table and wrestles it into the closet. She lugs the chairs upstairs, throws out paper plates and plastic cups, stuffs a trayful of cookies and half a honey cake down the garbage disposal, followed by the rest of the champagne. When her house is her own again, she collects all the baby gifts in one carton. She'll spend tomorrow writing thank-you notes. Most of the gifts are items of blue clothing, but someone has given the baby a silver Kiddush cup in anticipation of his Bar Mitzvah—Esther supposes she ought to be grateful that, unlike some tribes, Jews don't circumcise their sons at thirteen—and there is also a pair of tiny nail scissors cunningly shaped like a stork. Esther nearly overlooks them. They are concealed by the white flannel blanket she'd wrapped Jesse in today. She folds and smooths it carefully, then unfolds and holds it up to the light. No mistake. There is a fresh rust-colored spot where her eight-day-old son has paid his membership dues. Despite her stitches, Esther sits down hard on the floor, buries her face in the soft little blanket, and empties the tank for the second time that day.

The doctor, himself a nice Jewish boy from Brooklyn who came upstate to medical school and stayed on, refuses to perform circumcisions for any but religious reasons. There is no medical benefit, he says flatly, and so no reason to hurt the baby. He is devout, both as a doctor and a Jew, and this is a dilemma for him. But the Law is Law: the rite of circumcision is a sign of the Covenant with God—the child must surrender his foreskin in order to be considered a Jew. The Book of Genesis makes that perfectly clear.

To Esther nothing is clear except that her week-old son must have the tenderest part of his body mutilated. She could have refused, defied her family—Owen would have backed her up— but then her son wouldn't be a Jew, and that seems tantamount to self-betrayal. It would be like declaring herself an orphan: Jewishness and family are that intertwined.

For Owen the question is much simpler. He is a Jew only in the strictest technical sense: his mother is Jewish and he is circumcised. According to the Law, that makes him a Jew even though he was confirmed in the Episcopal Church at prep school (his father thought it would be good for business connections later) and even though his mother— born a Nussbaum—invites them to Cambridge every year for Christmas, complete with tree, stockings, and plum pudding. Owen has never lived as a Jew, but he understands Esther's complicated feelings: though she will be miserable at what transpires today, she will be eternally uneasy if it doesn't.

The circumcision is scheduled for the doctor's lunch hour. The day is bright and bitter; Esther has bundled the baby in a snowsuit and heap of blankets. This is the first time they have taken him out since the trip home from the hospital. Owen drives, while she sits in back with the car seat, holding her hand in front of Jesse's face to block the glare. She has pulled his knitted cap down over his eyes and soothed him with his Binky. All that shows from the mound of blankets is his tiny nose and the busily working pacifier. Owen's face in the rear view mirror is as sharp as a hatchet. He's scarcely spoken a word and did not sleep well.

Following in a caravan are two Cadillacs and a Lincoln containing the assortment of relatives who have made the trip from Ohio. Everyone troops into the doctor's office led by Esther's mother in her mink coat and matching hat, bearing trays of cookies and chopped liver for the celebration afterward. The nurses seem a bit nonplussed—the doctor doesn't do many circumcisions and certainly none that are *catered*—but Esther, who often discreetly intercedes for her mother, interpreting and smoothing the way, ignores everyone. She sits on one of the elegant striped couches and carefully tugs off the baby's cap and snowsuit so the cold air won't be too much of a shock when they go back out. Owen stands over her. He is polite, barely, when someone suggests that he sit down or at least take off his coat. Jesse peacefully sucks his pacifier. He has a velvety head, black eyes, and pink pomegranate cheeks. His nose is still flattened by its trip through the birth canal, and his head, where it battered Esther's tailbone during labor, still bears a bruise. Esther touches it gently.

"Touch him! Reach down and touch your baby!" the nurses cried, and Esther looked down to see a dusky crumpled little face between her legs, about to wail.

"Tell him he's safe," the doctor added, and Esther realized that he was out, he was Jesse, he was born. She laughed like biblical Sarah, reaching with both hands to pull the slippery little body onto her belly.

"I don't believe it!" she kept saying, laughing and kissing Owen, kissing the baby's wet head as the doctor stitched her up.

She had felt from the start that it would be a boy, though her mother, who claimed the gift of prescience, had predicted a girl. When her mother learned of her error she was silent a moment, then, characteristically, turned it into a personal triumph after all by declaring that Esther must have inherited her ESP.

Now, holding the baby in the same waiting room where she has spent three years waiting to hold a baby, Esther wishes for once that her mother had been right. Jewish girl babies only get named: there is nothing to cut.

The doctor is running late. The children restlessly page through picture books. Esther's mother strokes the fur sleeve of her coat and contemplates the chopped liver tray, which she has festooned with curly radishes and dyed blue turnips carved into flowers. Cutting things into fancy shapes is her specialty—her signature, she likes to say. At home she has a scrapbook full of pictures of the masterpieces she has produced with her knife.

The last patient, a career woman in pinstripes and pearls, is called into an exam room. She carries a telltale red folder and glances sharply at the baby as she passes, reminding Esther of her own red folder, her own three long years of testing and chart-keeping, watching women with big bellies in the doctor's waiting room. She still can't quite believe that the baby in her arms is her own, that she doesn't have to give him back. You aren't supposed to get your heart's desire; that's not how life works; and besides, she already has Owen. How much more can she get away with? None of this feels real.

The entire first week has been surreal, in fact. At first she hallucinated, seeing the baby's face loom huge beside the bed, hearing him cry, thinking Owen was handing him to her to nurse, even when both were fast asleep beside her. The one time she ventured out, to the drugstore, she kept hearing people say "Jesse, Jesse." Maybe they were really saying "Yes," or "Let's see," or maybe nothing at all: she heard "Jesse" and hurried home. Things had just started to settle down when the first Cadillac arrived.

"Esther and Jesse?" says the nurse in the doorway.

Everybody stands up and follows her down the hall. Esther notices for the first time how smartly her relatives are dressed, as if going to Temple for the High Holidays. Only she and Owen look *schlumpadinka*—she in a baggy maternity jumper, Owen unshaven in a dirty ski jacket and scuffed boots.

In the examination room the nurse takes the baby from Esther and lays him upon the white-papered table where Esther herself has lain so often with spread knees and someone's gloved hand inside her. The nurse begins to unsnap Jesse's sleepers.

"I'll do it," Esther says quickly. Jesse hates to be undressed. The only time he really cries is when air or water touch his naked skin. Esther covers him with her hand, which just spans his small chest. She bends close so he can see her face. Jesse frowns, hiccups, loses his pacifier.

"Now Esther," says the nurse firmly—everyone here knows Esther; they were all glad she finally got pregnant; but after all, this is their lunch hour— "why don't you take your people back out while I get the baby ready?"

Esther, accustomed to obeying at the doctor's office, picks up her purse, but Owen says: "I'll stay." The nurse, glancing at his face, just nods.

Everyone else, murmuring, glancing at watches, heads back to the waiting room. Esther's arms feel dangerously light; she can smell the baby on her shoulder. Why does she do what she's told, trot placidly along with the pack? They are not "her" people anymore, not the way Jesse and Owen are hers. When the nurse calls them back down the hall, Esther charges ahead. She can hear Jesse's outraged howls through the door.

The doctor is inside. When he moves his broad back, she sees the baby spread-eagled naked on a white plastic form just big enough to hold him. His arms and legs are strapped down and there is a thick cotton pad wedged against his groin, ready to catch his blood. Jesse's face is purple, his screams hoarse already. Esther bursts into tears.

Her mother pours the kosher wine while her father passes

out mimeographed prayer sheets. The doctor dips the pacifier in wine and puts it in the baby's mouth, but Jesse spits it out—he will not be pacified. Next the doctor tries a piece of gauze soaked in wine, but Jesse's screams, forced to the back of his throat, only intensify. The doctor shrugs and glances at Esther's father, who takes his cue and begins to read the service. Someone hands Esther a box of tissues, which she uses in great handfuls, taking a distracted satisfaction in the waste.

The doctor selects an instrument. Esther looks, then doesn't look, then looks again. Does she have the right to protect herself from this? Can Jesse protect himself? He is here because of her; she forbids herself to look away.

The worst part is not the knife but the scissors as the doctor works them in his hand: snip, snip, as if cutting cloth, not human skin, not *Jesse's* skin. Then he uses a socket wrench to force the snipped skin down. The tool has to remain in place for three minutes. The baby keeps up his dry, furious, muffled sobs. Behind them, Esther's father reads the service in a special singsong cadence as if it were an incantation. Blood continues to well up from the tip of the tiny penis.

Owen never takes his eyes off his son but reaches out an arm for Esther. She leans against him, fixed on the sight of their baby gagged and strapped to the table with a large cold piece of steel affixed to his most vulnerable place. This is a *mitzvah*, a blessing? This is a scene from a horror movie.

"Amen!" cry Esther's relatives as the service is concluded. Jesse is officially a Jew. The doctor says "*Mazel tov!*" and strips off his gloves to pump her father's hand as if they have single-handedly saved the Jewish people from extinction.

The nurse is explaining how to dress the baby's wound, but Esther can't take it in. She blows her nose and mops her face because she is afraid to let her family see what is in her eyes. Why are they here? Why are they doing this to her child? It can't be a matter of *belief*—no one has ever asked what she believes. That's not the important thing in Esther's family. What matters is tradition, symbolic behavior. You cut off a baby's foreskin because Jews have always cut off their babies' foreskins, not because you believe that once upon a time in the desert God gave the first Jew this command, or even because you think a God who would require babies to suffer such pointless pain is worth believing in. If there *is* a God (Esther asks her relatives, furious and silent), what makes you think He's benign? Or even in His right mind?

The nurse leads the family back out to the waiting room, where Esther's mother has set out trays of delicacies bristling with frilled toothpicks. She is in her element now, discoursing upon Jewish customs and etiquette for the benefit of the doctor's staff.

Esther and Owen stay behind with the doctor, who puts the baby back in Esther's arms. Jesse is still crying, though without tears—he is too young to produce them. Esther unbuttons her blouse, asks for more Kleenex. Owen hands her rough brown paper towels instead.

"Listen," says the doctor gently. "The bad part's over. He's going to be fine."

Jesse will not be comforted. He refuses to take her nipple.

The doctor smiles, stooping to put his large melancholy face close to the baby's. "Listen, pal, come back in eighteen years and I'll let you throw the first punch."

Owen makes a noise that sounds like laughter, but when Esther looks up he is leaning against the wall in tears, clenching the sodden contents of an entire box of Kleenex. The only other time she has ever seen him cry was when he talked about his father's death. He does not hide his face but shows it to her, distorted by tears, as if to say *See?*

The doctor laughs softly. "That's why you got paper towels," he tells Esther. He claps Owen on the shoulder, rests his hand on the baby's head, then goes out to try her mother's chopped liver. Esther and Owen stay behind until, like Jesse, they weep themselves dry.

On the way home, Esther's parents stop to pick up the deli tray she ordered for lunch. Owen takes the baby upstairs. Esther's mother, still in her mink hat, is "doctoring" the deli tray, tucking parsley, radish roses, and spirals of carrot among the cold cuts.

"Is the tray okay?" Esther says, meaning: who are you trying to impress now?

"Well, the *ham* is nice and lean," her mother replies in a voice which suggests that the tray is appalling.

It takes Esther a moment to get the message. Then, foolishly, she says: "But you don't keep kosher."

Her mother gives her the look of iced fury she reserves for occasions when her judgment or expertise is called into question. "It's just not the sort of thing you serve at a *bris*," she retorts.

Esther is speechless. Or rather, she can think of nothing to say—short of "I'm sorry," which would constitute complete self-betrayal—that would not blow open the huge crack running through the center of the family, something everybody, especially her father, has been desperately shoveling over for as long as Esther can remember. She would like to point out that her mother requested cheese as well as meat on the platter, that the children are drinking milk, that last night they ate shrimp cocktail: why is her logic so selective? And what is the point of keeping kosher for one meal? Is God so easily hoodwinked? But Esther knows it has nothing to do with God. What matters is beautiful performances: the family is her mother's private repertory company and today they are performing "Good Jews."

Esther's father opens the first bottle of champagne and fills the glasses. "Here's to Jesse," he says, raising his own. "May these be the worst tears he ever has to shed."

"Amen," says Esther's mother briskly and hoists her new video camera to her shoulder. "Now say Jesse's Hebrew name for the camera."

"Jesse's Hebrew name is *Yishay Ya'akov*," says Esther's father obediently.

"No, no, look up."

He looks up, clearing his throat. "Jesse's Hebrew name is *Yishay Ya'akov*."

"In memory of?"

"In memory of your father— "

"His great-grandfather on his maternal side..."

"His great-grandfather on his maternal side..."

"Jacob Gutmann..."

"Jacob Gutmann..." He waits for his next line.

To Esther it seems like some perverse ceremony, with her mother administering an oath and her father swearing in. As her mother aims the video camera around the table, feeding everyone lines ("Now Missy gets the biggest bagel because she's the oldest cousin, right? I always make something special for each of you, don't I? What do you like best, my bagels or my blintzes? Missy, look at the camera."), Esther tries to think how her mother got the idea they were naming the baby for Grandpa Jake—a short, paunchy, aggressive man Esther barely remembers. He died when she was seven. "Jesse" is just a name they like, she and Owen, and the fact that it begins with J is a coincidence. But Esther's mother, characteristically, assumed that the name was chosen to please *her*, which is itself an odd assumption since her father never liked her much. She was the fourth girl in a string of five; he had hoped each time for a son. Plus, she was the tallest, strongest, most robust of the girls, and that had irritated him even more. Esther's mother bore the full force of his displeasure and fled into marriage at seventeen, surrendering (she said) both her youth and her dreams of becoming a famous artist or actress.

But if she surrendered her youth, Esther thinks as she watches her mother point the camera, controlling all the conversation, then she has also somehow remained infantile. Doesn't she realize that all you hear on these videotapes is her loud imperious voice, the voice of the infant-tyrant?

"Here's your wine, dear," says Esther's father, setting the

glass down beside her mother's plate.

"One minute, Gil!" Esther's mother snaps as if he has made some kind of demand. "Can I please finish what I'm doing?"

Esther takes the risk of letting her jaw drop and looks around the table. Everyone is very busy unfolding napkins, pouring milk, cutting up food for the children. She contemplates the possibility of telling her mother that she is full of crap, that she cannot get away with this behavior just to indulge her love of self-drama. But even as she's rehearsing this speech, conversation resumes and, as usual, the moment passes.

Her father rises again to bless the bread. He has accepted the unjust rebuke silently with no trace of resentment. Esther knows why. He is the same kind of husband as he is a Jew —the important thing is not to question or articulate belief but to behave according to familiar patterns. He likes to tell how his own mother used to say that family was *geknipt und gebinden*, knotted and pasted together. Esther's father would never dream of cutting those knots, not even metaphorically, not even in the privacy of his own heart. How could he? *He'd* had a mother who never went to bed on Thursday nights. She stayed up to prepare for the Sabbath, cooking, cleaning, baking. And since her three children all liked different kinds of cake, she made each child his own, from scratch, every week. They would find her sleeping at the table Friday morning, surrounded by fresh bread and pastry. It was on this same table that her children had learned to crawl. She considered the floor too dirty (despite its daily scrubbings); so, using rolled-up towels as barriers, she would put the baby on top of the table and spend the afternoon racing around the sides to head him away from the edges. No wonder Esther's father makes sentimental speeches about Family; no wonder he is willing to sacrifice anything to preserve the illusion of harmony. A family is a little civilization unto itself, with its own history, laws, codes, and discontents.

They begin to eat. Esther notices that nobody passes up the ham. She should have called her mother's bluff, spoken out

about self-delusion and hypocrisy. But challenging her mother
—the infant-tyrant around whom a protective cult has sprung
up—would invite the same kind of alienation as refusing to
circumcise the baby. Esther doesn't want to be estranged from
her family; she just wants them to let her be. She does want
Jesse to consider himself a Jew; she just doesn't want him to be
coerced to behave as one. She wishes her parents really knew
her, but she takes care never to reveal herself. Nevertheless, she
reveals herself in little ways, just enough to strike sparks with
her mother. She rubs her aching head.

Esther's father notices and leans forward to say
sympathetically: "In three days he'll forget all about it and
everything will be healed."

Perhaps because Owen is not here to exchange ironic glances
with, or perhaps because Esther is simply too cowardly to
take on her mother, she remarks: "The doctor refuses to do
circumcisions anymore except for religious reasons. He says
there are no medical benefits and that causing the baby so
much distress for cosmetic reasons is unforgivable."

Esther's father keeps his eyes on his sandwich—he knows
when to leave a subject alone; he's had over forty years of
married life to perfect his knowledge—and she feels ashamed,
remembering how he'd cradled the baby in his arms and
sung him a Yiddish lullaby about a pomegranate, bouncing
a little on the downbeat, oblivious to the video camera and
stage directions. But before she can say something palliative,
her mother replies: "*That* isn't true. There are *many* medical
reasons for circumcision."

Esther goes positively hot with fury—her mother lacks the
grace to give up even this much ground—but hears herself say
coolly: "Have you read the articles?"

"I certainly have," her mother replies. "And I consider myself
quite knowledgeable on the subject."

There can be no response to this, of course, except "I'll bet
you do," and Esther gulps champagne to keep from making
it. Her mother's education has largely been provided by

afternoon television, but to challenge her openly would bring on the rupture Esther dreads. Instead, she pulls her sandwich to pieces on her plate, and the silence spreads around the table as her mother eats on in offended triumph.

There's a sudden indignant cry from upstairs—Jesse having his dressing changed—and everyone laughs. Everyone but Esther. Jesse hates to be undressed. Hates the touch of air on his skin. On the changing table he kicks and twists and flails his tiny fists. She tenses, listening, but the crying stops. Meanwhile, the laughter has released everyone from her mother's spell. The clatter of silverware and chatter resume.

"You know, you were pretty lucky," Esther's sister-in-law tells her. "My cousin just had her third miscarriage."

"Hilda's daughter is in the hospital for toxemia," one of the aunts observes. "She's only six months along."

"The girl who does my nails is having twins," says another. "*She's* in the hospital too—contractions at only nineteen weeks. They say it doesn't look good."

"My neighbor's baby had a skull that never closed," adds a third. "It only lived a few hours."

"You were very lucky," the aunts chorus.

Esther agrees. "I thought it would take much longer. But I was already six centimeters dilated when I got to the hospital."

"That's wonderful," says a cousin. "With my first, I started pushing too soon—my cervix swelled up and I had to start all over again. It was horrible."

"I can imagine," Esther says quickly. "Waiting to push was the worst part. It's so much harder to *not* do something."

At this point Esther's mother takes over again with a long story about a young man who got one girl pregnant while engaged to another who happened to have no ovaries, and all the complications that ensued. Everyone pays rapt attention, even Esther's father, who must have heard this story countless times. Esther sits like a rock, letting the words break and flow around her. Until her mother's monologue, she had been enjoying the shared mother-talk—her first as a bona fide member of the club.

It reminds her of a remark her mother made the day before, when they were alone in the house with Jesse, waiting for Owen and Esther's father to get back from the hotel with the first load of relatives. Esther was nursing Jesse in the rocking chair, and at first her mother critiqued her technique: Esther was not burping the baby in the right place (towards the side, a little under the arm, was better), and she was not trying hard enough to keep him awake between feedings ("He'll keep you up all night; he'll take advantage.") But Esther just kept rocking and murmuring, and after a few minutes her mother said: "You know, when I was trying to nurse you, they told me to put molasses on my nipples."

Esther looked up. "You nursed me? I never knew that."

"I tried," her mother said with a reproachful sigh. "You wouldn't take the nipple."

Esther ignored the sigh and risked a small revelation of her own. "Jesse wouldn't nurse at first either. They said it was because I have flat nipples and he's got a high palate. I had to use breast shields till he learned to suck."

"My nipples were fine," her mother replied. "You just wouldn't take them."

Sensing danger—any minute now her mother would start on how Esther had drained all the calcium from her body and left her with serious dental problems—Esther switched the topic to some child-abuse cases in the news. But despite the rebuke, she was touched by the fragile intimacy of this conversation. Her mother had never spoken to her as one woman to another, and she wondered, as she nursed the baby and discussed public events, if it put their relationship on new ground. Her mother was apparently thinking along the same lines, for, as they heard car doors slam outside, she said something about Esther one day knowing the satisfaction of adult conversation with one's child. Though Esther felt a foolish glow of pleasure at this indirect commendation— both "adult" and "conversation" were suspect terms when her mother used them—she was relieved to be distracted by the crowd of aunts and cousins. Intimacy, in their family, was about as authentic as her mother's videotapes.

As if proving her clairvoyance after all, Esther's mother chooses this moment to glance at the stairs and say reproachfully: "It's a shame the baby can't come to his own party. He won't even be on the video."

Esther expertly ignores the bait. Owen had forbidden her mother from filming the *bris*—it was one of the few things he insisted on. But how long can they go on protecting the baby? Sooner or later he'll have to submit to the camera, to the hokum and pageantry, to the whole religious fantasy. He'll have to learn, as she did, to swallow his indignation along with the bagels and blintzes. It's the price of belonging, she thinks as the aunts rise at last to clear the table, of *geknipt und gebinden*, if you don't want to cut ties.

But how to teach Jesse that without betraying him? How old will he have to be before he understands that the survival of any civilized society, large or small, depends upon a certain amount of courteous hypocrisy? And will he despise her in the meantime, as she'd despised her own parents and chafed under their bonds? Will being free at home to *speak* —to acknowledge the tacit conspiracy, the family totems and taboos—make the crucial difference? It will have to, Esther decides. She can only bend so far.

There is the usual prolonged leave-taking among the aunts, but her mother's goodbye is cool. She simply nods at Esther's ritual "Thanks for everything, Mom" and kiss on the cheek. The thanks are her due, the nod implies, even if Esther does not mean them. She is still stewing over the challenge to her authority: to reject that, after all, is to reject the image of herself as expert which she has spent so much energy—her own as well as everyone else's—and so many years cultivating.

Esther hugs her father goodbye. He means well; he means *her* well, but he has practiced the habit of deference too long. He will be an indulgent and loving grandfather, but an unreliable ally. He's spent too many years trying to fill a leaking bucket: her mother's thirst for attention, admiration, and appreciation—for the love her own father refused her—can never be satisfied, no matter how much of a cult the family makes of her, no matter how much damage is done in trying. Of course, Esther has never had the guts to speak up for *him* either. Guilty, she hugs him again.

The jangling of the door harp has long since died away when Esther looks up from the blanket she has been using as a handkerchief. Her face is hot and swollen again, but her house is back in order; except for the big bag of garbage, there is scarcely a trace of her family's visit. Esther opens her cramped fingers to find that she is still clutching the stork scissors. Gently, she puts them down.

Upstairs, she eases open the bedroom door. Jesse and Owen are asleep, the baby humped into a ball on her husband's shoulder, one little fist flung out as if in defiance.

"I learned something today," Owen had said as they mopped their faces in the doctor's office. "My son is a fighter. He won't easily submit."

Jesse is a fighter, but he lost today's battle. It was Esther's interference he submitted to: after a week of soothing care, of responding to every need the moment he made it known, of fostering in him the sense that the world is a safe place, she had caused him to be strapped to a table and cut with a knife. And she would do it again, for the same complicated reasons.

In his sleep Jesse turns his head and opens his mouth in a soundless mew. He's getting hungry. Just the sight of his round cheek and pursed lips makes her eyes prick with fresh tears. She thinks of Hilda's daughter, her aunt's manicurist, her cousin's neighbor; she thinks of fever and accidents and the awful specter of crib death—so much peril, within and without.

Gently she pulls up the blind to let in the late afternoon light. Outside on the lawn below, children are playing war with snowballs; when one receives a direct hit, he falls thrashing in mock agony to the ground. Soon—sooner than she thinks, everyone tells her—Jesse will be among them, running, leaping, growing taller, moving further from her arms each year. Will she know him any better than her parents know her?

As the light touches Owen's face, he opens his eyes and looks at her calmly. Immediately her loneliness subsides. She has been too cut off from him and the baby today: if real intimacy comes from knowledge of the beloved, then this is her true family now. Jesse stirs again, grunting and smacking his lips. He turns his head from side to side, rooting, inching his way down Owen's chest as if he intends to set off on his own.

"He thinks he's one of the big boys," says Esther.

"Yeah," says Owen. "He wants to go hang out with the three-month-olds."

"In front of the corner toy store."

They smile a little, the first time all day. Then Jesse lets out a cry, clearly a summons, and Esther feels her bra dampen in response. She kicks off her shoes, settles on the bed next to Owen, and, as the children outside stagger and die in the snow, unbuttons her blouse to feed her son.

ROCKS

T he baby is six months old before my brother comes to see him, bringing apologies and a suitcase full of pricey toys he can no longer afford.

"I didn't know you had F.A.O. Schwarz on the Coast," I say, holding up a stuffed yak.

"We've got everything on the Coast," says Jonathan. He has, in the family vernacular, *gone California*, and still looks like a hotshot Beverly Hills broker—lizard shoes, paisley tie, hair short on top and long in back—though he hasn't touched the market since the crash of '87. Instead, he's been struggling to get his own business underway, doing public relations for companies selling stock, which (according to my mother) is going to be wildly successful any day now. My mother does not know and must *never* know (according to my father) that Jonathan has been living off his credit cards, or that my father, whose name he submitted as a credit reference, has been receiving decreasingly polite calls from the companies. My father has been making discreet payments on the bills, he tells me, but neither Jonathan nor my mother must ever, ever know. I can't imagine how my father thinks Jonathan accounts for his shrinking debt—a general amnesty for brokers, perhaps? But the crash, and his firm's downsizing, and his subsequent conviction that he was destined to be his own wildly successful boss are what kept him from attending Jesse's bris.

"Be glad you missed it," I tell him. "It was bloody and barbaric and awful."

"Oh really?" He looks around at the boxes I've been packing. That kind of talk makes him uncomfortable. Besides, we all know that Mom long ago cornered the market in bitterness—everyone else has to make do with light irony.

Since I love my brother, I usually respect the family taboos, but Jesse's bris cut something loose in me and now this reticence seems irritating. Worse than irritating. To cover, I take him upstairs to see the baby napping.

"You know who he looks like?" I say.

Jonathan stoops till his face is level with Jesse's. "Uncle Lenny? They've got the same hairline."

Uncle Lenny is another dangerous subject. Did he or did he not molest his granddaughter? No one will talk about it.

I look down at the top of Jonathan's head, where I see silver strands. Our mother, too, went silver prematurely. I don't take after that side of the family. "He looks like you," I tell him. "When you were a baby."

"Really?" He's pleased. If his marriage to Delilah had lasted longer than two years, he would probably be a father now himself.

"Except you had all those curls," I add. Neither of us mentions the birthmark that covers half his cheek and has long been concealed by his glossy black beard. It's possible he's forgotten it, forgotten the taunts of other children and the unthinking remarks of teachers.

But I remember the ringlets, the swollen purplish cheek, the half-solemn smile as if he were trying to mimic my father. Long before he could understand, I used to sit by his crib and read him stories. I lugged him, half-sliding off my hip, all over the house and yard. I was eight and thought of him as *my* baby. A good thing, too—soon after his birth, my mother sank into one of her depressions and spent most of the day in bed. My father learned to cook and I learned to change diapers, fix bottles, and work the washing machine. I managed surprisingly well. But then she got better and took the baby back, and I reverted to being a clumsy lump of a child who generally dwelt in a fog. For a long time, especially after my first marriage ended, I thought Jonathan had been the only baby I would ever have. It took Owen and me three years to conceive Jesse—three years of charts, thermometers, hormone shots, and therapy—and even now, even when I see him sleeping in his crib, I can't believe it's happened. The truth is, I never expected to be happy.

"He's long, isn't he?" Jonathan says softly.

"Like you and Uncle Mel. He's got the tall gene."

Jonathan grins. "I played golf with Mel last time he was in L.A. He told me the baby was so long when he was born, they had to let down the cuffs on his Pampers."

I give him half a smile. Uncle Mel is the family joker. He also cheated our father out of a business a long time ago, but that, of course, is not something we discuss.

"God, look at him *sleep*," Jonathan whispers, as if the baby has done something clever. "Wish I could sleep like that."

"Your ulcers acting up again?"

Jonathan's stomach ulcers and high blood pressure are another thing my mother must never ever know about.

He pulls a wry face. "Them and Clay."

Jonathan's friends are legion, but Clay's story has assumed almost mythic proportions in our family. Clay is a successful young broker who managed to survive the crash, largely due to the munificence of one wealthy client who admires his chutzpah. Two years ago, Clay's girlfriend Carissa decided it was time they got serious. He was leery and asked Jonathan: "If I get her a ring, how much time will it buy me?" Then a chronic bellyache—she and Jonathan used to share Tums—turned out to be something ominous. She beat the cancer but lost both ovaries. Clay was at the hospital every day; the engagement was announced, the date set. But during this time, Clay was also dating—that is, screwing on the floor of his office—a temp secretary named Arlene. She had been married at seventeen, divorced at eighteen, and had a baby that died. Naturally she got pregnant again. The baby was born soon after Clay and Carissa's wedding. Arlene wanted to call him Clay, but when Jonathan talked her out of it, she settled on Nike, after her favorite sneakers. Clay was crazy about his son.

Eventually, of course, he had to tell his family. Carissa forbade him to speak of the child or see him on her time, which meant evenings, weekends, or holidays. Clay's parents were thrilled—since their son's wife is sterile and their daughter an embittered lesbian, they figured this was their only chance for a biological grandchild. Carissa's parents were horrified. When she went East with Clay at Christmas, her mother called from L.A., screaming so loud over the phone that everyone in the room heard her call Clay "that bastard with the bastard" who would make Carissa get sick again and die.

Clay tried to abide by Carissa's rules, he told Jonathan, but he kept slipping up—leaving Arlene's checks where Carissa could find them, making thoughtless remarks about bikes and baseball gloves. Meanwhile, Arlene kept threatening to kill herself if he didn't divorce Carissa and marry her immediately. When Carissa told Clay he had to choose between her and Arlene/Nike, he came up with the kind of bluff that had made him so successful in the market: he would stage a mock separation, move out temporarily; Arlene would be lulled into a false sense of security; Carissa would be scared into seeing how unreasonable her demands were, and Clay would buy himself enough time to figure out his options. At first he moved into a three-hundred-dollar-a-day hotel suite, and then —when he got tired, he said, of living alone—into Jonathan's modest post-crash apartment, where he sleeps on the couch, dodges hysterical phone calls, and keeps Jonathan up all night talking.

But Jonathan doesn't want to dwell on Clay's problems. He's brought me a videotape of the wedding, which my parents attended and which my mother, who loves Clay, has never stopped raving about. "The *color* scheme," she keeps telling me, "was *peach* and *aquamarine*." We slide the tape into the VCR.

Jonathan pours himself a glass of scotch and sips, wincing, while the tape rolls: *Klay and Carissa's Glorious Day!*

I hit pause and look again. It can't be a typo. Clay spells his name with a K?

The credits continue: Klay and Carissa's wedding stars Klay and Carissa; it is produced by Carissa's parents, directed by the rabbi, and co-stars the ushers and bridesmaids. Jonathan is (Special Appearance By) Best Man. First we see baby pictures of the two stars. Fade into swans, a fake pond, lush greens. A string quartet plays. Carissa appears backstage in her wedding gown, looking like an angel until she opens her mouth. Her voice is thin, nasal, inclining toward shrieks. I can well imagine those midnight calls.

The ushers appear—there's Jonathan. My stomach gives a lurch. Why should the sight of my baby brother make it do that? He towers over the other young men, sleek in his custom tuxedo. Except for the silver strands, he still looks like the young prince who married Delilah Sugarman and stood ready to inherit her father's vast enterprises. But the last eight years have been filled with unaccountably bad luck. Through a dirty trick, Delilah saddled him with a large debt just before the divorce became final; their lawyers are still hammering it out. Then there was the crash, his struggling new business, new debts, his ulcers and blood pressure. Girls keep dumping him. His car keeps getting broken into. Every time he flies, the airlines lose his luggage or keep him circling for hours above one city or another. Even his dog was snatched.

How did it happen? How did my life get to be so good and his so awful? It was always the other way around. And seeing what's happened to Jonathan, how can I trust my own happiness? Sometimes when Owen's been gone a while, I imagine the policeman coming to the door, the slow heavy knock: a drunk driver, a patch of ice, a stray bullet. And Jesse —all it would take is one of his ambitious lurches when I'm carrying him down the stairs. Once I told Owen that FDR was full of shit: there's *plenty* to fear. "He was talking about banks,"

Owen said dryly. But he knew what I meant. In his house, you joked about such things. In mine, you never mentioned them.

Now Klay and Jonathan are coming down the aisle, Klay talking the whole way. Then the bridesmaids in strapless peach taffeta with huge bows across their bosoms. Then Carissa, crying already on her father's arm. Klay takes her hand, murmuring nonstop—no doubt he packed his nose just before the ceremony. The camera zooms in for a close-up of Carissa's eyelashes. Klay and Carissa promise to cherish and honor each other forever. Jonathan looms behind them. Is he remembering his own wedding day? What is he thinking when the rabbi says that the home is a sanctuary, the kitchen table an altar? What, for that matter, is my mother thinking at that moment?

Klay winks at the camera as the rabbi pronounces them man and wife. Jonathan places the wrapped wine glass— really a light bulb, because it makes a more satisfying crunch —beneath Klay's heel. Klay stomps, then grinds it underfoot, grinning so hard it makes my own face hurt. The newlyweds embrace, the audience applauds, the rabbi signals someone at the back, and dozens of peach and aquamarine balloons fill the air. Fade-out on the balloons.

Jonathan hits pause so he can refill his glass. "So what do you think?"

The scotch must have made him reckless. No one in our family ever wants to know what anyone *thinks*. Once, after a family reunion, my father got careless and asked me, happily, what I thought. "Well," I said, testing the waters, "it was quite an ordeal." Instantly the smile fell from his lips. "What do you mean, *ordeal*?" he said stiffly, and I had to work fast to repair the damage.

But Jonathan is my brother, my ally, my old comrade-in-arms. "Well," I say. "The rabbi's speech had me all choked up."

Jonathan rattles his ice. "Isn't he great?"

"Oh, come on—the kitchen table an *altar*? What is he, a Druid?"

"He's a nice guy. He's one of my golf buddies."

"Who isn't?"

He blinks. "What do you mean?"

"Why do you always paint a happy face on everything?"

"I don't."

"Jonathan, you do." I wait, but he gives me nothing. I have to do it myself. "For instance, how would you describe our childhood?"

He sips and winces. "We had our problems, but every family does."

"That's it? Come on, Jonathan, the first thing we did when we got home from school was tiptoe past the kitchen to check Mom's mood. You think that's normal? How many times did we sneak out and stay away till Daddy got home and it was safe to go back? What about the midnight raids when she came bursting into my room, yanking clothes out of the closet and dumping them on the bed? That wasn't *Mommy Dearest*. That was us!"

He sighs. "It was so long ago. Why get worked up about it now?"

"Because," I say and stop, swallowing tears. For me it's always there, a pressure under the skin that rises often and threatens to burst.

Even as a muddle-headed child I knew mothers weren't supposed to terrify their children, throw daily shrieking fits about how unappreciated they were and how nobody loved them, and be so sullen and prickly and critical the rest of the time that it made intimacy impossible even if you wanted it. But how could I say any of this, even if I could have formed the language for it, in a house where not just words but *thoughts* were censored? "Get that dirty look off your face!" my mother snapped time and time again. She broke into my juvenile diary, where I had written what was unspeakable—*I hate my mother!* —page after page of it, and berated me bitterly, as if I were the unnatural one. For years I was afraid to write anything real about my family—no, not afraid: I blocked it. I signed up for a creative writing course in college, but had to drop it because, as I told the instructor, I couldn't think of anything to write about.

"How can you be so forgiving?" I manage to say. "She was a bully."

He shifts, rattling his ice. "It's not like she beat us."

"Do you know, I don't have a single memory of her showing me affection? No spontaneous kisses, no pats or touches, no memory of sitting on her lap. At least Jesse will always *know* I love him."

Then I burst into tears after all. Jonathan puts his arm around me, as he used to do even when he was small. After a while he says: "You shouldn't let this stuff get to you. It's all water under the bridge."

He's serious; he means it. He used the same words last summer when he went to his ten-year high school reunion and saw his old friend Christopher Joy. "Whatever happened to Christopher?" I asked when he told me about it. "You were such good friends till tenth grade, then suddenly we never saw him anymore."

"Oh," said Jonathan, "he just started hanging out with the antisemitic crowd." He said it as if Christopher had briefly decided to vote Republican.

"Is there any trace of that now?" I asked, and Jonathan laughed.

"We're not kids anymore, everyone's mellow," he said, adding again: "It's all water under the bridge."

There was also a girl at the reunion, someone Jonathan described as "off-the-wall," which meant she'd been perceived and persecuted as a misfit. Her high school years must have been misery. Now she was a recovering alcoholic. She told Jonathan she expected the reunion to be excruciating. "I couldn't believe it," he told me. "Why would you come all the way from New Jersey and spend fifty bucks for a dinner if you expected it to be excruciating?" He couldn't or wouldn't let himself imagine why you'd come, what would *drive* you to come. He refuses to understand the need for vindication.

I go upstairs to wash my face and check on the baby. When I get back, Jonathan is watching the video again. Klay feeds his ulcers, but he can't stay away.

"Just in time for my big speech," he greets me.

"*Come on down!*" An MC is doing a Monty Hall impression as each member of the wedding party enters to applause and whistles and "Hey-O" Johnny Carson cheers. Now Jonathan comes striding up the red carpet in his Gatsby tuxedo, teeth gleaming in his tanned face. The potted palms are strung with twinkling lights. It's Oscar night. Where's the paparazzi?

Jonathan fast-forwards. "Here we go."

Now the video-Jonathan stands up and gives his beard a nervous stroke. Only two other people—my parents, sitting among the guests—know the significance of that gesture. He's stroking the birthmark, as if to make sure it's still concealed. It's something he's done since he was first able to grow a beard.

"I've known Klay and Carissa a long time, and I've watched their love grow stronger and stronger," he begins. "They are truly a unique couple, inasmuch as they agree on so many different topics, such as health food, exercise, love for animals, and a strong drive to always improve themselves."

I am doing something painful with my teeth. Of course weddings are made for banalities, but Jonathan is *my* brother—we are products of *that* household. How can this drivel satisfy him? How can he be proud of it?

"Over the past two years we've had a lot of good times: dinners at the Rangoon Club, the Improv, brunch at Tony and Luigi's, and staying up till four A.M. to watch *Combat*. Let me say this"—is that a lisp? — "you are two of my dearest friends. May your dreams and desires be exceeded only by your love for each other. To the bride and groom!"

"To the bride and groom!" And five hundred tulip glasses go bottoms up as the band plays *Love Is A Many-Splendored Thing*.

Jonathan hits pause. "I was so nervous," he says. "I had to turn my feet out like a ballerina's so my knees wouldn't knock."

"Well, it didn't show," I say. "You would have made a terrific rabbi."

He chuckles. If he had any notion that I was being nasty, I'd feel ashamed of myself. As it is, I only feel lonely. I wish Owen would get home.

Now Jonathan fast-forwards through the dancing and testimonials, stopping here and there to listen. Klay's anorexic mother wishes the newlyweds "health, wealth, and happiness —whatever they want."

"What *they* want," his father adds. "Not us."

"Whatever makes *them* happy," his mother concludes, clearing everything up.

"We want to see babies!" says a guy who evidently just got in from Mars. "Lots and lots of babies!"

"Klay!" exclaims a lantern-jawed young woman with a single cross dangling from one ear. "Okay, so, we made it this far, okay? And you got married today, and I was gonna cry, and I don't cry, Klay, okay? So it was really gorgeous and wonderful, and good luck, and it might be tough, but like I said, good luck." This, I am disappointed to learn, is the embittered lesbian daughter. I'd hoped for some hint of articulate rage.

And here are my parents at last, my father in his rented tux, my mother in a little black hat complete with feather, veil, and twinkling beads. My father clears his throat. "This affair has been very special and beautiful and— " He looks at my mother.

"Memorable," she finishes crisply, taking over in her best lady-narrator voice. "Klay and Carissa, it's a joy to be here and share this *very* beautiful evening with you on your wedding day. We thought Jonathan's toast said it all, and we wish you the best in life, and all our love, and we only hope you'll be as happy as we are." She lifts her wine glass in the air and holds it there, till the cameraman gets the idea and pans slowly to someone else.

Now the guests are dancing the hora to an especially sobby rendition of *Havah Nagilah*, Klay flinging up his legs like a place-kicker. In the background I catch a glimpse of Jonathan, not dancing, one hand inside his tuxedo jacket. Rubbing his stomach, no doubt. Then, finally, the last rites: Jonathan, taller than everyone else, easily snags the garter. He looks surprised but tucks it into his pocket as the ushers slap him on the back. The tape ends with the bride and groom thanking everyone for their good wishes, and the bride thanking the groom for showing up. "I'm a very lucky guy," Klay declares, squeezing Carissa. Fade-out on the kiss.

Jonathan rewinds. I wish Jesse would wake up. I wish Owen would get home. I need my other life. Jonathan smiles at me, lifting his eyebrows: *So?*

"Do you remember once when I came home from college and Mom was on one of her rampages?" I say, not really intending to start this again. "Everything about me offended her: my manners, my attitude, the way I looked and spoke."

The smile vanishes. He fingers a roll of Tums.

"When it came time to leave for the airport, she locked herself in the bathroom. Daddy didn't want me to leave without saying goodbye. He wanted us to make up. I started crying. Mom came out of the bathroom. I was bawling something like 'I was never pretty enough for you, I was never popular enough for you!' But Daddy didn't *hear* what I was saying. He put one hand on Mom and one hand on me and literally shoved us together, saying *'That's* what I like to see.' Then he drove me to the airport and I made my escape."

"You know what Dad's like."

"Oh yes. Peace at any price. Neville Chamberlain Sapperstein."

Jonathan looks pained. He hates this. He and Owen are the only people I ever say these things to, and though Owen cares, he didn't grow up in our house and doesn't know whether my depictions are accurate and therefore reserves a part of his judgment: he listens, but doesn't *know.* Jonathan knows, but won't speak.

"It's the truth," I say sharply. "What about Mel? Or Lenny?"

Tall, jovial Uncle Mel cheated my father out of his share

of a business they owned, obliging my newlywed parents to move to a new town, go into debt, and start over again. My father never spoke about it, never reproached his brother, and never let my mother reproach him either. Uncle Lenny was my mother's favorite brother-in-law, husband to her oldest sister. She used to tell us how much fun he was when she was young: "If we drove over a bump in the road, he'd back up and do it again. I used to sit on his lap and steer while he worked the pedals." Years later, we heard that Uncle Lenny had molested his twelve-year-old granddaughter. Of course this was something that had to be hidden from my mother. My father seemed to put both incidents out of his mind altogether, something he has an uncanny knack for doing.

"You know why he's like that," Jonathan says now.

"I know. Losing his own father so young and all."

My father once told me his earliest memory: creeping into bed with his papa and sharing his big pillow. After his father died and Mel ran off to get married, my father, who was still in high school, had to support his mother and sister. He might have succumbed to bitterness, but instead he chose to reverence family—to sacrifice anything, in fact, to preserve the illusion of family closeness and harmony.

Jonathan and I are sitting side-by-side on the couch, gazing straight ahead as if we are taking a trip. "Jonathan," I say softly. "Remember the pact?"

He briefly shuts his eyes. I have committed a violation.

After my mother's second suicide attempt, my father sat us down and swore us to silence. I was seventeen; Jonathan was nine. We were never ever to mention it again—not to outsiders, not to each other, and especially not to Mother. He always calls her Mother when he talks to us; you can hear the capital letter in his voice, as if he thinks he's still referring to his own tiny, Yiddish-speaking, self-sacrificing mother.

Not only must we never mention it, but we would all have to try "extra-special hard" to show Mother our love. This, I longed to point out, was begging the question: how could I love someone who had terrorized and humiliated me, and whose departure would come as a relief except for the pain it would cause him? But I knew he didn't want to hear what I really felt. The closest he'd ever come to acknowledging it was a tense short speech he once delivered in my bedroom after a rough session between my mother and me. He said not to make him choose between us, because if he had to, he would choose her—she was his wife. I was ten; I had no idea what he was talking about except that he was saying he'd at least *chosen* her: me he'd just been stuck with. Some years later when I heard the old saw that you can choose your friends but not your family, I felt as if I'd been socked in the gut.

The pact consisted of pretending to believe my mother had been in the hospital with meningitis instead of having her stomach pumped. It also meant "showing our love," as my father put it, "with little gifts and notes and things," and telling her frequently how much we loved her. In short, we had to woo her. For his part, he would take her out to dinner, to the theater, on vacations; he would make her life more exciting and glamorous—give her something to live for, he implied, since her children apparently weren't reason enough.

In those days, in that little town, "therapy" meant physical rehabilitation, what you did after a stroke or traffic accident. Psychiatrists were only for loonies. My mother began seeing one; we pretended not to know and it was never mentioned in front of us. No one ever suggested that Jonathan and I might be angry or confused, that *we* might need to talk. In fact, my father made us swear our silence on a Hebrew Union Prayer Book (another piece of irony, since by that age I no longer believed in God). For years I thought, superstitiously, that even if I confided in a total stranger sitting next to me on the bus, somehow my father would know and I would be atomized by my own betrayal.

Even Jonathan and I have not discussed it, although—obeying my father in letter, if not in spirit—we make oblique references and talk our own form of shorthand. Now he crosses and uncrosses his legs. I am not doing his blood pressure any good. If I love my brother, why don't I just let him be? Why don't I just go talk to a shrink like everyone else?

But I know the answer to that: a shrink would be a stranger; he would know only what I told him; it would be *my* problem, *my* therapy, all *me*. But Jonathan was there: he *saw*, he *knows*. I don't want insight—I want vindication. Confronting my parents would bring on a complete rupture, which I dread. That leaves Jonathan, fellow witness and survivor.

I wait, forcing an answer. Finally, looking into his empty glass, he says: "That was all a long time ago. She's mellowed out."

"Like Christopher Joy? She just hung out with the antisemitic crowd for a while?" He looks at me with pained bewilderment, and I feel like a bully myself. "Jonathan, we've buried it, but the stink has never gone away."

"So what do you want?" At last, an edge of anger. "You want to bring on some big catharsis, make everybody talk about it? You know what that would be like."

Oh yes. A great crisis, just like the old days. Shrieks, tears, slamming doors, pain, betrayal, violation—with no strong chance of anything good coming out of it.

"Look," Jonathan goes on. "My philosophy is you accept what you can't change." He gives me a very level, earnest, and intent look. Then he bumps his fist to mine. "Rocks, remember?"

I remember. It's what we used to say to each other when we were still trapped at home, under my mother's power. "Rocks" was shorthand for "*Water's wet, rocks are hard, and Mother's Mother.*"

What is, is. And since we are powerless, we must endure. His philosophy hasn't changed since he was nine. I had no idea he was so much like my father.

I smile. I nod. He is my brother but also my guest, and you can't get blood from a stone. Or a rock. But when will we talk about it, Jonathan? At the funeral? Sitting shiva? When we're dying ourselves?

Then, miraculously, my other life intervenes. Jesse cries, awake and angry that I haven't anticipated his waking and stuck the nipple in his mouth already. I've never been so glad to hear a cranky baby in my life. We go upstairs. As usual, he's stranded himself in a corner of the crib, tangled in the blanket, but as soon as he sees me, the crying stops. His eyes, so dark they're almost black, go wide at the sight of Jonathan. I nurse him in the rocking chair while Jonathan stands at the window looking down at the parking lot. Maybe he's embarrassed. Maybe he's bored. Maybe he's thinking about business. How is it possible to tell what Jonathan really thinks?

Downstairs, I get dinner started while Jonathan holds Jesse on the couch, talking to him softly. Jesse kneels on his chest, looking earnestly into his face and drooling on his paisley tie. I keep coming out of the kitchen to watch them.

"This is fun," says Jonathan, nuzzling the baby's head. "I could get used to this."

I almost make a crack about booking Arlene, but then I don't. Jonathan and Jesse get down on the floor to practice crawling. Jesse squirms madly after the remote control like a soldier going under barbed wire.

"Like this, like this," Jonathan tells him, getting up on all fours. I remember when he himself learned to crawl—for the longest time he could only go backwards. Jesse manages to get up on all fours but only rocks and teeters, bobbing his head like a circus horse. When that doesn't get him anywhere, he squawks. To distract him, Jonathan makes a whooshing sound like wind blowing through the trees. Jesse climbs up Jonathan's chest and lays his hand on Jonathan's mouth to see where the sound is coming from.

I look at the two of them on the floor, my two babies, and for no clear reason I'm crying again.

But then Owen comes home, dropping his briefcase with a thump, yanking off his tie and flinging it across the room. His suit jacket flies after it as Jesse screeches with excitement, flapping his arms to be picked up. Owen swings him high in the air. Jonathan gets to his feet; they shake hands; Owen opens wine; I bring out crackers and cheese and some strained pears for Jesse. We sit around the table and tell Jonathan about the house we just bought, and suddenly everything seems okay, cheerful, normal—the past behind us, where it belongs.

We eat early so Jonathan can catch his plane to New York. He is meeting Klay, who has promised to line him up with some big clients. We leave Owen chasing Jesse, barking as the baby shrieks with delight and squirms across the carpet.

"You ought to get stuff like that on videotape," Jonathan tells me as we pull out of the parking lot.

"That's Mom's thing, not mine."

He grins. "You know what she told me last week? She said: 'People don't want to be videotaped, and I know they're bored watching the films, but I just love doing it.'"

"That's what it is to live in a pre-Copernican universe," I say, and Jonathan gives me a wry laugh. We're back on familiar ground now—this is how we're used to talking about family. You could draw a cartoon of us right now and caption it *The Saving Distance of Irony*.

On the way to the airport he tells me about his latest ex, a twenty-year-old Amazon—he always goes for big, glamorous, hard-to-please women who push him around and then drop him. This one is a fingernail tech at a Beverly Hills salon.

"She does them with acrylics, fiberglass, linen, silk, and precious metals," he says in the same voice he used to quote our mother. "She airbrushes them with Zodiac signs, palm trees, and tiny pictures of rock stars."

"This is a joke, right?"

"Wrong. She's even working on battery-powered nails designed to look like Sunset Strip at night."

"And *she* dumped *you*?"

He laughs again. At the airport I give him some animal crackers in a baggie. He tucks them into his pocket, then hugs me hard enough to bring me to my toes.

"Hope they don't lose your luggage," I say.

He bumps my fist with his, then disappears through the sliding doors—tall and dapper, leather bag slung over his shoulder, looking from behind like the young hotshot he used to be. Then the cab behind me blasts its horn, which means get the hell out of the taxi zone, and when I look again Jonathan is gone.

As I hit the Interstate, I think of him returning to L.A., gingerly approaching his car, hoping the windows aren't smashed again, driving wearily home to his tiny apartment, steering with one hand while he rubs his gut with the other. He won't have been temperate in New York—Klay likes tequila, spicy food, cigars—and perhaps the ulcers are oozing again. I think of him negotiating those monster freeways in the dark.

How did we come to trade places, Jonathan and I? I was the late-bloomer and slow-learner; he was the crown prince, destined for great achievement and early retirement. My mother used to scream that I was stupid, contrary, clumsy. She used to scold that if I kept on eating, I'd be as big as a house and no man would marry me. Nor was I allowed to cross my legs, as it would "spread the calf," or bite my lips, lest they grow swollen and huge. I rebelled to the point where they dragged me to child psychologists, grounded me forever, held bribes over me: the penny loafers all the other girls were wearing, for instance, instead of the corrective oxfords I was ridiculed for. But Jonathan was handsome, well-mannered, sweet-tempered, a boy who knew how to hold his mother's chair and give her his arm. For him great things were in store, while I, as she told me innumerable times and as I'd spent much of my life demonstrating, was headed for disaster. But somehow things got turned around.

I try to imagine how Jonathan would account for all this, but all I can hear him say is "Rocks." We have grown into two very different people. Yesterday when I was packing boxes, I came across some old family photos I'd taken with me when I left for college. In one picture, I stand in front of our old Pontiac in the days before my father could afford Lincolns. I am six or seven; we are on our way to Temple for High Holiday services. My hair is tortured into a tight frizzy perm; I am wearing pointed glasses; my belly sticks out. My mother has put a felt beret on my head, white gloves on my hands, lipstick on my mouth, and, around my shoulders, a "mink stole" made of cotton fur to match her own real one. Her hat, like my beret, is tilted rakishly. She has assumed what I always thought of as her Miss America pose: three-quarter angle (to show off pointy bosom and play down breadth of hip), chin up, eyelids haughtily drooping, lipsticked mouth in a phony gracious smile. She wants to be seen as glamorous and statuesque, but the unhappy lump of a girl at her side spoils the effect. My face tells you everything you need to know about my childhood.

The other pictures are more of the same: Jonathan and I baring our teeth in obedience to the ritual command--"Say *cheeeese!*" (and its implicit command: *Be happy! Be loving!*); my parents on their way to a country club dance (the country club that used to blackball Jews); Dad doing his best to get his arms around everyone at once. All of the pictures are posed.

Looking at them—especially those of me stuffed into clothes that were too tight, too hot, too fussy, with the only protest possible showing in my eyes, and then only until my mother noticed and snapped "Get that look off your face!"—reminded me freshly of why I left home the first minute I could and went as far as I could and never really came back. And they reminded me, too, of what our family has forfeited: real intimacy, love based on real knowledge of each other. And that made me angry all over again, so I took the photographs outside and dumped them in the trash.

Later, carrying another load to the dumpster, I came across some of them blown free, scattered in the alley, those familiar faces startling against the damp concrete. But though it made me uneasy and kind of sick, I stepped right over them and kept going.

Jonathan would never have done that. Jonathan is more their child than I am, and always has been, so what's the big deal? Except you've got rocks in your head, Jonathan, if you think you can put the past away and it will stay put.

I rub the tears out of my eyes, then see I'm going almost ninety. I ease my foot on the pedal, check the rear view mirror for cops. Got away again. I am getting good at getting away.

As I turn off the Interstate, I realize that it's still light out. We have reached that point in the year when it seems spring is really here, though it's hard not to think winter doesn't have a few more tricks up its sleeve. Still, there's no denying that pale blue evening light, the willow trees shaking down their long green hair, the new maple leaves like wrinkled infant hands. By the time summer comes—by the time even I am convinced —we will be in our new house, our first real house, Owen and Jesse and me. Tonight, in fact, we're taking Jesse to Sears to look at dishwashers: it will be his first major appliance.

I will never get used to my own life, I think. Then I say it out loud. And then, coasting down a hill lined with trees that in a few weeks will be one big pink cloud, I repeat it like a vow.

SOURBALLS

Yes, another wedding story, but this one's funny. It's almost totally dialogue too. What can I say—I come from a big extended family of talkers who held many large events. This particular situation— the split between the A list guests and the B list—did not actually happen to me: I read about it in a Dear Abby column. Nor is every guest based on a real person. But the talk, *though more elevated at times than anything I ever heard from my own mishpacha, is true in spirit and flavor. I wanted to keep the focus on that extended family, which is why I wrote the story in the plural first person and why few characters are named. The sourballs are absolutely real.*

But take it: if the smack is sour
The better for the embittered hour;
--A. E. Housman

W e're the out-of-town crowd, the B-list, not cool enough for the reception. We went to the ceremony, of course, and we'll go to the dinner tonight, but this afternoon, while Marci and Mitchell's friends attend a champagne reception, the rest of us--a dowdy assortment of cousins, uncles, and aunts--are scheduled for a bus tour of the Finger Lakes. However, one thing Marci can't control is the weather: a sudden snowstorm turns the bus around before we've even seen a knuckle.

Those who don't want a nap end up in the bar, just down the hall from the reception. We can hear their jazz combo doing Gershwin. We push tables together, liberate the bartender's bowl of beer-nuts, and sprawl out. We are a poet, a scholar, a jokester, an etiquette maven, a retired dentist, a carpet salesman, a scattering of consultants. One of us, a teenager, has *Don't* tattooed across one hand and *Panic* across the other. One has a secret: blood in his urine. He's waiting until after the wedding to have it checked out so he doesn't cast a pall on the festivities. In the photos, afterward, we will search his eyes for hints of what he must have been feeling. One of us, as completely Jewish as the rest, prays to Saint Anthony whenever she loses something. Another has a shy bladder and needs props to distract herself—how many words can you get out of *Head and Shoulders*?—before it will let go. One of us, a compulsive gift-giver, always pressed his own things upon playmates—toys, clothes, books—until they backed off in distaste. Now he tries to buy rounds for the whole bar, but we don't let him.

At first the drinks we order are staid: lite beer, wine spritzers, one Bloody Mary. Later we'll try the Buttery Nipples and Crack Baby Shots and maybe a Smirking Priest. Conversation is slow until the poet says: "Well, what should we call ourselves?"

"Rejects," says the teen with *Don't Panic* on her hands.

"Wallflowers," says another cousin, recalling her youth.

"Victims," snaps the maven. "It's a disgrace what they did to us, a *shandeh* and a *charpeh*, and it's not very Jewish."

We eye one another. She's the oldest woman at the table, thus the authority. Has she just declared open season on the wedding?

"The bride did look...striking," one of us ventures.

"Was that dress made of real feathers?" asks someone else.

The maven snorts. "She looked like the ghost of Big Bird."

"Someone should've called PETA," the teen snarls, and everyone relaxes. It's open season.

"The white silk top hat did seem a bit much. Now if the

groom had worn it—"

"I went to this wedding once that was held on a beach: the bride wore a white bikini and the ring went on her toe. Afterward, we had to write their names in giant letters in the sand and build them a castle. I felt, like, four?"

"I went to a wedding at an aquarium. The lighting was fabulous and the bride dressed like a mermaid. But I think it was insensitive to serve sushi."

"I went to one that started at midnight. As we left at dawn they handed us coffee, a bagel, and the morning paper. Now *that* was fabulous."

"If I ever get married," the teen says bitterly, "I'm walking down the aisle to *Highway To Hell*."

"I went to one where the bride's father had died two years before. She walked down the aisle with a big portrait of him under her arm and set it on a chair so he could 'watch.' So okay, but then in the middle of the ceremony they stop for this PowerPoint presentation on her father's life, ending with a shot of him in his coffin. By that point we would have killed for a drink. Or Prozac."

We tip our glasses, look at each other through the empty bottoms.

"I heard Marci made her bridesmaids sign up for boot camp at her gym."

"I heard her best friend started referring to herself as the Maid of Horror."

"I heard Mitchell's mother doesn't want to be in the pictures because she went off Weight Watchers, but she wants them to airbrush in one of those silhouettes—you know, all black, just the profile?"

"Interesting," says the scholar. "Like those medieval portraits where death or the devil is tucked into the crowd as an admonishment."

"*Meshugas!*" cries the maven. Craziness.

"We went to a wedding in Canada where there was no bride at all," says the poet.

"How can there be no bride?"

"Two grooms. They both wore kilts. The invitations were pink triangles."

"Oy! A little too Auschwitz if you ask me!"

"Well, that's the idea. It was a political wedding."

"All weddings are political," says the teen.

"So what were they pronounced: husband and husband?"

"You have a better suggestion?"

"Were there two little men on top of the cake?"

"No, it was an abstract symbol."

"Nothing abstract about two brides with beards."

"Keep those pink triangles coming, folks! They don't get it yet."

"Listen, you know my friend Lucille?" says the maven. "Her son Ezra?"

"The doctor?"

"He went to medical school but he doesn't practice. He lives at home and takes care of her, but mainly he writes Broadway musicals that never get produced. All that money for medical school and he's still sleeping in the room with the cowboy wallpaper. The other day Lucille told me he tackled a kitchen full of dirty dishes. 'Turn on the radio,' she told him, 'it'll make the time go faster.' And you know what he said back? 'I'm my own radio, and who says I want time to go faster?' Such a boy."

"And a *faygeleh*? That's what you're telling us?"

"Yes, but he never brings them home."

The poet shrugs. "The heart wants what it wants."

"Well, the heart is a *schmendrick*!"

"What did you think of Marci's invitations?" we ask the maven to steer us back off course.

"A mess," she replies. "It's always a mess when stepparents are involved—whose name goes where, which personal pronouns do you use: *my, our, their*—I tell you, we never had such *tsuris* when I was a bride. And the misspellings!"

"They misspelled?"

"'Honor' and 'favor' should be spelled *our*."

"What are we, Masterpiece Theater?"

"I hope you mean Masterpiece Theatre," says the jokester, but no one gets it till she spells. She is not a very good jokester. She adds: "Am I the only one who thinks it's funny to call Save The Dates STDs?"

"The best wedding invitation I ever got was to a second wedding for both. It said: 'Since we already have two of everything, no gifts please. Reception and garage sale immediately following the ceremony.'"

But the maven is implacable. "You should say 'request the honour—our—of your presence' when the ceremony takes place in a house of worship—"

"Such as Saks," the jokester puts in.

"—and 'request the honour—our—of your company' when it takes place somewhere else."

"What about requesting the pleasure?"

"That's just for the reception."

"Should 'pleasure' be spelled our?"

"*Pleasour?*"

"Please sour?"

"Like sourballs."

"Ooh, sourballs, remember sourballs?"

Everyone's face goes soft in instant recollection. The aunts —there used to be ten, they made a minyan—always had an arsenal of sourballs in their purses: hard, pastel, wrapped in cellophane that made loud crinkling noises. Sourballs were the family's official antidote for everything from carsickness to bar-mitzvah jitters. They were our first aid. Sourballs really were sour—they didn't get cloying like sweet candy could— and they lasted a long time in your mouth, though they could get sharp enough to cut your tongue. "Have a sourball" was the panacea for a crying child, a depressed teenager, a worried mother, an impatient father. You couldn't complain and suck on a sourball at the same time. Sourballs always won.

"There's our name!" exclaims the jokester. "The Sourballs!"

We applaud and bump fists.

Some of us order whiskey sours out of a vague futile longing. Nobody wants those days back. We just sort of want the taste in our mouth for a while.

"I knew a girl who handed out wedding invitations at her uncle's funeral," one of us offers. "She said he was only an uncle by marriage, so it was okay."

"Once I got one—I swear—from the bride's fetus. He wasn't born yet, but his mother had him issuing the invitation from her uterus."

"I got an invitation that came with a card asking for help with their mortgage instead of a wedding gift. No kidding, they gave the 800 number and everything."

"*Oy*, where they register these days!" says the maven. "Radio Shack, Best Buy, liquor stores, stockbrokers! They register for gift cards—50, 75, 100 dollars! No shame!"

"Marci and Mitchell registered for his-and-hers iPhones."

"I hear they gave her a Breakfast-at-Tiffany's shower. Everyone wore elbow-length gloves and a little black dress. They tried to raise Audrey Hepburn on the Ouija board."

"Is everything a fantasy now?" the poet asks.

"I think so," says the scholar. "If you're affluent enough."

"Don't the poor fantasize?"

"They fantasize about eating."

"I knew someone who had a Self-Enrichment Shower. She got lessons for ballroom dancing, wine tasting, scuba diving, two foreign languages, plus tickets to the ballet."

"I hate it when they register," says our most sophisticated cousin. We were surprised she didn't make the A-list—she's a very sharp dresser. "When they open the gifts, it's so self-congratulatory: 'Oh, I picked this out and you bought it for me. Don't I have exquisite taste?'"

"I hear the trend now is to get the bridesmaids to write the thank-you notes. Because the bride is so stressed and preoccupied."

The maven says a naughty Yiddish word.

"Well, Marci did have two engagement parties, two bridal

showers, *and* a gift-opening party."

"Listen to this: I know a gal who lives with a fella twenty years older than she is—they just had a baby, *baruch ha-Shem* —but he lost his business and he's heavily in debt. Yes I know, such *tsuris* you wouldn't wish on anyone, but here's the thing: they're having a pretend wedding. The *chuppah*, the gifts, the cake, the dancing on chairs, the whole *schmear*, everything but the rabbi and documents, because she's afraid if they're really married, she'll be legally responsible for his debts. She wants the gifts, she wants the party, she wants the ring—she just doesn't want the *tzimmes*." The mess.

"Whatever happened to 'for better or worse'?"

"Weddings make people nuts. I got an invitation that said: *A money dance will be included at the reception.* In other words, stuff your pockets, come prepared!"

"I got one that said food stamps would be accepted. And they tucked in a blank savings deposit slip. I thought: why bother calling us 'guests'? Why not call us 'serfs' and be done with it?"

"At some weddings the bride gets 'kidnapped' and you have to pay a ransom to get her back."

"Sometimes they auction off the centerpieces."

"I went to a reception once where you had to pay a cover to get in. It was set up like a casino with games and everything, but you didn't get to keep what you won—it all went to the honeymoon fund. Instead, you got wedding favors. Mini picture frames."

We consider this glumly.

"What do you think *we'll* get?"

"Sourballs."

"Mini picture frames. It's always mini picture frames."

"It's M&M's, for Marci & Mitchell," says one of our West Coast cousins, dragging up a chair. She's A-list, in Halston and a winter tan. "Can I hide out with you?"

"What's wrong with the reception?" we say. "We heard it's the place to be."

She shudders. "They won't let me drink in there. Because

of my ex's new wife. She's pregnant and all of 23 and they're afraid I'll make a scene."

"You're welcome to make a scene here. We're starved for entertainment."

"Also food."

"Bartender!" says the West Coast cousin. "A new round for everyone!"

"And what about you?" we ask a chubby man in a tight suit, also hiking up a chair. "Are you a refugee too?"

"I'm with a different reception. You're having more fun than they are. My name is Eugene."

"Welcome, Eugene! You can be an honorary Sourball for the rest of the afternoon."

Eugene buys the next round and we teach him to say "*L'chaim!* To life!"

"Did you see how uncomfortable Marci looked?" says our West Coast cousin. "It was the torsolette. You know how they got that dress zipped? They had to tie her hands with a long ribbon, hook the ribbon over the door, and pull her up until she was on tiptoes. Then they hooked the torsolette as tight as it would go."

"I heard she needed Valium to get through the ceremony."

"Did you see those bridesmaids? I heard she wanted them all to go blonde so her black hair would stand out."

"Did you see those shoes with the hollow heels?"

"What was *in* those?"

"M&M's for Marci & Mitchell."

"They should've packed them tighter so they didn't make maraca sounds—maybe then the girls wouldn't have cha-cha'ed down the aisle."

"I heard Marci wanted to carry fasces instead of a bouquet, but they had to draw the line somewhere."

"What's a fasces?"

"An axe blade sticking out of a bundle of rods carried by a magistrate in ancient Rome as a symbol of authority," says the scholar. "They revived it in Fascist Italy."

"I thought having her birth father walk her partway down the aisle, then her stepfather take her the rest of the way was a good compromise. But what if you had a string of stepfathers?" says the West Coast cousin, who sees a lot of that sort of thing. "Imagine the traffic jam."

"I've always wondered why the bride circles the groom seven times. Is he, like, roping her in?"

"It's part magic, part symbol," says the poet.

"Magic?"

"Where do you think religion comes from? By circling the groom, the bride throws up a barrier to keep off evil spirits, not to mention the designs of other women and temptations. Symbolically, she binds the groom to her, creating a new family circle."

"The *Kabbalah* would say that circling is how she enters his *s'ferot*, the mystical spheres of his soul, which correspond to the seven lower attributes of God," adds the scholar.

"Did you see that one bridesmaid mouthing something to her boyfriend while this was going on? That'll look great on the video!"

"Still, you know...when he said those words, in spite of everything, it kind of gave me shivers."

"Weddings always make me cry."

"Which words?"

"What the groom says when he places the ring on her finger: *Behold, thou art consecrated unto me with this ring, according to the laws of Moses and Israel.* It's just so ancient. It's such a long chain that's lasted through so much crap—and here we still are with our *chuppahs* and bagels. We're still here."

"Because we're crazy. Jews are freaking nuts."

"Specifically, *Jewish* weddings make me cry."

"What was that bit at the end? It looked like the rabbi was giving them operating instructions."

"He was, basically. He gives them the Seven Blessings, which cover everything from the creation of the world to the creation of a family. He tells them that our true job is *tikkun olam*, to repair the world."

"I like the words they used to say at weddings," says Eugene. "*Those whom God has joined together, let no man put asunder.* That's a good word, *asunder.* And I don't mind naming God and man."

"You're right," says the poet. "That is a good word."

The teenager gives a loud sigh, finishes another Coke, and dumps her purse out on the table.

"Are you doing your nails?" we ask. Her nails are painted black.

"I'm lubricating my cuticles."

"Oh, can I do mine?" someone says.

She's willing to share. We all lubricate our cuticles, even Eugene. Then we take turns going through our purses and wallets, trading photos and explaining anything of interest. We cheer when the maven's purse yields a few grubby crinkly sourballs, long forgotten.

"Who wants?" says the maven.

Some of us partake. They aren't half bad with a martini.

But the bowl of beer-nuts is empty and we start eying the bartender's dishes of olives, little onions, and maraschino cherries.

"What are they eating over there?" we ask the West Coast cousin.

"Little bites to tide us over. Mini-tamales. Spicy dumplings. Onion-and-sage tartlets. Tiny potato pancakes with horseradish crème."

We're groaning. "And you *left*?"

She shrugs. "Got to save some room for dinner. Did you see the menu? Tataki of fresh tuna rolled in peppercorns, sesame, and coriander seeds with garlic chips and rocket, followed by roast Barbary duck with corn crepe, shallot compote, and merlot jus."

"And for dessert?" we croak.

"There's going to be a Viennese table, but the official dessert is a *croque en bouche.*"

"What's that?"

"A tower of cream puffs. It's a traditional French wedding cake."

"Are we French?"

"And I think there's going to be a chocolate lava thing. They're all the rage." She looks around at our hungry faces. "Why don't you guys order a sandwich?"

"When roast duck awaits?"

"That *she* paid for?"

"Forget about it!"

Instead, we order drinks that sound like food: Apple martinis. Clementine cosmopolitans. Cantaloupe mojitos. Anything that comes with an edible garnish.

"What's the best food you ever had at a wedding?" one of us asks as we wait for our drinks.

"Once there was this mashed potato bar. I never saw anything like it. It was like a Cold Stone Creamery with an array of toppings: onions, bacon bits, caramelized leeks, you name it, made to order and served in a martini glass."

"I had something like that, only it was a risotto station."

"Nothing beats good old rack of lamb."

"Except prime rib crusted in lavender and black pepper..."

"Or butternut-squash ravioli in sage brown butter..."

"Can we talk dessert? Cheesecake lollipops, bite-sized tiramisu in espresso cups with edible chocolate spoons? *Gevalt!*"

"An old-fashioned egg cream bar, any flavor you can imagine."

"A wedding cake shaped like a French Rococo vase covered with gold leaf, filled with sugar paste and lilacs."

"Italian sponge filled with Chantilly cream, soaked in pear liqueur, covered in pale green buttercream and marzipan pears that looked so real you could sink your teeth in and taste the juice."

"A second wedding I went to had Spider-Man and Wonder Woman on top of the cake."

"Well, I went to one that had Spider-Man and Spider-Man on top of the cake."

"Apparently we don't attend the same kinds of weddings."

"You're not supposed to put a bride and groom on the cake for a second wedding," says the maven.

"So you just leave it bare?"

"Flowers atop a cake are lovely."

"As Dr. Johnson observes, remarriage is the triumph of hope over experience," says the scholar.

"Another doctor? Is this one also a *faygelah*?"

"The best wedding cake I ever tasted was a pink pistachio torte filled with white-chocolate truffle cream and marionberry preserves."

"You guys are making *me* hungry," says the bartender, refilling our beer-nuts bowl.

"Did you know there are gardenia blossoms in the urinals?" says the scholar, who has just returned from the Men's, where he found a bride's magazine full of sulky models who look like young vampires waiting for permission to hunt, skinny girls dressed in enormous gowns like opera costumes—no, like stage sets, as if the things need to be raised and lowered by wires. We tear out the best pages and pass them around, giggling.

"I heard there's a poet in here," says a desperate new voice, and we turn to see Mitchell's best man with a book under his arm. "Dude, I could really use your help."

He orders a new round of drinks—the bartender gives us double garnishes—and wedges in another chair. The book turns out to be Bartlett's *Quotations*. The best man is frantically trying to put together his toast for the dinner in a few hours.

"What do you think of this: *May the best day of your past be the worst day of your future*?"

We groan.

"Okay, okay." He flips pages. "What about: *To the lamp of love —may it burn brightest in the darkest hours and never flicker in the winds of trial*?"

The poet grabs the book. "Give me that. Ah! *Marriage has many pains, but celibacy has no pleasures.* One can always count on Dr. Johnson."

"The same guy? Any relation to the pharma company?"

"I know one. Tell Mitchell to cover Marci's hand with his. Then say: *Cherish this moment...because it will be the last time you'll ever have the upper hand.*"

"Whoever said that must know Marci."

"How about: *Love is like quicksilver in the hand*?" says the best man.

"What, it poisons the tissue?"

"*Love is the triumph of imagination over intelligence.*"

"Stay away from Mencken," says the scholar. "Nietzsche too."

"*Love is blind and marriage is the institution for the blind*?"

"You're getting warmer."

"You think I should just do jokes?"

"No," says the poet. "Listen." He closes his eyes and spreads his hands:

I am my beloved's, and my beloved is mine, that feedeth among the lilies.
Thy hair is as a flock of goats that trail down from Gilead.
Thy teeth are like a flock of ewes, which are come up from the washing;
Who is she that looketh forth as the dawn, fair as the moon,
clear as the sun, terrible as an army with banners?
How beautiful are thy steps in sandals, O prince's daughter!

Thy navel is like a round goblet, wherein no mingled wine is wanting;
Thy two breasts are like two fawns that are twins of a gazelle.
This thy stature is like to a palm-tree, and thy breasts to clusters of grapes.
I said: 'I will climb up into the palm-tree, I will take hold of the branches thereof;

and let thy breasts be as clusters of the vine, and the smell of thy countenance like apples;
And the roof of thy mouth like the best wine, that glideth down smoothly for my beloved,
  moving gently the lips of those who are asleep.

The entire bar is still. Eugene and the bartender weep silently.

"Are you crazy?" says the best man. "I can't say that."

"Why not?" says the poet. "Has anyone ever said it better? You think Toastmasters has anything on Solomon?"

"But it's embarrassing, talking about breasts like grapes, her navel, her hair like a—a flock of goats. They might be offended."

"Offended because you're quoting the Bible? Classic *Tanakh* literature?"

"Well, not when you put it like that."

"It's about love," says the scholar. "Two rapturous lovers talking about each other. Just quote the parts you're comfortable saying."

"Yeah!" says the best man, suddenly enthusiastic. "Maybe that *would* be better than the usual thing. They'll remember it for sure!"

He heads out to find a computer, his seat claimed by two new refugees, our cousins the twins, tugging at their bridesmaid gowns and ordering frozen daiquiris to cool off.

"It's boiling in there!" says one.

"And these ruffles are torture!" says the other.

"We haven't had to dress alike since our ninth birthday party."

"We should've known we were in trouble when she wanted us to make origami place cards—"

"And come up with a signature drink for the reception—"

"But we didn't realize it was hell until the rehearsal, when she made us *skip* down the aisle!"

"Did you *see* us?"

"It was *mortifying!*"

They drop crushed ice down their bodices and collapse

against each other with a sigh.

"Did you hear about the honeymoon?" says one.

"No, where is it?" we ask. "Buckingham Palace?"

"Close. One of those resorts with butlers who adjust your chaise."

"And stand there while you sunbathe to spritz you with mineral water."

"And mop up your wet trail. And serve you drinks in the pool."

"Not just drinks—they serve you *dinner* in the pool!"

"What else do they do?" we ask. "Scratch your nose? Wipe your tush?"

"Don't be silly: nobody shits in a place like that."

"But if they did, they would do it in the pool!" They collapse in giggles.

Our teenage cousin sighs. "This family is *so* screwed up."

"Not really," says the bartender. "I have relatives who use every family occasion to get hammered. They were so drunk at my grandmother's funeral that they barfed into the grave. Now that's screwed-up."

"At my niece's wedding, her stepfather hit on every woman in the room," says Eugene, "including his ex-wife and the bride's new mother-in-law. It caused a riot. The police had to break it up."

"I've seen basset hounds in bridesmaid gowns," says the bartender. "I've seen a Border Collie as Best Man. It tried to herd the wedding party."

"See?" says the jokester. "We're perfectly normal."

"Not for Jews," insists the maven. "A wedding day is supposed to be a personal Yom Kippur for the bride and groom, a day of repentance and forgiveness. They're supposed to fast before the ceremony. That's what the bride's white dress is all about. And the groom is supposed to wear a white *kittel*—it looks like a lab coat—over his suit. Repentance! Forgiveness! Fasting!"

We take this in.

"So all right then," one of us replies, "we're in an excellent position. We're fasting, sort of. And who better to forgive the bride and groom than *us*, the wronged guests? We'll forgive them. It's a wedding present *and* a mitzvah."

"Everybody wins! Fill the glasses!"

"*L'chaim!*" yells Eugene.

"Speaking of dresses," says one of the twins, hitching up her bodice, "does anyone know *why* we need six guys dressed like penguins and six girls in identical dresses standing up there with the bride and groom? Are we supposed to catch them if they make a break for it?"

"Actually, that's not too far from the truth," says the scholar. "Marriage by capture used to be the norm, so the groom needed friends to help him kidnap the bride and hold onto her."

"So the bridesmaids are what, decoys?"

"Something like that. In ancient Rome you needed ten witnesses to make the wedding legal. To confuse envious spirits lurking at the altar, witnesses dressed exactly like the bride and groom. In medieval Europe the bride and groom walked to church with their friends. The men all dressed like the groom and the women like the bride to confuse any witches who might want to curse the happy couple."

"Of course where we live, all the *men* dress like brides," murmurs the poet.

"That's also why they unroll a white carpet when the bride walks down the aisle," the scholar continues. "People believed evil spirits lurked in the earth. The white runner denotes purity and the kiss was a legal bond that sealed contracts. And the wedding cake was originally a small bun broken over the bride's head to symbolize fertility."

"God, does everything go back to ancient Rome?" says the teenager.

"Of course not," says the maven. "Jews go back way before then."

The scholar polishes his glasses with a cocktail napkin. "If you mean is everything we know now spiraled through a past we can only dimly make out, anchored in the mud of an ancient world that looks about as familiar to us as the soil to a sunflower, then the answer is yes."

The teen groans. "This is supposed to be my *weekend*." She gets up and stalks out.

"Just yes?" we ask.

"Yes, and if people studied history the way they study take-out menus, we would live in a very different world."

We are all silent.

"Man," says the bartender respectfully. "You really know how to kill a buzz."

The poet defends him. "He's only saying we have to read the past."

The maven provides unexpected support: "The old rebbes say that every human being is tied to God with a rope. If the rope breaks and you tie a knot, it just brings you that much closer."

"Hey!" Our teenage cousin is suddenly back. "It stopped snowing!" She gives us a huge unexpected grin. "Let's go write our names in the snow! Let's write: *Thanks for the tour!*"

We look at each other. No one has gloves or hats. It's almost dark outside. We've been drinking all afternoon. We're a bunch of weak-eyed, soft-bellied, middle-class Jews, one with a tumor, one with a shy bladder, one a compulsive giver, one a fan of a Catholic saint, the rest with our own secrets and blind spots, all of us certifiable.

"Let's build our own bride-and-groom," says someone with an evil smile.

"Let's build a freaking wedding party—including the B list," says another.

"All at the same damn reception!" adds a third.

Our teenage cousin jumps on top of a chair and holds up both hands for quiet. Her eyes positively gleam. "Let's make a pile of snowballs for when the newlyweds come out!" she whispers, and the room erupts into cheers.

The bar clears out in an instant.

We love weddings.
They always make us laugh.

MERRILY, MERRILY

This is possibly the most autobiographical story in the collection —so much so that for a long time, I couldn't read it without re-experiencing the panic and even longer before I could read it without tears. This is the story of my daughter's birth. Don't worry: it has a happy ending, something I wish I'd known when I was living it.

I thought I was already an expert in worry, but Molly's birth was like a post-doctoral fellowship. The first thing I worried about—it seems like a luxury now—was that I wouldn't be able to love her. She was an accident, too soon after Jesse: it would push him out of babyhood before he was ready; my body was finally my own again; we didn't have the money; and how could I possibly be pregnant again? It had taken three years of charts, drugs, and thermometers to conceive Jesse. How could my body just fix itself? What a time for things to go right!

But what bothered me most was the feeling that I was betraying Jesse, popping that brilliant bubble we'd been floating in from the start. I knew that if both babies were crying, I would go to Jesse first. How could I not? We had a history. Which made me feel even guiltier about the poor child I would bring into the world and not love.

Then, in the midst of the 24/7 nausea—*that*, at least, was no different—I found out the baby was a she. When they told me, I dropped the phone and screamed. And from that moment, though I knew it would be hard, the baby no longer seemed like a mistake. As Owen pointed out, we might have tried for another three years and ended up with another boy. This way, he said, at least you got your girl.

I got my girl. That's what I said when they pulled her out and turned her over. Relations with my own mother had been rocky for years, and I'd always had trouble making female friends. But now I had a chance to get it right. Now I had Molly.

But not quite. Because the delivery had been fast and rough, she was terrifically battered and they wouldn't let me hold her. She had two shiners, cauliflower nose, hugely swollen cheeks. Long bruises streaked her body. One nurse said her left hand looked funny—crooked, with a thumb like a small finger—but nobody paid attention then. She just looked too awful. They took her away, and the doctor spent a long time stitching up my unusually large episiotomy.

That night I hemorrhaged, leaving bloody footprints all over the floor, and they called my OB back in at 3:00 a.m. to do an internal.

"This is a nightmare," I told him between gasps.

"The worst is over," he said, pulling out a large slippery blood clot. "Behold the culprit!"

He was in a jolly mood for someone who'd been called out of bed in the middle of the night, but why not? He'd negotiated a tricky delivery, done some creative stitching, and solved the bleeding problem. We had just about reached the end of his jurisdiction. Now the pediatricians took over.

The first indication that the nightmare wasn't over was the way the doctor hesitated. I was ready to nurse the baby and I didn't understand why the pediatrician was still hanging around. He seemed elderly, tentative, a little embarrassed. When he said she had a heart murmur, he hastened to add that it was probably nothing. Over the next day or so we heard about dozens of people whose heart murmurs mattered no more than a freckle or a mole. I worried a little, indulging myself. But no one seemed to think there was cause for alarm.

Yet doctors kept coming to see her. "It's not a *good* murmur," one of them mused. He was talking to himself, not me. That's when the fizz started prickling my stomach.

On Thursday, when we were supposed to be discharged, they decided to keep her another day because her bilirubin count was 18—her liver couldn't process all the broken blood vessels caused by her rapid violent birth. Her little nose was golden, her eyeballs the color of weak tea, and there were long mustardy streaks along her back and legs. That's okay, we said. What's one more day? Think of the parents who have to leave the hospital empty-handed.

That afternoon Owen brought Jesse in to meet his sister. Her eyes were still swelled shut, but when we sang Jesse's favorite song, "Row, Row, Row Your Boat"—which she must have heard in utero since he demanded it night and day—her lids fluttered and she managed to squint at us. Jesse was more impressed by the TV high on the wall and the sink that operated by foot pedals.

After they left, the baby nursed, but I kept nuzzling her, frowning, trying to remember how Jesse felt when he was two days old. She seemed a little warm. I'd been so hot throughout the pregnancy that I didn't trust my judgment, yet the habit of worry made me mention it to the nurse.

"She feels all right to me," said the nurse. "Try to get some sleep."

I eased onto my side and closed my eyes.

Next thing I knew there was yet another doctor standing by my bed. I was groggy; it took a moment for his words to sink in. *Special Care*, he was saying: Molly was in Special Care, the hospital euphemism for where they sent critically ill babies. As the doctor talked, I opened my eyes wide to keep the tears from spilling over. He was talking about temperature, dehydration, breathing rate, heart failure. My baby might die. He didn't say that. He very carefully didn't say that.

I had only one question and I didn't ask it, because I knew doctors don't give you that kind of answer. I called Owen but he wasn't home yet. I tried him every five minutes. I walked around my room a hundred times. I cried until my eyes were as swollen as Molly's, till I could feel my contact lenses scrape against the lids. I called Special Care three times. "Nothing has changed," they told me. Everything had changed. Worry, I discovered, had been my private protection racket: if only I worried enough, none of the things I worried about would actually happen.

Then Special Care called me. They wanted me to come right away. The "right away" jammed an icicle through my heart. I stuffed my pockets with tissues and hurried out to ask the nurses for directions. They hushed as I approached, studying me with professional sympathy. In other rooms, mothers held their babies and chatted with guests, balloons and fruit baskets by their bedsides. Their worst worries were what mine had been forty-eight hours ago—lost sleep, sore nipples. I stared, uncomprehending, at the nurse who gave me directions until she took my arm. "Come on," she said. "I'll walk you."

As we approached, I could hear a baby screaming, its little cartoon-voice raw. Was that Molly? My guide melted away— I hope I thanked her. Molly was enclosed in a plastic box. Pasted to her skin were disks like metal nipples, each clipped to wires that hooked her up to a monitor that pulsed and rippled. Her face was purple, the lips cracking, lined in black. Her little arms and legs were stiff with outrage. I thought I was already weeping, but vast new reservoirs of tears unleashed themselves. There was a physical but disembodied pain, like the phantom pain amputees feel, as intense as anything I'd experienced in labor.

"Hold her," they urged me. "Maybe she'll calm down."

I sat on a stool and they put her, a bundle of wires, in my

arms. My stitches throbbed, but I was glad. I think I believed —the worse the nightmare got, the more magical my thinking became—I was siphoning some of the pain from Molly, diverting the evil spirits. I was utterly panicked. I thought I might be looking at her for the last time. I tried to sing "Row, Row, Row Your Boat," but nothing recognizable came out. I put my cheek against hers. She was burning. Her little tongue kept poking out, dry as cotton. She couldn't have anything to drink; they were waiting for the ambulance from Crouse, where there was a better Intensive Care for newborns. The ambulance team would give her an IV. "Please, can't I just wet her lips?" I begged, and they finally let me dampen a piece of gauze and touch it to her mouth. Her furious crying broke when she felt the gauze, and she sucked eagerly for a moment. Three hours ago I'd been nursing her.

Then a nurse tapped my shoulder. Owen was on the phone. We spoke tersely. In the background the baby screamed. I felt a perverse pride. My baby had enough life in her to rage. Then I thought that if she died, all she would have known was pain, terror, and rage, and I couldn't speak anymore. The ambulance team arrived, surrounding Molly. Her screaming seemed to escalate. How could she possibly scream any harder? A nurse tugged my elbow. I had to sign papers.

I packed. I paced. I waited for Owen. Last night I'd been worried about sibling rivalry. Now I was thinking about tiny coffins; I was ruling out suicide because Jesse needed me. I wanted to call the police, report a crime—I wanted to race through the corridors, breaking glass, shrieking: *Give me my baby!*

It was eleven p.m. when we finally walked into Neonatal Intensive Care at Crouse. We had to scrub our hands and arms and put on masks and itchy yellow gowns that tied in the back. We did each other up, like playing surgeon. The nursery was full of isolettes blinking and buzzing. It took me a moment to recognize Molly. Then I grabbed Owen and cried: "What did they do to her head?" It had been partially shaved. She looked like a tiny tonsured monk with tubes attached.

"It was for the IV," the nurse explained. "Sometimes they can't find a good spot anywhere else."

Our daughter lay in her isolette as if she'd been flung there, naked except for a diaper and sunglasses fashioned from cotton balls and surgical tape. The isolette was fitted with fluorescent lights that bombarded her skin, breaking down the bilirubin.

"At least she seems quiet," said Owen.

"We gave her a little sugar water," said the nurse. "We had to —she was just wild."

Owen nodded, sharing my grim satisfaction. No child of ours would slip gentle into any good night. I remembered how Jesse had raged and fought at his own circumcision—he spat out the wine-soaked gauze; he would not submit; he would not be pacified. And I remembered how my father had leaned down to blow gently across his face, as he'd done with me when I was little and sick. I used to think he did it to cool me off. Now I knew it was to blow the evil spirits away.

"There's a parents' lounge down the hall," said the nurse, pushing us gently along. "Why don't you wait there?"

"Can I touch her?" I asked.

"Not now. Maybe tomorrow."

I pressed my hands against the isolette, leaving a perfect set of prints.

We saw lots of doctors that night, cardiologists and neonatologists who kept popping in with good news and bad news like vaudeville comedians. One said Molly's defect seemed small, another confirmed she'd been in heart failure, a third noted that some of her valves were leaking and the blood vessels to her lungs were connected in the wrong place. A fourth said he would order a brain scan since her upper-body flaccidity might be caused by a tumor.

"What upper-body flaccidity?" said Doctor Number Five the next day. There was no tumor. And leaky valves were normal under the circumstances. They ordered more blood tests, echocardiograms, x-rays, EKG's. And we began to get used to the incredible fact that *doctors disagreed.*

Thus began our new life. Each morning we called the hospital to find out Molly's bilirubin, breathing rate, oxygenation, and temperature, noting down the numbers. We kissed Jesse goodbye, gathered the bottles of breast milk I'd pumped overnight, drove to the hospital. Each time we trekked down the hall, freshly scrubbed and gowned, bearing the parcel of tiny jars with their inch of grayish milk, I was terrified we'd find an empty isolette.

Then when I saw her, naked, blindfolded, the IV taped to her head, sensors pasted to her stomach, little heels dotted with needle marks, I would be overcome with relief and misery. I was not stoic about it. I stuck my arms through the portholes and sobbed as I stroked my daughter. There seemed to be no limit to the amount of tears I could produce.

Owen didn't cry. He asked questions. How many holes in her heart? How big? Located exactly where? What had caused them? What was the prognosis? What were our options? He began reading cardiology textbooks and photocopying dozens of pages. His questions were so aggressive that the doctors began asking if he was a medical student. They seemed relieved that he was not.

Gradually the other doctors began deferring to the geneticists, who somehow came out on top of the heap. Finally they sat us down and gave us their conclusion.

Molly had a rare syndrome that involved the heart and upper extremities, hence her crooked hand and peculiar thumb. But we were lucky, they said: babies with this syndrome were sometimes born with no fingers, or hands, or arms at all. And with much bigger holes in their hearts. The geneticists were quite cheery about it. They were pleased to have solved the mystery, told us what a pleasure it was to talk with us, how much they'd enjoyed examining Molly and drawing our family trees. Before they left, they made sure we understood that Molly's defect was not our fault: she did not inherit it from either of us and it was not the result of anything I'd done or taken during pregnancy. A gene had mutated. It was a fluke.

"But what does this mean?" I kept asking. "What kind of life will she have? Could she drop dead in the middle of hopscotch?"

The doctors smiled at what they took for verbal extravagance. Oh, they were nice enough: you couldn't blame them for being so *interested* in Molly's *case*—they were already planning a paper. The nearest to brass tacks we could get them was that her heart might heal itself, might heal with medication, or might require surgery before the age of two.

"Of course, we have a very high success rate with that kind of procedure," the cardiologist assured me.

"Yeah," I said, "but do any of the parents survive?"

He gave me that smile again.

Her hand would need orthopedic surgery followed by physical therapy. And there was a fifty percent chance that any children she had would inherit the condition—with no guarantees, of course, that those cases would be mild. The doctor dropped that one on us on his way out the door. "But that's a decision she'll have to make herself," he called over his shoulder, as if he thought we might have other ideas.

"My God." I turned to Owen. "What a legacy."

Owen knows me well. "It's *not* your fault," he replied.

But it certainly wasn't hers. Yet here it was, the inception of a curse that would haunt all the generations to follow—if there were any. Perhaps she would choose not to have children. She would ask me about pregnancy and childbirth, and I would have to word my answers carefully. She would grow up haunted by this question of risk, and when she fell in love, the love would be tainted with it too.

But at the moment the blindfolded baby in the isolette was much realer than the woman she would become. Owen read *Cardiovascular Research* and *Pediatric Cardiology*. I brought her frozen milk, stroked her head and her smooth little back, so hot from the bilirubin lights, and sang:

> *Row, row, row your boat*
> *Gently down the stream*
> *Merrily, merrily, merrily, merrily*
> *Life is but a dream*

Twice the doctors named a discharge date and then reneged because her bilirubin shot up or her breathing climbed back into the eighties. They were cautiously optimistic, but I didn't really believe anybody: not doctors, not nurses, not even Owen. As long as she was in Intensive Care, I had a shard of ice stuck in my chest. Pessimism has always seemed truer to me than anything else.

When the doctors said I could try nursing Molly again, everyone was cheered. "This is where we left off," I told her, cradling her carefully in my arms. But something was different now. The baby labored to suck. She started, stopped, resumed, rested. She dropped the nipple, looked for it frantically, howled. I put it back in her mouth but she thrashed her head wildly, as if she couldn't tell she had hold of it. When I finally got her calmed down, she sucked a little, then closed her eyes. I sang to her and she fluttered her lashes but lost the struggle and sank, exhausted, into sleep. The nurses nodded sympathetically when I told them. Typical cardiac behavior, they said. Watch out if she breaks into a sweat or starts turning blue—watch out for choking. It's hard to suck and breathe at the same time when you've got a hole in your heart. Finally the doctor put her on formula. "At least this way we'll know she's getting enough," he said.

And so, in addition to bilirubin and breathing rate, we became engrossed in how many ounces she consumed each day. "When she's steadily gaining, we'll let her go home," the doctor promised. But I kept thinking about my cousin's baby who was born with a hole in his heart the size of a quarter. He desperately needed surgery, but the doctor didn't want to do it till he weighed 25 pounds, and his parents just couldn't get him there. Every time he gained a pound, he'd catch a cold and lose it. When he was two and wearing the clothes of a nine-month-old, he had the operation anyway. And got better. But that didn't mean *my* baby would. Maybe my family had used up its quota of luck.

The last day of August was a Friday, Labor Day weekend. "Let's shoot for Tuesday," the doctor said. I nodded, fresh tears already burning my eyes. He put his hand on my shoulder, adding: "I just don't want to see her come back." I imagined a midnight run to the hospital, paramedics, oxygen tanks, and had to shake the vision off.

By Saturday she had gained two grams. Breathing was still down, bilirubin okay, all systems go. I was elated, joked and chatted with the neighbors instead of avoiding them. Sunday morning she had dropped a gram. "Don't let it get you down," said the nurse. "It's normal to go back and forth. Tomorrow she'll be up again." But by Monday she had lost the other gram. Monday night I finally got to sleep by repeating like a mantra: *Don't get your hopes up/She's not coming home.* Even so, when I dialed the number Tuesday morning I was shaking. "Well, the doctors haven't made their rounds yet," said the night nurse, "but she's down another gram." I nodded, though she couldn't see. I was too full of tears to speak.

Owen had class so I went to the hospital alone. I scrubbed and gowned myself, expert by now, and walked into the nursery. The nurses were feeding the babies.

"*There* she is," one nurse sang out.

"They just signed the order," said another.

When I continued to stare at her, she added: "Molly's going home!"

I dropped my purse. My arm went dead and my purse slid

right onto the floor. And then, for a change, I burst into tears. It was a mistake, it had to be a mistake, but I wasn't asking any questions. I just knew she'd be okay if we could only get her home.

And she was. At her first check-up, she'd gained five ounces —almost one for every day she'd been home. We held her constantly. Even Jesse seemed to regard her as his own personal baby. He brought her his trucks and beloved blankie; he took off his shoes and put them on her feet; and once, when I saw crumbs on her lips, I opened her mouth and scooped out a soggy lump of Fig Newton.

As her bruises and jaundice faded, Molly turned fair, with a dimple in her right cheek just where Jesse has his. She waved her arms in slow motion as if practicing tai chi, and when I stroked her forehead, her mouth formed a perfect little o. I could scarcely believe it. I'd thought surely this time disaster had caught up with me. Yet here she was—round blue eyes, hypoplastic thumb, and sweet downy head with the hairline of a sixty-year-old man.

Still, I felt a peculiar sadness when my stitches stopped hurting and the lochia dried up, a nostalgia for childbirth itself. I wanted to go back and do it right—have a perfect unbruised baby, a baby with a blissful future. We were cheated out of our honeymoon, Molly and I. My body seemed to feel its own regret. One night, long after my milk had dried up, I got up to get her a bottle and was amazed to feel the front of my nightgown grow damp.

But we *were* lucky. Some of those tiny babies in isolettes wouldn't go home for months. Some never would. There were children in the hospital elevator—skinny, translucent, bald little children—on their way to chemotherapy. Every time I saw their mothers I wanted to apologize for our astonishing and undeserved good luck.

Which doesn't mean I've stopped worrying about Molly. I'm frightened every time she has a cough or seems sluggish or won't eat. I'm going to imagine losing her for the rest of my life.

I even worry about her in retrospect, which is the weirdest thing of all. I go over and over that scene in the hospital when they took her away, compulsively imagining how it might have turned out, how we might have gone to the NICU to find a crash cart and a team working on her, how they might have turned to us at last, exhausted, saying "We're sorry." I actually break into a sweat thinking about this. It's like a story Owen told me about how he climbed down an abandoned well to rescue a cat. There was no one around for miles. It was winter, icy, dark. He never stopped to think about whether he'd be able to climb *out*. This happened twenty years ago, long before I knew him, yet I can't think about it without fear twisting my gut, and I catch myself whispering: *"Owen, get out!"*

He laughs when I tell him these things. He says my motto is: "Why worry later when you can worry now too?" He reminds me that I used to worry about whether I could love a second child. I look at the back of Molly's head, and the swirling pattern of hair makes me weak. She will be different from other children: she will need surgery; she will have to be careful about infections; she may never have children of her own. This last is the hardest—already I ache for Molly's own pain. Owen is right about me. And yet there are days, warm sunny autumn days, when I can imagine a time when that mutated gene will not be the most important thing about her. When I say this to Owen he smiles and says the day is so fine, we should take the children for a walk.

The children. I'm not used to the sound of it yet. We put them into the double stroller, which maneuvers around corners like a stretch limousine. Jesse sits as far forward as he can get, like the figurehead on the prow of a tiny ship, eager to thrust himself into whatever's coming. Molly lies in back, tentatively kicking her feet against the light blanket. I push first. The sun is warm. The leaves are golden yellow. Somehow there seem to be as many underfoot as there are still clinging to the branches overhead, so that the whole world glows under a brilliant blue sky—the colors of a medieval manuscript. We talk about Owen's students, Jesse's new words, Molly's next appointment. Then Molly starts to make the high sandpapery sound that means she's hungry. Jesse twists around to look at her, then lets out an uncanny imitation of the sound. Molly stops fussing and looks at him, or at least in his direction. I could swear there's a bemused expression on her face.

"Bee," Jesse says, prodding her with a chubby hand—he means "baby"—and I realize suddenly that I have made him a brother and her a sister. I have made Owen a father. There are invisible threads knotting and tangling the four of us together forever.

Then I think of the mothers on the hospital elevator, of all lurking peril and untapped bad luck, and I want to bend down and blow gently across my children's faces. But Jesse has lost interest in Molly and begins saying: "Out. Out," and Molly resumes fussing in earnest. Automatically, Owen and I both lean over the stroller and begin a round of "Row, Row, Row Your Boat." I am laughing, and instead of asking why, Owen just puts a hand on the stroller and helps me negotiate a bend. Our arms collide and we don't move out of the way.

FAT PENCILS

This is another true story, faithful to real events and feelings, though perhaps a bit more dramatic than what I experienced. (There was only one pack of pencils left, but no Virginia Slims lady to grab them first.)

"**D**o they let you take blankies to kindergarten?"

Jesse's quick feet slow as they approach the big doors, and Esther's heart clenches. *They*, already? *They*? Her exuberant, generous, mischievous son—the same child who sang "I happy, I happy," as he rode in his stroller, drawing affectionate looks from total strangers—already sees himself at the mercy of a vast impersonal system? She stares at the handful of forms she clutches, full of numbers representing this child, this unique combination of quirks and qualities named Jesse Sapperstein Muldoon.

"I don't know, Jess. Why don't we ask?" she says in her we're-all-reasonable-creatures voice. Such a lie, but he doesn't have to know yet.

Ahead of them, Owen holds the big door open—an institutional dark-red door like the one at Stutzman Elementary, where Esther served her own time. Where Mr. Kipp, sixth-grade science, often remarked: "Say, you're a husky one, aren't you?" Where Miss Horoff— "Miss Horror," fourth-grade geography—paddled her in front of the class for whispering. Where gym class and recess meant not play but humiliation, with nowhere to hide. She puts her arm around

Jesse as they pass through the door.

Kindergarten Orientation turns out to be a series of speeches for parents in the "Auditeria" while children meet their new teachers and take a ride on the school bus. Parents hear from the principal, the PTA, the school nurse, the counselor, the transportation facilitator, the room mother association, the coordinator of instructional support. They are given hand-outs on clothing requirements, snack money, book orders, medications, screening tests, bus safety, parenting classes, holiday bazaar, fire drills, report cards, whole language approach, lice, and mandatory supplies. Mandatory supplies is what does Esther in: each child has to *bring to school tomorrow* eight large primary crayons, a pencil box, an art smock, a bottle of glue, safety scissors, a paintbrush, a box of tissues, and two primary pencils.

"He has to have all this by *tomorrow!*" she whispers to Owen, half-expecting Miss Horror to swoop down with the paddle. "Why didn't they tell us sooner?"

"I'm sure it can wait a few days," he murmurs sleepily.

"And what the hell are *primary pencils*?" she whispers, this time expecting to be thrown out of the Auditeria for saying "hell."

Owen does not share her sense of urgency, but the woman beside her whispers that primary pencils are fat ones, supposedly easier for small hands to manipulate.

"He doesn't need those," Owen says when she explains on the way home. "He's been using regular pencils since he was two."

"But that's what they want him to have." *They!*

"We've got plenty of stuff at home. Crayons, most of a bottle of glue, and he can have one of my old shirts for a smock."

"No!" Esther says sharply. "I want him to have new things. I want him to have what everyone else has."

Owen shoots her a look which means it isn't wise to say such things in Jesse's presence, which she already knows. Jesse is sucking his thumb and holding his blankie to his cheek, eyes closed, but Esther knows he's not sleeping. She wants to tell Owen that this isn't just a matter of keeping up with all the Ryans and Ashleys and Brittanys: she wants Jesse to have new things so that the occasion—starting kindergarten, entering the *system*—will seem shiny and thrilling and irresistible to him. So he'll remember it that way. So that maybe his childhood will be different than hers.

After picking Molly up at the sitter's, Esther drops them all off at home, leaving Owen to deal with the children's dinner. First she tries the office supply store, where she finds a bright new pack of jumbo crayons, a green bottle of glue, a package of different-sized paintbrushes, and a cunning pair of red safety scissors shaped like Mickey Mouse. At K-Mart she gets the tissues and a yellow pencil box that looks like a school bus. At the art supply store she finds an orange oilcloth smock with pockets in front to store brushes. Now she has everything except the pencils. She tries Ames, Walmart, and Target, stopping at every drug store along the way. Everywhere she goes she sees fancy *skinny* pencils. No one has any idea what she's talking about until a woman behind her at Customer Service says: "Oh, I got those last year at Schmidt's."

Esther streaks out of the parking lot across town toward Schmidt's, an old-fashioned general store which sells a little, but just a little, of everything. Every light she hits is red; then the parking lot is so crowded she has to park up the street at a supermarket.

Her heels make anxious clacking sounds on the old-fashioned wooden floor as she rapidly cruises the aisles. Paper, binders, staplers, tape, pens, pens, pens, *pencils*. Neon, geometric, pastel, scented, Barbie, Batman, Power Rangers, Star Wars—and *there*, swinging from a lone peg, one packet of Husky—*husky!*—Primary Pencils!

Snagged, just as she spots them, by a woman who drops them into her cart on top of the crayons, pencil case, glue, scissors, paintbrush, smock, and carton of Virginia Slims.

If she'd only come here first! Dejected, she plucks a package of overpriced Power Ranger pencils that will delight Jesse—he won't know till school starts how she's failed him—and follows the woman to the checkout.

"Thirty-two ninety-one," the cashier says.

There is a lengthy and embarrassing pause as the woman digs through her purse. "Damn," she says finally. "I thought for sure I had another twenty." She looks up. "You take Visa?"

"No credit cards," the cashier says firmly. "Cash or checks." Then she adds: "With proper ID."

The woman shrugs. "I left my checkbook at home," she says with the kind of laugh people use when nothing is funny. And then, though Esther cannot believe it, she takes all of the school supplies, *including the fat pencils*, off the belt, leaving only the carton of cigarettes, which she pays for and tucks under her arm as she strolls away.

Esther snatches up the packet: two long pencils as thick as her finger, one blue, one red, "for primary school and checking." Checking what? She doesn't care—she can scarcely let go of the packet long enough to let the cashier scan it. Twenty-five cents. With tax, twenty-seven. Peace of mind will never again come so cheap.

"Could you believe that?" the cashier says. "She puts the school stuff back and keeps the cigarettes."

Esther carefully counts out the coins. She doesn't want to make any mistakes.

"Takes all kinds, I guess," says the cashier, ringing it up. "I feel sorry for the kid."

But though Esther feels sorry for the kid too—Esther feels sorry for *all* kids—she has been transported by this miracle, by the fact that she can now go home with the exact right pencils, and Jesse will not have to begin his career by being made to feel conspicuous, inadequate, wrong. Tomorrow he'll embark, with brand-new supplies—and his blankie too, damn it, for he *is* an absolutely unique combination—without having to make a single apology. Esther gives the cashier a blinding smile as she accepts her treasure, because she knows now that he, and she, are going to be okay.

FORTY-FOUR LIGHTS

I actually don't remember much about going to Lizzie's preschool class to talk about Hanukkah. I assume it went well because she's still speaking to me, but the real point of the story is Esther's uneasy truce between tradition and fact, between the desire to expose lies and illusion and to protect her children from uncertainty.

sther is pacing in the hall. She would like a sip of water but the fountain is tiny and low, and the narrow skirt of her suit does not encourage stooping. She has come straight from the university. On either side of the fountain, Boys and Girls doors stand open and she can see tiny sinks and toilets. She would like to use one of those toilets, but her Ruthless Control pantyhose will burst if she tries to crouch that low. Through the pane in the classroom door she watches Miss Tammy clap her hands to make the children pick up their toys. It's Story Time. Esther is nauseous.

She checks her supplies again: menorah, candles, matches, dreidels, little mesh sacks of chocolate coins. Should she put the candles in now or later? Will it set a bad example to light matches? Will it set off smoke alarms? What if Miss Tammy opposes gambling in preschool? What about the other parents? Molly is the only Jewish child in class. Esther knows how that feels. She stayed away from Jesse's class, but Molly asked her to come. Begged her. Thought it would be the coolest thing to have your mom barge in and explain why you're a freak.

No, no, that's you and *your* mom, Cousin Trudy the analyst

would remind her: *you're* the one obsessed with not repeating history. Molly's just having fun. Don't get in her way.

Besides, Molly doesn't yet realize what it means to be the only Jew. Esther's grandparents kept impeccably kosher homes, refused to use electricity on the Sabbath, tore their clothes at funerals—not the sissy split ribbons modern Jews use but their real everyday clothes—and sat on the hard floor to mourn. Esther's parents joined a Reform Temple, ate bacon and shrimp but went to services every week, observed major holidays, and made their children do the same, until Esther left for college at seventeen and lost track of the Jewish calendar completely. The only time she knows it's a holiday is when her father wishes her a *shanah tovah* over the phone or her mother sends buttery *hamantaschen*. Or Hanukkah gifts.

At first, when it was just Esther and Owen, they opened all the gifts right away. But this upset her mother, so, feeling foolish, they waited for the start of Hanukkah and opened one each night. They didn't bother lighting candles. Owen had never celebrated Hanukkah—his father had been a lapsed Catholic and his mother, though technically a Jew, was completely non-observant. Her parents put up Christmas trees and handed out Easter baskets, so she did the same. She knew less about being Jewish than four-year-old Molly. Owen said he wasn't anything.

But now, after years of trying, they have Jesse and, unexpectedly, Molly, and despite the clichés, it *does* seem important to be something. To make sure the children know what they are—and what they are not. Though if you grabbed Esther's arm this minute and asked her why, her mumbled answer would have more to do with history than with God. Recent history, that is. Because since she started teaching at the university, ancient history has become way more problematic.

Now the preschoolers are busily and inefficiently arranging chairs into a circle for Story Time. Only instead of a story today they will have Esther, who starts pacing again, clutching her index cards. It's not as if she doesn't know her way around a preschool classroom, but today is different. Today isn't about gluing cotton balls to paper plates. Today she actually has something to *teach* them. And whenever she has to teach, she gets stage fright. Without her index cards, she would turn to stone. Maybe that's what Lot's wife saw when she looked back over her shoulder: an auditorium full of college freshmen waiting for their lecture in Western Civ.

The index cards don't just give her something to say, they give her someone to *be*: a profess-or of history, a modern woman who knows things. Her specialty is ancient art, but between the Internet and the university library, she can plug enough gaps in her knowledge to do a decent job with the survey class. Often, as she preps, she discovers that there are conflicting stories of an event—and why not, she tells her students: history isn't the past, it's only language about the past, the story that got recorded the most, repeated through the centuries in lecture halls like this one, where students memorized what teachers said, where textbooks and chalkboards were high-tech innovations. At this point, her students always laugh.

So she shouldn't have been surprised, in prepping for this little talk today, to discover that there are conflicting versions of Hanukkah. But she was. Perhaps because Hanukkah is regarded as a minor holiday, mainly for children: candles, presents, gambling with tops and chocolate coins, eating jelly doughnuts and potato pancakes. What possible reason could there be to dissemble?

But, following a path which grew ever rockier and alien, she found out. Which left her—leaves her—with the historian's classic dilemma, something not unlike a parent's. Or a member of the Sapperstein clan. She chews the corner off an index card. Up to her neck in complicity, Cousin Trudy would say.

The standard version of Hanukkah describes the 166 B.C.E. revolt that Judah Maccabee and his small guerrilla band waged against huge Syrian forces occupying their land. That victory might be considered miracle enough, but there was a mysterious coda: when they cleaned up the desecrated Temple, there was only enough oil to keep the great Menorah lit for one day. Yet the flame, which represents the presence of God, must never be allowed to go out. A runner was dispatched to the nearest town for sacred oil, though everyone knew it would take him four days to get there and four days to get back. And yet that tiny bit of oil somehow lasted for all eight: the flame never went out. That was the miracle of Hanukkah, festival of lights.

The historian's problem is that although Hanukkah is the most historically documented Jewish holiday, no mention of the miracle is made until the Middle Ages, a thousand years later. Why would that be? Wouldn't such an astonishing event, proof that the Children of Israel were indeed God's chosen, be trumpeted far and wide?

There are further complications: the Maccabees turned out to be religious zealots who forced their fanaticism on others —not the stuff heroes are made of. And, ironically, despite the amazing victory over the Syrians, the Maccabees' descendants adopted Syrian culture after all and persecuted their fellow Jews. Then there's the debate over whether Hanukkah existed as a real event or whether, as the numerologists argue, it was fabricated for political reasons. And of course the contemporary customs of gift giving and house-decoration have more to do with Hanukkah's proximity to Christmas than with any Jewish tradition.

Esther shuffles the cards. How much to tell? How much to explain? These children know nothing about "the Jewish Christmas." How much does she owe to Molly? To Jews? To history? But there is no time to weigh it all out—a beaming Miss Tammy throws open the door and Esther drops her cards.

"Look who's *here!*" Miss Tammy cries. "It's Molly's *mommy!* Can we say a big hello to Molly's mommy?"

"Hi Mom!" Molly yells, bouncing in her seat. "That's my mom!"

"Molly's mommy has come to tell us about something very special," Miss Tammy continues.

"We have Hanukkah instead of Christmas," Molly announces.

"Well, not exactly instead of," says Esther, fighting her pantyhose to pick up the cards.

"It lasts eight days and I get a present every night!" says Molly.

"Whoa! You get eight presents?" says a boy in a Spiderman shirt.

"Boys and girls!" Miss Tammy is clapping.

"Nope, *more*, 'cause I get some from my Grammy and Poppa."

"Molly," says Esther, finally making it into the room.

"How many do you get?"

"Well, I get some from Uncle Jeff and Aunt Nancy—"

"Boys and girls!"

"And some from Uncle Mark and Aunt Caroline. They come in the mail."

"I love mail," sighs a girl in a Little Mermaid headband.

"I get birthday presents in the mail," says another.

"How many?" asks Spiderman.

"Boys and girls!" Miss Tammy's hands must be smarting.

"Here, look at this," Esther says. Prying off her pumps, she manages to kneel and strew the box of colored candles across the rug.

"Crayons!" squeals the Little Mermaid.

"Nope." Esther begins fitting them into the menorah.

"Do a green," someone suggests.

"Do a pink," someone advises.

"Do *all* pink," the Little Mermaid urges.

But they hush the moment Esther strikes a match. "I light the one in the center first because it's the *shamash*—the helper candle. See how it's higher than the others?"

"It's the boss," says a boy in fire-engine overalls.

"That's right. On the first night of Hanukkah, the *shamash* lights one candle. The next night, two. And so on, till the eighth night, when it lights all eight candles. Like this!" She wiggles it back into its holder and the menorah is fully alight. For a moment they gaze, as humans have always gazed, at flames which dart and shimmer, stolen from the gods.

Then Miss Tammy recovers. "So, how many candles would we need for the whole holiday? Anyone?"

"A million!" yells the fireman.

"Not quite," says Miss Tammy. "Let's count together." She holds up both hands, fingers spread.

"Ten!" shout the children.

"And?" She does it three more times. "Ten and ten and ten and ten make…anyone?"

"Ten!" yells the fireman.

"Not quite," sighs Miss Tammy. "They make forty. Plus this many." She holds up four fingers. "How many is that?"

"Forty-four!" shouts Molly, blushing with pride.

"Very good, Molly. Forty-four candles, boys and girls! Isn't that a lot of light?" Miss Tammy looks to Esther for endorsement, but Esther is busy watching the flames. Forty-four lights. She is forty, Molly—the child they weren't supposed to be able to have—is four, Owen is forty-four. What would the numerologists make of that? She feels hot.

Peeling off her suit jacket, she kneels on the rug. "When I was little, we decorated the whole house for Hanukkah. We made endless paper chains. Each person in the family had their own menorah and lit their own candles."

"Whoa!" says a World Champion Wrestler. "That's more than forty-four!"

"A lot more. When we lined them up in all the windows, they lit up the whole street." This is nearly fiction, but surely permissible under the circumstances. "And after we lit the candles and opened presents—" there is a brief yell for presents — "*then* we played dreidel."

She takes out one of the bright colored tops and spins it in the middle of the circle. The children burst out shouting when it falls: "Can I try? Can I try? Can *I* have a turn?"

Esther holds it up. "Do you know why we play with dreidels?"

"I know! I know!" Molly shouts, squirming in her seat.

Esther smiles. "Long ago there was a brave family called the Maccabees who lived in a land ruled by a wicked king. The king wanted everyone to do things *his* way all the time—"

"Just like Jeremy," one boy observes darkly.

"No sir! No sir!" cries another—Jeremy himself, no doubt.

"And this king wanted to take everything away that the Maccabees loved: their schools, their books, their language, even their children—everything that made them who they were. And he got away with it too, until a brave man named Judah Maccabee decided to fight."

"Was he a ninja?" asks a rather small boy.

"Yes, in a way. Now, Judah went to see all his friends to make plans to fight the king, but the king's spies were everywhere —" She drops her voice and the children lean forward. Even Miss Tammy leans forward. "So whenever anyone suspicious approached, they pulled out these little tops and pretended to be gambling. That's how they planned the rebellion, and we do it today so we'll never forget." It occurs to Esther that she has no idea whether any of this is true. But the children are waiting. "And you know what? Judah Maccabee and his little group of friends fought so hard and so smart that they beat the wicked old king with all his powerful armies!"

The children cheer. Someone's chair tips over.

"The good guys *always* win!" Molly announces, and no one corrects her.

So they spin the dreidels and pretend to gamble with the chocolate coins, and, thanks to Jeremy, invent a new game called Human Dreidel, which involves spinning across the floor and crashing into your friends. Miss Tammy has to clap numerous times to bring them to the table for Snack Time.

Esther perches on a tiny chair, munching a graham cracker and thinking about what she has not said. She has given them fantasy, not history. She has not told them why the candles are lit. She has not explained the oil, the eternal flame, the eight-day run, or the miracle. She has not mentioned God.

The candles burn down to nubs as the flames waver and the sky outside fades. It is time to go home. Time to see Owen and Jesse, climb into her sweatpants, help the children glue endless paper chains, grate potatoes for *latkes* she hopes will turn out less soggy than last year's. And for what? So Jesse and Molly will remember? So maybe someday they'll make soggy *latkes* and light menorahs for their own children? Tell a story that has no more substance than a fairy tale? So one more generation of Jews might know what they are, and what they are not? *What makes a Jew a Jew? He remembers.*

But why does it matter so much? Why cling to something whose tenets she doesn't believe in? *Because us freaks stick together*, she can hear Trudy say. Because five thousand years of persecution tend to cement a tribe, no matter what their internal arguments might be. Because she can't imagine herself as something else. Because if her children were raised something else—or *nothing*, like Owen—they would be strangers to her.

Yet that only gets you so far. Especially if you read history.

How much to *tell* them? How much to tell?

Other mothers are arriving, zipping their children into parkas, exclaiming over the gold coins, picking up the daily masterpiece from the Art Shelf. Esther, getting up to gather Molly's belongings, catches sight of the classroom reflected in the darkening windows. Phantom mothers and children going about the business of life. What would they say, these mothers, if she'd told their children that after receiving the Ten Commandments that both religions are based on, the Jews, fleeing Egypt and invading Canaan, had not just razed the city of Jericho but murdered every living thing there: man, woman, child, and animal. To show how fierce and merciless the invading horde would be, so all Canaanites would fall before them. Joshua fought the battle of Jericho and the walls came tumbling down, oh yes, but this wasn't quite how they taught it in Sunday School. This wasn't quite so different from a Nazi *aktion.*

What a shock that had been to discover. What macabre distortion it had given the traditional songs she'd been teaching the children: *Hanukkah, oh Hanukkah, come light the menorah/Let's have a party, we'll all dance the hora.* Dancing on blood, on bones. What other crimes, lies, propaganda lurk buried beneath the stories of wonders and miracles that are supposed to provide the basis for faith?

But does that not apply to all religions? She suspects a historian wouldn't have to dig very deep to discover the answer. There are bloody secrets that must be kept to preserve the status quo. Just as with governments. Just as with families.

Molly is tugging at her arm. She stoops, feeling her pantyhose rupture at last in a starburst of runs, and looks into the face of this miracle, her child. How much truth does she owe her? How much truth does she *know?*

"Mom!" Molly is saying. "If we put menorahs in every window, will they light up the street?"

Esther smooths the round baby cheek and gives her the lie, the beautiful lie, hoping that its very beauty, smug and irritating, will give her what she needs now and someday lead her down the broken path of history.

"Molly," she says, "they will light up the world."

A CUP OF KINDNESS

Although this story invents a different fate for Esther's parents than the next one, it's based on real events and takes a closer look at Esther's marriage than any other story so far, giving the reader a glimpse of the intimacy and comfort of an enduring relationship.
At least that's what I thought when I wrote it.

It's only nine o'clock and the children are wild. They've stretched a sleeping bag over the kitchen steps and piled cushions at the bottom. Jesse and Molly hold the bag taut at each end while the third child—Annabelle, their mutual best friend—takes a running leap and surfs it on her belly, landing in a screeching heap.

"Ow! Ow! It hurts!" she cries, giggling.

"Let *me* try!" Jesse yells.

"No, my turn, *my* turn!" Molly shrieks.

Esther and Owen, spying from the dining room, each clutch their own bellies: fifteen years of marriage and they're still in sync.

"'Ow, it hurts, let *me* try'?" Owen repeats, amazed. "I thought we had rational children."

"No children are rational," says Esther.

"*I* was a rational child. I built a clavichord."

"Yes, and look how you turned out."

They pick their way through the minefield of toys in the living room, staying out of sight so the children won't think they were spying. Not that the children are remotely aware of their presence: they have a full schedule of activities—drawn up by Molly, the family list-maker—planned for this, their very first New Year's Eve party. Esther has seen the list. It includes: "Getting undressed while jumping up and down," "Spying on parents," and "Eating snow." Other refreshments consist of Tootsie Roll pops dipped in chocolate syrup, Mountain Dew mixed with milk and chocolate syrup, and matzoh spread with chocolate syrup. And Esther has given them a bottle of sparkling grape juice with real wine glasses to drink from. "Now, no drinking and driving," she warned when she put it on ice.

"Just driving you crazy!" Molly cackled, seizing her from one side just as Jesse seized her from the other. They crushed her in the middle, chanting: "Group grope, group grope!" till she threatened them with the sprayer on the sink.

"Think they'll remember this party?" she asks Owen as they shut the bedroom door on the tumult below.

"What's to remember?" Owen stretches out on the bed with a groan. They both tend to groan these days: it's a middle-aged form of breathing. "They're screeching like alley cats, making a huge mess, stuffing themselves with junk, and refusing to go to sleep. No different from any other night."

Esther tosses him the remote. "I'll go check on Pop." Pop, short for Poppa, what he'd called his own father. What her children had always called him until her mother died and he became a *baal teshuva*--a master of return, a born-again Jew-- and insisted on the Yiddish *Zayde* instead.

Gil hears Esther on the stairs and catches a fragment of the children's joyous *tumel* below. He smiles, despite a pinch of disapproval. This New Year's Eve business is an arbitrary blip on an arbitrary calendar. Though Esther was raised in a modern Jewish home, they were observant. She knows that the real New Year comes in autumn, at the beginning of the month of Tishri. She knows it's a Day of Judgment, when the fate of every living creature is inscribed in the Book of Life, a time for examining your soul and taking stock of your actions—not this excuse for wild drunkenness, this defiant orgy at the start of winter.

"Pop?" She raps on the doorframe. "Dad?"

He puts down his book so she can see the title: *Pirke Avot: The Wisdom of the Fathers.*

"I came up to see if you needed anything," she says softly. He is wearing a *yarmulke* but looks like anybody's grandfather in every other respect. White hair. Glasses. The handsome cardigan she sent for his birthday. Maybe that, too, is a message.

He has been so subdued, so alone these last two years. Gloria was his queen and he was her court. When her heart suddenly stopped beating, his did too. Only it didn't, leaving him bewildered as well as bereft. For over a year the only people he wanted near him were his *minyan*, the men he goes to *daven* with each day. But now he has ventured out again to visit his children, to walk a little, to breathe the air.

He finally smiles and her shoulders ease. "I've got my tea," he says. "If I want something else, I'll get it." He pauses. "They're having fun?"

Encouraged enough to perch on the edge of the bed, she gives him a we're-all-adults-now grin. "We'll be lucky if the house is still standing in the morning."

Gil wants to say something about *Purim* or *Pesach*—both stories of escape—being more appropriate holidays for riotous celebration. But he holds his tongue. That's something the last twenty years have taught him. He has learned that in America families can be fragile things. In the old country, his parents' world, you were united against a common enemy. Here the opposing forces are more likely to come from within. Both children divorced (but, *Baruch ha-Shem*, remarried) and all that turbulence between Esther and her mother. Things only calmed down when her own children were born, and he, Gloria, and Esther learned to avoid any conversation that involved the words "religion" or "tradition." It's a fragile peace that they've kept going for ten years.

Of course things got a little tricky when he resumed the Orthodoxy of his childhood. It comforts him, but he tries to be accommodating: keeps everything in his suitcase when he comes to visit, eats off paper plates with plastic utensils in this non-kosher household, and performs the necessary rituals alone up here in the guest room. The family knows he won't turn on lights or ride in a car on the Sabbath; he knows not to expect Owen (let alone Jesse when he's of age) to join him for the morning prayer which thanks God for, among other things, not making them women. It's live and let live—far from ideal, but, unlike some of his Orthodox friends, he doesn't have to sit *shiva* for anyone still living, and he gets to see his grandchildren, those imps, and hear them call him *Zayde*. When they remember not to revert back to Pop.

"Well!" Now Esther feels silly for sitting on the bed. What's there to talk about? The past, when her mother was alive? The heartache they gave each other over what kind of daughter Gloria wanted versus what kind of person Esther turned out to be?

She looks at her father in his sweater and neat skullcap. Each time he visits he seems smaller. Maybe they don't need to talk. Maybe it's enough just to have him here, to know he's in the room at the top of the stairs, that her children have the chance to know him.

"Okay then, Dad." She gives him a kiss. "I'll say good night." She knows better than to say "Happy new year."

She shuts his door and stands a moment, remembering the times she sneaked out of her parents' house, defying curfew in pursuit of adventure, especially a thrilling New Year's Eve. Part of it had to do with impressing her friends, the rest with a superstitious belief that as went the Eve, so went the year. But though she pursued it relentlessly, this ideal New Year's Eve always fell short. One boyfriend actually broke up with her at midnight. Even after she met Owen, their New Year's Eves usually consisted of staying in and ordering out. The main difference was that back then they could manage to keep awake until the ball dropped and the world erupted in song.

And in fact, though it's scarcely ten as she comes down the stairs, there's singing already. The children are practicing. She holds open the bedroom door so Owen can hear:

Should old containers
be unlocked
so we drink up all the wine?
We'll take a couple
aspirin then,
and wake up feeling fine!

"Should what?" Owen says, shutting off the Food Channel and struggling up against the pillows.

"They're making up their own words. Didn't you ever do that as a kid? You know: *Jingle bells/Santa smells*…that sort of thing."

"We only listened to classical music."

"Even in school?"

"You know what kind of schools I went to."

She does: the choicest private schools, from kindergarten on. His parents, particularly his father, had the highest ambitions for him—until he dropped out of Harvard, joined one of the radical groups that sprang up like fungi in those days, and moved to Georgia to help mobilize the working class. Getting the crap beat out of him by machinists who weren't interested in the Revolution was the first step on what would prove to be a long journey back to reality. Too bad his father didn't live to welcome him home. Too bad they never got to talk it out. Esther knows how big a hole it left in Owen—one reason why they're raising their own children so differently.

She stretches out beside him with only a little groan. It's good to lie down, to stop thinking, stop doing. To hold Owen's hand. To float with him on the big bed as if it were a raft. To listen to their life.

The children have broken out the noisemakers already, which means they've also found the glittery top hats and the bag of colored popcorn she bought instead of confetti, hoping more of it would end up in their bellies than stomped into the rug.

The bed is a raft and the house is a ship, with her father out of sight but not out of reach at the top of the stairs, and the children below, boiling with energy, making the ship go, and Owen and Esther in the middle: steering, watching, listening.

The children sing again, louder. They crave an audience. What will they say about their own parents when they are grown?

"Hear that?" she says. "*A couple aspirin* instead of *a cup of kindness*. There's our brave new world."

"Then they'll need lots of courage." Owen says, his voice thick with sleep. "Lots of aspirin too." He draws the quilt over both of them. "But they don't have to do it alone."

"I know, they have us. And Dad."

"And Google." He snaps off the light.

"What time is it?" she murmurs.

"Almost eleven."

"We'll never make it."

"It'll still be New Year's in the morning."

There is a fresh wave of whoops from downstairs, then the song again. *They'll* make it, Esther wants to tell him, smiling as she drifts: they'll be counting down each second until the new year, the new era, the new age. They'll be up until it's tomorrow. But she is asleep now, and the house sails on.

FOOL AT THE FEAST

This story is the capstone of the collection. It was the last story I wrote about my "old" family—my family of origin—and it pretty much says what I needed to say. And anything I may have left out is covered by the story-within-the-story, "Blood and Milk." Some characters in these two stories are composites, some drawn strictly from life. Nearly all events in "Fool" are factual, while the central event in "Blood" is invented, but both stories are honest. I think what distinguishes them from the other original-family stories is Esther's ability, finally, to move past the bad memories of childhood—not forgetting them, certainly, but putting them aside. Writing the stories did that for me and made a new relationship with my parents possible. My mother and I made peace without ever talking about it, without a big catharsis, without even acknowledging the trauma and damage. I found to my surprise that I did not need to say these things to her, because I had already said them here.

> *Better a fool at the feast than a wit at the fray.*
> Sir Walter Scott, *Ivanhoe*

"Hi! Hi! Good to see you!" I wave at the couple in the hall as the elevator doors close.

"Who were they?" Trudy asks.

"No clue. Best assume we're related to everyone in the hotel."

The doors open in the lobby on a massive group of Sappersteins clumping like a colony of giant protozoans.

We have gathered for a great event many months in the making: my parents' fiftieth anniversary party, to be held at their elegant country club, the one that used to blackball Jews. Everyone is clutching the Hospitality Bags we received at check-in, which my mother decorated with gold glitter and bows and stuffed with candy, chips, cheese crackers, safety pins, stain remover, bubblegum, breath spray, peanuts, refrigerator magnets, pencil sharpeners, beef jerky, soap bubbles, and a jump-rope. Everyone has received the same bag, even Great-Aunt Dora, who takes tiny steps within the cage of her walker, obese diabetic Cousin Roz, and Uncle Shlomo, who keeps so kosher that he takes a box of matzoh and rebbe-certified peanut butter with him whenever he leaves the house —you never know when you could be stranded in a snowstorm and forced to live on *traif* from vending machines.

"Esther, *mommeleh!*" Roz, known in family vernacular as The Planet, tackles me as Trudy slips away. I am engulfed in a cloud of Opium as Roz, Aunt Honey, and the twins Mira and Shira all pile on. Hugs, shrieks, clanking bracelets, lipsticky kisses, someone's earring caught in my hair, *hello, hello, it's been so long, how* are *you, mommeleh?* Why are they so excited, why all the yelling? They're glad to see *me?* Despite my capacity for self-delusion (something Trudy constantly points out), I know they're screeching because I'm Gil and Gloria's daughter: I swing from a branch of the family tree, linked to them by a ribbon of nucleic acid. That's what "family" must mean. Because if it means those who know you, those whose intimacy is based on *understanding,* then the only people you could say I'm related to would be Trudy and Owen. Jesse and Molly too, I hope, as they grow.

But family—mine, at least—is based on ritual, not understanding. Bar mitzvahs, weddings, funerals, circumcisions, seders, and feasts. And once in a while something more august, in need of many more appetizers and desserts, such as this fiftieth anniversary party.

The chartered bus arrives to take us to my parents' house for a "little welcoming get-together," as my mother puts it. The real party will be tomorrow at the country club. But the guests know my mother: sensing an imminent and spectacular feed, they surge forward. I spot Owen, his face ruddy from wiped-off kisses, and the children, racing from aunt to aunt, begging for treasures from their Hospitality Bags. Molly wants the candy and toys—no surprise there—but Jesse is avid for the little rings of safety pins. He has some project in mind: I will have to keep my eye on him.

"How you holding up, Beaut?" Owen says when I reach him. "Beaut," shortened from "Beautiful," is what he's called me ever since we first started courting. Any claim to beauty I once had has long departed, thanks to twelve years, two children, and constant proximity of bread crusts and cookies, but the fact that he still calls me by this name is one of my sweetest consolations. I take his hand as we line up. The children, lords of the school bus, have already swaggered on board to sit independently, watching us clumsy adults with undisguised condescension and glee. Molly breaks form long enough to grab me as I pass, and I cup her plump cheek. It feels just like it did when she was a baby, scarcely a minute ago. I locate Jesse giggling in the back with Roz, then sit down beside Owen, still holding his hand. The thing about love is it gives you so much to lose.

At my parents' house the spread is laid: stuffed cabbage, stuffed kishke, stuffed capon; brisket and herring and a whole salmon steamed to perfection in the dishwasher; kugels, knishes, kneidlach, and an entire table of vegetables and molded salads. And that's not counting dessert or the special dishes made for Uncle Shlomo and The Planet.

"My buttons are popping already," Trudy says as we wedge ourselves onto the bottom step, plates on our knees. Owen has escaped to the basement under the pretext of overseeing the children's table. I well remember my own exile at that table, listening to the adults chatter above, wondering what it was like to live in the world as a grown-up. I thought they must all be free of the restrictions, threats, and corrections which burden a child's life, but none of the grown-ups I know seem unburdened. None seem to savor their freedom. And now that I am entitled to sit upstairs, I listen for the shouts of my own children below, wondering how we seem to them.

"You know what my problem is?" I ask Trudy. "When we were young, I felt like I was impersonating a kid, and now I feel like I'm impersonating a grown-up."

"That's a symptom, not a problem," Trudy says, then points with her fork. "*That* is a problem." She is watching my mother migrate from group to group, urging everyone to take more and basking in their praise. "She made enough food to feed the neighborhood."

"She *is* feeding the neighborhood. She books space in the neighbors' refrigerators, so she has to invite them. So," I add with a tiny thrill of triumph, "you agree my mother is a problem?"

"Nice try," she says. "The problem is what's between the two of you."

So I tell her about one Hanukkah when they drove all the way from Ohio with four cartons of presents for Jesse and Molly. "Except most of them weren't really presents—they were things like batteries, boxes of Jello, bubblegum, pencils."

Trudy nods. "Hospitality bags."

"All wrapped individually to make it seem like a lot. I mean, the children don't *need* four cartons of presents, but they were bewildered when they opened one and it was a box of Jello. Their expectations got raised too high—it wasn't good for them."

"And of course you sat your mother down and explained all of this."

"Before we could even open anything, we had to heap them all on the dining room table so she could tape it—the treasure, the abundance. She wanted to revel in it a little longer, and she wanted documentation. Everyone who saw the tape would see *her*—her stylishness, her munificence. Lady Bountiful meets Auntie Mame."

That was the year Hanukkah started on Jesse's birthday, so the next afternoon we had a party. The birthday project, decorate-your-own-sweatshirt-with-glitter-paint, was a complete bust: the paint came out in huge globs that never dried and the tubes emptied instantaneously. The whole project took three minutes, and I'm still scraping glitter off my kitchen floor. Then my mother, who taped it all, insisted we sit down and watch the tape so everyone could be bored twice. After the guests left and we cleaned up the mess, with Molly fussing and Jesse so wired he'd be up till midnight, my mother—who had stocked the kitchen with $90 of delicatessen food, including four racks of baby back ribs she'd personally doctored—said in a tone of deep concern that I looked tired, so maybe she and Daddy ought to Just Go Now. This was a bogus offer, of course—we hadn't had dinner or lit the Hanukkah candles, and they'd driven eight hours to see us. What she really meant was I wasn't showing adequate gratitude, enthusiasm, and appreciation. Of course no one could ever appreciate her sufficiently, though my father has spent his life trying. So when she offered to go, I just said: "No, no." But she acted like she hadn't heard me: she repeated what she'd said, and again I replied: "No, no." But, incredibly, she just kept talking, more of the same, right through my reply until I heard myself shout: "*I said no!*"

The words hung in the air like a dialogue balloon, and for a moment everyone froze. Then my mother stiffened and withdrew, the embodiment of wounded dignity, and observed quietly that they would leave whenever I wished (as if I were trying to hustle them out the door, as if the point weren't *not* leaving).

"Well now," says Trudy, turning her wide-eyed gaze on me. "How do you think you got in that jam in the first place?"

I steel myself. "What do you mean?"

"Why do four-year-olds need to decorate glitter-shirts? Why isn't Musical Chairs good enough? Why did they get to take home the shirt, plus a prize, plus a goody bag, plus a balloon? Why did there have to be a whole canopy of streamers and balloons?"

I sigh. "Oh. Because I'm just like my mother?"

"Well, your mother wouldn't have made that admission. But you engineered the excess. You set up the kind of situation she's used to dominating. You collaborated. What did you expect?" She points the fork at me. "You and your mother have these little skirmishes in order to avoid a holocaust."

She returns to her blintzes looking pleased with herself, but she's right. I am like my mother. When I shouted *"I said no!"* I instantly recalled shouting at Jesse that same morning. I'd sworn never to bully and terrify my children, but I yell at them more than I can bear to think, and my hand is too ready to smack. I'm good at restraining it, but the impulse is there, my temper always verging on out-of-control.

From where we sit, I can see my mother taking more cheesecake out of the refrigerator, and I remember the day my father brought home a calendar with a woman's face on the cover and hung it up there. When I came in, he pointed to the face and said: "Who does this remind you of?"

I said: "Sophia Loren?" It looked like Sophia Loren.

He said: "No-o-o," in an encouraging way, and I got it.

"Mom?" I said.

He turned to my mother. "What did I tell you?" His pleasure was untarnished by the fact that I had obviously inferred the correct answer from him.

It was also in this kitchen that I met Janie, our babysitter. My mother was interviewing her when I came racing in to ask for waxed paper to make the sliding board more slippery. She introduced us, and I—why did I do this? —took Janie's hand, kissed it, and said something like *"Enchanté."* My mother laughed, which surprised me: normally she didn't find me amusing, but perhaps she laughed because Janie was there to provide an audience. I recall it now with mortification. Why did I do things like that?

Trudy grins. Oh. Same reason. My mother taught me both things: extravagant rage and extravagant pretense.

"Are you this smug with all your patients?" I ask Trudy.

"No, no, infinitely smugger with patients who actually pay." She touches the tines of her fork to my arm—an old game.

"Stop," I say, but fork her back.

Down in the basement the children's shouts escalate as ping-pong turns into wall-ball, where, with a paddle in each hand, you hit as many ping-pong balls as possible off all four walls simultaneously. That means my brother Jonathan is down there, because he invented the game and holds the title of Grand Master. Owen is still downstairs too, probably nursing a glass of syrupy wine, as oblivious to the balls whizzing around him as a nucleus bombarded with atoms. No doubt he is contemplating his article on the new theory that the shape of the universe resembles a potato chip—the curved ones that come stacked in a can. He's frustrated because his models keep disappearing, especially when the children are around. When Roz heard about it, she shouted in that big raspy voice: "Hey Owen! Is the universe Flavorful Ranch or Sour Cream and Chives?" Owen just smiled. He has a wonderful capacity to go away.

There's another shriek of laughter from below, and I nudge Trudy. "Come on. Let's go work off the blintzes."

But as we get up my mother dings her little bell, the kind used to summon bellhops. The Planet has something to present to my parents: a memory book full of old photos and typed reminiscences that friends and relatives have sent at her request. My mother acts so surprised—one hand actually laid over her heart—that I know she got wind of it somehow. My father looks on as she turns the massive pages, reading aloud in her best Lady Narrator voice about visits and vacations, births and bar mitzvahs, unions and reunions, and many a catered affair. In tones of hushed modesty, my mother reads praise for her party favors, her towering pyramids of sugared fruit, her lifelike chopped liver sculptures. My father beams but doesn't get into the act until they come to the letter written by his brother Mel, the family jokester, and, at 6'3", the Big Guy, like Jonathan, like Jesse will one day be.

Mel's letter is about playing football on the streets of Pittsburgh, about the time their ball broke the window of the kosher butcher on the corner. "It smashed through the glass and landed smack on the counter where he was plucking chickens," the letter says, "and he came roaring after us with a cleaver in his hand. My legs were twice as long as Gil's, but somehow he beat me home. I scrambled under my parents' bed and had to say 'Move over!' because he was already there!"

Over the laughter my uncle cries: "It wasn't just the window, you understand—it was that *pigskin* landing in the middle of a kosher shop. He had to scrub the place down with boiling water and take a blowtorch to the oven under rabbinical supervision!"

My father is weeping with laughter, clutching his brother's arm. The only times I've seen him laugh with such abandon were when he watched old Jerry Lewis or Danny Kaye movies with my brother and me. But I've never seen the mischievous ten-year-old in him. Even in photos as a child he looks somber, responsible: the son who supports his mother and sister when Mel runs off and gets married, the young man who fights in France while Mel spends the war safely at the naval base in Norfolk.

"Did you know my dad wanted to be a doctor?" I ask Trudy.

"When was this?"

"After the war. He wanted to go to school on the G.I. Bill and become a pediatrician."

"He would have made a good one. What happened?"

"He met my mother. Ten days after he got out of the army."

For the last fifty years my father has been in carpets and flooring. He started as a salesman and eventually bought the business. When he met my mother, he was still supporting his own mother and sister. Mel contributed almost nothing to their upkeep, but that, of course, is not something we discuss. Nor do we mention how Mel cheated my father out of his share of the small carpet business they started together, which forced my parents to move to Ohio and start over. My father seems to harbor no grudges: is this goodness or denial?

"I wish I could have known him back then," I murmur. "Both of them. I wish I could have *met* them."

"Your presence might have been awkward to explain."

I nudge her and she nudges me back, but I am watching my father wipe his eyes and clean his glasses with his handkerchief, the spotless white handkerchief I have never known him to be without, often used to dry my own tears, for I had a very damp childhood. I am remembering something my mother said when she asked me to give the toast tomorrow. To prepare, I'd sent them each a list of questions about their early days together. In reply, she told me that my father, who never talked about his war experience, had sworn that if there were ever another war, he would run away to Mexico to live in a cave. He'd also said that he hated the army uniform and would never wear a tie again, and indeed wore open-necked shirts the whole time they were courting, which, my mother said, simply wasn't done in those days and elicited many a disapproving look. My father, Mr. Responsibility, who took care of his mother and sister (and his sister's family) all his life, who was twenty minutes early for every appointment, and who has spent the last fifty years in a suit and tie.

My mother said when they came back from their honeymoon—a weekend in a local motel—they had $60 between them and were $300 in debt for their bedroom set; they lived in a third-floor walk-up and shared a bathroom with a family on the second floor; there was no refrigerator, but in winter they would feast on ice cream kept on the ledge outside the window; and when her own parents finally came to visit, they were so appalled that they swore never to come again and didn't. When I think of my parents in those days —young, ready for anything (imagine my father even *talking* about running off to live in a cave), just starting their great adventure together, everything still ahead of them—I get an ache I don't entirely understand, an ache that gets muddied and mixed up when I listen to my mother now, taking over again, reading tributes to herself aloud in her over-animated, over-enunciated manner, then punctuating each one with a health update on the sender: "Oh, he's been so terribly ill this year with pancreatic cancer," or Parkinson's, or Alzheimer's, or prostate surgery, until The Planet says plaintively: "Aunt Gloria, don't you know anyone who's healthy?"

With this mild insurrection the party begins to break up, people standing and stretching, starting their own conversations, or ambling over to the buffet for more dessert. Reluctantly, my mother closes the memory book, and my father, always tuned to her frequency, leans over to say they will take it to the party tomorrow, put it on display, make an announcement that anyone who wishes may come and read. My mother, who would rather do the reading herself, under a spotlight and in front of a microphone, nods and smiles bravely. After all, having people know how much you're loved by other people is better than not having them know, even if you can't tell them yourself.

Trudy disappears. I go in search of my own small tribe.

And before you know it, we're all back at the house eating again, this time a huge breakfast buffet. I could easily consume my weight in my mother's sticky buns, for which I feel more frenzied lust than I've ever felt for any man. When we stagger away from the table, a whole day stretches in front of us, nearly seven hours until we gather at the country club. Trudy, wearing a T-shirt that says *Let's Put The Fun Back In Dysfunctional*, heads upstairs to take a nap on my old bed. But

Owen and I have two restless children to entertain. What is there to do?

We drive around and show them landmarks of my youth, which they're too young to care about and which don't actually exist anymore. Here's dear old Stutzman Elementary, where Mama was paddled for whispering by Miss Horoff in fourth grade and praised for her vocabulary by Mr. Wancey in fifth. Except that Stutzman Elementary has been turned into a warren of Borough Administration offices, and the playground where I tried desperately to make myself invisible is now a parking lot. Next is Westmont Middle School, whose mild sandblasted facade suggests nothing of the terrors it held when it was still Westmont Junior High, where I walked the gauntlet each morning as Rose Pagano and her fellow thugs ridiculed and pursued me. Nor can you see anything of the old Corner Store across the street which sold long penny pretzels for an actual penny. Now it's a Hess's Mini-Mart. I am not, however, sentimental about the past. The Corner Store may have disappeared, but so did Rose Pagano.

Eventually we wander back to the hotel, where the children take the sheets off the bed and make a tent with the hoarded safety pins. Owen lies on the bare mattress, hands linked beneath his head, thinking about the shape of the universe. I want to ask if he'll let me choose his tie tonight, if he'll polish his shoes and clip the two little hairs that stick out of his nose and spoil his classic profile, but I can't afford to alienate him. Other than Trudy, he's my only ally, the one person who knows me.

Finally Owen takes the children down to the pool. Since I don't appear in public or anywhere else in a bathing suit, I stay behind with Trudy. We drag pillows and a giant bottle of Diet Pepsi into the children's tent and recline in luxury.

"So, *girlchikl*," Trudy begins. "What are you wearing?"

She means to the party. My mother would like to see all the women in evening gowns, all the men in white tie and tails, and the children in miniature versions of each. "You're the mind-reader," I say. "You tell me."

"Plain black dress, knee-length. Black sandals with chunky heels, and handmade silver-amethyst earrings that set your dad back fifty bucks."

Of course she knows I use my father's credit card to buy my clothes and the children's clothes, things for the house, even some groceries. He gave me the card when I left for college: it has my name on front, though the bills go to him. I don't want to think about how much they add up to. At first the card was only for emergencies, and I rarely used it. Then I started using it for essential items, like a new winter coat. Eventually, as my body kept expanding and contracting, I used it to buy all my clothes. And now the children grow so fast and have so many needs. Owen is rather austere when it comes to things like silver-and-amethyst earrings, but my father never mentions how much I'm spending, though it's steadily increased over the years. He always sends me a new card when the old one expires. Jonathan, once his broker, says Dad's in good shape and I shouldn't feel guilty. I tell myself he wouldn't let me have it if it were a burden. I tell myself I'm spending my inheritance now, when we need it most. I tell myself I'm not a loathsome parasitic deadbeat who's never grown up.

"*Anyway*," I say, "can you guess what my mother's wearing?"

"Let's see. Got to be gold. Floor-length, though she passed reluctantly on the cathedral train and tiara. Sequins, though, definitely. And earrings down to her shoulders."

"You nailed it."

"Size two," she adds. "Or maybe zero."

I take a moody swig of Diet Pepsi. My mother, who used to be *zaftig*, has worn tiny sizes ever since she injured her back and had to start wearing a heavy brace that zips, laces, and hooks. The doctors warned that any excess weight would do further damage, so she whittled herself down by following first the all-protein, then the all-fat diet. Those were not happy years in our house, but the weight came off and stayed off. It took me ages to realize that the way she managed this, in light of her gargantuan appetite, was by throwing up after dinner every night. I heard her sometimes, of course, and saw weird stuff floating in the toilet, but attributed that to the family myth of Mom's "nervous stomach." It wasn't until a family dinner at an expensive restaurant, when my mother excused herself to go to the Ladies' Room, that I intercepted a glance between my cousin and her husband, heard him murmur: "It's such a waste to buy her dinner," and realized what most of the family had known all along. Even my father was in on it, I discovered, as I watched him fix a glass of iced tea the way she liked it—squeeze of lemon, packet of sweetener, straw—to slide across the table when she sat back down, a little smeary-eyed and moist, but trim as ever.

As for me, I've been an eight and I've been an eighteen. ("Not *been*," Trudy interrupts. "*Worn*. You are not your dress size.") The dress I'll be wearing tonight, if the sticky buns permit, is a ten. I chose black not just because it's slimming but because it's severe—I'll feel less like an idiot when I get up there to sing The Family Song With Accompanying Hand Motions.

Trudy grins. "Oh no. Hand motions?"

Oh yes. The Family Song is largely a figment of my mother's imagination—she wants to belong to the kind of family that *has* a song, so she arbitrarily chose the silly old cowboy tune my father sometimes sang when we were little. It has lines like: "I'll be hanged if they're gonna hang me: *beep beep!* Why, I'll sue the penitentiary: *beep beep!*" The song has no inherent relevance (don't rob mail trains? don't get lynched?) and little personal significance. My father sang it sometimes on car trips. Jonathan and I liked chiming in on the "*beep beeps.*" This hardly makes it the Sapperstein Anthem. It would make more sense if we learned "their" song— "To Each His Own"—and sang it safely from our seats while they danced. But my mother requires massive public testimonials, so we'll have to pin on the toy sheriff's badges and stand up there in front of everyone and sing the song with hand motions.

"Show me," Trudy demands, so I demonstrate, feeling like

one of the Supremes. When I "flash my badge" I could just as well be singing "Stop! In The Name Of Love!"—which, come to think of it, would make a more relevant anthem. I hitch my thumbs under suspenders, pull train whistles, and point guns. Trudy never stops laughing.

"Oh, the aunts, the aunts," she says finally, wiping her eyes. "Gloria is priceless."

"Glad you're amused."

"I'm not minimizing your struggle. I'm saying it's part of something bigger. Look at her sisters. Goldie is her biggest fan —your mother can do no wrong by her, thus she never runs the risk of incurring her wrath. Honey never stops talking, I mean never. Even if she has nothing to say, she'll repeat what you just said in case anybody missed it the first time around. If you're in the car, she'll read aloud every street sign, every billboard, every bumper sticker she sees. Lois says "Uh-huh" to everything everyone says. Your husband could be calculating the shape of the cosmos and she'd be agreeing with every word that came out of his mouth. Faye worries about everything. She's worried that if Joshie doesn't keep his grades up, he won't be a National Merit Scholar, and he won't get into a good college, and he won't find a decent job, and all the money the family spent on his education will be wasted—Joshie is eight years old! This is nuts, Esther, this is very, very nuts."

"Is that a clinical diagnosis?"

"You bet. And your mother cannot be challenged no matter what. There is no talking to her: there is only agreeing, flattering, and seeking her expertise. Control and power are the underlying issues for them all. Faye and Gloria compete for it; Honey never had any, so she talks to make herself look involved; Lois and Goldie don't want it, so they agree with everyone."

I take another swig from the bottle. "Maybe I should share those views tonight."

Trudy grins. "You'd be a smash."

"I'll have to *get* smashed to give that toast. You know

what I'm like in front of an audience. Remember my toast at Jonathan's wedding?"

"Everyone remembers that, which is why you'd better not get smashed tonight."

I'd burst into tears and babbled about my baby brother and had to be led from the room by my solicitous first husband, who was only too glad to make his escape, both from the room and from the family. In the end it scarcely mattered, since Jonathan's wedding lasted longer than his marriage.

Tonight is different. Tonight is about the past, not the future. A marriage, not a wedding. And it will be me standing alone in front of three hundred people—my parents' friends, family, and business associates, including a boy I had a crush on in high school who is now a state senator with an eye on the governor's mansion—trying to summon the kind of language equal to the occasion, the kind of language people expect, without choking on my own bullshit.

"It's got to be either bald truth or bullshit?" Trudy asks. "No points in between?"

"No, there are points, I found points," I say. "Taking that course helped."

Last spring, at Trudy's suggestion, I took an adult ed course: "Writing Your Family History." That gave me the notion to interview my parents separately about how they met and what their first impressions were. Instead of grand words of praise, I wanted to reconstruct a moment, perhaps *the* moment, when a chance meeting turned into something else and our history began.

But what happened on those Tuesday nights when I put a casserole in the oven and left as soon as Owen got home, driving into town with all the traffic coming the other way, seemed bigger than that. Our final assignment was to write a five-page scene between two family members. What I had in mind was a skirmish between mother and daughter. What came out of my pen was more like—what was the word Trudy used? —a holocaust. Thirty-eight pages worth. I called it *Blood and Milk.*

"Okay, Scheherazade." Trudy settles against the pillows. "Let's hear it."

"All thirty-eight pages?"

"You know you want to."

I get my notebook and another liter of Diet Pepsi and scramble back into the tent.

Blood and Milk

...only a motion away

—Paul Simon,

Mother and Child Reunion

I am in the middle of childbirth, rocking frantically in the chair, commanding Gordon to rock me, accusing him of not rocking hard enough and of smelling like meatloaf besides— when my mother, critical, demanding, a hypochondriac who hates doctors, enters a hospital five states away with stomach pain. I am hooked up to a fetal monitor, twisting my feet in rapid circles to get through contractions while the nurses urge me to go limp, go with it, go with the pain, till I use up precious breath shouting "Fuck off!"—when the surgeon opens her up and finds that she is full of cancer. I am hyperventilating, trying not to push, using every ounce of effort I can dredge up, spitting raspberries instead of genteelly blowing feathers, my body bearing down anyway all by itself, weird grunts escaping me, Gordon and the nurses shouting "Don't push! Don't push!"— when they wheel my mother into Recovery and wait for her to wake up. Later Gordon swears I howled like a dog. And I am reaching down between my legs and hauling the baby onto my belly like a slippery exhausted fish, kissing its slimy head, when the worried Recovery Room nurse calls my mother's surgeon back in. I ask my OB: "Is it a boy or a girl?" and he replies, deadpan: "I wouldn't know. It's the father's job to check." So Gordon lifts the tiny bottom and says: "It's a girl!" and, like biblical Sarah, I laugh and laugh. This is my last baby, and after two boys, my longing for a daughter is ferocious. When my mother's surgeon finally tracks us down, Gordon takes the call. I am holding the baby, nudging her lips with my nipple, murmuring to let her know she's safe, and I scarcely notice his hurried conference with my OB in the hall. Later he says the doctor told him not to upset me, because it might affect the milk.

"Whoa," Trudy interrupts. "The mother goes into the hospital with stomach pain and they find out she's full of *cancer*? No clue before that?"

"It happens," I say irritably. "Anyway, this is fiction."

"Is it? I thought it was history. Go on."

I can't sleep at all that night. The baby sleeps, but I trade war stories with the nurses who come to check on us until even they tell me to be quiet and get some rest. But it's no use. After the baby nurses again—no problems so far—I simply hold her, thinking tiny velvet dresses and pinafores, thinking French braids and girl-talk, thinking now I have a chance to get it right.

It's not until Gordon brings us home, until Max and Toby are jostling to get right in the baby's face and see if she looks more like ET or Yoda, that I learn my mother is lying in a hospital bed "in a coma-like state," as her doctor says when I finally get him on the phone. It appears that the anesthesia weakened her already depressed system, which is why she hasn't woken up. He cannot say if or when she will.

"Have you started treatment for the cancer?" I ask.

He doesn't hesitate. "At this point, there's little we can do except make her comfortable." It's evidently an answer he's given hundreds of times.

I put my coat back on. "Call the airport," I tell Gordon. "I have to go."

"You can't go," he says. "You just had a baby."

"I have to go." My older brother Nathan is in Zurich on bank business. My younger brother Ronnie just got a job after sixteen

wretched months of unemployment—he can't ask for a leave of absence now. My father's been dead for five years. I have two aunts, both in nursing homes. I have to go.

"Pretty slick," says Trudy. "You deactivate or disarm everyone else in the family, leaving only yourself in a position of power." She waves me on.

"Sandy can go," Gordon says.
"Sandy's the daughter-in-law. I'm the daughter."
"Then we'll come with you."
"No, the boys would be miserable. I'll be okay. I'll just stay with her till Nathan gets home or she dies, whichever comes first."
Gordon looks worried. He's thinking that I haven't grasped the situation, that I'm delusional again. It's true that after each of the boys was born I underwent a mild psychosis—a few hallucinations, a little paranoia, some irrational thought patterns. No big deal. It goes away when you start getting some sleep and your hormones settle down. There's nothing I haven't grasped. My mother is dying.

As I step off the elevator, my stitches give a giant throb of recognition. The body has its own memory: this hospital smells exactly like the one I just left. On this floor, though, the rooms are dim and quiet. No TV, no infants wailing, no boisterous visitors bringing flowers and balloons. The last time I visited an oncology floor was ten years ago, when Pinky died. She was my mother's closest friend. There was nothing pink about her at the end.
My mother's room is also dim and quiet. Our nurse escort bustles right in, but I pause at the door. There she lies in her coma-like state with surprisingly little equipment—only an IV and a call button lying within reach atop the crisp sheet. The other bed is empty.
"She breathes by herself, but sometimes it's irregular," says

the nurse, taking my mother's pulse.

I take Emmy out of the carrier and lift her warm sleepy weight to my shoulder so I can touch my lips to her head. I have not seen my mother for two years. Her grand curly pouf of silver hair has gone yellow and flat. Her face sags without its usual animation.

"She's still wearing her hearing aids," I say, though I didn't know she had two of them until now.

"Oh yes, talk to her. They say hearing is the last to go." She wipes my mother's mouth with a damp sponge and smooths on some lip balm. "There. Now I'll leave you two alone."

"There's three of us," I say after the door has closed.

It takes me a while to approach the bed. "Mother? It's Isabel. I had the baby—a girl this time. We named her Emma. Emmy."

She probably wouldn't remember the doll I had when I was young. It looked like a real baby, with rubber skin that was soft and warm. I called her Emmy because when I rocked her at night, crooning her name, I thought that was the sound of love itself.

"Me," says Trudy.

I look up. "What?"

"Me, me, me. That's what you were crooning. 'Em-me-me-me, Em-me-me-me.' That's what the sound of love was for you."

"So I'm just a narcissistic whiner?"

"Well, you were also a child who didn't feel adequately loved. Go on."

I pull up the chair, using a pillow from the empty bed to cushion my stitches. Emmy stirs against my shoulder, looking for the nipple in her sleep. My breast throbs in response, a painful throb which makes me nervous. I had a lot of trouble nursing Max. The week he was born was surreal—I went seventy-two hours without sleep. I was a wreck, life was something out of a Dali painting, but try as I might I could not sleep. When I closed my eyes I would see the baby's face looming gigantically before me, or I would think Gordon was handing him to me, even though both were asleep beside me in bed. I had constant flutters in my stomach as if I were about to go onstage.

Part of the problem was that nursing had become such a struggle. The baby screamed, turned red, screwed up his face, whipped his head frantically from side to side. I kept trying to stuff my nipple in his mouth, but he simply wouldn't take it or he'd spit it out a moment later. Then he'd whimper piteously. I wanted so much to make it work, to nourish my child with my body—it seemed like the essential act of mother love, surely what little girls yearn for when they instinctively clutch their dolls to their chests. But the baby was starving, he was dehydrated, this couldn't go on. So I gave up and put him on formula. With the very first bottle, he was transformed. He made contented noises while he sucked, swallowed rhythmically, nodded off like a tiny junkie.

I tried again with Toby, but—as if competing with Max already—he was even worse, and I gave up sooner. But I still have hopes for Emmy. Being a girl might make a difference. My milk has come in right on schedule, and she is snuffling a little, scrubbing her face against me. Soon.

"The boys are fine," I say aloud. "But so competitive. They fight over who answers the phone, who goes through the door first, who gets which hanger to hang up his coat. Once I found Toby crying his heart out, and when I finally got him to tell me why, he said: 'I'll never be older than Max, never!'"

Emmy gives a tiny grunt.

"Max says some funny things too. Apparently he thinks there's some correlation between age and bra size, because when we were walking through the lingerie department at Sears, he pointed to a bra and said—at the top of his voice— 'Look, Mom, forty-two: that's your size!' And the whole store turned around to get a look at this size forty-two."

Emmy is fussing now, a series of tiny hacks with much internalized agitation. She isn't used to making noise yet. I settle her in the crook of my arm, open my shirt and help her latch on the way the nurses showed me. There's a sharp pain as she starts to suck, but it subsides. Her eyes close again, her hands make little fists as she swallows.

"Look," I say softly so she won't startle. "Look, it's working."

But no one's there to look. Gordon's missing this—I've deprived him of the first few days of his baby's life. But what else could I do? I know what's expected of daughters.

Halfway through, I stop to change her diaper. She's still full of meconium, the tarry residue from my own intestines. When her body finishes clearing that out and her umbilical stub falls off, we will finally and irrevocably be two separate people. I pat her, but she doesn't want to burp; her head lolls drunkenly against me.

"Not yet, little miss," I croon. "Emmy..."

Then I jump out of my skin when I hear my mother's voice—at a tenth of her power but unmistakably her voice—say in exactly the same crooning tone: "Pinky..."

I spin around, clutching the baby. My mother looks unchanged, but she has definitely spoken. It sounded like a greeting.

"Wait. Who's the extra brother?" Trudy interrupts.

"What?"

"Ronnie is obviously Jonathan. So who's this Nathan guy? What's he doing there?"

"I wanted her new family to mirror her old family: two boys and a girl, so you can sort of see one superimposed on the other. You know: the past doesn't stay put."

"I've heard that," she says dryly. "So why a banker?"

"Because if I had an older brother, that's what he'd be. Successful, driven, independent."

"Everything you're not, in other words." She waves me on.

In the dark I am jerked awake by the feeling that someone has sat down on the bed. The luminous face of my watch tells me

I've slept an hour. Emmy, swaddled and capped, sleeps in the curve of my arm. My mother lies unmoving, barely a bump beneath the blanket. How can she be so diminished? She was the terror of my childhood. I was not the daughter she'd had in mind—I was dumpy, with weak eyes and bad hair; I was clumsy, gauche, oblivious, with a knack for blurting out stupid remarks (when Pennsylvania came out with new license plates featuring the Liberty Bell, I stopped in astonishment as we were walking through a parking lot and exclaimed: "Look! This one's cracked!"). At school I was the goat.

And she, a high school knockout in her day, a ringer for Betty Grable who eloped at seventeen, has spent her life trying to reclaim that early pinnacle, to be glamorous and influential, an authority in matters of taste and etiquette, the center of everyone's attention as she was the center, the black hole, of our own little universe. Every night at the dinner table we would hear dramatic reenactments of indignities she had been forced to undergo that day or triumphs she had achieved despite insurmountable odds, recounted word-for-word, in tones of quiet dignity or ringing denunciation, often with a hand laid over her heart. Even those who deferred to her expertise seldom deferred enough: my mother was insufficiently appreciated and let us all know it. My father tried, but nothing could ever plug the leak in her bucket. He wooed her all his life: trips to New York and Las Vegas, flowers for no reason, scavenger hunts with rhyming clues and little boxes hidden all over the house. It wasn't enough. She broke down on a regular basis, shrieking that no one cared, ripping up photos and cards and valentines we'd made her, shutting herself in her room and, twice, swallowing handfuls of Valium. Then we'd all have to woo her back to life, as if she were a reluctant virgin and we the amorous swains.

Trudy is covering her eyes. "You weren't actually thinking of publishing this, were you?"

"Not unless I'm dead."

"Oh good."

As for friends, though there were sycophants enough to provide a steady flow of gratification, I could see that aside from my father she had a strained and artificial relationship with everyone except Pinky. They were childhood friends, went to Sunday School together, rode the trolley downtown to look at clothes in the big department stores. Pinky was the only person who wasn't flayed alive for not deferring to my mother's expertise. "Is that a new lipstick?" she'd say. "Let me see." And when my mother handed it over, Pinky would drop it in the trash and bury it with coffee grounds. "You can't wear coral— how many times do I have to tell you? Rose shades, rose! And no frosted."

Pinky herself wore only aggressive shades of pink, head to toe, and decorated her house the same way, despite having three sons. "Me, I like pink," she would say, deadpan. Pinky was nobody's fool but her own. At the end, after she'd lost all memory, the part of the brain that names and recognizes things stopped working. She didn't see chair, bed, table, floor: she saw blotches of color. It was a kind of blindness, the doctor said— like being a newborn.

There's a sigh from the other bed. I raise my head to look at my mother. "Are you dreaming?" I ask. "Can you hear me? Do you know I'm here?"

She probably wouldn't take much comfort from my presence: she'd prefer Nathan-the-success or Ronnie-the-baby. We all got locked into our roles early on. Oh, Ronnie will agree with me on the phone that she's seriously impaired, but that doesn't seem to dampen his devotion. And Nathan calls her every Sunday, reports on his own two boys, inquires after her health and investments. He won't discuss her with me at all. His lips actually get stiff and he'll say: "She's my mother, Isabel."

Trudy laughs. "Nathan is your super-ego."

"Well, you would know."

I call my mother occasionally. She describes in animated and painstaking detail the health concerns of people I've never met, repeats words of praise showered on her for her cooking or flower-arranging or scarf-tying, gives me elaborate instructions on preparing some fancy hors d'oeuvres she's had great success with; I tell her the latest cute things the children have said; then we hang up.

I've only been home once since my father died. Until I met Gordon, I never even liked the word "home"—I always associated it with dread. As a child, I tried always to be the last one in the house after school, hanging back until my brothers got home and I could tell, by the pitch and volume of her voice, what state she was in. She had the stamina to shriek for hours about our rooms, our clothes, our attitudes, our behavior, our posture, our expressions, and, especially with me, our appearance. Nathan looked sober and grown-up in his crewcut and black-rimmed glasses; Ronnie had dimples and ringlets; but I was a great disappointment. I didn't sparkle. I didn't even gleam. In my mother's presence I tried to be as dull as possible, which she mistook for sullenness. She berated me, but if I let my face or voice betray what I was thinking, all hell broke loose: bitter diatribes about lack of gratitude and respect, slammed doors, burnt dinners, and complete withdrawal until my father made me apologize, even when there had clearly been no transgression. Once when I was twelve, for instance, I was coming out of the walk-in closet in my room, shutting the door behind me just as my mother came in with a stack of fresh laundry. Instantly she pitched the laundry onto my bed and, with a look of triumph that chills me to this day, flung open the closet door, expecting to see some evidence of wrongdoing —a smoldering cigarette, perhaps, or an empty bottle of gin— but there were only the usual rows of dresses and shoes. She kept peering, though. She didn't want to miss anything: a half-finished pipe bomb, a counterfeit printing press. She took a good long disappointed look, and when she finally turned around, I could not for the life of me keep the contempt out of my eyes. She flew into a shrieking rage, and, nine hours later, my father had me knocking on her door to apologize. She never accepted an apology, though. She always said: "No, you're not," or "It's not enough."

"Actually," says Trudy, "she was right on both counts."

"Whose side are you on?"

"A forced apology isn't sincere. And even if it were, it wouldn't be enough for your mother. The two of you needed to find a whole new language, a different way of talking to each other. You needed to imagine each other's point of view, which you couldn't do because you were a child. But she should have been able to imagine yours. She was the grown-up."

"Where were you? Why couldn't you have said all this *then*?"

Trudy laughs. "I couldn't have said any of this then because I was the same age as you." She waves me on again.

There's no more sleep tonight. I spend the hours holding Emmy and gazing at a tree in the parking lot which, as the darkness lifts, turns into a feathery golden puff. In sunshine it must be brilliant, but in this raw gray light I can trace the skeleton beneath the leaves. Autumn teaches a useful lesson. By the time you reach November, what was unthinkable in July now seems inevitable. I hope death works the same way, though it didn't for my father. For him there was no warning, no chance to accept the inevitable. One minute cheerful, upright, putting my mother's special little cushion in the car, ready to drive her to the mall, the next lying flat on the driveway, eyes reflecting sky. A clot, the doctor said, a clump of dark blood in the wrong place. It cut him out of his life with surgical precision.

When I was small, he'd dance me around on the tops of his shoes, singing: "Is you Iz or is you ain't my baby? Is you Iz or is you ain't my gal?" And I would squeal: "I is, Daddy, I is!" And my mother, famous for having no sense of humor, would snap: "Don't teach her bad grammar—she'll end up in a trailer park."

I look at her now, so flat and inconsequential under the blanket, a vanquished dinosaur. The T-Rex, Nathan and I called her when we were little, because she roared and her approaching footsteps struck terror. Oh how we quaked when her shrieks summoned us to our rooms, where we found her dumping the contents of drawer after drawer. They had not been tidy enough. And the bedspreads, such torture. I could never get mine right, especially the slippery part that folds over the pillow. And the towels, which had to be folded in halves, then thirds, with the stripes matched up like gift-wrapped parcels. And the sheets. It's agony to fold a sheet perfectly, especially a fitted sheet, if you're a child with stupid fingers. But most terrifying of all was the shower curtain, new and expensive, with a vinyl inner liner, a muslin middle liner, and the fancy outer curtain made of velvet brocade. It fell in great loops and folds like a theater curtain, held back by gold tasseled ropes. I was enchanted and promptly took a shower. I didn't realize you're only supposed to put the plastic liner inside the tub. The velvet curtain was "ruined"—that is, it showed faint scalloped watermarks—and I thought my mother would scream the house down.

My father was loving and warm, though he didn't protect us from her. He's the one who should be here now to shield her the way he did all his life. No one knew her secrets: the depression, the spending sprees, the fits of rage. Oh, and the vomiting—

Trudy interrupts. "You only thought we didn't know about that."

—I was thirty before I realized that "Mom's nervous stomach" was just her way of maintaining a size two. And she hadn't been in the hospital with either meningitis or pneumonia: she'd been having the Valium pumped out of her stomach. We were all in on the conspiracy: my brothers, my father, and me. It's what passed for closeness in our family. Now Nathan is a successful banker who works all the time and is never home, and Ronnie

has an ulcer, is too nice a guy, and can't hold onto a job. But except for the occasional brief psychosis, I'm pretty much okay,

Trudy bursts out laughing. "Kant was right."

I sigh. "Remind me."

" ` We see things not as they are but as we are.'"

"Oh, that."

The golden puff in the parking lot has fully materialized. When the day nurse comes in to change my mother's diaper, I change Emmy's and my own: the lochia is still flowing heavily. The nurse, Jackalene, talks to my mother the whole time. When I come out of the bathroom, she comes over to admire the baby, then takes a closer look.

"This baby's just been born," she says, then peers at me. "Child, don't tell me you're here by yourself?"

"No, I'm here with my mother," I say. It's supposed to be a joke, but Jackalene frowns. "My brother will come in a day or two. And my husband will come if I need him, but we have two little boys—"

"Boys or not, you need him." She steers me over to the empty bed. "This is too much for someone who just had a baby. What's your name?"

"Isabel. And this is Emmy. My daughter."

"Okay, Isabel, you lay down and rest with Emmy-my-daughter. Your mama's not going anywhere, and I'm going to see you get a breakfast tray."

"You have children, Jackalene?"

"Only three from my first marriage and two from my second. So you know you can listen to me. I want you to stay off your feet till that bleeding lets up, you hear?"

"Red Alert," says Trudy. "Female Authority Figure off the port bow. Regress! Regress!"

"Maybe," I say. "But she's a kind Authority Figure."

"And one who does imagine your point of view."

As Jackalene goes out, Emmy's eyes open. She looks watchful and severe. Her invisible brows draw together when I trace her hairline with my finger, and when I touch her cheek, her mouth opens on that side—a reflex: feed me.

I turn to ease the stitches and look at my mother. This is the same hospital where she had me. What was that like, to sit up against these pillows and study my small unfamiliar face? Was she curious? Did she wonder what I would say and do and think? Did she hope to know me? Or was I more like an accessory, a new purse or hat? All my life I have waited for my mother to want to know me, and now it's too late. Not just because of the coma, but because neither of us knows how to be any other way with each other. She'd have to be a different person. So would I.

Suddenly I gasp, startling the baby. The boys! My boys! First I disappear into the hospital, then come home with a new baby and disappear again. Do they think I've abandoned them? Are they crying for me right now? What kind of person forgets her own children?

"Now for a little post-Freudian shamanship." Trudy rubs her hands together. "Something like: 'Perhaps this suggests a certain suppressed ambivalence about motherhood'?"

"I love my children," I say swiftly.

"Of course. But with a love completely pure, completely...unadulterated?" She grins at the pun. "Go on, go on."

I struggle up—everything hurts—pull the phone over, and dial the number. It rings and rings. I'm not sure I dialed right. I'm not absolutely sure I remember my number. Where are my boys?

I wipe tears away and look at my mother. The nurse said hearing was the last to go. "Mother?" I say. "Mom? Did I tell you what Max said? He asked me if Earth is the biggest planet, and when I said 'No, Jupiter is twelve times bigger,' he said: 'Wow, it must have a lot of states.'"

My father would have loved these stories. I remember when

Max was born how he held him and sang a Yiddish song about a pomegranate, bobbing gently as if at prayer. He never got to see Toby at all. And Emmy, his first granddaughter—how he would have adored her! To see him hold her would be like looking back in time to see him holding me.

"Ah," Trudy murmurs without opening her eyes.

"And you know what Toby asked me? He wanted to know if it was good for married people to have the same color hair. And when I was wearing my baggy old maternity pantyhose, he asked why my legs were slobbering. And Max said—"

My mother's eyes open and my heart slams against my ribs.

"Mom?"

My mother's eyes close.

"Mom, it's Isabel. I had the baby—it's a girl, look!"

But she's as still and closed as before. Did she hear? Does she know?

"Probably not," says a voice behind me. "It was just a reflex."

At first I think it's Jackalene, but I turn and see a face floating near the TV high on the wall, a warm, cheerful, freckled face I never expected to see again. Pinky.

"Hello, mommeleh," she says. "It's good to see you too."

"Terrific," I say. "Full-blown psychosis. I wondered when it would kick in."

"Let me see that precious girl." The face floats nearer and now I can see more of her. She's wearing a pink beaded jumpsuit and flamingo earrings. Her voice is low and tender. "Such a shayneh maideleh! *Such a* zeesa punim!*"*

A pretty girl, a sweet face. I can't help feeling proud. "She's not nearly as red as Max and Toby were. And no jaundice at all."

Pinky sighs. Death agrees with her: her wavy hair is black and thick again, her teeth perfect. "I always wanted a girl."

"I know you did, Pink. You used to tell my mother how lucky she was."

"I offered to swap—she could've had the pick of the litter."

The flamingos quiver when she shrugs. "But I had to buy three sets of pajamas with trucks on them, and she got to go shopping for you."

"Well, if it's any consolation, I used to wish you were my mother," I say. "You were so calm and cheerful. And warm, always so warm."

"That's how I was made, Iz. I was also made lazy and sloppy —remember what a mess my house was? It drove your mother crazy."

We both look at my mother, whose hair and skin seem to fade against the immaculate glare of the hospital sheets.

"That's how she was made," Pinky goes on. "Some things you can't change."

"Some things you can," I say. "Especially if they involve tormenting smaller weaker human beings."

"'Tormenting,' Iz? That's not a little strong?"

"You don't know, Pinky. You were never in her power." I reach for the box of tissues. When I turn around, Pinky is gone. I wanted to tell her how jealous I used to be that she was friends with my mother. How could my mother be anyone's friend? How could she laugh and talk with Pinky, be warm and loyal and tender and devoted when she couldn't be any of those things with me? All my life I've had trouble making friends with other girls. I still do—it never works, it doesn't last. Gordon is my only friend.

I pull the phone over and call again, but there's still no answer.

"Well, it's about time," Trudy says. "I was wondering when I was going to show up. I know, I know— "She holds up her hand. "This is fiction. But Pinky's me."

"A little," I concede.

"Go on. Let's see if I do me justice."

I think I doze. Nurses drift in, tend to my mother. The doctor comes and talks in my direction without saying anything new. Feeding Emmy wakes me up because it hurts. Jackalene brings me food, which I don't want, and little cartons of milk which don't quench my thirst. Toward evening I leave Emmy surrounded by a fortress of pillows to go wash myself in the bathroom and make the mistake of looking in the mirror. The harsh light reveals a new loosening of flesh under my chin. What is the word for that? Wattle. Here is my first wattle, a preview of damage yet to come. The Spanish have the right idea when it comes to talking about bodies: they say "the," not "my," distancing themselves. I am not the wattle. But look at those vertical grooves above the lips, between the brows, etched more deeply than before, etched deeper by the moment because every time I look at my face I catch myself pouting like models in magazines. I've been doing it all my life, even now—three days after childbirth, seeping blood and leaking milk, sleepless, seeing ghosts, staring at myself in the ghastly bathroom light, while in the other room the woman who tormented my childhood with predictions of ugliness—Don't cross your legs: it spreads the calf; Don't bite your lips: it makes them fat; Don't eat so much: you'll be big as a house and no man will marry you —lies wakeless, her own face as worn and creased as a paper bag. The mother.

"This is one thing that was better in the old days," Pinky remarks, just above my shoulder. At the moment she's the size of a flying squirrel. "It was dark in those shtetls—you didn't have to watch your face deteriorate. For illumination we pay a price."

We look at the humming green light, which sounds, if you really listen, like a high-pitched mantra recited by a computer at breakneck speed. I turn the water on because I don't want to hear: I'm afraid I'll start understanding. Behind me Pinky enlarges, her face wavering and indistinct.

"Why are you haunting me?" I say.

"Who says you're the one I'm haunting?"

As we turn to look at the motionless figure on one bed, a chirp and a series of tiny clicks and smacks comes from the other. The fresh pads in my bra grow damp.

"That's what's haunting you," Pinky says, disappearing piecemeal like the Cheshire Cat.

Emmy's grunts grow frantic; she turns her head as best she can, seeking me. I scoop her up, but just holding her against my breast makes me wince, and when she latches on, I break into a sweat. I must have cried out, because a young nurse looks in, then returns with Jackalene, who snaps on the overhead light.

Jackalene lifts my shirt. "Girl, you have an infection—see these red streaks? And you're all swelled up. I know it hurts." *She sends the young nurse to find the resident on duty and get him to authorize some Dicloxacillin.*

"Can I still breastfeed if I take it?" *I ask.*

"You can—it won't hurt her." *She watches as I gingerly touch Emmy's lips with one inflamed nipple. When I gasp again, she shakes her head.* "But if it's that bad, with everything else going on..." *She glances at my mother.* "Nothing wrong with giving that baby a bottle."

To my embarrassment I start to cry. "I wanted it to work. She's my last chance."

"Last chance for what?"

"You know. To feed her. To be a good mother."

Jackalene throws a towel over her shoulder, takes the baby, and expertly extracts a burp. "Good mothers take care of themselves as well as their children," *she says. For a moment she looks grim, which confuses me. Is she calling Child Welfare? Are they coming to take Emmy away?*

"Paranoid thinking, Iz!" *Pinky whispers in my ear.*

Jackalene gives me another look. "What did you say?"

I rub my eyes. I'm so tired. "Could I have some Tylenol?" *I ask.* "And maybe a little Haloperidol? As long as you're up."

Emmy gulps the bottle right down and nods off. I sit on a chair between the beds and watch them both: my mother, who moves only to draw ragged breaths, and my daughter, whose breathing is imperceptible. They are both under spells. In a few weeks

Emmy will learn to smile, laugh, cry real tears. She will lie on her back, gurgling at her mobile, waving her arms and legs like feelers. In sleep she will make little whimpers and sounds of protest, her face scarcely ever still. Sometimes her hands will fly into the air, then float down slowly as if through water. Awake, she will stare at me intently, as if her entire survival depends on her ability to hold my gaze. When I nuzzle her or blow on her belly, she will reward me with rich chortles, grabbing fistfuls of my hair, kicking her fat legs.

Surely this is a baby's nature. Max and Toby were like this, and surely Nathan, Ronnie, and I were too. And surely it is a mother's nature to respond in kind, to hold the gaze, to nuzzle, to adore and be adored. Did my mother ever do such things? Was she capable of such tenderness? If so, how could it be so utterly extinguished in my memory?

"Could be your memory's wrong," suggests Pinky. She hovers like a levitating guru, wearing a pink tracksuit and high-tops.

"I may not remember my own infancy, but I recall Ronnie's very clearly. She wanted nothing to do with him. She stayed in her room with the door shut. We had to hire a baby-nurse."

"See? Postpartum depression, just like you."

"I'm psychotic, not depressed, and it goes away. Hers had nothing to do with hormones. She wasn't loving. Wasn't sympathetic to the child's point-of-view. Couldn't even imagine *the child's point-of-view. She was too much of an infant herself, a terrible infant with power over others."*

Now I'm too agitated to sit. I get up and pace.

"Listen," I say. "A few weeks before Ronnie was born, Nathan and I were playing in the living room. I was six, he was nine. We'd been cooped up all winter. Saturday morning cartoons were on, The Flintstones, *so Nathan and I started pretending we were dinosaurs. We got on our knees, curled our fingers and began roaring. We weren't touching, we weren't even near each other, and the noise was obviously playful—we were actually saying: 'Roar!' But my mother, coming up the stairs with a basket of laundry, eight months pregnant with a third child*

she hadn't planned on, decided we were fighting and punished us both. Then she imagined I stuck my tongue out at her—something I was much too frightened to ever do—and slapped my face."

"Parents make mistakes," Pinky says softly. "You've never yelled unfairly at Max or Toby? Never smacked them on the tush?"

"I have. But I know how to apologize, and my children get lots of hugs and kisses." I stop at the window and look for the tree, trying to get the tremor out of my voice. This always happens. I become that child again. Even under the best circumstances, my ability to project competence and dignity is precarious. "Then she told me to go downstairs and get the milk from the pass-through. It was still delivered in glass bottles then—I remember how cold and slippery they were. I was wearing my fuzzy slippers. As I hurried back up the stairs, clutching the bottles to my chest, I tripped and went sprawling across the kitchen floor. The bottles smashed. There was milk and broken glass everywhere, and my mother's voice was like the shards of glass, screaming that her life was shit and no one gave a damn. My heart was slamming as I picked up the glass, trying stupidly to scrape milk back inside what was left of the bottles. Then she stopped shrieking and seized my wrist. She said: Come here, you're bleeding. Only then did I realize that my hands were streaming blood, blood mixing with puddles of milk on the floor. I didn't feel any pain until she held them under running water. Afterward, I sat on the couch holding my hands in the air—the pain throbbed with my pulse, glowed red beneath the bandages—and watched her struggle to clean up the mess. I waited for my father to come home and punish me. He didn't, of course: he called her doctor."

I look at Pinky. "I used to wish for her death, until I realized how miserable it would make him. Then I wished for divorce, but only if he got custody. After her first suicide attempt, I stopped making requests."

Now Pinky floats higher and stretches, expanding like a

birthday balloon, pinkly transparent—I can look right through her at my mother lying in the bed.

"You know what I hate?" I say.

Her eyes are closed. She bobs gently against the ceiling. "Tell me."

"Mother's Day. It takes forever to find a card that doesn't lie. They're all full of this You-were-always-there-for-me/ What-is-a-mother?/Now-you-are-my-friend *bullshit. I have to search hard for one that says something neutral like:* Enjoy your day."

"But you send a card. You go and you search and you send it."

"And I hate the way the media, our whole culture, all our institutions presume that everybody had this wonderful Ur-mother. There are nauseating little poems in the paper, magazines do famous mother/daughter stories—Hilary and Chelsea holding hands and swooning, people call talk shows to share the best advice their mothers gave them, Dear Abby runs her treacly annual tribute—God, it's sickening! Not everybody had a mother who loved them."

Pinky opens her eyes. "But you send the card."

"Yes, I send it! If I don't, she gets all haughty and stiff on the phone. I do it for my dad. He did so much for me, spent so much money on me over the years, long after kids are supposed to be independent..."

"So it's fair to say you've been a conscious and willing participant?"

I take a step back. Pinky is now wearing a salmon-colored suit and pillbox hat like the ones Jackie Kennedy had on when JFK was shot. Oh, and the hat has a little pink veil—nice touch.

"Izzy, pay attention. It's fair to say you were complicit? You played the game, you held your tongue, you took the money. Am I right?"

I don't think the Dicloxacillin is working. I'm hot and sweaty, and my bra feels like an ace bandage. "Of course you're right," I say irritably. "You're my superego."

"Sorry?"

This is a new voice. A young nurse is standing in the doorway, looking apprehensive.

"I need to take your mother's vitals," she says.

I nod. As the nurse trades my mother's hospital gown for a fresh one, I remember the negligees she always wore at home: white, filmy, glamorous, something you'd expect Elizabeth Taylor to wear. She used to send me one like it every year for my birthday. I always gave them to Goodwill because I sleep in T-shirts. When did she stop sending them?

"Time gets away from you, Iz," Pinky whispers.

"How's she doing?" I ask the nurse.

She hesitates. I make her nervous. "Her breathing's slower."

I point to the underside of my mother's arm. "Are those bruises?"

"No, the skin is darkening because her circulation's slowing down."

She doesn't say what that means. She doesn't need to. I sink back down on the bed, almost squashing Emmy. I'd forgotten about her. And again I haven't thought about the boys for hours —a fine mother I am! It's like that dream I have, where I come out of the grocery store, put my bags in the car and drive away, leaving the baby in the cart. Then when it hits me, I can't turn around: the roads are one-way with no exits. I get further and further away, knowing some stranger is going to take my baby, and I wake up in panic.

"Isabel?" says the little nurse. "Are you okay?"

"My mother is dying."

"Let me see if Jackalene's still here." She hurries off.

Emmy's asleep, but I scoop her up anyway, ashamed of disturbing her for my own comfort.

"Where were we?" says Pinky.

"My complicity," I say bitterly. "Which I concede. But what about my mother, Pinky? Were we equal partners? She was the grown-up!"

"Which I concede. Absolutely. She messed up, Iz, and she didn't have the will or the ability to change herself—who knows

why? It could be a character flaw, it could be psychological, it could be brain chemistry for all we know. But that's not really the question."

I look at the flat bed where my mother lies. She is disappearing. There is hardly any of her left, and no chance in hell we can ever make real contact now.

"That's right," Pinky says softly. "You're the conscious one. It's up to you."

"What's up to me? What is there left to do?"

"Forgive."

"I can't. It's not in me."

"You're not an orphan yet."

"How can you forgive someone for not loving you?"

"How can you be sure she didn't?"

"How does any child know? I have no memory, not one, of being cuddled or caressed by her. No spontaneous embraces. No sitting on her lap. No affectionate touches. She took no interest in what I thought or felt. Even after I grew up, all she ever talked about was herself."

"Your mother was shy."

"Damn, I'm good!" says Trudy. I ignore her.

"Shy? She was overpowering—she dominated every social situation, turned every group into an audience."

"And she was afraid of you."

"Are we talking about the same person?"

"Don't you think she knew how bad she messed up? The thought was intolerable—that's why she talked non-stop. She was frightened of what might happen, what might be said, if she uncorked the bottle. And so were you."

I realize that I am patting and soothing the baby, though she is still fast asleep. I pull her pink blanket up so I won't wet her head with my tears.

"She was actually proud of you. And intimidated by you, by your college degrees and the books you read and your

intellectual husband. And she loved the boys."

"My boys?"

"Oh yes. Every time you talked, she'd call me afterward to report all the cute things they did. How Max told you to stop saying 'Bless you' when he sneezed, because from now on he was going to bless himself. How Toby wanted to know why there wasn't such a thing as Brothers' Day."

"She thought that was funny?"

"She told me, didn't she?"

"But she has no sense of humor."

"I'll tell you a secret about your mother, Iz. She wanted one."

"And I wanted a mother! A mother who knew me, who liked me! I missed out on all of that!"

"I know, mommeleh. She missed out on it too. It damaged you both. But a famous rabbi once said that mistakes should be forgiven when it's too late to undo them."

"Which rabbi was that?"

"Me, actually." She looks over at my mother. "It may be too late for her, Izzy, but not for you."

"Isabel?" Jackalene appears in the doorway. "How you feeling, hon?"

"Talk to your mother. Let her hear your voice," Pinky murmurs as she fades.

"Isabel?" Jackalene is feeling my forehead, my wrist.

"It hurts," I say. "There's hardly anything left."

She exchanges a glance with the younger nurse. "Now listen to me. Your husband called from the road—he's driving in with the boys, and they should be here in a couple hours. Your sister-in-law's on her way, too, and your brother's flying in from California—"

"Ronnie? But his job—"

"Don't you worry about his job—he worked it out. I want you to stop trying to handle everything, you hear? When this baby sleeps, I want you to sleep too." She eases me back against the pillows and pulls the blanket up.

As soon as the door shuts behind her, I sit up. "Pinky, come back!"

Her face flickers on the TV.

"Pinky, I need to know. Does my mother love me, yes or no?"

"Izzy, Izzy—they gave me a death certificate, not a Ph.D. No one knows what's in another's heart. Go, darling. Proceed on faith. Listen to her."

We both listen. My mother's breaths are ragged. Sometimes she goes five or ten seconds without breathing at all.

"Talk, Iz. You're running out of time." Pinky flickers out.

I watch my mother, what's left of her—the T-Rex who shook the ground of my childhood. She has run out of future. For me: a husband I love, two sons, a baby girl, a story I don't know the ending of. For her, blankness.

I can't let sorrow wipe out the past. I can't betray that lumpish gray child, that ancient pain, that rage. They made me who I am. But Pinky is right. Soon Gordon and the others will be here, soon we'll all be caught up in the rituals of hospital, family, religion. The time to speak is now, but only if I can say what I'm certain is true.

"I'm sorry," I tell her. "I've looked and looked, but I don't remember feeling any love, either for you or from you. From Daddy, a lot. But not you. It's just not in my memory."

"Is that all?" Pinky whispers in my ear.

"I wanted to love you." Now I'm crying.

"Anything else?" Pinky whispers in the other ear.

I look at my mother, so remote, almost a memory already. Soon like my father: only an image in my head, only stories I tell the children, only a handful of photos. I can feel the minutes pouring through my fingers.

And suddenly it occurs to me that my mother couldn't have told Pinky those stories about the boys, because they're only five and six, and Pinky's been dead ten years. So I've made it all up. The past is truly past. The dead are truly dead. I've been talking to myself all this time. And now that the spell is broken, I know I'll never hear Pinky's voice again.

"Mom," I say. This could be the last time I ever say the word. "I

wanted to love you. Did you want to love me?"

The baby stirs in my arms. I struggle to my feet and smooth my mother's impeccable sheets. I wipe her mouth with the sponge and dab some balm on her lips.

"Don't go," I say. "Don't go yet."

And, pulling down the blanket, I crawl into the bed beside her, one arm around her bony shoulders and one arm around my girl.

When I've been silent awhile, Trudy says: "I find it interesting that you couldn't kill her off."

"Well, it's not like the prognosis is good."

"No, that's clear. You rendered the mother powerless. But you couldn't actually go through with the death—you stopped short. How come?"

"You're the analyst. You tell me."

"Izzy, Izzy—zey gave me a Ph.D., not a death zertificate." Her Freud sucks. "How can we know another person's mind?"

"I thought that was your job."

"No, that's *your* job, and believe me, it's *work*."

The door crashes against the wall and a horde of two giggling wet children tumbles into the room.

"We beat him!" Jesse crows. "We took the stairs—"

"And he took the elevator!" Molly cuts in. "And we still beat him!"

Owen comes along in a moment, grinning as the children swarm him, declaring victory. They have no idea they've been outwitted.

"Did you enjoy your two minutes of peace and quiet?" I ask him.

"Did you enjoy your two hours?" he asks me.

"It was more like dread and quiet."

He knows I mean the toast. "You want to practice? We could gag the children and tie them to their chairs."

I decline his attractive offer and oversee their baths while he takes a nap. There are three things about him that I envy: he can take himself a million miles away, he can nap at will and wake refreshed, and he genuinely doesn't care what other people think of his appearance. With what I hope is great tact, I select his tie for the evening and drape it over his shoes, which I've just finished shining.

Once again Sappersteins are loaded onto the school bus, this time in beads and sequins, chiffon and mink. There are even a few tuxedos. The Planet, our self-appointed bus monitor, sets the tone for the evening by leading us in vigorous song, including "Three Cheers For The Bus Driver" with half the bus yelling "God bless him!" and the other half yelling "He needs it!" as we pull up to the country club, where my parents await.

My mother glitters head to toe; her earrings do indeed brush her shoulders; she is wearing a new pair of sparkling eyeglasses bought specially and leaning on her dressiest cane, the one with the lucite head. My father, who once swore never to wear a tie again, stands proudly by in his black tux, stiff white shirt, and a cummerbund made of gold lamé to match her gown.

"Damn," Trudy mutters in my ear. "I should've worn my medals."

There is another lavish spread of hors d'oeuvres: shrimp and bacon and scallops and caviar and salmon and all kinds of things with cream cheese. I lose track of Owen and the children as soon as we walk in. There are at least three hundred people in the room, many of whom I haven't seen for twenty-five years. They keep grabbing my arm and saying: "I bet you don't remember me!" Most of the time I can come up with the name: what's harder is keeping the dismay off my face when I gaze into the ruin of theirs. Twenty-five years does a lot of damage. Here's Lucille Leiberman who, it was rumored, had an affair with the rabbi when he first came to town. See what gravity and time have done to this face—who would be seduced by it now?

"Sure, I remember you, Mrs. Leiberman! How are Joey and Beth?"

And here's Sheldon Pinsker, whose pure tenor in the Temple Choir once commanded even my attention. And the Marty Nabalsons, and the Harold Yetnikoffs, and Florence Plotkin, and Irma Lustig, and poor chubby Mr. Bovitz, my old Sunday School teacher, who we teased unmercifully, mooing and calling him Mr. Bovine, myself included—I, who knew so well how it felt to be mocked and despised.

"Oh, take off your hair shirt," says Trudy. "There's a whole school of psychology devoted to identification-with-the-oppressor. Well documented—look it up."

All of them have shrunk. Their heads droop—they have to look up to say hello—and they move with the gingerly gait of those who know their bones are brittle. The women have drawn eyebrows where their own used to be and colored their gray lips pink. The men have grown fur in their nostrils and ears.

"Circulate!" Trudy hisses. "If your mother sees you hiding in the corner, you're cooked."

"Mr. Mittermeier!" I exclaim. "Of course I remember you. What's Ellen doing now? No kidding! Mrs. Tinkelman, how are you? Yes, they are—that tall man with the nice tie over there and the little boy blowing through the straw at that little girl's hair—*Jesse, quit it!* She's six, he's seven. Well, thank you very much. Hello, Mr. Grossrosen, Mrs. Grossrosen! Gee, at least twenty years. Yes, unbelievable! Well, thank you very much—so do you! Dr. Gottlieb! Sure I do!"

Backing up, I bump into Louie Litvak, who used to be the goat at Sunday School. He had problems reading English, let alone Hebrew, and his social skills were worse than mine. Once he farted, and all the kids ran screaming from the room, holding their noses, Louie among them, as if he thought he could escape his own stink. Identification with the oppressor again.

"I'm telling you, it's classic," Trudy murmurs.

Louie was the only Jewish kid I knew who didn't leave town after graduation. He never even applied to college. Instead he went to work managing his father's dry-cleaning business, eventually joining as partner, then buying his father out. Now he owns a chain: they pick up and deliver, catering to the aging Jewish community. His red hair has turned auburn, he's camouflaged his weak chin with a beard, and he's wearing an eight-hundred-dollar suit. He married a girl from a big Catholic family, who promptly converted and presented him with four sons—the next generation of the dry-cleaning dynasty.

"Louie Litvak!" I say.

"Actually, it's Louis," he says. "You look great, Esther. Better than high school."

I give him what he wants. "You look fantastic, *Louis*. You're a whole new person!"

He chooses to misunderstand. "Yeah, we're doing okay—it's a good little business. A service people need, and we treat them right. Have you met Peggy, my wife?" On the lips of Louie Litvak, the words *my wife* are a cry of triumph.

I am introduced and congratulated for having parents who stayed married for fifty years. I congratulate Peggy for having been fruitful and multiplied.

"Yup, four boys," Louie says, socking his fist into his palm. "An heir and three spares."

Peggy laughs, though this must be a joke she's thoroughly acquainted with. Perhaps she knows something of those Sunday School ordeals, perhaps even of the day when everyone ran out of the room, screaming and holding their noses.

"So you're not sorry you stayed in town?" I ask.

"Hell, no!" says Louie Litvak. "Business is good, our families are here—the kids spend as much time with the grandparents as they do with us. We have it good, don't you think?" He looks at Peggy.

"Very good," she says, taking his arm.

"Besides," says Louie. "We get away a lot. We take the boys to Disney World, we go skiing, we take cruises."

"Anytime we want a long weekend, either set of grandparents is happy to take the boys," Peggy adds. "We've been to San Francisco, New Orleans, Santa Fe."

"Chicago," Louie continues. "Vegas. New York lots of times."

I can't believe it. I'm jealous of Louie Litvak, of the life he leads in a town I couldn't wait to see in the rearview mirror. I'm jealous that he's close to his parents, that they're involved in his daily life, that they know his children as well as he does.

"What about you?" Louie says. "Weren't you some kind of artist?"

"No, I *studied* art. Now I dabble in different things, but I actually get paid to teach Western Civ, the big survey class. I'm just an adjunct, nothing fancy."

Peggy asks me to point out my children, but before I can hunt them down and pin them with my gaze, I am slapped—well, it's a combination of slap, hug, and shake—one arm around me and the other around Louie, and a familiar voice says: "Hey, hey, hey! What's the story?"

Louie's chest expands a little more as he turns to shake the hand of State Senator and rumored gubernatorial candidate Jay Finch. Jay and I edited the high school newspaper together. Every day when he walked through the door, he said "Hey, hey, hey! What's the story?" Every day I struggled to think of a clever comeback.

"So what's the story, Esther?" he says now, still hugging my shoulders. "You've had twenty-five years to think up an answer."

"The story is you, Jay," I say. "You've always been the story."

He lets out a big laugh, though I doubt if he gets it. For the last two years of high school, I was sick in love with Jay Finch. He was everybody's pal, a brain who was on the best of terms with jocks, preps, nerds, hippies, and greasers alike. He was that rarest of creatures: a high school boy who didn't judge you by your looks. I looked okay—a little overweight, with an unfortunate weakness for granny gowns—but Jay and I had a mind meld, a sublime rapport. The trouble was, he didn't know it yet. So I conceived a plan: I would have a party and invite him. Something would happen. I hadn't given any parties since the sixth grade (when the girls in my Sunday School class came because their mothers made them), and I had none of the prerequisites for a decent bash: no access to beer, no room to dance, no monster sound system, and no absentee parents. My mother froze hors d'oeuvres weeks in advance: tiny quiches, pigs-in-blankets, cheese straws, stuffed mushrooms. I knew it was doomed, but I went ahead anyway.

There was a girl who ran with the popular crowd—Colleen Clemmons. Ordinarily, I was beneath her notice. But shortly after I started inviting people to the party, she started saying hello to me in the halls. Then she started passing me notes in class. The notes were chatty, about nothing in particular at first—as if she were resuming a conversation that had been interrupted—but gradually zeroed in on Jay. Was he fun to work with, did I like the shirt he wore, had I heard what he said about such-and-such. And finally: was he coming to my party?

I wasn't stupid. Well, not *that* stupid. I knew I was supposed to invite her so she could connect with Jay. I knew I was being conned, and I fell for it anyway. No one had ever tried to seduce me for any reason, and I found it impossible to resist. I thought if I did this for Colleen, I would be the matchmaker, the confidante, admitted to her exalted circle of friends. In some ways, that would be even better than being Jay's girl.

The party was a bust for everyone except Colleen and Jay. I played my folk records, my mother served her hors d'oeuvres, and everybody cleared out by ten, smoked dope in the woods, and went for pizza afterward, all except Colleen and Jay, who disappeared.

On Monday, I passed Colleen in the hall and tried to catch her eye. She stared straight ahead. On Tuesday I said "Hi, Colleen."

I didn't exist. I went into the girls' lavatory and cried. On Wednesday I stayed home from school. When I returned, I was firmly back in place on the food chain. Colleen married Jay the day after they graduated from Ohio State.

Which, in itself, is no big deal. So I was dumb and pathetic. So she was cruel and manipulative. I can take better care of myself now. And I'd make a lousy political wife. What bothers me is the myth they propagate about how they met. Whenever Jay is in town pumping hands and wooing voters, talking to my father and other businessmen, he's always sure to mention (with that arm-around-the-shoulders shake/hug thing) that he met his future wife at Gil's daughter's party. And my father laughs. Not because he thinks it's funny—he laughs with *pleasure*, because he's being singled out, because it's a brush with greatness, because he himself is a naturally modest man. Jay makes us seem clever, as if we conspired to make a good thing happen. And then my father tells me about it when he calls—in that same happy voice, with that same laugh. So what should I do? Tell him we were used? Kill his pleasure? I'm beginning to think there is no such thing as old pain—it doesn't mature the way skin does.

"Sure it does," Trudy murmurs. "It's called *growing up*."

I nudge her and she nudges back. We are cruising the outer edges of the room, having backed away from Jay as soon as he switched his beam to someone else. He continues to work the crowd skillfully, first ascertaining where people live. If they're from out-of-state, it's nice-to-meet-you and so long (no point in burning bridges—many a former governor has occupied the Oval Office). If they're Buckeyes, he's there to ask: "What's the story?"

We find the air more breathable at the edges, and besides, I'm trying to locate the children. There are so many adults in the room that it's like having *no* adults. The smaller children are flying under radar, crawling beneath food-laden tables, reaching up to pluck an olive or cracker, zigzagging around shiny pants legs and fancy skirts, filching maraschino cherries from the bar, ignoring a parent's beckoning hand as Jesse and Molly are ignoring mine. One of my mother's brainstorms was to buy disposable cameras and heap them in a basket for the children to use. The children will be the party's documentarians.

"I hope she's prepared for a lot of stomach and butt shots," Trudy says, watching them aim their cameras.

A waiter goes by, and I pluck a glass from his tray. "At least I'm not the only fool in the family."

Trudy snorts. "Are you kidding? It's our legacy, what we inherit instead of fine china. Remember Roz's accident?"

"When she drove her car through the garage wall into her son's bedroom?"

"Right. You know what Honey's comment was? 'They don't make houses the way they used to.'"

We giggle. "So the clinical term for this would be...*denial?*"

"I prefer *complicity.* Which you are in up to your eyebrows."

"You mean the money and credit cards."

"And the way you've turned your unhappy childhood and impaired social skills into art, thus gaining a degree of control."

Now it's my turn to snort. "Art? I keep telling you, it was just an assignment in a family *history* class."

"And I keep telling you that you don't know the difference. All you know is what you remember; pardon me, what you *think* you remember; pardon me, what you've been *telling* yourself you remember. All this time you've been talking to yourself. That's what you know."

Another waiter goes by and I snatch another glass. A child cries "Mommy!" but for once I don't turn around. There are at least seventy-five women in the room who still answer to "Mommy."

Trudy's not through. "You've never admitted what an adroit player you are in this game. That's why you couldn't kill off the mother in your story, and that's also why you silenced her. It was just another standoff. If you can't confront these things on

245

paper, what makes you think you could do it in life?"

"So what if I don't? There's a lot to be said for détente. Live to fight another day."

"You won't always have that option. Once they're dead—" I flinch, but she keeps talking— "you'll be stuck with the guilt and regret, no hope possible."

"What am I supposed to hope for? A breakthrough? A catharsis? My mother's suddenly going to be a different person? I don't want to go down those old roads, Trudy. I couldn't stand to see my father cry again."

"Then acknowledge your role as an *active* player. Every family is its own little culture with its own subtext. You're fluent in yours."

Trudy is getting tiresome. I'm glad when Owen turns up to say that my mother wants everyone to find their table. The orchestra, led by another old classmate of mine, a tubby avuncular guy named Eddie Gasvoda who looks just like he did in high school, which is just like Theodore Roosevelt, is playing "To Each His Own" and already small boys are stepping manfully about the floor with their grandmothers. My mother occupies her favorite spot in the universe: behind the microphone, in the spotlight. With my father beaming beside her, she welcomes us and begins the ritual of presenting the family. As she calls our names, we must rise and maneuver our way between crowded tables to join them in front. I can feel three hundred pairs of eyes assessing the breadth of my bottom. Then I'm standing safe with Molly, Jesse, and Owen. Jonathan completes the roll call. Here we are! The Happy Sappersteins, with Sapperstein blood, genes, and pathology. What was the word Trudy used? Subtext. Yes, our very own Sapperstein subtext, which tells all these nice people that they are supposed to applaud now, so they do. Molly takes my father's hand and my hand and makes them clap in front of her, laughing in delight at her power.

Now my mother starts on the aunts and cousins. As she calls names, people must wave from their seats. Molly and Jesse start waving back, and pretty soon the whole room is doing it.

"Now the in-laws!" calls my mother. "Tables nine and eleven! Wave, everybody!"

Everybody does. If you don't, it looks like sabotage. This is good old-fashioned emotional coercion, another Sapperstein tradition.

"Now, tables five and six—raise your hands, guys, get them high! You're the twelve-and-under table, our official roaming photographers."

I don't see Trudy, but I can tell from Owen's suppressed smile that he, too, has noted all the crotch shots.

Then neighbors, friends, people from Temple, my mother's manicurist, my father's business associates, even an old war buddy he's stayed in touch with. Everybody waves and is waved at. It's like a gigantic twelve-step meeting, but what's the addiction?

More applause—my hands are burning, can we please sit down? Rabbi Tinkelman steps up to lead the blessing. He's got a packed house tonight, better than some High Holidays even, and with the prospect of a phenomenal feast to come, he's going to take his time, do it up right, let that sonorous voice ring half a beat behind the guests'. Molly leans back to look up at him as though gazing at a tree.

And now—yes! We are released. Already, swift waiters are delivering plates of shredded beets with goat cheese in a cold terrine. Jesse and Molly escape to the children's table where they're served chicken fingers and miniature pizzas. Uncle Shlomo over at table eight is using a plastic knife to spread peanut butter on the matzoh lying on his paper plate. The only thing I feel like eating is sticky buns. But when the waiter comes around with wine, I hold out my glass.

"You sure?" Owen asks.

"This one's the last," I say. He's right: I can't hold my liquor. But in a little while I'm going to stand up there and make a speech to people who remember what I looked like in seventh grade. I need this one.

The band resumes playing, and Peggy Litvak gets up to teach the Funky Chicken to the kids. She flaps her arms and cackles and struts as I watch in awe. So that's what it's like not to be crippled with self-consciousness. Now I know what turned Louie the loser into Louis the mensch.

The waiters bring caramelized cauliflower and sea bass with caper-raisin emulsion when the music changes to show tunes, and Eddie takes the hand-mic onto the floor, heading straight for my parents' table. He takes my mother's hand as if he's going to kiss it and pulls her gently to her feet as the band launches into "If Ever I Would Leave You," from *Camelot.* My mother stands, leaning on her Lucite cane as Eddie goes creakily down on one knee and sings about her hair streaked with sunlight, her lips red as flame, about seeing her run merrily through the snow. He is singing about who she was at twelve. But a delighted smile pulls at her lips—she tries to restrain it, but she's bursting. *She* doesn't see this serenade as corny or ingratiating. Her eyes glisten. As Eddie heaves himself up, still singing, she lays her own bejeweled hand over his, the one that's holding the microphone, and gazes into his eyes as if he, personally, has just written this song specifically for her: *"No? You wouldn't leave in springtime? Why is that?"* With her chin tilted high, the skin of her throat seems taut, young again.

I feel a stab of grief I am at a loss to explain. My mother is neither lovable nor loving—not to me, anyway. But standing there clutching her bouquet, leaning on her cane, she seems frail. An elderly girl. She, the fearsome T-Rex whose footsteps thundered and shook the ground of my childhood. I don't understand this sorrow. Just tonight she betrayed me again. It happened in the Ladies' Room, where she was troweling on more lipstick and I was hiding in a stall, taking a breather. My mother was talking to Faye, the worry queen, about Faye's young grandson who talks to an imaginary friend.

"Doesn't mean a thing," said my mother, the expert. "He'll grow out of it. Esther had one too—I used to hear her talking aloud in her bedroom. She called her Trudy—no, wait, it was

Cousin Trudy!" They had a good laugh. Then my mother said: "And you see how well Esther's turned out. They outgrow just about everything."

I was shocked to hear her say I'd turned out well, but too furious to think about it. How dare she trivialize Trudy as something infantile, to be outgrown like a teddy bear! Trudy is my twin, my foil, my second self—it's my *mother* who's imaginary!

"Two hearing aids and still deaf as a post," Trudy murmurs in my ear.

That makes me smile. I watch my mother as Eddie finishes the song and she kisses *his* hand amid thunderous applause. And now my father, pretending jealousy, claims the microphone and signals the band, which breaks into "S'Wonderful," a much better song. My dad has the only true voice in the family, and he is entirely unabashed to be singing a public love song to his wife. Has he forgotten the bulimia, the suicide attempts, the shrieking, the years of depression, the blighted atmosphere, the children's dread? Or does it no longer matter? How do you get it to no longer matter? Jonathan once told me to wad it up in a ball and throw it away. But Jonathan had high blood pressure and an ulcer by the time he was twenty-five. Do you tell yourself that the past exists only in memory—all in your head, like imaginary friends—so all that counts is the now? I know what Trudy and Kant would say: even the now is in your head.

My father is singing to my mother:

> *You've made my life so glamorous,*
> *You can't blame me for feeling amorous...*

He means it. She's made his life glamorous. He feels amorous. I'd thought the gleam on my mother's skin was her new pearlized make-up, but my father has it too: they're actually *happy*, despite everything.

The waiter comes around again, but I put my hand over my

glass. Soon I must take the microphone and lead the guests in a paean to their hosts. My mother said, when she assigned me this honor, that they didn't want any "eulogies"—her word—which meant she didn't want the kind of extravagant praise that gets showered on the dead. My toast is the other product of that course in family history. I can't imagine what they will think of it.

But first it looks like we have more singing to do. My parents summon us again—Jesse has apparently been in a ketchup fight and Molly has lost a shoe—as my mother explains that we are about to perform the Sapperstein Family Song. All of the guests have been given a little booklet containing the lyrics and a tin star. I would like *not* to pin the star on my dress, but I see right away this will not be an option. We pin on our stars. We sing, with hand motions, my mother leading the way:

> *I was standing on a corner in Arizona*
> (swing arms, look jolly),
> *I was standing there not doing any harm*
> (palms up, innocence personified),
> *When along came the sheriff of the county,*
> *and he flashed his badge* (grab lapel, show tin star)
> *and grabbed me by the arm* (arm flies
> up in the air—what a tall sheriff!)
> *He accused me of robbing the mail train* (point finger gun),
> *He said I was the leader of the gang* (stick
> thumbs in armpits and swagger),
> *He escorted me before the judge and*
> *jury* (hands out in handcuffs),
> *And the verdict was that I was gonna hang* (clutch throat).
> *I'll be hanged if they're gonna hang me,*
> *Beep, beep!* (pull train whistle)
> *Why, I'll sue the penitentiary!* (shake fist)
> *Beep, beep!* (pull train whistle)
> *I may never be forgiven, but I sure ain't*
> *tired of livin'* (shake head)

I'll be hanged if they're gonna hang me,
Beep, beep! (pull train whistle enthusiastically)

"One more time, everybody sing!" my mother shouts, and the guests pick up their little booklets and sing, slightly bewildered but obliging. Jesse and Molly like the "beep, beep" parts, and Owen goes along with good grace. Somewhere in the room Senator and Mrs. Finch sing with fixed smiles on their faces. At the end of the song, my father grabs the mic and says: "Ladies and gentlemen, you are now duly deputized!" The whole room laughs, and I kiss his cheek because he is having fun.

Everyone sits. I get the folded paper from my purse and smooth it. Owen also has a copy in his breast pocket and there are two more copies back at the hotel—I'm taking no chance of being speechless.

The anniversary cake—a tiered mountain of frosting, gauzy gold ribbons, and tiny blinking lights—is wheeled out; bottles of champagne are uncorked; but the waiters, schooled by my mother, stand back and wait for me. Owen gives my hand a squeeze to let me know he will not be contemplating the cosmos while I undergo my ordeal. The paper can't get any smoother. I approach the microphone.

At first I stand too close and my voice sounds like bad Marilyn Monroe. I step back. I begin.

"A few weeks ago, Uncle Mel called my brother in California, looking for a wedding picture of my parents so he could have it enlarged for tonight. Unfortunately, the only wedding picture that exists is the portrait in their bedroom, and short of sending Cousin Roz in disguised as a plumber, we couldn't think of a way to smuggle it out." This gets a laugh.

"I woulda done it!" The Planet yells from her seat, getting an even bigger laugh.

Encouraged, I go on. "So in lieu of a portrait, I would like to sketch a scene—not the wedding itself, but a moment— *the* moment—when it all began, when two lives crossed, and instead of each continuing on its own trajectory, began to move in tandem."

The waiters are discreetly delivering big slices of golden cake and filling champagne glasses in readiness for the toast. I don't look at my parents. I'm revealing more of myself than I have in decades—not since a college boyfriend broke up with me and I called my father in tears, knowing I'd made a mistake as soon as I heard how uneasy he sounded. The last time I revealed myself to my mother was in junior high, when I gleefully described what make-up I would buy with my birthday money, and she promptly vetoed all of it. I am also revealing more of Gil and Gloria than most of these guests have known, and I don't know how my parents will react to that.

"Fifty-one years ago today," I go on, "in an elegant ballroom on the seventeenth floor of the Pittsburgh Palace Hotel, a very young woman crashed a wedding reception with her sister."

There's a flurry of giggles at the word "crashed," and I hastily add: "It was considered okay in those days to drop in just to hear the music and dance, not eat or drink or anything."

Now I'm worried. My mother considers herself an expert in etiquette, and she is so easily offended. Will she see this as sabotage? She is capable of suspecting me of the basest motives. Once when I got caught skipping class in high school —the only time I ever tried it—she said during a bitter harangue: "And don't put your faith in condoms, Esther, because they don't always work. *I* should know, all right?" I was so embarrassed at hearing the word "condom" (I was a virgin until my junior year of college, despite what she thought) that the implications didn't sink in until later. Then I realized she'd been talking about *me*—they hadn't wanted me, I'd been an accident. It took me twenty years to find out she'd been referring to Jonathan, beloved son and favorite.

Distracted, I hurry on. "I would like to tell you that while she was sipping champagne, she saw a stranger across a crowded room and suddenly it was some enchanted evening—" Big laugh. This is the *South Pacific* crowd. "But that's not what happened. She drank nothing, not even ginger ale, and the nice young man she met was named Abie Fein. They chatted; then he said he wanted her to meet his buddy and tapped the shoulder of another young man who was leaning on the bar, apparently *beating* on another guy's *eyeglasses* with a swizzle stick. He was ten days out of the army, and he was wearing yellow socks."

The room roars with laughter. I look around, waiting for the noise to die down, and finally risk a glance at my parents. They're holding hands. My dad is laughing, my brother leaning across the table to grasp his shoulder, laughing. Everyone's laughing! Gil Sapperstein, responsible, reliable, the most grown-up person in the room, the guy who supported his mother and sister, the biggest mensch in the family, the self-made success who began with nothing, bought the company, retired, and still goes in five days a week, *Gil!*

I go on with new energy. "When he turned around, what did she see? A young man with a shy smile who appeared to be blushing violently before he was even introduced, though it turned out to be sunburn. Along with those yellow socks, he was wearing his blue high school graduation suit, which was baggy because he'd been living on Army rations."

There are affectionate murmurs, everyone's face turning from me to my parents to me again.

"When he looked at her, what did he see? A pretty girl, tall, with curly hair and red lips. She was wearing a sophisticated dress of black crepe, cut low. He had no idea she was only sixteen, and she had no intention of telling him."

Now the laughter and glances are for my mother, which she loves. So far I don't think I've embarrassed either of them, though they could see this as presumptuous—speaking from their points of view, going into their heads—or even condescending. If I ruin this moment, my mother will never forgive me.

"So they met," I go on. "They chatted. Her impression of him was: 'pleasant.' His impression of her was 'pretty.' So why wasn't that the end of it? Why are we all sitting here today? Why aren't you all someone else's relatives and friends? Think of it: they could have just kept going, traveling their separate paths, *and everything would have been different.* What made them stop, hover, start moving in sync? What was the moment of transformation, and what made it different from all ordinary moments?"

I'm losing them: people look puzzled, squinting. This is not what they expected; they don't know what I'm getting at. Owen does, and I suspect Jay Finch does, but this speech is for my parents, a gift from me: their personal legend.

"I haven't had enough champagne to explain *why* or *how* —" There's a merciful ripple of laughter— "but I think I can pinpoint the moment *when.* For her, it was when he led her to the dance floor: his hand on her back gave her the oddest tingle between her shoulder blades. For him, it was when they jitterbugged: he spun her out and saw her poised at the end of his arm, ready to come spinning back to him—and he knew. But since you don't always believe what you know, they danced with other people and lost track of each other in the crowd. When it was time to leave, she spotted him at the door. Her back still tingled, but since he was fortified with something a little stronger than ginger ale—" Another laugh; we're back on familiar ground— "she wasn't convinced he'd remember her. So she did something very daring for those days. She wrote her name and number on a cocktail napkin and tucked it in his pocket as she passed him on her way out. She didn't dare look him in the eye—she didn't even know if he noticed. But the next day he found it, he remembered, he called, and the rest, ladies and gentlemen, is history."

The guests gaze at my parents, grinning. I don't think anyone's ever seen my father even slightly tipsy. And my mother, the etiquette queen—crashing a reception, boldly pursuing a young man! We all look at Gil and Gloria, trying to see the outlines of who they were fifty years ago. I feel a little like the son in Delmore Schwartz's story—the one who dreams he's in a theater watching a film of his parents courting, and leaps to his feet shouting: *Don't do it! Nothing good will come of it, only remorse, hatred, scandal, and two children whose characters are monstrous!* I still wish I could have met them before disappointment and illness warped everything. But would I want to stop them?

"I mean that literally," I go on. "She could not know, when she committed that small act of daring, that she had set in motion a profound series of consequences. My father could not know, when he dialed that number, that he was making history. He thought he was just continuing the dance —forward and back, my turn, your turn—but in reality they had embarked upon a fifty-year odyssey that would transform their lives and create new ones, an odyssey that has brought us to this room today."

I have them again. Even the waiters are standing still, listening to me, the remains of the feast scattered across the tables. *It's all a feast,* Trudy murmurs in my ear, *not just the credit cards and cartons of presents, not just the sticky buns and blintzes, but all of it, boundless possibility and peril.*

"There is something heroic about a marriage that has lasted this long," I say, talking over her voice but listening too. She wants me to admit that I mean some of the schmaltzy things I'm saying. "It tells us something about the character of the man and woman, and it tells us something about the power of loyalty."

Trudy's right about one thing: it's never going to untangle, that thorny knot of grudges. It's never going to disappear entirely, but the older I get, and the frailer my parents grow, the duller its barbs seem to be.

So the past doesn't matter anymore? That unhappy child with her useless rage—she's gone? All that matters is doth time fly and do we die, and one day I'll be able to see and hear my parents only in memories, in dreams, and at this I almost gulp down the champagne before I've proposed the toast. Five years ago I would have told my mother (if she were safely in a coma): *You never loved me, so I never loved you.* Now I'm not sure. I don't know what I feel. It isn't love, exactly. I don't want to exaggerate, I don't want to rewrite history, but I see time running out, I see their outlines etched upon the air, ready to disperse.

"In slipping that napkin into his pocket, she made him a husband and father; in dialing that number, he made her a wife and mother; they changed each other's destiny and made us a family forever." My voice cracks, but I raise the glass: "So please join me in a toast: to fifty years, to family, to Gil and Gloria!"

And the whole room rises, glasses raised, and bursts into spontaneous song: not "To Each His Own," or "S'Wonderful," but, unbelievably, no one cracking up, no one's eyes rolling besides Trudy's: "I Was Standing On A Corner In Arizona." They sing as if it were an alma mater, an anthem, a hymn to family foolishness and the opiate power of love. Then, finally, we can all sit down and eat.

SOCIAL SKILLS

This happened, and I'm still mad.

Sitting on the gurney, waiting for his next psychiatrist, Jesse remembers the story his parents tell about the emergency conference called by his preschool teacher, the woman his parents referred to as Chicken Little. They sat in her tiny office clogged with shelves of self-help books while Jesse was supposed to occupy himself down the hall in the playroom. But as the grown-ups talked, he pushed one of the chubby, plastic, kid-sized chairs out of the playroom, up the hall, and into the crowded office, where Chicken Little was telling his parents that their son fit the profile of several books on the shelf, which she would be glad to lend them.

"What precisely is the problem?" Owen said in his politest voice, always a danger sign.

Jesse was nearly four. The teacher described how, while she was reading a book at Story Time, Jesse would get up and walk around the circle, explaining the story to the other children, making sure they understood it. "The problem is," she concluded, "Jesse always has to be the center of attention."

She broke off and they all looked at Jesse, who had just pushed his chair into the geographic middle of their little circle. Owen and Esther burst out laughing, but the teacher grimly plucked a book from the shelf and held it out: *How To Raise Your Disturbed Child.*

Now, sitting on the gurney, Jesse mutters: "So we'll just pick up where we left off," and a nurse passing in the hall stops cold in her tracks.

"Who are you talking to?" she says. "Do you see them? Are they in the room with you?"

Jesse is interviewed by five psychiatrists. By number three he anticipates the questions and gives his cheerful answers in advance: No, he's not going to harm himself; he has no wish to die; when he said "I have no friends," he meant at Music Camp—possibly because every hour there is structured: when you aren't in class, you have to go to Daily Activity, which might be tag, clapping games, relay races, or scavenger hunts, none of which holds the least interest for him. So he sits off to the side and reads. This summer he's reading Tom Clancy —intricate spy thrillers full of technical detail. Some of the counselors give him uneasy looks: he's twelve—he's supposed to be into Harry Potter. Bedtime is 9:30; flashlights are confiscated. Other than his roommate—with whom he gets along very well, incidentally—when would he have a chance to make friends?

And yes, he did say "I should just shoot myself" to the custodian who was setting up chairs for Intermediate Bassoon. The guy asked how he was doing. Jesse's got a cold and summer colds are the worst because they feel surreal— (each psychiatrist writes something in his chart at this point: Jesse is sure they are noting his use of the term *surreal*), the dorms are not air-conditioned, and temperatures this week have hit the nineties. He can't breathe through his nose. He can't sleep. His head hurts. He *is* learning a lot in bassoon class—he made his own reed—but Daily Activity is so boring and pointless—why is it mandatory if it's supposed to be recreational? —and every hour of the day is so regimented that yes, he said it, but *it was a joke*. Sixth-grade humor, his mom would say, same as his dad's.

But the next thing Jesse knows, he's sitting in the Mental Health Unit of the Cayuga Medical Center being evaluated. Lots of little chats, lots of little notes. He doesn't mind. He's always liked grown-ups. And the hospital is air-conditioned.

"Jesse, I understand you give your counselors math problems to solve," one doctor says. "I'm wondering why you do that."

"It's a tradition."

"A camp tradition?"

"No, my tradition. I started it last year. There was more time to talk because the schedule wasn't so tight."

"What sort of problems do you give them?"

"Like: how many 1-liter Pepsi bottles will fit into a 20-ounce bottle of Coke and vice versa?"

"How many?"

"625 and 1.6, respectively. One guy got it. There was a follow-up question: which is a better deal? The answer is Pepsi, by .00055 cents per milliliter. Nobody got that one, but I taught my roommate how to figure it out." He smiles at the doctor and the doctor smiles back.

Music Camp is really a college campus where a week of intense tutorials is given to students who are nominated by their music teachers and who pass the audition. At the end of the week they give a concert. This is Jesse's second year. He plays clarinet and bassoon. Last year Esther and Owen were impressed by how much progress he made, and Jesse couldn't wait to go back.

So Esther is astonished to get a call from the camp saying that Jesse is suicidal and has been taken to the hospital. In a week? Her bright, happy, talkative child changed this drastically in a week? She tries to imagine it and fails. No, not Jesse.

After the shock she's annoyed, first with him—what's next: jokes about bombs in airports? —then with whoever leaped to the wrong conclusion and made this huge fuss. She knows what he said. In any other context, no one would give it a second thought. But for the custodian, then the counselor, then the camp director, it must have been a red alert: *Dead kid. Liability. My ass.*

But by the time they get to the hospital, she and Owen are laughing. Sure, schools are paranoid these days, but the public is litigation-happy, no doubt about that. You can't really fault them for erring on caution's side. And Jesse's a kid, for all his precocious ability. You can't really expect a child to know how an adult, let alone an institution, is going to interpret what he says. It's all just a big misunderstanding, inconvenient and expensive, but typical Jesse, a good anecdote. And insurance should take care of the cost.

They collect Jesse's things and sign him out of the hospital with the blessing of all five psychiatrists, who have found him to be "not in jeopardy." On the two-hour drive home, Jesse keeps them laughing with impersonations of the medical and camp staff. Then, since he hasn't practiced yet today, he hums his part of the score for tomorrow's concert.

After dinner, while Jesse fits his bassoon together, Owen calls the camp to find out what time they need to be there tomorrow. Esther takes one look at Owen's face and runs upstairs to pick up the extension. The camp director, a man who spent forty years in the public schools, fifteen as superintendent, is on the other end. She understands right away, as he goes on in the plodding tone of a born administrator about Jesse's unhappiness and lack of social skills, that they are not going to let him come back for the concert.

Owen, ever rational, tries to pin down the terms. "But what do you *mean* by 'social skills'?" he says in the so-calm, so-polite voice Esther dreads. She can detect just a hint of tremor. "You don't mean that he doesn't talk, because you just got through telling me he talks to *everyone*. And if you mean the relay races and scavenger hunts—well, if you were required to join in some recreational activity that you found pointless and dull, but you refrained from saying so and instead sat with a book quietly off to the side, not making a fuss, I would think you'd demonstrated a high level of social skill, rather than the reverse."

"I'm sorry," says the director. "I know how upsetting this is. Our staff is deeply upset. And I know Jesse is deeply upset and unhappy."

"You don't know anything about him, you son of a bitch," Owen says in that calm deadly voice, but then Esther jumps in.

"Look," she says, "he doesn't need 'social skills' to play in this concert. All he needs to do is follow the score and watch the conductor, and there's no disagreement about his ability to do *that*. It's one afternoon: *we'll* be there the whole time; *we'll* be completely responsible for him."

"I'm sorry," says the director. "I just can't."

"The hospital released him! Five psychiatrists concluded that he's no threat to himself or anyone else! *He's not suicidal!* You want to talk to him yourself?"

"I can't."

The director's voice is growing smaller, as if he's backing away from the phone, but Esther goes on. "If you really cared about Jesse, you'd let him come and reap the benefit of his week of hard work. He wants to do it: he's practicing right now—he made his own reed, for God's sake! But you aren't thinking about *him*, are you? You're thinking about your own discomfort."

"I'm so sorry," says the director again and very softly hangs up.

Owen is all for immediate and direct action. Drive down anyway, confront the bastard, make him say it to Jesse's face.

Esther, after some tears of pure fury, says: "No—how would that make Jesse feel?"

They both swing around to look at their son, who is cradling his bassoon and watching, amazed by this intensity of feeling on his behalf. "It might feel kind of weird," he says.

"Okay, a letter campaign," says Owen. "Letters to the editor of all papers in the area, letters to music teachers, to schools, to —"

"Again," says Esther, "how would Jesse feel? Does he want to make this a public issue?"

Jesse fingers the keys of his bassoon. He is still wearing his hospital bracelet. "I'd have to think about that," he says at last.

Esther gets the scissors, cuts the bracelet off, then stands back and considers her son—almost as tall as she is, forehead bubbling with the first pimples of adolescence, dark eyes brilliant, feet enormous, voice unbroken. She considers his exuberance, his intelligence, his soft-heartedness: if an animal dies on TV, he has to leave the room. The director, who has probably spent his professional life singing the praises of diversity, has hung a sign around Jesse's neck that says *Disturbed*. He didn't tell Jesse they were taking him to a hospital. He didn't tell him they were sending him home and that he couldn't come back to play in the concert. He didn't ask him any questions or listen to any answers.

Owen's face is grim. He's writing letters in his head.

Esther puts her arms around her son. "I'm sorry, baby. We tried."

His chin rests comfortably on her shoulder. "It's okay. I can just play my part for you."

Jesse's comforting *her*. You don't get much more skilled than that.

But this is how the world works. Those who run it carry a box under their arms, a small box with a tight lid. If you can't be stuffed into that box, then you're suspect, or damaged, or some other damn thing. She cups his smooth cheek. "You have to be careful around people who have authority over you, because some of them are fools, and they can hurt you. They can hurt a lot of people."

"How do fools get to *be* authorities?" Jesse asks.

"Other fools put them there," says Owen.

"Kind of a chicken-and-egg problem," Jesse says. "Who was the First Fool...what's it called, Dad? The prime mover?"

"That's what it's called," Owen replies, softening.

"And if you know enough to ask the question," Esther adds, "then you know there's no answer."

Jesse's eyes narrow as if he is calculating pennies and milliliters. Esther pulls him close, resting her face against the springy hair which used to smell of baby shampoo, the kind that promised no tears.

"Okay, Mom," he says after a moment of this. "Can we get started now?"

NIGHT COURT

This did not happen. But many of Molly's ("Sap's") qualities are drawn from real life. I leave it to the reader to determine which.

T he highest-ranked item—fifty points—was the hooker, but Sap started with the frat trophy, which was number two and nearly suicidal because all the frats were having parties tonight. A scavenger hunt was such a lame idea that Dregs had made all the items absurd: where would they find harpoons or donkey-baskets on Halloween? Sap figured everyone would simply go for the fifty-point hooker, trolling the bars and a few notorious streets. She had the same idea, but with a slightly different strategy that just might give her the crucial edge. But first she had to kill a few hours, which was why she started with the trophy.

While the frat boys stripped to underwear and body-surfed in beer poured over the concrete basement floor—a tradition of this house and the reason she chose it—Sap, who pretty much looked like Halloween every day, had no trouble getting past the bouncers. She crouched by the trophy case in the dark living room, waiting for just the right song. When it came—heavy metal, cranked all the way up, *so* last century— she wrapped her precious denim jacket around her fist, told herself it couldn't hurt worse than an upper-cartilage piercing, and punched the glass. It worked perfectly. The singer was still yowling, the bass throbbing when she stuffed the largest trophy into her backpack. She tucked her jacket in too so her bustier would distract the bouncers as she strolled back out of the house. They would never remember her face.

The night was balmy for October, though the courthouse steps were cold beneath her butt. Still, no one she knew was hanging around. That meant no one else had realized that hookers get busted and arraigned every night, even on Halloween. She could catch one coming out of Night Court and offer her a deal—half the prize plus some recreation—to salvage a wasted evening. With any luck they'd beat everyone back to Dregs's place. She grinned. Those slackers would probably all get distracted and come back empty-handed anyway.

Now her bottom was numb, but she couldn't risk the lobby —her piercings always drove metal detectors crazy. Usually her pink Mohawk drew the visual human equivalent, but tonight she was barely rating second glances. That brought back flashes of the bad old days, when she was either ridiculed or ignored, before her parents got disgusted with public school and took their children out.

Jesse-the-prodigy actually *liked* being invisible, giving no thought to how he looked or what he wore or where he rated in the court of public opinion. Of course he was the one born with thick hair and long eyelashes. *His* pimply stage lasted fifteen minutes. Easy not to care when you were smart and good-looking. When your college kept heaping money on you so your parents didn't have to shell out tuition. When everybody loved you despite your caustic tongue that could shred a person faster than the stupid Light Saber you used to tote everywhere.

Sap looked down at her heavy black-laced boots. Shit-kickers, they were called in her mom's day. She wished she had something to kick now. Why was she freezing her ass on the steps of the courthouse? The scavenger hunt's IQ was dipping with the temperature.

But as she stood up, the big doors slammed open, yielding

the night's haul of evil-doers, most looking no older than Sap. Her attention fixed on a young woman who yanked off a blonde wig and dropped it on the ground like a used tissue, raking both hands through brown hair carefully cut to look rough and choppy. But it was her working clothes Sap had to stare at: a bikini top made of pink feathers that continued halfway down her arms; a red jewel wedged in her navel, a full pink tutu, finished off by the very latest spiked caged booties. Sap dragged her eyes back up to the girl's face, only to find the girl staring at her.

"If you attached your head to my body," said the girl, "we'd make a spectacular bird."

For a moment Sap had no idea what she meant. Then she remembered her own pink hair. "Oh," she replied. "I guess." Brilliant. What would Jesse have said?

The girl reached out and ran her hand over the 'hawk. "Very like a tufted crest. Quite a display."

For some reason Sap shivered. The girl grinned—perfect teeth, too—then turned and trotted on down the steps.

"Wait!" cried Sap, following. "There's something I need to know!"

The other girl half-turned.

"Are you—a hooker?"

The girl stared Sap up and down. "Why? Are you?"

Sap, too, glanced down at herself. "Oh, you mean the bustier? No, I made it. I make everything I wear."

"Really? Everything?"

"Well, not the boots. But everything else I re-con. Reconstruct. For instance, this jacket used to be a pair of jeans —see, it's upside down: the fly still works and you can still pull a belt through the loops. But I've never made anything as exotic as your outfit."

"Thanks. I had a little help."

"So, um, are you?"

"Am I what? An independent contractor in the professional sex industry?"

Sap blushed. "I didn't know that's what it's called."

"Yes, I'm independent. Pimp-free." She stuck out a manicured hand. "Cherchez les Femme. How do you do."

Sap scowled. "I'm not an idiot."

"Did I say you were?"

"I know what *Cherchez les femme* means."

"Did I say you didn't?"

"It's not a name. It means: *seek the ladies.*"

"A good working name for someone in my line. Call me Cher."

"I'm Sap." At the other girl's raised eyebrows, she added: "It's a nickname."

"I didn't think it was a description. When I started out, someone suggested combining the name of my first pet with my hometown street. I got Butter Wood out of that. Kind of sexy, don't you think?"

"What was the pet's name?"

"Butterball. Big goofy Yellow Lab."

"We've got a Yellow Lab too. They *are* dumb and happy."

"Later I started using the name Buffy."

"Not in honor of the Slayer!"

"Big fan."

"Me too! Team Angel or Spike?"

"More like Team Faith, but if I had to choose, definitely Spike."

"Me too. That leather coat!"

"Shall we stroll? I mean, of course, in an entirely non-professional sense. That way you can explain why you're asking such invasive personal questions."

Sap followed her down the steps. "First I've got to ask one more."

"I doubt there's any way to stop you. You look like you can stand a lot of pain."

Sap touched her face. "You mean the piercings? They don't hurt as much as tattoos."

"This night is a true education. What's your question?"

"Are you really set on Cher or could we go back to Buffy?"

"Why?"

"It's just that I have no respect for Cher as a musician, but I have real affection for Buffy—I used to watch it with my mother and brother—so if I'm going to be saying your name all night, and it's not your real name anyway, I'd much rather—"

"Fine! I'm Buffy. Take a breath."

They walked a few steps, then the girl—Buffy—said: "But why are you going to be saying my name all night? Do you want—"

Sap blushed for the second time. "No, I just want to borrow you."

"Let me get this straight," Buffy said three blocks later as they hit the main drag and merged with a stream of ghouls, pirates, vamps, sexy nurses, half of Congress in plastic masks, and at least one Bo Peep of questionable gender, "you and your friends are having a party—"

"Not a *party*," said Sap. "We don't have *parties*."

"Okay, union meeting, whatever. And you decide to do a scavenger hunt."

"I know it's lame."

"And one of the items on said hunt is a hooker—"

"I didn't realize how that sounds. I know you're not an—"

"In fact, I am the most valuable item on this list, which is why you went for me first."

"Well, second, actually."

"I was second?"

"I had to wait till Night Court let out. And the second highest item was a fraternity trophy. So I stopped at a party and stole the biggest one in the case."

Buffy halted so abruptly that Presidents Reagan and Clinton crashed into her. "Watch it, bitch!" snarled Reagan, and Buffy absent-mindedly flipped him the bird. "*You* stole a trophy from a frat house," she repeated. "While a party was going on."

Sap shrugged, with difficulty. "It's in my backpack. Heavy as shit, too. I would've taken something smaller, but I thought in case of a tiebreaker, Dregs might award points according to size. You know how guys are." She stopped. Buffy was chuckling. "What's so funny?"

"Just the universe talking to me. Doesn't it talk to you?"

Sap scowled. "Not so I've noticed. I wish it would."

"Maybe you need to listen harder."

"So will you come? I'll split the prize with you."

"What's the prize?"

"He didn't say exactly."

"I'm not interested in beer, weed, or happy pills. I'll do it if you'll make me a bustier like yours."

Sap stared. "Really? You like it that much?" Her voice actually squeaked. "Do you want it exactly the same? Because I saw this great embroidered satin at Prescott's—"

"We can talk about that later. Do we have a deal?"

Sap stuck out her left hand. Buffy gave her the look people usually did when she stuck out her left hand but gripped it. Her own fingers were bumpy with rings whose stones sparked like real ones under the streetlamp.

"So what's next?" Buffy said. "Got a limo for me?"

"No limos. No taxis, no trains, no cars. We're allowed to bus it or walk."

"Is this guy into pain?"

"He just doesn't want to make it too easy."

"Uh-huh. And is he playing too?"

"Um—"

"That's what I thought. So where does he live?"

"South Side."

Buffy groaned. "Of course. Come on."

"In those?" Sap glanced at Buffy's caged stilettos.

"I'm looking for a bus stop, idiot. If you think I'd walk all the way to South Side, you drank too much frat punch."

She really could walk in those things. Sap had to catch up with her. "I didn't drink—"

Buffy smiled. "I know."

"You know? Something the universe confided?"

"What, you have no beliefs?"

"I believe in God."

"Really?"

Sap pushed up her left sleeve and held out her wrist. They could just make out the blue letters. "It's *chai*. Hebrew for *life*. For a long time I wanted to be a rabbi."

Buffy looked her up and down again. "Well, aren't you a bundle of contradictions."

"Look who's talking."

"*Moi?*"

"You look like a hook—sex industry professional—but talk like a debutante. What's up with that?"

"Tell you my sad story someday." Buffy picked up the pace. "Where's the damn bus? Let's walk to the next stop."

They wove their way through gladiators, witches, Batmen, brides of both persuasions, too many hippies, and the occasional banana, as the street narrowed and the music pouring out of bars grew louder and raunchier. Buffy sang along to everything, dancing a little, raising her arms, and she could *dance.* Even those few moves attracted sharp attention from whatever gangsta or zombie was sharing the sidewalk.

To distract her, Sap said: "I want to hear that sad story *now.*"

"Really?" said Buffy. "Is that on the list? Are there points?" Then she relented. "Nothing much to tell. Crack mother. Foster parents, Catholic school—hence the correct speech. But bad blood will out, and here I am back on the streets again."

Sap laughed. "That's totally bogus."

Now Buffy laughed. "*Bogus!* Are we in a movie? *Buff and Sap's Excellent Adventure?*"

"I guess I picked that up from my mom."

"Your mom says 'bogus'?" Buffy looked thoughtful. "Tell me about your family."

"My mom's cool. Sympathetic. She writes stories all the time—probably writing one even as we speak. My dad's a cosmologist, conservative but funny. Mostly. But my brother's an asshole."

"How an asshole?"

"He's perfect. And don't think I haven't noticed you totally changed the subject."

"I told you there's—" She stopped, glancing over her shoulder. "Shit! He must have followed us." As Sap started to turn, Buffy grabbed her arm. "Don't! Keep walking."

"Is it your boyfriend?"

"I don't have a boyfriend."

"Your *pimp*? You told me you didn't have one!"

"He's more like a business partner. He doesn't control me, but—"

"Then why are we running from him?"

They took a sharp right down a dark street, Buffy walking on the balls of her feet so her heels wouldn't clack. Not just walking now either—they'd broken into more of a trot.

Sap started to repeat the question, but Buffy sliced her hand through the air. No more talking. They kept turning, then cutting through bars, ignoring the raucous welcomes and protests as they squirmed through the crowd straight out the back exit. Sap had no idea where they were. When at last they pulled up in an alley to get their bearings, both were panting.

"If he's not a pimp, why would he mind the scavenger hunt?" Sap managed to whisper.

Buffy shut her eyes. "You really are a lamb, aren't you."

Sap looked down at her shit-kickers, trying not to smile in spite of the danger. "Lambie" was her mother's pet name for her. She would rather be shaken in a sack of rattlesnakes than admit it.

"This is a business," Buffy was saying. "You don't go *borrowing* its prime assets. What, you think he'll accept a share of my new bustier?"

"All I know is you don't run from a *business partner*."

"Depends on the business," Buffy retorted.

They emerged cautiously onto an empty street. For a while they walked, keeping an eye out. Sap had no idea if they were heading in the right direction. She did notice Buffy was limping. Gone were the costumed partiers. They didn't even see an open bar, only run-down buildings and lots of trash piled at the curb. The street looked dead, except for a group of young boys approaching on the other side. Their sagging pants defied gravity.

"Trick-or-treaters, maybe?" Sap murmured.

But they seemed too intent for that and they weren't holding any bags. As they passed on opposite sides, Sap watched out of the corner of her eye. The boys were watching them. After a moment she risked a glance back. The boys had crossed the street and were now following. She gave a muffled groan.

"They look about *eleven*," she muttered.

"Those can be the most dangerous," Buffy muttered back. "Out to prove something."

"They're closing the distance. Do we run?"

"Can't anymore. Not in these shoes."

"Take them off."

"Do you see all this broken glass?"

Sap wished Buffy really were Buffy—a few roundhouse kicks and problem solved. Sap could swing the backpack, but she didn't know how to fight. Why hadn't she ever studied karate? Because Jesse hadn't. He'd been content to fake it, shooting his little Star Wars videos, both Jedi Master and Director: murky tales of Knights and Dark Siths battling with plastic Light Sabers, Sap forever cast as a miniscule villain, tripping over her mother's black raincoat, following his lead like every other kid in the neighborhood.

"They're closing," Buffy murmured. "Get ready."

Sap eyed the garbage heaped on the curb. "Hold on." She grabbed a hunk of cardboard from the trash—an insert, the kind that comes inside a large carton—and dropped it over her head. Screeching like a caffeinated chimp, she began staggering, stumbling, flailing her arms. Both Buffy and the pursuing boys came to a dead halt. Sap squawked louder, spraying spit.

Buffy was quick to take her cue. "Stop it, Bernadette! You

are *not* having another fit, do you hear me? Stop drooling and control yourself! If you mess your pants again, *you* are cleaning it up this time! Bernadette, can you hear me? Did you take your meds? Bernadette!"

Sap squealed, snorted, and careened, knocking over garbage cans, banging the cardboard collar into the street lamp, making Buffy leap out of the way. Then she squatted, grunting, threw back her head, and yodeled like Tarzan swinging from the vines. When she looked up, the boys were gone.

"Absolutely brilliant!" Buffy hugged her, tearing the cardboard away. For a moment they clutched each other, grinning. Then Buffy reached down to yank off her stilettos. "*Now* we run."

"What about the glass?"

"Run in the street!"

So they raced down the middle of the deserted road, glancing up every side street until they saw traffic. By the time they were safely back to civilization, both were sweaty and panting. Sap pulled off her jacket.

"How are your feet?" she asked.

"Kind of shredded. I'll live." Buffy, still panting, had started coughing too.

"We're getting a cab." Sap stepped off the curb to look for one.

"No! Contest rules!"

"Screw the rules—your feet matter more."

Buffy coughed. Then, spotting a coffee shop with a blinking cup, she wheezed: "Let's chill for a moment and think this through."

After dropping into a booth, they gulped down two glasses of water each and ordered hot chocolate and pumpkin pie. But Buffy kept coughing and her breathing was rough.

Sap touched her arm. "Are you okay?"

Buffy rasped: "I was…hoping…to avoid this." She opened the

pink satin bag slung across her chest and took something out, cupping it in her hand, turning away.

Sap recognized the movements. An inhaler. "I had asthma too for a while. Why are you all secret agent about it?"

Buffy let out a sigh. "It just seems so dorky. I mean, shouldn't I be shooting meth in the bathroom?"

"Hey, I got dorky covered. I grind my teeth. I'm supposed to wear a Sleep Right No Boil Dental Guard to bed."

"Supposed to?

"It's too dorky even for me, even when I'm alone, which is always." She blushed, wishing she could take that part back.

But Buffy was studying Sap's bustier again. "No one who makes something as beautiful and delicate as that could ever tolerate a Sleep Right No Boil Dental Guard."

Sap knew it was pathetic, but the words got past her teeth. "You really think it's beautiful? And delicate?"

"As are you."

Now her face flamed. Delicate? In her shit-kickers? Besides, she had no illusions about the way she was built. *Zaftig* was the Jewish term for it. *Curvy* was what her mom said, but then her mom loved her. Whereas Buffy was tall, lithe, willowy, graceful, sylphlike—Sap ran out of adjectives—and *still* curvaceous. Extremely so. Sap gulped the rest of her cocoa to account for the heat in her face and signaled the waitress.

"Decaf, please," she said. "With skim milk."

"Same here." Buffy was grinning. "Well, since you saw my asthma and raised me one tooth-grinding, now I'll see your tooth-grinding and raise you one insomnia."

Sap forgot everything else. "You too?"

"Don't tell me."

"For *years*. So bad my parents took me to a shrink. You?"

"Well, Catholic school, you know. They just tell you to drink hot milk. Did you get any good drugs?"

"Tons of drugs, but the side effects were deadly. Either they make you hyper or zombify you or give you a rash or make you fat. I seem to be sensitive to everything. So now I just stay up till I fall down."

"So do I. Did you ever read this story by Nancy Kress about children who are genetically engineered not to need sleep at all?"

"From *Beaker's Dozen*! I love that story! It was like they had twice the life spans of everyone else. Of course, they were lonely too. Till they found each other."

Their eyes met. Sap wondered if the coffee was really decaf. Her pulse was throbbing like the bass in that stupid frat house.

"My mom gave me this book of poems about insomnia," she said. Oh, brilliant. Her mom again. And *poetry.*

"Your mom gives you books? Mine just shares her drugs. Sometimes."

"With my mom it's all about words. Everything's a story."

"I'd like to see that book sometime." Then, misreading Sap's face, she snapped: "Oh, *what*? I read the menu, didn't I?"

"I wasn't thinking you couldn't read. That's not what I was —"

"No, you were surprised I like poetry. A whore who likes poetry is like a dog who can talk."

"That is *not*—"

"Maybe I'm putting myself through college—ever think of that?"

"You are? What's your major?"

Buffy's eyes dropped. She reached for Sap's right hand and ran her finger over the defective thumb. Shocked, Sap looked at it too: tiny, shaped like another pinky, practically useless— how she hated the damn thing, always interfering with her grip, her ability to carry things. She'd learned to sew and write left-handed, but she never got the hang of throwing a ball or swinging a bat—or a Light Saber—and mean kids never missed an opportunity to jeer. She remembered her mother coming to school once, passing out homemade cookies, whispering to her worst persecutors that Molly's deformed thumb was a sign of immense intelligence. They didn't buy it. They liked those cookies, though.

"See me one insomnia," Buffy was saying, "and raise me... whatever *this* is."

Sap was tempted to wrench the misshapen thing back into hiding, but the stroking felt good. She sighed. "It's a freakish rare syndrome that affects the upper limbs and heart. I was lucky. Some kids are born with flippers or no arms at all. I just got a hypoplastic thumb and weak hand. And a hole in my heart that's supposed to close on its own."

Buffy stared at her. "You have a hole in your heart? And you were *running*?"

"Well, *you* have asthma."

They glared at each other for three seconds, then broke into grins.

"I guess we'll be the death of each other," Buffy said. "So does this syndrome thing run in your family?"

"No, I am the first freak. Founder of the curse. A gene mutated when I was conceived. But now all issue of my loins stands a fifty percent chance of inheriting, with no guarantee that those cases will be mild. My mom explained it very carefully. Not your typical sex talk."

"So that's one of the things you lose sleep over."

Sap shrugged. "What do you lose sleep over?"

Buffy bugged her eyes out. "Hello. Hooker. Chased by pimp. What do you *think*?"

"Oh, so now the word is permissible and you do have a pimp."

"Keep trying to trap me. The term is permissible among friends."

"We're friends now?"

"If you have to ask, you're worse off than I thought."

"I *am* worse off than you thought."

"Cut that shit out. We've been friends for hours and I'm sick of it. What's your major?"

"Hey, I asked you first and—"

"What's your goddamn major?"

"Something really candy-ass. You never heard of it."

Buffy heaved a sigh and waited.

Sap gave in. "Fiber Arts."

"Makes perfect sense."

"Yeah? Well, my brother is double majoring in math and physics. He's been taking graduate courses since he was a sophomore. He wins merit scholarships that pay his way. He built his first computer from scratch when he was nine."

"You're beautiful."

"What? I am not."

"Stand up."

Reluctantly, Sap got to her feet and watched Buffy study the bustier with its colored zippers, ribbons, and laces, all hand-stitched in contrasting embroidery, and the jeans patched with fabrics that looked as if they came from a 16th-century bazaar.

"You are beautiful, talented, original, and clever," Buffy said at last. "That scheme back there was brilliant and courageous. If I were any of those things, I wouldn't need to work so hard to charm you."

"You're charming me?"

Buffy sighed. "Apparently not."

Sap signaled for more decaf and studied the other girl, who had dipped a napkin in her water glass and was wiping off her dark eye make-up, performing the Merlinesque trick of growing younger by the moment.

"What *is* your major?" she asked again.

"Hooker, remember?" Buffy snarled. "Barely literate."

"Cut that shit out. We've been friends for hours and I'm sick of it."

Buffy turned her head. "Don't you think you better call your scavenger guy? You're going to lose your prize."

Sap felt the old sting. Shut out. But she only replied: "Let me see your feet."

When Buffy didn't move, she added: "When you said 'Stand,' I stood. Now stick out your damn feet."

Buffy glared but slowly untucked her legs—her feet must be freezing, Sap realized—and extended them on the seat. Sap got up and bent over them. They were a mess: blood-streaked, bruised, embedded with dirt and grit.

"Shit," said Sap. "We should have taken care of this right away. I'll ask if they have a first-aid kit."

"No! They'll kick us out or call a cop."

Sap scowled but slid in beside her, put the feet on her lap, dipped a napkin in water and started cleaning. They looked better when she finished—nothing still bleeding—but she'd have been happier with antiseptic and bandages. Still, years of competing with Jesse had made her resourceful.

"What the hell are you doing?" said Buffy.

"You can't possibly put those Iron Maidens back on, and you can't walk out of here barefoot." Sap finished pulling off her boots and socks.

"Well, no offense, but I'm a six and those look to be—"

"They're nines. Don't worry." Sap wound her long socks around Buffy's feet like bandages, tucking the ends in neatly, then began padding the boots with napkins laid flat. When she emptied their napkin dispenser, she grabbed one from the next booth.

Buffy started to giggle. "And you'll be wearing?"

"The Iron Maidens."

"Are you my wicked step-sister? They're size six! And they're Jimmy Choos!"

"So I won't buckle 'em. I'll tippy-toe. We'll all survive."

She finished lacing her boots onto Buffy's small feet and grinned. It was a good look with the tutu and feathers. More balanced. Then she squeezed her own big feet into the little booties.

"Holy shit," she said, trying to balance.

"Holy is right," Buffy said. "Jimmy *Choos*."

"I'll *shuffle*. At least as far as the taxi."

"No! No cabs, remember?"

"Will you forget about the stupid scavenger hunt?"

"But I'm your prize. Your top ticket item."

Sap gave her a pained look. "You're not a prize. I mean, you *are*, but—" She shook her head and yanked her cell phone from her jeans, viciously punching the numbers.

"Ow," said Buffy, "Ow, ow, ow," and Sap snorted, unable to suppress a laugh. She listened for a minute, then punched it—gently—off.

"No one's there," she said. "Either it's over or they went elsewhere. So the issue is moot."

"Really."

"Really."

"Well, I'd better check in too." Buffy slid off her tiny purse and plucked out an even tinier phone, pointedly tapping in the numbers with great delicacy. She, too, listened a long grave moment, then snapped the phone shut.

"Too late. He's locked me out."

"You *live* with that guy who was chasing us?"

Buffy studied the tabletop. "He likes to protect his investments. And he's very strict about curfew."

Sap looked down too, studying her freakish thumb. Then abruptly, with her good hand, she snatched Buffy's purse, shoving her backpack across the table in exchange.

"Ah," said Buffy softly. "The great reveal. A bold move."

"Every minute with you makes me bolder," Sap said.

"What if you don't find what you're looking for?"

"You could just tell me."

"I could."

"But if I'm right about you, I'll find it."

"Tell me your theory."

"I'll tell you after I corroborate it." Sap gave her a mocking grin. "Can you say 'corroborate'?"

"My major is cultural anthropology. It makes my parents crazy. But this university has a fantastic program."

Sap sat up straight. "Go on."

"You've got my bag, not to mention my phone. You might as well look."

"All right. Since you give your kind permission."

"You would have done it anyway, brat."

"I was losing patience."

"Now me, I'm made of patience."

"*Fuck me!*" Sap practically howled. The waitress and other customers turned to stare. "Your fucking *name* is Patience!" She was holding open a slim wallet.

"See why I prefer Buffy? Or Cher? Or anything else? Actually, I go by my middle name, which is Alden. Old family name. That's what my friends call me. Of whom I have very few, incidentally."

Sap lowered the wallet to study her. "Alden. It suits you. So, no foster parents. Or Catholic school?"

"Choate, actually. Did you look at the rest of the name?"

Sap glanced at the wallet again. This time she whispered: "*Fuck me.*" She stared at the wall behind the counter where miniature boxes of breakfast cereal were stacked like children's blocks. "It's not just a coincidence?"

"Nope, I'm an heiress and a scion and a black, black sheep. They're actually going to start stamping the family name on every cornflake now so people know they're getting the real thing. Imagine how possessive they are about their only child. According to my mother, I should be at Finishing School majoring in husbands. According to my father, at Harvard, on track for an MBA. But I don't have the slightest interest in husbands, business, or breakfast cereal. I prefer bagels myself."

"So how did you happen to get busted for prostitution?"

"First tell me your theory. Was it cor-a-bor-a-ted?"

"I figured you had to have real ID or the cops wouldn't have let you go. And I don't think real hookers carry purses. Too easy to get snatched. And your face—you just don't look hard enough. Especially after you wiped off the make-up."

"I knew that was a mistake."

"Which brings us back to my question: how did you get busted?"

"*You* got me busted, brat."

Sap just stared as Buff—no, Alden—unzipped the backpack and yanked out the frat trophy. Alden laughed, reading the plate. "It's for community service. Who knew?" She shoved it across the table. *I'm not a hooker—I just play one on TV.* I was at that party. This is my Halloween costume."

Sap groaned.

"Someone discovered that the case had been smashed and the prize trophy was missing, and this genius was just far gone enough to call the cops, who promptly busted everyone for underage drinking. They let us go with a warning, but that's why I was at the police station, Ms.—" She yanked out Sap's wallet and flipped it open. "Muldoon? What kind of name is that for a nice Jewish girl?" Then she looked again. "*Your* name is Molly?"

Sap's head was buried in her arms. "Molly S. Muldoon. S is for Sapperstein, old family name. My friends call me Sap."

"Why don't you like Molly?"

"Makes me sound like I'm five. Why don't you like Patience?"

"Makes me sound like I'm ninety-five. Pick up your head and talk to me."

Reluctantly, Sap did. Then she had to drop her eyes. "Alden, I am so, so sorry. First I got you busted. Then I insulted you by making all kinds of offensive assumptions. Then I got us chased—hey, who *was* that guy? You don't have a pimp!"

Alden smiled. "I had to distract you. And you have nothing to apologize for."

"Yes, I do. That gang who chased us, your battered feet, your asthma kicking up—none of that would have happened if I hadn't butted into your life."

"Oh, I would have had a pleasant evening being mauled by drunken frat boys."

"Then why did you go? And why wear something so... provocative?"

"It was a social obligation between my group and theirs. And I wore this to torture them."

"Your group? Shit, you're in a sorority."

"I couldn't help it—I'm a legacy. My parents wouldn't let me have an apartment. And God forbid I live in a public dorm!

It was the sorority house or nothing. That was the only way I could avoid Finishing School—I was limited to universities that had chapters of my mother's sorority." She rolled her eyes. "That's how they decide things. Take pity on me."

"So who did you call just now?"

"The time." Her eyes narrowed. "Who did *you* call?"

Sap grinned. "The weather."

"I think I've met my match," Alden said softly.

"*Bashert*," Sap muttered.

"My shirt?"

"*Bashert*. Yiddish word." She forced herself to add: "It means destined."

Alden laughed. "The universe is talking to you after all." She reached out to trace the Hebrew letters on Sap's wrist. "This means what again? Life?"

Sap nodded. The rings on Alden's fingers *were* real. She wondered if the jewel in her navel was real too.

"What do your parents think of your look?" Alden asked.

Sap shrugged, aware that their hands were clasped. "The pink dye is temporary, the 'hawk combs down, some of the piercings come out. I'm the gray sheep of the family."

"Nothing gray about you. You are an exotic bird of brilliant plumage."

"My brother's the brilliant one. Ow!"

Alden had pinched her.

"I'm going to pinch you every time you say something like that."

"Okay," said Sap, rubbing the spot.

"And if I'm not with you, I want you to pinch yourself."

"I'll be black and blue."

"Better than gray." Alden took hold of her chin. "I mean it."

Sap felt a great hot rush, as though her whole body were blushing. She also felt like weeping. And she was way too aware of her feet in Alden's shoes. "Are you really locked out?" she blurted.

Alden let go of her chin. "Yes. The sorority house has

antiquated rules."

"Well, I can't sign guests into my dorm after midnight either. But my folks only live a half-hour by train—and when my brother left home, I inherited the basement. It's nice: bedroom, bathroom, living area. First-aid kit. And a private entrance."

"Just one bed?"

Sap felt the rush again. "It's a queen."

Alden smiled. "Good. You call a cab to take us to the station. I have to leave a message on the housemother's machine so she knows I'm not kidnapped."

Sap groaned. "I can't believe it. A sorority girl."

"I won't tell if you won't."

"I think I'd prefer the hooker."

"No, you wouldn't."

Sap drew a breath. "Can you tell I've never been with a girl before?"

"But you've wanted to." Alden stood up, held out her hand. "Come on, Molly. Seek out new life and new civilizations."

Sap wobbled up, holding onto Alden. "I just can't imagine what my mother would say."

"I won't tell if you won't," said Alden again.

But the truth is, my Molly: I knew, I know, I've known. For almost as long as you have. And you will always be my lambie.

BOXES

Obviously, this story—with its touch of magic surrealism—did not happen. It is a true story anyway. The details about young Jesse are all drawn from life, and the story's core truth reflects Esther's feelings about the new distance between her and her son, something the real-life model for Jesse claims he doesn't remember.

I t appears while she's creaming the butter and sugar. Behind her back while she's swaying to the oldies, the radio loud. When she turns for the cinnamon, she stumbles over it —a box clotted with clumps of string, pulsing to the beat as if there's a giant heart inside. Esther stares at the thing. The twine is tangled and snarled all around it like a thorn bush, like the briar forest growing over the castle where a prince lies in enchanted sleep. Wary, she crouches, plucking at the knots. Her blunt nails are useless, so she grabs a knife. The box's pulse quickens as she saws and the knife bucks, biting her finger. Blood drips, but she manages to pry up a flap. "Oh no!" she whispers. Just what she feared: Jesse, crammed inside, all knees, elbows, and weedy hair, his face the reflected blue of his computer screen.

His face flickers, and multiple Jesses peer up at her, disasters overlapping like a thumb held down on the remote: Jesses flunking-out/dropping-out/breaking-down/overdosing or meeting-the-wrong-girl-and-running-off-to-get-married-in-Vegas. Everything she worries about, all at once.

Esther shoves the box away, her heart kicking so hard that anyone else would be gulping aspirin and dialing 911. But she knows the catalyst for this sorcery. It was the song she'd been crooning tunelessly, mindlessly, just before the box appeared —a dopey song popular when *she'd* been a college student, waitressing one summer in a diner where it played constantly: *Sometimes...all I need is the air that I breathe, and to l-o-o-ve you...all I need is the air that I breathe, and to l-o-o-ve you.* It stuck, and whenever Jesse caught her at it he'd substitute his own words, crooning to the dog: *Sometimes...all I need is the hair that I sneeze, when I r-u-u-b you....*

She sticks out her bleeding finger and gives the flap a poke. Twelve-year-old Jesse bursts from the box, knocking her onto her butt as he springs through the air. She recognizes his *Dance of the Cold Lamb Fairy*, adapted from "The Nutcracker," which he improvised one afternoon from pure joy when he discovered there *were* lamb chops leftover from dinner. Leaping across the kitchen, he kicks and twirls in size twelve sneakers, flourishing a lamb chop in each hand. Esther laughs till she desperately needs to pee. This is the Jesse she knows —bursting with exuberance. The Jesse who organized luger rides with sofa cushions down the stairs, who persuaded the neighborhood kids to tie their bikes behind his to make a train that had one speedy moment of glory before its inevitable Waterloo. Who brought her the stick from his first lollipop, saying: "Here, I don't like the bone." Who listened at six to Owen talk about teaching in a Catholic school and asked earnestly: "Daddy, were you ever a nun?" Who demanded suspiciously, at seven: "Are you using child psychology on me?" Who built his first computer at nine. Who scored 1600 on his SATs, despite having been schooled at home, and won two merit scholarships to college.

"Where did you go?" Esther asks the boy with the crazed hair and impish intelligent gaze. "What happened to you?"

But he isn't there. The kitchen is empty again except for the box, pulsing faintly. Esther, still on the floor, gropes for her spatula and swirls it through the dark interior. There's some resistance, then the spatula comes out entwined with a sock

—the holey tube sock that Owen tossed into the fire during a camping trip one summer, prompting Jesse to burst into tears. What they finally got out of him was that it was like killing the sock. He couldn't bear for anything to die. He was eight.

Taking a breath, she plunges her hand inside. Her fingers touch slick paper—a photograph. She holds it up, then clutches it to her chest. Oh, they'd *had* to take a picture of that! Otherwise, who would believe a child could fall asleep standing straight up? But here's the proof: her engine of protest, her bottomless fount of energy and will, asleep on his feet, arms dangling, cheek pressed to the wall. He must have been five, with that round tummy and the persistent cowlicks he'd named for each Teenage Mutant Ninja Turtle, plus the Talking Rat Sensei.

She looks up. Something has changed. The box's pulse has been replaced by a deep resonant hum. The timbre reminds her of how Jesse's voice changed at fourteen. In the grocery store—he was offended if Esther went shopping without him —he would imitate the velvet tones of a *National Geographic* narrator, so crisp and dramatic, pretending the tumbling piles of kiwis were lemmings trying to find their way to the cliff: *And thus we leave them to their fate, at the mercy of the instinct which drives them, letting nothing impede their self-destructive urge to find their way to* (dramatic pause) *oblivion*. Meanwhile, kiwis would be rolling and tumbling like small furry creatures as he juggled to keep them off the floor, and Esther would be laughing too much to scold him. Or, at the top of that booming voice, he'd teach her whatever he'd learned in physics that day, and everyone else in the grocery store would learn too, from Produce to Dairy to Frozens. Or he'd turn into an agent of the Secret Swiss Police, which was so secret even the Swiss hadn't heard of it. Esther would ask him questions just to hear his accent:

But where is your headquarters?
Vee haff no headquarterz. Vee are too zecret.

But if you have no headquarters, how do
you get your assignments?
Zey do not give me azzignmentz. I am too zecret for zat.
Then how do you get anything done?
*No one knowz what zee Zecret Zwizz Polize does,
not even zee Zecret Zwizz Polize!*

It could go on and on—he was a natural master of the absurd.
But he was always ready to help—reach a can from a high shelf,
run to open a door, carry someone's heavy bags. "Such a good
boy," all the ladies said, and Esther would agree, stroking that
maniac hair. He was that rarest of creatures—a teenager who
preferred his parents' company. He liked to do his schoolwork
on their big bed, lying between them, then watch a movie
together afterward. He and his father would walk the poor dog
for hours, arguing politics and philosophy—the dog never got
a word in edgewise—in their ceaseless game of *More Logical
Than Thou*. He hated, at that point, to be reminded about the
sock.

Esther eyes the box, which has gone still. "What happened
to you?" she asks. She gives it a tap, then a nudge. She almost
expects to see them pop out, a springy accordion of paper-
doll Jesses—clever, exuberant, kind, sweet-natured, and oh-
so-reasonable—then morph abruptly, like a scary jack-in-the-
box, into Evil Twin Jesse. The person he suddenly became
in his last year at home. Someone distant. Someone Esther
didn't recognize. Someone who said: "I don't care anymore
about protecting people's feelings." By which he meant *hers.*
Considerate, helpful Jesse, who had always taken out the
garbage and carried in the groceries, now strolled past
unconcerned. He let her move furniture and shovel snow
and struggle with suitcases by herself. His face was carefully
blank, his gaze elsewhere. When he bothered to speak, it was
to critique her driving, planning, financial, and culinary skills,
not to mention the way she arranged dishes in the cupboard.
Her heart was a rock her son kicked, hands in pockets,

whistling.

"Where did Jesse go?" she asked Owen, weeping.

Owen wasn't worried. "He'll be back."

Esther consulted books, which called this strangerness a stage some teenagers go through to help them separate, especially when home life is good. Teens subconsciously fear they'll have trouble breaking away, so they sabotage their relationships to make leaving easier. And the books echoed Owen: once the break is established, the kids come back.

Esther took no comfort. Her chest felt as if it had been gouged with the heart-shaped cutter they used to make cookies on Valentine's Day.

She reaches for the box. She wants the Cold Lamb Fairy. The Secret Swiss Police. The black-haired baby with bright pink cheeks, the four-year-old who kept interrupting Reading Circle to explain the story to the other children, the twelve-year-old who studied calculus but memorized poems by Frost and Poe because he liked their sound. She wants to *hold* him again. But none of them are in the box. Then again, neither are Evil Twin Jesse nor Jesse the Disaster—not that she really expected them: she has too much faith in him. What she does fear is Brilliant Jesse, who's taking grad courses already and winning prizes, becoming too immersed in work, isolated, not connecting: *remember the stupid song, damn it—you need hair to sneeze AND someone to rub!* But that's not what she sees either when she finally hauls the box onto her lap, opens it up, looks into its darkness.

The box is empty. A good bit smaller than she'd thought as well. The right size for sending *rugelach*, actually, with room to tuck in a few bags of cashews, because God knows the boy could use some extra protein. Might as well do what she's always done: feed him. They don't stop being your children no matter how alien or mysterious—no matter what *schmucks* they temporarily become.

She does hope it's temporary and not the person he's finally grown into, the way he finally grew into size fourteen feet.

Gazing at the box, she could swear it's just inched a size or two larger. Room now for a batch of mint brownies, too, his favorite. After all, the mixer's already out.

Her finger's still oozing and for a moment she considers letting a drop or two fall into the batter. But then she decides it's probably uncool to hex your son and gets a Band-Aid from the cupboard, along with the Mint M&M's.

That should hold him for a while, that should hold them both. At least until the next box appears in her kitchen, tangled with string. *Genipt und gebinden*, knotted and pasted, as her *bubbe* would say.

Only she, of course, was talking about family.

LUMPY, BUMPY, STUMPY, BOO

or Miss Patty Will See You Now

This is another story drawn from life. I still don't know what kept me silent for so long.

Will I be appropriate?
Will I sport a fabulous wig? Or a bald dome signed by supporters and painted with pink daisies?
Will I have to miss:
- seeing my kids grow up
- meeting my grandchildren
- getting a novel published
- retiring to the beach with Owen and the dog?

Will I get to miss:
- seeing my parents die
- living on without Owen
- failing to publish a novel
- burying the dog?

I've named the lump Stumpy. It's on the left, underneath, close to the areola, dark, almost black. I didn't know they could be black. It was a little globe at first. Now it seems to be flattening. Spreading. *Like a patient etherized upon a table.* I was keeping an eye on it. That's what the wisdom of the world tells you to do with things that matter. Fix your eye on them. Even newborns frown, hiccup, catch your eye with that severe gaze and hold on like life depends on it. Keep your eye on the ball. *By thy long gray beard and glitt'ring eye, wherefore stop'st thou me?*

And oh, the very first, the Giant Eye in our living room each morning: "Romper Room," where Miss Patty would hold up her Magic Mirror and deliver her potent incantation:

> *Romper, Stomper, Bomper, Boo,*
> *Tell me, Magic Mirror, do!*
> *Are all my playpals good today?*
> *I see Susie, and Bobby, and Nancy, and Tommy,*
> *And Peter, and Sharon, and Billy, and Cindy....*

I listened in terror for my name. I knew if she ever looked through that horrifying thing and said "Esther" that I was dead, dead, dead, because I was *not* a good Romper Room playpal. I was not *good*, though I was asked that question earnestly and often by adults. I gulped chocolate syrup from cans in the refrigerator, I stole objects off dressers and dropped them out windows to see them plop into the snow, I framed my brother by rolling down the stairs and claiming he'd tripped me, I told grown-ups what they wanted to hear. Why else would they ask if we were good?

Long after "Romper Room" was replaced by the likes of "Sesame Street," it occurred to me that Miss Patty was never going to say *Esther* any more than she was going to say *Shlomo* or *Habib*. Not with *that* Magic Mirror.

But you only have to *think* you're looking into the abyss for the abyss to look back at you. It's funny, really. Here you are with three university degrees and 54 years of living the contemplative life—writing everything down, rewriting it twenty times—but when the skull and crossbones pop up on your left boob, what do you do? Nothing. You don't tell anybody. You don't do research. You don't write about it. You don't make a will. You don't even think about it, except for those dreams about teeth falling out, piling up on your tongue. You just ignore it. For three and a half months, you have nothing to say.

Then you experience sixteen straight days of nausea, headaches, diarrhea, and fatigue, and you think: holy crap, did I go straight to chemo and nobody told me? You *feel* sick, and it scares you. The word "meat" makes you want to hurl. Stumpy is a lump of meat in your breast. A squatter. And suddenly you're on the phone to the doctor—what? They can't see you for three weeks? Outrageous! This is a *lump in your breast*! Where are their medical ethics? In three weeks you could be dead! What? Yes, of course you can come in Monday before office hours —you'll come at midnight, bring a tent, wait outside for doors to open—it'll be just like Black Friday.

No, of course I don't talk like that. Not to the *doctor*. Not Gloria Sapperstein's daughter. Until I was ten my mother made me dress up and wear white gloves to go downtown for doctors' appointments.

I am appropriate.

Yes, I will be there. Monday. First thing. Before the office opens.

Thankyouverymuchforfittingmein.

Then I'm lying on the bed waiting for Owen. The children have been home for a few days. Now they're packing to go back to school—I hear them squabbling over ownership of a flannel shirt. If I hadn't waited so long to get pregnant, I'd be looking forward to my grandchildren's graduations, not my children's. I try to imagine the two of them middle-aged: softening bellies, loosening jowls. I wish they'd try to get along better. When they want to remember us, they will have only each other.

It's a summer Friday. Not much happens in the lab on Friday. If Owen could only come home early. If he could just sense that I need him and fix me with his own giant eye—what else are telescopes for? Romper, stomper, bomper, boo. Come home, Owen, I'll tell you.

"Hey."

I turn over, the sense of teeth heaped on my tongue persisting a moment too long. I look at the clock. "You're early."

"Not much happening." He sits beside me, the bed dipping. "No better today?"

I look at him. A tear slides down my face. I hadn't realized how much I want to tell. To get this in motion.

He quickens, frowns. "What is it?" Picks up my hand. Already my ring slides, loose, over the knuckle. "What is it?" he says, his voice changing.

"Monday," I begin. "First thing."

HANDMAIDENS
OF THE PRECIOUS
BLOOD

In this story, which could be a sequel to "Boxes," Esther continues to struggle with her son's baffling detachment. While the events are true, the perceptions are solely mine.

T he desert is rust red. Ahead, the peaks of the Sangre de Cristo Mountains glow like sunset though it's barely noon. Owen lets the rented Jeep slide into the middle of the road as it rounds the killer curves. He assumes no cars are coming the other way. Esther, however, has always lived according to the opposite principle: there will always be unseen obstacles hurtling toward you, with smashing and pain to follow. But she doesn't tell Owen to slow down, ask how he knows no one's coming, or criticize his driving. That's because their son has done such a stellar job of chastising and correcting both of them all week long.

This is their vacation. They've come to New Mexico to visit Jesse, who is spending his third summer working at the Los Alamos Lab. There's a certain glamor in a Lab job, despite constant security checks, ubiquitous assault rifles, shouting protestors who crowd the fence on the anniversary of Hiroshima. But Jesse's field isn't physics anymore. He's a theoretical mathematician working on his dissertation: a problem in cohomology no one's ever solved. He thinks this will be his last summer at the Lab, which is why it's so frustrating that the system lost his paperwork and he's been hanging around for two weeks, waiting for clearance.

Esther tells him that when he leaves, he should hang his ID badge on his rear view mirror as a trophy. It's a joke, but Jesse shakes his head.

"Totally illegal, Mom," he says, as if she proposed driving around with an open can of Bud.

"Why?" she asks. "Because it blocks the view?"

"It's illegal to advertise the fact that you've worked here. Operatives could capture and torture you for information." He gives her a pointed look. "Or they could capture your friends and family."

"Operatives?" Esther murmurs, but Owen shoots her a look. It means: *don't let him think we aren't taking him seriously.* She wants to retort: *are you kidding me? We still have safety locks on the drawers at home.*

But instead she studies her son in the vanity mirror on her visor. Jesse's hair is pulled back into a thick curling ponytail, red glints sparking in the hard New Mexico sun. Esther has always envied him that hair. Since starting college Jesse has been growing it long, then having it cut and donated to make wigs for cancer patients. He says he does it for the free haircut. If so, he inherited this parsimony from his father, whose favorite sayings include what he's not made of and where money doesn't grow. But Esther has her doubts. Beneath Jesse's cynical surface, her tenderhearted boy still exists—dormant, perhaps, but not extinct.

Now she asks: "Are these operatives as dangerous as the Secret Swiss Police?"

Jesse doesn't answer. Either the phone is too absorbing or he doesn't want to play, doesn't want to recall the time when he was her most devoted companion. So she asks Owen: "You remember the door?"

He lifts his brows, so she goes on: "At preschool. I made the egregious mistake of pushing open the door for Jesse and me. He threw a fit. I had to go stand a block away while he started over, doing it *all by himself.*"

Owen laughs. "I remember when he asked that old lady whether she was going to die soon."

"Remember when he ran away?"

It really hadn't been running away. He'd simply packed all his Power Rangers and biked off in the snow to move in with his friend Andrew, not because he was unhappy at home, but because he thought Andrew would benefit more from his full-time counsel and companionship.

"How about the time he fell asleep standing up?" Owen murmurs.

"We've still got the picture."

She glances back at Jesse, who frowns as his thumbs fly over the tiny keyboard. Where did he go, that boy with the wild curls and lustrous gaze of the never-bored? The one who sought out her company and hardly ever stopped talking? She waited through college and grad school, through the sparse visits, the occasional phone calls which consisted of asking Jesse questions, perpetually interviewing him, since he volunteered so little about himself. Why did he stop letting her know him?

But Owen is speaking now, raising his voice as he wrestles the alarming curves. He's telling Jesse how he had to rewrite practically the whole dissertation for a grad student whose committee he chairs. "She should give me co-authorship," he jokes.

But Jesse doesn't laugh. Instead, he delivers a lecture on the perils of plagiarism, warning Owen that software programs are being developed to catch similarities of language, flagging them even if they're not quoting a published source. "They exist now and future use of them will be more widespread, so you shouldn't regard yourself as invulnerable," he says.

Owen and Esther exchange another glance, hers pained, his amused. The whole week has been like this. Jesse is capable of relaxing, having fun—he paddled the whitewater raft so vigorously that the guide had to tell him to ease up: he was unbalancing his parents' side—but he never misses an opportunity to chide or correct them. Esther forgot to bring sunblock: they got a disquisition on the dangers of skin cancer. When she asked why the water shoes she brought him didn't fit, he said: "Just because I have big feet it doesn't necessarily follow that all big shoes will fit me." As rational as a syllogism. When Owen inquired about the kinds of apparatus they had at the Lab, Jesse replied: "The collective form of the word is *apparati*." When Esther said "Santa Fe," meaning "Taos," Jesse pounced, even though the context made it clear.

He could have let it slide. He could let a lot of things slide—out of grace, out of affection. God knows Esther's done enough of that with her own parents, who have grown blurred and fragile in their late eighties. She had a rocky childhood with lots of turbulence, but now that they're slipping away, she can't bear the thought of a world without them. Will it have to come to that before Jesse feels the same?

"Look," he says, pointing. "Handmaidens of the Precious Blood."

Before Owen swoops past, Esther glimpses the wind-crumbled remains of a convent wedged into a niche in the iron-red cliff. "What a name! Did conquistadors build it?"

"Doubtful," he says dryly. "The order wasn't formed until 1947, and they've since moved to Knoxville."

"Did they try to convert the Indians? Does the blood refer to human suffering?"

"No." Jesse reads from his phone: "'One of the most pervasive images in religious iconography shows people nursing at the spear wound in Christ's body, nursing like a babe with its mother. The precious blood refers to a life-giving substance freely given.'"

"So they equated blood with breast milk," Esther murmurs.

"There are pictures." Jesse thrusts the phone at her. The pictures show sturdy nuns in crimson habits and butcher aprons hoeing weeds, feeding chickens, mopping floors. What strikes Esther most, besides the brilliant habits, is the sunny smile on each nun's face.

"They look so happy," she says.

Jesse leans back, reading aloud. "'The Jemez people migrated here around 1275. They were a powerful warrior culture that built large stone fortresses atop the mesas, four stories high with up to three thousand rooms. Other pueblo tribes called on them for help when under attack.'"

Esther gazes out at rusted trailers, collapsed shacks, red dirt yards. "What happened?"

"The Church." Jesse scrolls down. "But the Jemez united with other pueblos and expelled the Spanish for twelve years, starting in 1680."

"Twelve years." Kindergarten through high school. "Then what?"

"Then the Spanish reconquered and the Jemez Nation was moved into the single village of Walatowa. They lost all their ancestral lands. This is what they ended up with."

But as they speed past hand-painted signs for fry bread, mutton stew, and hominy tamales, Esther keeps picturing the nuns' blissful smiles. What would it be like to feel such peace, such certainty that you were in the right place doing the right thing? Did the Handmaidens—or the Jemez, for that matter—ever feel the need to reinvent their families?

"Interesting history lesson," Owen says.

But Jesse's phone vibrates and he twists in his seat for the illusion of privacy. They listen to his terse syllables without understanding. When he ends the call, his face is blank.

"Something important?" Esther ventures.

"My advisor at the Lab. The paperwork came through. I start tomorrow."

Owen and Esther both let out a glad cry.

"What a relief," Esther adds. "No more wasted time."

"I haven't been wasting my time," says Jesse. She's irritated him again.

"No, I know, I just meant they've been wasting *you*. Now they only get you for six weeks instead of eight. Their loss is all I'm saying."

Jesse regards her with his remote gaze. "Mom, you have a peculiar idea of how these things work. The only person who knows I'm here or cares whether I produce is my advisor, and I'm not even sure about him. Nobody else gives a fuck."

Esther stares back. She has never heard him say "fuck" before. Jesse's speech has always been remarkably circumspect, even prudish. "All I'm saying is that I'm on your side. I will always be on your side, especially when someone doesn't appreciate you."

"It's not a matter of *me* against *them*. There are no sides."

Esther puts her sunglasses back on and faces front. What is he saying? Does he really believe she has no stake in him? Why won't he accept what she offers? She wills herself not to cry: she doesn't have a handkerchief and Owen would ask what's wrong and she would only repeat: where did Jesse go? Why doesn't he *like* me anymore?

She recalls how aggressive and critical Owen became when he was first appointed department chair. The pressure at work was intense and spilled over at home. He was snappish, his voice taking on a caustic haughty tone, speaking as if there were only two extreme positions possible on any question. ("You don't want to rake leaves? You'd rather spend the day napping?") Once when he was off on a tear, cowing both Molly and Esther, Jesse stood up to him, saying: "Take it easy, Dad." This took courage. His voice trembled. But Owen was too heated to see it. He just wheeled and shouted: "Take it EASY? I'll start taking it easy when everyone else starts pulling their weight!"

And another time, when Jesse was starting to draft personal statements for his college applications, he showed a copy to his parents. Owen gave him the bluntest of criticism: don't do that, do this and this and this. Esther, watching, saw Jesse's eyes fill with tears, though he wouldn't let them spill over. Was that the moment he began growing his hard shell? But there doesn't seem to be any old resentment between father and son. Owen—much calmer these days—doesn't worry about Jesse's connection to the rest of the family. The two of them can talk for hours, though never about anything personal. *She* is the one with the problem. And both Owen and Jesse would tell her that it's of her own making. And maybe they're right. Maybe instead of shrinking from Owen's shouting (her mother's rages still fresh in her memory), Esther should have stepped in, shielded her children. Maybe Jesse needed a champion more than a pal. Maybe this punishing distance between them is the consequence.

Opening the vanity mirror again, she pretends to check her lipstick but watches Jesse's face. He sprawls in the back seat, earbuds on, eyes closed, but she knows he's not asleep. She wants the Cold Lamb Fairy. The Secret Swiss Police. The velvet-headed baby who nuzzled her neck. Is this the person he's finally grown into, the way he finally grew into size fourteen feet? Will he ever feel the pull of blood to blood?

They reach the top of the mountain and start coasting down the other side, nothing but solid rock to the left and plummeting red cliffs to the right. There is not even a guardrail —nowhere for the car to go if the worst should happen. For a moment she pictures it: flames, terror, blood. Then Owen starts tapping the brakes, Jesse's thumbs fly across his phone, and Esther recalls him telling them that the plane which dropped the bomb on Hiroshima was named Enola Gay, after the pilot's mother. The bomb it dropped was called Little Boy.

Her Cold Lamb Fairy has evolved into a fully competent adult now, no one's object of amusement, but perhaps he is not quite finished evolving. Perhaps she is not either.

"*Genipt und gebinden,*" she murmurs.

Owen says: "What?"

But she only gives a soft laugh she would have trouble explaining, and, as Owen slides toward the middle again, opens her eyes to see what's coming.

ATTACHED

This is a story that comes with a warning: if it were a movie, it would be rated R. I thought about leaving it out of this collection, but no other story focuses exclusively on Owen's and Esther's marriage. Originally, I wanted to show some of the compromises long-married couples make, how each learns to accommodate the other, sometimes in unconventional ways. I thought at the time that this is part of what makes a marriage endure, part of what grown-up love means. This story represents the joy of long intimacy and, what was, for me at least, the peace of abiding love. The fact that I turned out to be wrong does not diminish the truth of Esther's thoughts and feelings at the time.

Naked? Or fig leaf? Just burst in on him stitchless, still twitching from five orgasms, or struggle into the byzantine little nightgown, which means figuring out the ties, arranging her breasts, and making sure the damn thing's not inside out. Naked is easier. And more efficient — skin against skin right away. But in all the years they've been married, she's never walked in front of him naked, not even since losing all the weight. She doesn't look bad for an old bat, but gravity does have its grip. Of course, he's in the same boat: slackening muscle, softening belly, thinning hair, and how far would they get without the precious blue pill? Still, it's always worse for the woman, and if she sees a hint of anything cross his face—

The solution hits her, elegant in its simplicity. She just takes off her glasses and leaves them behind in the guest room.

Everything a safe blur, she crosses the hall to their bedroom, where her husband, wearing only briefs, looks up from his spy novel. "Have fun?" he asks.

She tries for modesty. "Five times."

He laughs, reaching out. She hops onto the bed, sliding her body against his. Skin to skin. Nothing better. He ditches his own glasses and kisses her. He's never learned to kiss properly but then she's never tried to teach him—it always seemed too soon, until, inevitably, it seemed too late. She never wanted to remind him that she was the one with more experience. She's not sure kissing *can* be taught, except in romance novels, which is where she now experiences most of her kissing. *Their* kissing—except for rare moments when everything meshes —is bumpy, awkward, without the prolonged contact and tongue play that lets passion build. Apparently this is what he thinks kissing is. What does he know? He reads spy novels.

Stroking and squeezing her all over, he pauses to nip each breast—not something she's crazy about, but maybe she used to be, when her breasts were big and full—then sinks his fingers between her legs.

"You're drenched." He looks up, intent, focused completely on her.

She squirms, tiny bolts shooting through tissue already swollen. Abruptly he replaces his fingers with his mouth and she moves with him. She never used to experience pleasure this way except vicariously, in books. But the half joint she smoked in the guest room has resurrected dead nerve endings. Weed has turned out to be *her* Viagra. And even though her husband—like every other man she's been with—performs oral sex as if he's eating pizza, she's able to ride the trailing ends of pleasure. She won't have any more orgasms—that's the point of the guest room, and five really are enough—but his tongue feels cool against her heated flesh, and it's clearly turning *him* on. They won't be wasting that expensive blue pill tonight.

He surges back up, fumbling, and she reaches down to help.

She steers, he shoves—this is her favorite part—then they are fully connected, attached in every sense possible. Now he takes over. Though she longs to clamp his waist with her thighs and thrash like crazy (slammed up against a wall always does it for her in the books), she knows they have to be careful. The erection is precious. An endangered species. His ambition is keen, but the damn blood flow is unreliable. Gravity again—always tugging till it sucks you down for good.

So, to protect him—to protect them—she follows his lead. He likes to keep things tight, changing angles every few minutes, though basically locking her in place. She knows if she lets her hips churn, either he'll come right away, depriving him of the steady build and intense finish he craves, or he'll lose the necessary friction and possibility of climax. He'll end up going soft, while she strokes and strokes his back as if erasing the disappointment.

So no twisting, no bucking, no flipping him over and grinding down. After all, she's had her five. When they were younger, she'd have had five, six, or even seven lying right next to him—Christ, at the start she could do it while he was inside her: he'd lift up a little, she'd concentrate, stroke herself, then she'd be coming while he surged back in, storming her gates. Amazing. With other men she'd always faked orgasm, too shy to show what only her fingers could manage to do. With Owen, she was relaxed enough, secure enough, to actually reach climax while he thrust inside her. It was her favorite part. Yet at the time she still considered it—her, them—defective: the *man* was supposed to make the woman come, they were supposed to climax *together*, it was supposed to just *happen*. But now? What wouldn't she give for just such impaired, defective, substandard sex? Lying next to him doesn't work anymore: watching her, he gets stimulated too soon, and when it's time to join in, his desire has already peaked and blood flow will not cooperate. Hence her exile to the guest room and subsequent return for stage two.

Far from ideal, but better than no touching and no pleasure.

They've experienced that too. Might still be experiencing that if she hadn't decided, after their youngest left for college, that she wanted to transform her body, revive their sex life, and most of all, restore that delicate intimacy—the tendrils that connect them as a *couple*, not just housemates. Something that now seemed wilted if not altogether withered on the vine. She knew she'd have to be the one to speak: despite his intellectual and professional aggressiveness, Owen has always displayed a curious passivity about his emotional life. As if, though he values sex and love, he wouldn't mind adapting himself to a life without. So it was up to her. It took three weeks to work up her courage: she wrote it out first as a manifesto, then read it to him in the car so he couldn't escape, bursting into tears when he reached a hand out halfway through and gripped her knee. And now, in addition to their Saturday dates, he sometimes reaches for her in the middle of other nights, ordinary weekday nights—he doesn't have to reach far, since they sleep entwined again as if they were newly-married. No O's for her on those nights, but it's still exciting: waking to his hands squeezing, running up and down her flesh. Of course, blood flow being unreliable, he can't always finish, especially without the blue pill, but they curl up and go back to sleep, telling each other they'll save it for Saturday, and Saturday will be better than ever. As long as the gods of gravity smile.

He's starting to drive into her now, really pound, a good sign. His face is clenched—mouth twisted, one eye screwed shut like a snarling pirate—and he's finally making some noise. *She* talks, but he, the world's most argumentative person, always clams up during sex. If she gasps: "Babe, it's so good, isn't it good?" he'll say: "Yeah." If she croons: "What would you like to do to me right now?" he'll say: "This." So when little groans finally start escaping him, she knows it's safe to throw her hips into gear. This is her favorite part. They clutch and grind together, his mouth an open sneer of pain. She bumps him hard, drawing a gasp, then clamps down to wring every bit of pleasure she can for him. After all, *he's* only getting one orgasm. He jerks, seizes. She clenches, grips. Locked together, they groan.

Afterward they lie still, hearts banging, breath jagged, occupying each other's bodies. Her face is pressed into his neck so she can't see, can barely breathe, but it's good to be covered. Pinned. Pierced. It's good to bear his weight. There's something elemental about it, like getting a vitamin she didn't know she needed.

"Hey, you almost came that time," she jokes when they've caught their breath.

He lifts his head. "That was...incredible."

"It was nice to have your undivided attention."

"You always have my undivided attention."

"Oh, that is such a lie."

They laugh, kissing. Short, warm, affectionate kisses. They do those very well. This is her favorite part. Lying together, still attached. She runs her hands down his back. She knows every bump, mole, irregular patch. At one time she believed the only way she'd ever have incredible sex would be to enter one of her romance novels, via some virtual-reality apparatus, and share the heroine's point-of-view—actually *experience* those erotic scenes instead of just imagining them. That would be so thrilling it might make real sex obsolete.

But now she knows it wouldn't give you this. Lying under a man you've argued with for twenty-five years, whose skin you could map, and whose pleasure matters as much as your own. No virtual experience could give you that. Though she wouldn't mind trying out the technology.

Gradually she realizes that her husband's breathing has become far too even. Her strokes turn to taps. "Are you asleep?" she says in his ear.

"Just resting my eyes," he mumbles. The standard male reply.

Feeling him starting to slip out, she resists, but he lifts his weight and with an audible plop unplugs himself. This is the part she hates: the sense of loss. Of course he feels no such thing—women are the ones to be filled and emptied—so she covers with another joke, calling: "You know your duty," as he stalks, stiff-legged, to the bathroom.

"We might be out of washcloths," he replies just to get her goat.

"We better *not* be out of washcloths and we better not be out of washcloths *first*."

In response, a clean cloth sails out of the bathroom and lands on her stomach, making her laugh. They long ago established that, considering what he leaves behind, etiquette demands he see to her cleanup before he sees to his own. Besides—as she points out when necessary—she's lying on *his* side of the bed: he'll inherit the wet patch.

She takes her turn in the bathroom, retrieves her glasses, and escorts the dog (who has been dozing unconcerned in his favorite corner) to the kitchen to let him out. More fluid seeps down her leg. "Thanks, honey!" she yells up the stairs, cleans herself again with paper towels, lets the dog inside, locks the doors, turns off the lights, escorts the dog back upstairs. This takes a while as the dog is hobbled by arthritis. Though it seems impossible, this bright yellow boy, who tottered straight to her feet only twelve years ago when the other pups, all black or brown, came boiling out of the breeder's pen, is now a cantankerous limping old codger.

When they reach the bedroom, her husband, back in briefs and undershirt, is lying flat on the bed putting in the eye drops that prevent glaucoma. His lamp is off.

"Feeling sleepy yet?" he asks, hopeful.

"Pretty soon. You go ahead."

"Just rest my eyes," he mumbles. Shameless. The dog curls up beside him, a substitute wife, and he throws his arm over the thick blond fur.

She goes back into the guest room, finishes off the joint to reactivate the buzz, then begins to stretch and hold positions. She makes it up as she goes, just pursuing what feels good: twisting, bending, reaching, reaching further. Push the good ache a little. Not as supple as she was in her twenties, of course, when she practiced yoga with boyfriends for the sheer sensual pleasure. These days she *works out* six days a week: dance class, free weights, grim hours on treadmills and bikes that go nowhere, topped Saturday mornings by the great Juggernaut: dance followed by step followed by circuit training. Keep that weight off. Tone muscle, build bone. Beat back age and infirmity despite two bum ankles and a wonky knee. Saturday is also date night. No wonder she needs stretching afterward. And weed.

Fake naked yoga also provides opportunity for contemplation. It's hard to avoid confronting the most fundamental truths with the effects of gravity dangling before your eyes. After all this time, it's still a shock. You just don't expect to see your own flesh drooping away from the bone. Your skin ruching, crinkling. Your veins rising and asserting themselves in 3-D. You don't expect your body to literally let you down.

But there's still so much sensation in the muscle, which is why she likes to be squeezed, why stretching feels so good. Why her husband has learned to grip her hard, giving her pleasure and holding on to what's there to hold onto. They grip each other. You have to if you're going to hold on at all.

Legs wide in the air, each hand grasping a foot, she has an unencumbered view of her personal landscape: the raised red scar from gallbladder surgery, silvery stretch marks from pregnancies, loose ripples from weight loss, and there, where her body neatly splits, pink fleshy ruffles peeking out. This is a sight that once would have mortified her, but now she likes the design. Likes the one place where she's still tight, pink, and shiny. Likes the way it still mysteriously accommodates a man.

So if she were summoned before the High Council of Girlhood Dreams and Womanly Fulfillment and required to give an account of herself? She knows women who would be horrified by her marital arrangement and women who would kill for it. Yes, she wishes her husband instinctively craved physical contact the way she does. She wishes he were more passionate, more spontaneous—more *wild.* She would like a little wild. Yes, she thinks it's equally hilarious and pathetic that most of the physical touch she gets these days she gives herself. But she also knows, and this is solid, that you can only change yourself. And *compromise* is only a bad word when you're talking about other people. She smiles, gazing between her splayed legs at the suitcases stored safely away in the guest room closet. She's not going anywhere. And this is what she'd tell the High Council: *you* are the monsters, you crowners of fairy princesses and hooders of Little Riding Reds, you prescribers and ordainers and constructors of quizzes in your great glossy magazines. So what if her climaxes are less intense now and she has them in the guest room? At least she has some. And her husband has his with her. Five years ago the two of them weren't even touching. Sometimes you have to let go of everyone's script, including your own.

Back in the bedroom, she prods the dog till, grumbling, he hauls himself to the far corner of the bed. She turns off her lamp, curls up just out of reach and waits, grinning in the dark. She can't help it. This is her favorite part.

Her husband stirs. "About time," he mutters and, reaching, pulls her under his arm, filling his hand with her breast.

"That's nice," he sighs, as he does every night. She hooks her ankle around his calf. They are attached again. Soon the soft breaths against her neck tell her he has fallen back to sleep. Her eyes close. She can still feel the shape of him inside her.

THE CROOKED THING

O love is the crooked thing
There is nobody wise enough
To find out all that is in it
Yeats, *"Brown Penny"*

T his is not the final Sapperstein story I planned to write. That one, about an aging marriage and an aging dog, would have illustrated the peace of compromise and acceptance, of long intimate connection, of facing together whatever the final season of life brings. It would have been a story about a marriage which endures because it has been carefully tended.

Now I cannot write that story, because it would be a lie. So instead, let me tell you a different story: short, with long consequences.

One June day a woman came home from getting a haircut in the middle of the afternoon and found her husband's car in the garage. She thought he must be sick—that was the only reason he ever came home this time of day. But when she got inside, two big suitcases stood in the kitchen, and her husband was waiting to tell her that their marriage was over. Thirty-two years together, two children, and it was over.

His reasons were vague. "For some time now we have been going our separate ways," he said, which was news to her.

She was having an excellent marriage. She thought they were close, they had a *rapport*. "We're both weird but we're weird in the same key," she'd told him once, and, amused, he'd agreed. He'd even told her just a few months ago that he felt closer than ever to her now that he was writing his memoirs and sharing all sorts of painful things about his youth.

But it seems he's met another woman, something he won't admit for a long time, though he remarries one month after the divorce is final. He tells her he has already rented an apartment, furnished it from garage sales, and hired a lawyer. He says she'd better get one herself. And then he's gone and she tries to breathe around the hatchet sticking out of her heart.

The worst thing about the split, besides the brutal way he broke it, was that he said he'd been thinking about leaving ever since the children were born. The children are now twenty-five and twenty-seven. That means that all the memories of all those years are now tainted. All the times he said "I love you," called her beautiful, held her at night—all the trips and projects when she'd remarked what a good team they made and he'd agreed---all of that is now suspect. One night, while they still lay entwined, she said: "Everyone should have a person they can lie naked with, skin to skin. You're my person, and I'm yours. No one else gets to touch us like this." And he'd agreed. Was any of it real? Has she been deluding herself all these years? How is it possible that he could hide his true feelings for so long? She would have bet her life that they were one of the few couples who would make it all the way. And he—he who'd been so big on loyalty and fidelity—how had he turned their marriage into this crooked thing?

Now that she's alone in the big empty house, every object is a reminder, every memory a stab:

- The phantom ring that keeps sliding around her finger though she put it away in a drawer.
- The commercial on TV they used to ridicule—she keeps turning her head to share it, but no one lies on his side of the bed, no one sits in his chair.
- She sees the title of a book he would like, then has to remind herself: "That's not your business anymore." He's not her business anymore.
- She realizes it will never matter again which color toothbrush she uses.
- No tap or step or creak in the house is his or will ever be his, but her traitorous body keeps anticipating, keeps listening for the rumble of the garage door.
- She has to keep dragging his dining chair away from the table after the well-meaning housecleaners repeatedly replace it opposite her own again.
- She cries when she finds the old Lactaid pills she carried for him in her purse.
- She understands now why old people eat dinner so early: to hurry the day along, bring it sooner to its end.
- She looks constantly for reasons to keep going. Her children are the first, last, and best reason.

Someday she may understand. Someday the crater in her chest may close. Or she may die still mystified and bitter. But in the meantime, she wants her children, and perhaps their children, to know just what wrecked the family. *She* would have fought for it, but she was given no choice, no vote, no chance. She's realized that she no longer knows the man she's spent more than half her life with. Perhaps she's never known him. Perhaps he's been doing a bang-up job of impersonating her lover and partner. She marvels at his hitherto unknown capacity for deception.

And she writes about it because she wants her children to know her—and sometimes you are defined by what you have lost.

But, it turns out, sometimes you can redefine yourself.

I've realized, with help from my therapist and support group, that maybe he and I were not such a great match after all, even at the beginning. Despite the fact that we are both writers, we never communicated well. For example, he told our daughter that when he started experiencing religious feelings, he did not trust me enough to talk about them because I had said so many acerbic and cynical things about religion. I wouldn't have ridiculed him—I would have been interested and supportive—but I'd given him no reason to believe that.

And when he said he was disillusioned with some family members, instead of listening and inquiring and trying to understand why he felt that way, I leapt to their defense, attacking him instead. But now, since I can imagine his point-of-view, I can accept my share of responsibility for the demise of the marriage, which means I no longer feel victimized or betrayed. He was right when he said we'd been going our own ways. I've realized that I crave solitude and have always *chosen* it: I just wasn't aware that I was choosing—I thought I was just being myself and that my husband instinctively understood and accepted me, but this turned out to be yet another unchallenged assumption.

I've also realized that happiness comes in different flavors. For example, a while ago my daughter asked me to send her some family photos for a scrapbook she and her father were making for his mother's birthday. At one time I would have found the experience of going through the photo albums unbearably painful: all those pictures of the four of us, happy and together. I would have focused on the loss. But now I was able to say to myself: *Yes, it was good, and you're lucky you got to have that experience. But you don't need to* keep on *having it in order to be happy now.*

The bitterness and resentment are gone because I understand myself better. This new sense of peace has made me more present and aware, which means I appreciate so much more. I actually feel grateful for gratitude.

As for the tainted memories, I made an executive decision: they're real, they're mine, and I'm keeping them.

Finally, forgiveness is no longer an issue. My life has changed drastically, but it turns out that I like the changes. I am no victim, thus there is nothing to forgive. I am learning, as the old saying goes, that happiness isn't so much having what you want as wanting what you have—a lesson I suspect I will *keep* learning as long as I'm alive.

ABOUT THE AUTHOR

Carol K Howell

Carol K. Howell, a 1985 graduate of the Iowa Writers' Workshop, has published over 60 stories in literary magazines and anthologies, including Epoch, New Orleans Review, Story/Quarterly, The North American Review, and Crazyhorse, written two novels on her own--one about Jewish witches in New Orleans and another about psychics and the Holocaust, and 3 novellas --as well as  Traffik Games and 2 upcoming novels with her collaborator, Sheila Hollihan-Elliot. After spending 30 years teaching college writing courses, she now leads public workshops and provides coaching and editing for individual writers. A trained dramatist and speaker, she is available for readings, book club online programs, and conference events.

BOOKS BY THIS AUTHOR

Traffik Games

A smart Texas ex-pat, an international supermodel, and bored spa friends take on the London Metropolitan Police in an exciting suspenseful romp when they accidentally encounter a case of human trafficking of teenage girls. They scheme and struggle to rescue the girls, bring justice to their obscenely rich abusers, and discover whether, despite everything, romance can flourish.

Also included –

Sample Book Club Questions

NGO's to contact for activism

AWARD WINNING STORIES IN THIS COLLECTION

1988: First Place *Nebraska Review* Fiction Competition ("Saving Soviet Jewelry")

1990: Third Prize *Oktoberfest* Fiction Competition ("The Seven League Boots")

1990: Second Prize *River City* Fiction Awards ("The Cutting")

1995: Finalist *Phoebe* Literary Awards ("Rocks")

1995: First Place *Stars* Holiday Fiction Contest ("Forty Four Lights")

2002: *The Bellingham Review* ("Redemption") nominated for a Pushcart Prize

UPCOMING FROM PALM BEACH PRESS

(novels)

SKYCLAD ON BOURBON STREET by Carol K Howell, is a contemporary tale about Jewish witches in New Orleans that blends realism with magic.

THE UNBELIEVABLE TALE by Carol K Howell, is the story of Ivy Perlman, a burned-out college professor in a dead-end job looking for a way out. Klara Löwe is an Auschwitz survivor working as a medium in a resort town famous for psychics. When a young woman who is Ivy's friend and Klara's protege dies mysteriously -- murdered apparently but impossibly by Nazis -- Ivy takes her place, determined to learn the truth.

WINGS OF MADNESS by Sheila Hollihan-Elliot and Carol K Howell, is a fictionalized biography of Gilded Age artist, inventor of camouflage, and possible madman Abbott Handerson Thayer. The story focuses especially on Thayer's troubled relationship with his daughter Mary.

WITH SEVEN FINGERS by Carol K Howell and Sheila Hollihan-Elliot, is a fictionalized biography of pioneering Modernist artist Marc Chagall, a fascinating blend of contradictions, arrogance, and insecurity. The story brings new light to his relationship with others, especially his wife Bella.

(novellas)

THE MAGICIAN OF BROOKLYN by Carol K Howell, inspired by Isaac Bashevis Singer's THE MAGICIAN OF LUBLIN, is a contemporary tale of a young Hasidic woman in Williamsburg who dreams of being a singer, something forbidden to Hasidic women.

THE EMPTY BOWL by Carol K Howell, tells the story of a young German woman working as a secretary in a death camp much like Auschwitz.

HAVDALAH by Carol K Howell, which references a ritual conducted by observant Jews at the end of each Sabbath, pairs Michaela, a cynical young woman and child of Holocaust survivors, with Eli, a young veteran of the Israeli wars who is suffering PTSD.

(story collections)

GITTEL'S GOLEM AND OTHER STORIES OF MAGIC REALISM by Carol K Howell, includes award winning stories Gittel's Golem, The Demon's Debut, Mrs. Cohen's Conversion, and more.

Made in the USA
Columbia, SC
11 January 2023

10012306R00180